BLOOD GUILT

BY
LINDY CAMERON

Bywater
BOOKS

Ann Arbor
2006

Bywater Books, Inc.
PO Box 3671
Ann Arbor MI 48106-3671

Printed in the United States of America on acid-free paper.

Bywater Books First Edition

This book was first published in Australia by HarperCollins*Publishers*, in 1999.

Cover designer: Bonnie Liss (Phoenix Graphics)

ISBN 1-932859-12-8

This one is still for you, Kate.

And always for Chele.

ACKNOWLEDGMENTS

A universe of thanks to:

My mum who never once said "you can't do that,"even when I wanted to be a famous scientist;

My sister Fin and outlaw Steve;

Sisters in Crime Australia, especially my fellow convenors—Carmel, Sue, Cathy, Katrina, Viv, Faye, Chele, Phyllis, Tanya and Robyn;

My best friends, the Special Girls of Yackandandah—Sally, Tricia, Jay, Kay, Jen, Rob, Kim, Jill, Marg and Trish;

The wonderful Fran Bryson;

Kate Lovett, whose support made this book happen;

And Chele for everything that matters.

Chapter 1

It was the sort of night that starts many a bad novel. Kit O'Malley was trying to decide whether to venture out into the midst of it or go back inside and have a long cold stiff drink. The rush of steamy oppressive heat colliding with the unnatural cold of the air-conditioned hotel lobby as she opened the door told her that outside was still not the place to be.

Raising her arm through the thick and putrid air to block out the streetlight, she glared at the storm clouds which were still doing what they'd been doing every night for a week—just hanging around, heavy and threatening, taunting a parched and overheated city with the promise of relief only to piss off before midnight and drop their bundles over Bass Strait.

The distinctive smell of rain in the air was permeated with the sweat, tension and extreme irritability of an entire population which had had just about enough, thank you very much, but couldn't do a damned thing to escape. Tonight did feel different though. The air was seriously full of something that indicated change. Kit hated that. It didn't necessarily mean a change in the weather; it would probably just be another downturn in the economy, a petrol strike or a sale at Kmart.

Kit's mad friend Brigit would say it was bad vibes or ions, that there were negative emotions running rampant through the suburbs because the moon was almost full, or because it hadn't aligned with

Mars or something. Whatever it was, it was producing a lot of shitty weather, not the sort a sensible person would want to be out in.

Kit was still trying to decide whether or not to go back and join Nick for a beer when a rogue wind, probably sent out as a scout for the raging gale that was almost certainly following, thwacked into the heavy door and pushed her back inside anyway.

"You know that light wind the Weather Bureau forecast would accompany the cool change?" she said to the two men in the small office off the hotel's foyer. "Well, it's about to destroy the street." She sat down heavily on a plastic chair and watched Nick and Simmons as they packed away their equipment.

"Is it raining yet?" Simmons asked.

"Don't be silly. It's either not going to happen or it's waiting till I'm halfway across the street to my car," Kit said, realizing she should have known from the moment she'd woken up that this was not going to be one of her better days.

It should have been Sunday, a day to roll over, stick your head under the pillow and pretend you couldn't hear The Cat demanding breakfast. Indeed it had felt like Sunday till that precious feline, yowling with a mouth full of something not quite dead, had leapt on top of her to show off the mangled catch of the day. Kit had launched herself from the bed, fighting off the effects of morning gravity, to chase The Cat out the back door. The daily newspaper had skidded across the patio and when Kit bent to pick it up she knew the day was not going to get any better. Thursday's *Age* meant one of two things: either it was Thursday or she'd been in a coma for four days.

And what should have been Sunday got progressively worse as Thursday wore on, culminating in a four-hour stakeout topped off by a meeting with a man who had nothing whatsoever to recommend him.

Not that Simmons is much better, Kit thought, watching the dishevelled detective as he tried in vain to hoick his trousers up over a stomach not designed to be contained by them. He gave up, as he always did, and his belt buckle slipped from view beneath a belly barely covered by a shirt too tight for pride to have had anything to do with the man's dress sense.

"You may as well go, Kit. We've got everything we need," Nick said, absently waving the cassette which held the recording of Kit's

2

meeting with the contemptible Jimmy Kerman. "We'll be able to pick up Manderson with this little lot."

"Yeah. Well I hope you've got enough on that sleazebag Kerman as well. The only thing worse than a drug-pushing pimp is a drug-pushing pimp who betrays his friends because he thinks it'll help him get on in the world."

Kit wanted nothing more right now than to wash off the stench of an hour spent with one of the most reprehensible human beings she'd ever had the misfortune to have to talk to.

"Hey, you and I know from experience you don't have to be a certified sleazebag pimp to be a Judas," Nick said, slipping an arm around Kit's shoulders.

Kit grinned. "Ain't that the truth. Got time for a beer before you go?"

"God, it's still like a sauna out here," Nick said half an hour later when he and Kit emerged from the Criterion Hotel. The wind, which had wreaked havoc in the street, had all but died down. "What a mess! Looks like a mad dog went through every bin in the street looking for leftover McDonald's."

"It's more likely that it went mad and did this *after* finding leftover McDonald's," Kit said, surveying the garbage that was strewn from one side of the road to the other. Emptied bins had been flung, rolled and battered, sandwich boards had deserted their posts to wrap themselves round telephone poles or leap through shop windows, and several parked cars no longer had windscreens. The footpath, where it could be seen beneath the collage of rotting refuse and flapping waste paper, was splattered with a few huge drops of rain, a sure indication that the black and heavy heavens were finally about to open.

"You going home now?" Nick asked, removing his jacket and slinging it over his shoulder.

"I wish. I've got one last stop. A client in Toorak."

"A client? It's after eight."

"When you work for yourself, Nicholas, your clients call the shots most of the time. The good thing about this deal is it's the last visit. You know, final meeting, give me the check, case closed."

"Two in one day. That's not bad." Nick followed Kit across the street to her car. "But aren't we getting a bit above our station by having a client from Toorak?"

"Absolutely, my dear," Kit said in her best posh voice. "And what's more I've got a new one to see there first thing tomorrow. O'Malley Investigations is going up in the world."

"I bet they don't pay any better, or on time," Nick said with a grin.

"Not that I've noticed, no. But at least my new client should be entertaining. From what I've read in the society pages even the wealthy eccentrics around town think she's a little weird." Kit opened her car door and threw her jacket onto the passenger seat.

"Listen, thanks for coming in on this tonight," Nick said. "You didn't have to. Even old Simmons appreciated it."

"Sure. I could just see he was bursting with gratitude."

"Hey, he bought you a drink. For him that means thanks from the bottom of his beer gut. My thanks, however, come from a little higher up." Nick placed his hand over his heart.

"I had unfinished business with Manderson, now it's over. Kerman also gave me info for another case I'm working on. So it was no big deal, except that you guys were covering my tail."

"God forbid that anything should happen to your cute little tail."

"Ooh Nick. I bet you say that to all the boys."

"Too right. Speaking of which, *you* may have a check waiting but I can hear a cocktail shaker being warmed up at my place. What's that noise?"

"What noise?" said Kit, feigning deafness.

"Sounds like a blowfly in a bottle."

"Oh, you mean that strangled blirp-blirping. It's my mobile. I dropped it earlier and it went into hiding." Kit bent down and fished around under the car seat. "Shut up you pretentious piece of plastic," she said, pressing the loudspeaker button as slipped the phone into its cradle on the dashboard.

". . . so I thought I'd take Diedre there. What do you think?"

Kit shrugged at Nick and whispered, "I believe Mrs. O'Malley's been at the sherry again."

"Are you there Katherine?"

"Yes, Mum. What do I think about what?"

"About taking Diedre to that lovely little place we went to that time."

"Which place, Mum? You really should wait till I've answered the phone before you start talking to me."

"Yes of course, darling. But do you think she'd like it?"

"I don't know which place you're talking about."

"Yes you do. You took me there. Or maybe it was your brother."

Kit glared at the phone as if it was responsible for her mother's mental leapfrogging.

"Mum, Michael has never taken you anywhere. He never has any money. He's starving in a garret, remember." Kit shrugged her shoulders and leaned over to give Nick a kiss goodbye before climbing into her car, starting the engine and pulling out.

"Well, there you are then. I knew it was you," her mother was saying.

"Okay it was me. Where did we go?"

"That little Japanese place in Chapel Street of course. Why are you asking me, Katherine? You took me there for lunch with Constance that day."

"Mum, I think maybe Constance took you there for lunch."

"Good heavens, so she did. You weren't there at all. It was Evelyn. Now how did I confuse you with Evelyn? You don't look anything like her."

"I should hope not. Evelyn's a good quarter of a century older than me," Kit said, taking off again as the lights turned green. "By the way, who's Diedre?"

"You know Diedre, darling."

"Oh, OK, if you say so, Mum," she said, shaking her head and making a left turn to run the gamut of Toorak Road traffic which tended to ignore all vehicles with a price tag below fifty grand.

Kit and her car were in dangerous territory now. This was where the locals, rather than walk around the corner from their fully serviced apartments to grab a fashionable sushi, spent fifteen minutes getting sports cars out of maximum-security garages just to give their personalized number plates an airing. The Range Rovers that cruised this street wouldn't be seen dead in the bush, the Stags were all driven by gallery owners, hairdressers and groupies, and the Mercedes always came in his-and-hers color-coordinated pairs. Pedestrians were fair game in Toorak Road, no matter where they bought their clothes.

Two cars in front of her a Volvo made an unsignalled U-turn while its driver adjusted his passenger's breasts, confirming the joke—the truth of which Kit had never doubted—that the only difference between a porcupine and a Volvo was that the porcupine had its pricks on the outside. Kit slammed on her brakes to avoid running into the back of a car that had obviously never ventured this far from the suburbs before. The driver of the maroon Torana festooned with bumper stickers boasting the sexual prowess of plumbers was demonstrating a perfect example of completely wasted effort in this part of the world—hurling abuse at a Volvo driver from this part of the world.

"Mum, I've got to go now. I'm about to do battle with the porcupines," Kit said.

Despite the weather, things here were as busy as usual for a Thursday night. The shops were open, spilling light and customers onto the footpath and sending subliminal messages out to Visa cards everywhere. Yuppies, dinks, professional groovers—whatever they were being called this season—were milling outside the right places to be seen, casually greeting or ignoring each other depending on whatever it depends on. Kit figured most of them never actually got inside these nightclubs and cafés, but had to be seen to be trying, and those who did came straight out again with their boutique beer or iced orgasm because it was too hard to tell at such close quarters if they really wanted to stand so close to the person whose pelvis was thrust up against their backside.

Kit finally managed to find a car park three blocks from the restaurant owned by Enrico Conte. All she had to do was inform her client that she had tracked down his ex-partner and found him to be living quite well in Apollo Bay on the proceeds of the cappuccino machine, jukebox, microwave, and thirty tables he had stolen from Enrico, not to mention the two months' worth of restaurant takings he had neglected to bank before disappearing with Enrico's second wife. Kit figured it would take about one cappuccino, from Enrico's new machine, to close the case.

She should have known that nothing is ever as easy as it should be. Enrico demanded to hear every single detail of the case three times over. He wanted to know what to do next about his ex-partner and, most of all, he needed Kit's womanly advice on how to get his wife back. Kit didn't have the faintest idea about the latter but as Enrico kept her prisoner with the best gnocchi in town she could hardly refuse his plea for a friendly ear. By the time she got home, however, it was after three a.m.

Barely six hours later she was driving down Toorak Road again, feeling decidedly grumpy from lack of sleep and suffering a slight case of déjà vu. The harsh light of day had little effect on the air of pretentiousness that ran the length of this road. All the nightclubbers were sensibly home in bed but now their mothers were out in force, armed only with their credit cards and a readiness to display their best "do I know you?" expression.

As she swung her car left off Toorak Road and down a couple of blocks Kit made a solemn vow never, ever again to make any appointments before noon. Her prospective client's suggestion that they discuss the case over a late breakfast had seemed generous at the time. But nine a.m. was not late. It was, in fact, without doubt, the most uncivilized time of the day to be out and about, no matter what the reason.

Kit was not at all in the right mood for trying to impress a new and wealthy client. As last night's storm had failed to eventuate the weather was still muggy and the temperature was already in the high twenties. The inside of Kit's car, even with all the windows down, felt like a sauna. She could almost see the heat rising off the dashboard and the smell of overheated plastic was getting right up her nose.

"Oh god, I hate mornings!" she growled as she tugged irritably at the skirt of her suit, knowing it would do little to prevent hard-edged creases forming at every point where her sweating thighs and back were touching the car seat. So much for power dressing. So much for getting up early enough to drag the iron out from its hiding place at the bottom of the basket of clothes she never wore because they never got pressed.

She made a right turn into the very heart of old-money territory—overstated mansions, tennis courts, electronically operated wrought-iron gates with rampant lions on the bluestone posts, a Rolls and a Range Rover runabout in every sweeping drive—and then a final turn into McGill Crescent, typically tree-lined and quiet with high walls that no doubt hid more than a secret or two. The tally-ho set were alive and well in this neck of the woods, spending their weekends riding innocent foxes to death and their weekdays working out ways to spend the extra money they'd made from the money they'd made the week before.

This was Kit's first call on Celia Robinson and her eclectic collection of bizarre statuary. It had only been two days since Celia had called to make this appointment so there had been little time for Kit to carry out the thorough background research she usually did on prospective clients—well, at least on those clients who had the courtesy to make appointments and didn't just turn up at her office. So most of what she knew had been gleaned from the pile of *Women's Weekly* and *New Idea* magazines, along with back copies of the *Business Review Weekly*, that her friends Brigit and Del had dumped in her lap in answer to what Kit had thought was a perfectly innocent question. *Everyone*, it seemed, had heard of Celia Everton-Orlando-Robinson. Where had Kit been that she didn't know of the woman's highly successful Australian-based international publishing empire, her tireless work on behalf of every worthy charity in town and her legendary habit of donating positively ghastly statues to any institution that looked sideways at her? Although generous to a fault, Mrs. Robinson, it appeared, was also a very strange woman, or as Brigit had said "definitely a Queen short of a royal flush."

Kit parked her car in the shade and made her way across the driveway which encircled a manicured lawn bordering an Olympic-sized fish pond.

Lucky fish, she thought, as she fought off the urge to take a swim with them. She put her jacket on instead, hoping it would hide most of the embarrassing creases. Don't be silly, even rich people sweat! No they don't, she argued with herself. They have air-conditioned cars and houses and business suits.

Kit stepped up onto the massive marbled portico, took a deep breath and reached for the bell. Her hand had barely touched it when the widest front door in Melbourne swung open expelling a blast of cold fresh rich people's air-conditioning. Dracula's long-lost cousin, dressed in black trousers, a white collarless shirt and braces, stood on the inside looking out and down at her from the palest face she'd ever seen.

This is a very tall person in desperate need of vitamins or sunlight, Kit thought. Her first instinct was to run; her second was to adjust the collar on her jacket so Mr. Anemia wouldn't get any ideas about breakfasting on her neck. If he says "you rang" we are out of here, O'Malley. She stuffed her hands in her pocket to keep them away from her throat and tried to smile.

"Ms. O'Malley, I presume," he said gently, with no trace of any Eastern European accent at all.

"Yes. I have an appointment with Mrs. Robinson," Kit said unnecessarily.

"Certainly. My name is Byron Daniels. Would you follow me, please. Madam is waiting for you in the Forum."

Madam? Kit followed the bloodless Byron along the marble-tiled mirror-lined hallway to a heavy curtain at the dimly lit rear of the mansion.

"Would you care for champagne or coffee with your breakfast?"

"Coffee, thank you," Kit replied.

He gave what appeared to be an approving nod, reached for the curtain and pulled it back to reveal double glass doors, one of which he opened.

"Mrs. Robinson is outside," he said, indicating that Kit should go through without him.

It took Kit a couple of seconds to adjust to the bright sunlight again but a little longer for the sight that was Celia Robinson to sink in. Swathed in a silk kaftan of bottle-green splashed with crimson and yellow, with bare feet at one end and a sola topee atop a head of très bouffant yellow hair at the other, she stood at eye-level with a very large penis, holding a silver goblet in one hand. The other hand was moving in a rapid circular motion accompanying the instructions she appeared to be giving to the body prone on the grass with its head in a fish pond.

All about her, as far Kit could see, were naked athletes, warriors, nymphs, dragons, gorgons, serpents and centaurs; hundreds of them standing, reclining and poised for action amid fountains, ornamental lakes, huge ferneries, lush rose gardens and flower-draped rockeries.

9

Kit wondered whether the heat and the ungodly hour of the day were making her hallucinate. She didn't quite know how she was going to contain the urge to roll about laughing—except to run away and hide till she could get control of herself. That could take months! She'd better get this over and done with as quickly as possible.

She put her sunglasses back on, raised a hand to her mouth to stop the smile that was ignoring her best intentions to appear calm and collected, and cleared her throat. Wrong! Celia Robinson swung around to face the patio, reaching out to clasp the penis of Perseus to steady herself as the kaftan swished around her stubby little legs and threatened to knock her off her feet.

"Ah, the private eye," she said grandly just as the head of the body on the ground came up for air—briefly. Kit was about to proceed down the cobbled steps to shake the woman's outstretched hand when she realized it was actually directing her towards the patio table set for two. "No shoes in the Forum please," she said. "The heels damage the lawn."

Kit backed into a chair, unable to take her eyes off the scene before her. Celia Robinson had thankfully returned to the task before her, whatever that was, and didn't notice the fresh rolls tumbling across the table and onto the ground as Kit clumsily sat down. Someone was watching though as she made a dive for the bread. She noticed the curtains on the patio doors drop back into place just as she sat down again.

Get a grip, for god's sake, O'Malley.

"Do you know anything about fountains?"

"Not a lot, no," Kit replied when she realized the question was meant for her.

"Pity. Neither does Mr. Burke here, I've just discovered." Celia Robinson swept onto the patio and pulled what appeared to be a small walkie-talkie from a pocket somewhere in the folds of the kaftan. "Byron. Byron. Come in, Byron."

"I'm right here, Mrs. Robinson."

Kit had no idea how the walking corpse had materialized so silently behind her.

"Good. Be a dear and bring out the breakfast. Oh, you'd better tell Burke to give up before he swallows any more water. We'll have to get one of the plumbing people in to solve the problem."

"What is the problem?" Kit asked as she watched Byron remove his shoes before venturing across the small patch of lawn. He tapped Mr. Burke on the shoulder and waited till the man was sitting up and facing him before he spoke.

"Damned if I know," Celia was saying as she settled herself amid miles of kaftan in the chair opposite Kit. "Every time we turn on the fountain the pond overflows. The outlet thingy must be blocked but Burke can't seem to find anything. The timer system also seems to have a mind of its own. The fountain comes on any old time it feels like it, which is a bit of a worry when the thingy is blocked."

"Yes, I imagine it is," Kit said, wishing she hadn't asked.

Byron appeared at the table with a tray. Kit nearly jumped out of her skin—she hadn't even noticed him going back inside. Breakfast was fresh fruit, icy-cold orange juice, toast and strong coffee. Kit wasn't used to eating at this time of the day, but it kept her hands occupied and helped to fend off an attack of the killer giggles.

"I have never had the need for services of your kind before," Mrs. Robinson began, getting right to the point. "I hope I am going about this the right way—by having you here rather than meeting in your office."

"I doubt there's a right way of hiring a detective, Mrs. Robinson. It depends on the case, and in this case your patio has a much better view than my office."

"My thoughts exactly and, please, call me Celia. The idea of hiring someone to follow my husband seemed so tawdry at first. But what must be done . . . It was really my solicitor's idea." Celia's gaze turned to the marble and stone multitude in her garden. She was obviously having difficulty dealing with this situation. "Douglas wanted to organize this for me, but I told him if it had to be done then I had to take control of the situation. He would have hired some grubby little man in a trench coat to hide in dark doorways and spy on Geoffrey with a telescope and dark glasses. I thought hiring a woman would be less . . . well, less tacky."

Celia looked Kit over as if her smart this-is-what-you-wear-to-meet-rich-Toorak-clients outfit somehow made tailing someone a classy affair, one that would be carried out in elegant surrounds with a glass

11

of Oloroso in her hand. Kit usually knew how to make her clients feel, if not happy, at least comfortable in their decision to resort to "services of her kind," but Celia Robinson was nothing like her usual run of clients. Short of promising to wear her best sequined evening gown should she have to hang around any darkened doorways, Kit doubted there was little she could say that would make Celia Robinson believe the situation was anything less than tacky. The woman was obviously more troubled about hiring a detective than she was about having a reason to do so.

"Well, I suppose there's nothing else to do but get this out of the way."

"You want me to follow your husband," Kit said, trying to help her out.

"Yes. You've no doubt done a certain amount of homework before keeping this appointment so you would know that Geoffrey is also one of my co-directors and the business manager of Orlando House, the publishing company founded by my first husband."

Kit nodded. She had managed to find out that much.

"Well, the firm that looks after all the company's financial and legal business is headed by my solicitor Douglas Scott. When his accountant discovered some, shall we say, discrepancies in some recent financial transactions made by my husband, he naturally informed Douglas."

"What sort of discrepancies?"

"Nothing alarming. By that I mean it hasn't been a great deal of money. Several thousand here and there, but all over the last eight months."

Kit decided to up her fee. If several thousand wasn't alarming then her services must be worth at least twice what she usually charged. "Did Mr. Scott ask your husband about the money?"

"Well, not at first because after all it is Geoffrey's money. He can do with it what he likes. In fact, saying that Douglas was informed of the discrepancy is not quite accurate. It was more a mention in passing over dinner one evening. To him, the accountant that is, it was simply a curious thing."

"But surely if your husband's been spending money his accountant would have to know the details. I mean, the books have to balance sooner or later."

"True. But Geoffrey was apparently evasive when asked for those details. He claimed he was trying to cover the costs on some aborted deal he had allegedly made on behalf of the company in America last year. That wouldn't have surprised me—about the deal being aborted, I mean. Despite having been OHP's business manager for the last eighteen years Geoffrey lacks the necessary judgement to initiate anything much on his own. We don't usually let him do a lot by himself."

"So Mr. Robinson made a bad call and then tried to cover it personally so OHP would not have to take the flak?" Kit said.

Celia shrugged. "Or more likely so that Mr. Robinson would not have to take the flak, as you call it, when we discovered he had used the company name in an unsanctioned deal of some sort. I mean, for all we knew then he could have been trying to buy a baseball team, a Republican candidate, or a fast-food franchise."

"With his own money though," Kit said, starting to wonder what the fuss was about.

"Oh yes. Which, as I said, he is perfectly entitled to do, but *not* on behalf of Orlando House without the Board's knowledge. Anyway, Douglas decided to follow the figures a little further and did some investigating on the quiet. He has always been suspicious of Geoffrey where money is involved and was particularly concerned about what this money was being used for. Oddly enough he has so far been unable to find out where it went, although he did discover another large withdrawal just one month ago. Thirty-five thousand gone. Just like that." Celia snapped her fingers to emphasize the point.

"I assume," said Kit, "that it was at that point your solicitor approached your husband with a few questions."

"Over drinks, just in passing." Celia smiled.

"Of course. So what was his story?"

"He claimed he was making an investment in a new publishing venture he was trying to get off the ground. He wanted to keep a lid on it until the matter was finalized, at which stage, he said, OHP may be interested in joining him in the deal."

"You don't believe that?" Kit said.

13

Celia raised an eyebrow as if to say, don't be ridiculous, who would?

"Keep a lid on it?" Kit said. "I gather that means he asked Mr. Scott not to tell anyone, including you, about this new venture."

"Exactly. But Douglas is more than just my solicitor. We've been friends for forty years," Celia said, pursing her lips as she pushed a slice of cantaloupe into her mouth with one finger.

"But your husband would know that. I mean, wouldn't he expect that you would find out?"

"One would think so, wouldn't one?" Celia said, raising an eyebrow. "But he told Douglas he was planning this new venture as a surprise. So Douglas agreed to keep it a secret."

"And then told you anyway," Kit said with a smile.

"Naturally."

"Did your husband give any clues as to what the venture might be?"

"Compact discs, of the information kind," Celia said in disgust. "Honestly, the man should know that Orlando House is being dragged kicking and screaming into the twenty-first century. We publish books. On paper, between covers. We may use computers to facilitate their publication but that is as far as I am prepared to go. We will not publish literature or anything else on little round pieces of plastic." She thumped the table and then looked quite surprised with herself. "I *am* sorry, Katherine."

Kit smiled. "I gather your main concern is that your husband might be using the Orlando House name for his own purposes?" she said.

Celia held out her hands, palms up as if she was weighing something. "Yes and no. As you gather I don't approve of this CD thing, whether he's using OHP as a front or not. More to the point, however, I don't believe that *is* what he's up to. Neither does Douglas. Because he can't trace the money it's his concern that this so-called venture may be something OHP quite simply would not want to be involved in. I wish to find out what it is before Geoffrey can retreat or cover his tracks." Celia left the hint of dirty dealings hanging in the air while she poked a strawberry into her mouth.

"Why doesn't Douglas just ask him straight out? He could threaten to reveal the big secret to you and then your husband would have to tell him." Kit was starting to think this whole case was a little strange.

Why was everybody else being so careful and secretive when it was Geoffrey's apparent skulduggery that was the issue?

"My major concern *is* the integrity of Orlando House. If Geoffrey is involved in something legal then I will have less of a problem with it, obviously. It will just be something that has to be dealt with. If, as Douglas suspects however, it is something questionable or even illegal then that is another matter altogether."

Kit wondered if Celia had any love for the man she obviously had so little respect for. "You don't think he's up to anything illegal, do you?" she asked.

"I believe my husband's sideline is a floozy," Celia answered matter-of-factly, taking a sip of coffee and looking seriously at Kit. "What do you think?"

Damn, was what Kit thought. All this for a floozy? She'd had the rising hope as Celia was talking that this was going to be a straight-forward daylight job of chasing a money trail and investigating any suspicious business ventures or acquaintances that the untrustworthy Mr. R might be involved with. But, although it had taken her a while to get around to it, Mrs. Robinson was indeed hiring Kit to hang around in darkened doorways with a telescope and dark glasses. The interesting stuff was obviously being left in the capable hands of the loyal Douglas Scott.

"I don't know, Mrs. Robinson—Celia," Kit amended. "Is there any-thing else that leads you to believe your husband has a . . . is having an affair?"

"I know my husband, Katherine. The amount of money involved doesn't seem, to me at least, to be enough for any kind of business venture—legal or otherwise. So what would that suggest to you?"

"Debts? Is he a gambler?"

"Only with my goodwill—as far as I know. Geoffrey married me for money, Katherine. He had enough before; now he has more than enough."

"Is it enough to *him* though?" Kit asked.

"Good question." Celia gave a short laugh. "Yes, perhaps it is a truth that a man in possession of a fortune must be in want of . . . more."

Kit smiled because Celia seemed so delighted with her little twist of classic Jane Austen. Downing the rest of her coffee Celia reached for the pot. "He already has a wife. I suspect he also has a mistress and that is not acceptable."

"I don't imagine it is," Kit said, holding her own cup out to the proffered pot.

"Don't get me wrong, Katherine. I don't actually care if he's being unfaithful," Celia said, emphasizing the "un." "What I don't want to have to bother with, at any time, is a scandal. Or blackmail. I know how sordid these things can get. Men just can't seem to help themselves when it comes to sex, can they?" She looked expectantly at Kit, who nodded—as expected.

"Maybe that's exactly what is happening," Kit suggested. "He may already be paying off a blackmailer."

"Well, the sooner we find out the better then," Celia stated.

"There's no chance he's trying to take over OHP?" Kit asked. She realized this was a bit farfetched but suddenly remembered an article she'd come across about the clever takeover of Milson-Carter in Sydney while doing her limited reading into Celia and OHP. That company, publishers of coffee-table books for the armchair traveller and a range of home-decorating magazines, had been literally taken apart and put back together by two very minor shareholders. While there had been speculation that the acquisition of shares had been achieved by coercion rather than free enterprise, nothing was ever proved. Rumors had been rife about some pretty weird skeletons in the closets of the Milson and Carter families, but their minders had closed the wrought-iron gates firmly in the face of the press to keep the old money in and the scandalmongers out. Maybe that was what Celia feared. An unfaithful husband and a conniving mistress could do a great deal of damage if they set their minds to it.

"No, my dear, I seriously doubt it," Celia was saying. "There is no way as far as Orlando House is concerned that my husband can get more than what he has."

"What about the other shareholders? Could he buy them out? I was thinking of the Milson-Carter thing in Sydney," Kit suggested hesitantly.

Celia laughed. "My husband, though co-director, is only a junior partner. Granted, so were the upstarts at Milson, but that company had a hundred or so shareholders. I am the majority shareholder of

Orlando House and I do not expect that to change. I own seventy per cent, the remaining thirty is split equally between only three other people: Geoffrey, my daughter Elizabeth, and our publisher Miles Denning. So it is an unlikely scenario. I trust Miles implicitly and hold him in the highest regard. And my daughter—well, Elizabeth is not much interested in the business at the moment. She has been living in England on and off for the last five years. She's trying to find herself, or something, away from the family influence, or as she calls it 'interference.' She's been gone six months this time."

"If she's not interested in the business . . ." Kit said vaguely. She regretted the implication immediately. Celia, on the other hand, didn't seem to find it inappropriate.

"Elizabeth would not sell her shares any more than I would, Katherine. They are her father's legacy and that means a lot to her. She may be stubborn, selfish and wayward but she would not abandon Orlando House and would certainly give nothing to Geoffrey. She does not approve of her stepfather."

Kit thought that "abandon" was a pretty strange word to use. It appeared Celia Robinson didn't have much luck with those close to her. She wondered what Carl Orlando had been like. She started to apologize for her lack of tact but Celia interrupted with a wave of her hand. "I have deliberated long on all of this. The questions you have raised give me confidence in your ability to deal with this matter efficiently and intelligently. That is all I ask. If my husband is having an affair I wish to be able to deal with *him* efficiently and intelligently. I shall probably want to kill him, though castration would be more fitting, but I will no doubt just manage to muzzle him for a while. If he's not having an affair then the answers to our questions lie elsewhere. One step at a time though. We begin with what I think is the most obvious."

Celia pulled herself up from the chair and motioned to Kit to follow her. She stopped by a set of shelves, inset into the low wall which bordered one edge of the patio near the door, and rummaged amongst the large collection of shoes that filled all the available space. Slipping a pair of high heels onto her tiny feet, she then opened the door and ushered Kit into the cool dark hallway. They made their way up a flight of stairs to a cedar-lined study furnished with two huge desks, a wall of books, several armchairs around an empty fireplace and the ghoulish Byron tapping away on a computer keyboard. His breathing was uneasy. Kit guessed he had just dashed up the stairs ahead of them.

"Is this your first husband, Celia?" Kit asked, indicating the large oil portrait hanging over the unbelievably ornate mantelpiece. Even if Kit hadn't already known what Geoffrey Robinson looked like she would never have assumed the debonair gentle-faced man staring down on her was the current man of the manor. Carl Orlando had been handsome indeed, his eyes showing a strength and integrity that could not have been simply imposed by the artist.

"It is," Celia said gently, placing a hand on Kit's arm. Discounting the exaggerated hairdo, which tended to make her larger than life, Celia was a short person. Kit was five-seven and Celia didn't even reach her shoulder. And she was round. Not fat, just round, though she could have been any shape at all under the tent she was wearing. Kit looked up at the painting again and wondered what the two of them would have looked like together.

"I painted this in 1969, five years before he died," Celia was saying.

"I'm impressed," said Kit honestly, returning her attention to this surprising woman who still had hold of her arm.

"By Carl?" she asked, pleased.

"And your skill, Celia." There had been love in this house at one time then, Kit thought, wondering why it should matter to her. It did though, and she felt strangely pleased that the love was still here, watching over this room at least, captured in the warm intelligent eyes of a long-dead man.

"Come, have a seat, Katherine. Let's get this tedious business out of the way."

Kit seated herself in an ox-blood leather chair opposite Celia who pushed a manila folder across the coffee table that separated them. "Byron has provided you with a copy of my husband's social calendar for the next fortnight," she said, tapping the top sheet of paper. "Geoffrey works till at least seven p.m. every day except Friday. The dates marked with asterisks indicate the evenings when I know he will be home or at a social function with me. So you will have some nights free." She smiled at Kit. "The other evenings, of which there are four, he could be anywhere. Sometimes he comes home for dinner and then goes out to his club, sometimes he dines out with clients, colleagues, business associates or god knows who. I've never asked him. On three occasions he will be attending official dinners; what he does afterwards is also a mystery. As you will see, there are also several times during the day when it may be necessary to keep an eye on him."

"Well, it certainly looks like I'll be busy," Kit said. And earning my money, she thought.

"I don't expect you to follow him day in day out, Katherine. Geoffrey is nothing if not organized. The periods marked will do for a start. We can decide in two weeks whether or not we need to change our tactics, or even if we need to continue. Now, I would like your first report in seven days. Perhaps we could meet again for lunch at noon on Friday. I would prefer that all information is exchanged in person. If you need to ask me anything and I'm not available you may talk to my personal secretary, Byron, and no one else, to arrange a meeting."

"Friday will be fine, Celia, and I can't foresee any need for contact before then."

"Good. Now, we have also included in this file a list of the friends or business associates whom I know Geoffrey will be dealing with according to *this* schedule." She tapped the social calendar again. "And a recent photograph of my husband, just in case you need to share the surveillance—I assume that's what you call it—with any of your staff."

My staff? thought Kit, taken aback. Where did she get that idea? "That will be useful, Celia, but I will be handling this personally."

"Excellent," she said. "I was hoping you would say that. That just leaves your fee." She turned her attention to Byron who obediently unfolded his long body from behind the computer screen and was at his mistress's side before she had uttered his name. He placed an envelope in her hand which she in turn passed to Kit.

"Celia, I usually just agree on a fee and settle the account at the end of the case," Kit said.

"This is an advance to cover you until our next meeting. Any costs you incur in the line of duty, so to speak, we can settle at the end if you keep a record of them. I am employing you for a service,

19

Katherine. I have always found it to my own advantage to pay for what I want before I get it, then it becomes a matter of trust. I do not want you to be out of pocket before you start. Will it be sufficient?"

Kit flipped open the unsealed envelope and pulled the check out just far enough to read $3000. For one week! She fumbled it back into the envelope and tried to place it casually on top of the papers in the Geoffrey Robinson dossier, though she didn't actually want to let go of it. "It's quite sufficient," she managed to say.

"Good. Then you begin tomorrow evening and I shall see you again next week. I will show Miss O'Malley out, Byron. You can carry on with, ah, whatever. Just carry on."

Kit stood on the doorstep and shook Celia's offered hand. "It has been a pleasure meeting you," she said.

"And you too, my dear. Despite the circumstances."

"Can I ask how you came to choose my agency, Celia?" Kit said, trying to make it sound like she did indeed have more staff than just herself and an insane black cat.

Celia Robinson's sudden smile was a tad disarming. There had been an attractive woman there somewhere before the hornets had made a nest on her head. "I went to school with your mother," she said. It was obviously of some amusement to her. "Remember, young lady, it is always *who* you know in this life that counts."

So Lillian was responsible for O'Malley Investigations taking on Pinkerton proportions, Kit thought as she got back into her car and headed back towards the office which would not, as Celia Robinson obviously thought, be abuzz with smartly suited detectives to-ing and fro-ing on all manner of operations covert.

Chapter 2

The headquarters of O'Malley Investigations measured approximately fourteen feet by twelve. What that was in metric Kit had no idea and no desire to find out—it would only reduce the spaciousness she didn't have. The imperial dimensions provided enough room to hold an impressive oak desk, three filing cabinets, two bookshelves, a kitchen sink, a pathetic potted plant of some tall variety in perpetual death throes, and two chairs—one for the only detective employed by the agency and one for the client. On the rare occasion that clients arrived in numbers greater than one, Kit simply borrowed a chair from her friend Del who produced, among other things, a feminist magazine in the front four-fifths of the Richmond premises.

A glass door opened from the main street into a small tiled hallway which featured two interior doors and a stairway going up. Kit didn't mind stairs when they went in that direction but, as her apartment was on the next floor, it meant she had to descend the damn things at least once a day. One of the strange things about suffering from vertigo was that coming down was always a lot harder than going up. A large sign on the first door off the hallway announced *Aurora Press* loudly in purple lettering. The fact that Kit's office had, until recently, been Aurora's lunchroom explained not only the sink that skulked in one corner, but why only the smallest of wooden plaques on the second door at the rear of the hallway indicated the center of operations for O'Malley Investigations.

When she'd first set up shop Kit had contemplated advertising her services with just a phone number, but realized that not all her clients would be happy meeting in the local pub or the Botanic Gardens. Whenever possible though, Kit offered to meet clients on their own turf, or at least neutral ground. She was certain, for instance, that Celia Robinson would never have paid such a large advance had she met with Kit beside a dying philodendron instead of a naked Greek hero.

Kit dumped a couple of books on the piles of paper scattered on her desk to anchor them before turning on the ceiling fan. It never cooled the room down but at least it moved the hot sticky air around, albeit in hot sticky lumps. She kicked off her sandals, hung up the collection of wrinkles that had once been the jacket of her light-weight suit and opened the connecting door to the front office. Aurora Press was deserted. They were probably still at lunch. After all, it was only three p.m.

Kit flicked the switch on the decrepit air-conditioning unit, grabbed a Coke from the fridge and dragged her chair into the doorway to try to get some relief from the heat. Putting her feet up on what was usually the client's side of her desk she opened the file on Geoffrey Robinson.

The photograph of the man in question was a black-and-white glossy taken, according to the details on the back, three months before in the Orlando House boardroom in St. Kilda Road. Geoffrey Robinson stood casually, one hand in a pocket of his immaculately tailored dark suit, next to a floor-to-ceiling window with commanding views of the city. A broad-shouldered man, large but obviously fit, he wore his hair in a sort of dry Wall Street look, combed back with precision to make a feature of his receding hairline. His eyes revealed absolutely nothing though his lipless mouth was spread in what for him possibly constituted a smile. His nose was neither big nor small, but his ears should have been pinned back from birth as they gave his face the overall appearance of a fruit bat, though he was nowhere near as cute.

Kit picked up the first page of computer print-out prepared by the bloodless Byron. It was headed "Week One," which began the next day with an afternoon of social tennis with friends in Brighton. This was marked with an asterisk which meant Geoffrey would be in the company of his wife, though try as she might Kit could not imagine Celia Robinson playing anything more energetic than bridge. Geoffrey's next appointment, at seven-thirty p.m. and underlined in red, was dinner at his club in Collins Street. What he did afterwards would perhaps reveal what Celia had called "the mystery" as this was obviously where Kit was expected to start. Despite Celia's misgivings about hiring a PI to hang around in dark doorways that was probably what Kit would have to do. Even her best sequined gown would not get her into the Patrician, one of the few remaining bastions of male exclusivity in Melbourne—if you didn't count leather bars like the Rod and Sergeant York's.

Sunday—the whole day, thank god—was marked with an asterisk so regular surveillance would be on hold till Monday evening when Geoffrey was due to dine out with Miles Denning, William Zaber, Marjorie Finlay, Greg Fulton and others at the Stone Garden from eight p.m. On Tuesday he had set aside three hours for lunch with one Ian Dalkeith, and the evening from seven p.m. onwards, though containing no appointments, had been circled in red and highlighted with a question mark beside the word "Patrician." Wednesday was a busy day: there was lunch with Marjorie Finlay and Miles Denning, an unexplained appointment out of the office scheduled for six p.m., and another night subtly circled in red and queried by Celia's meticulous personal secretary. Thursday involved yet another luncheon appointment, this time with a person or persons unknown, and some sort of publishing industry do at the Hilton from eight p.m. An asterisked notation beside the last appointment indicated that Celia would also be attending the function, but only from eight until ten-thirty. That was it for the first week. It was enough, even with an advance on payment for services rendered.

Kit ignored Week Two and turned to the page which listed Geoffrey Robinson's friends and associates. Miles Denning, as Kit already knew, was OHP's publisher; William Zaber was managing director of Zaber Ink, one of the largest advertising agencies in Victoria; Greg Fulton was marketing director of OHP's overseas division based in London; Marjorie Finlay was Fulton's Australian counterpart; and Ian Dalkeith, whose name rang a bell, was a local property developer.

Kit reached for the phone. It was time to ring Lillian and find out how her mother had gotten her into all of this. The number was engaged as usual. She waited a couple of minutes then hit the redial button. There was no ringing tone but she heard her mother muttering on the other end of the line.

"Mum? You must have been sitting on the phone."

"What? Who's that?"

"It's me. How many women do you know who call you Mum?"

"Oh, Katherine. The phone didn't ring. I was picking it up to call someone. You could have been anybody."

"I suppose so, Mum. Well, seeing you're obviously home can I come over for a coffee?"

"No, darling. I'm leaving in half an hour."

"Where are you going?"

"Adelaide. Connie and I decided we needed a couple of weeks of R&R."

"What on earth do you and Constance need a rest from?" Kit laughed.

"Very amusing, Katherine. We just feel it's time we gave some more of our money away to the casino. Is that all right?"

"We've got our own casino in Melbourne now, Mum. Why do you need to go all the way to South Australia?"

"It's a holiday, darling. The casino is just a bonus. I promise I won't lose all your inheritance, if that's what you're worried about."

"It's not the casino that's running down the value of my inheritance, Mum, it's the speeding fines you get every time you drive over there. They'll take your license away if you lose any more points you know."

"That's why we're flying this time, we—oh . . ." There was silence for a few seconds and Kit could picture her mother pushing a few strands of her slowly graying honey-blond hair behind one ear while being totally distracted by a pot plant growing or a sparrow farting on her windowsill.

"Mum? Hello?"

"Did you want anything in particular, Katherine, or have you just run out of coffee at your place?"

"Well, actually I wanted to ask you about Celia Robinson."

"Who?"

"Celia Robinson. She says she went to school with you, Mum. Short, round, outrageous hair, lots of money. You know, Celia Robinson."

"Oh, you mean Chel Everton. Haven't seen her for ages. I didn't know you knew her, darling."

"I didn't until today. She's given me some work. She said she got my name from you. So what gives?"

"Oh, isn't that nice, dear. Well, now that I think about it, I did bump into her about six months ago. We were both having a massage at Juno's and had lunch together afterwards. I'd totally forgotten about that. That's not like me."

Kit choked back a laugh. "So what did you talk about? I mean, how did I come up in conversation?"

"What a silly question, Katherine. Do you think I'm completely oblivious to your existence when you're not standing right in front of me to remind me of where you came from?"

"No, of course not, Mum. I didn't mean that," Kit said. Sometimes I wonder though, she thought.

"Besides it was ages ago. I expect we talked about the usual things old school chums talk about when they haven't seen each other for years. Not that we were actually chums at school. But you know how it is—common ground and all that. Chel was the sporty type, and you know I was never interested in all those balls and bats and things. She, however, was into everything. She was sports captain in our final year and the star hockey player. The whole bit. Every girl at school had a crush on her; she was our champion."

"Are you sure we're talking about the same person?" Kit just couldn't picture the Celia Robinson she had met that morning with a jolly hockey stick in one hand setting young schoolgirl hearts a-flutter as she inspired the school team to victory.

"Honestly, Katherine, I thought your father and I had taught you better than to judge people by their appearance." Lillian sounded quite miffed, as if she'd failed dreadfully in teaching one of the great lessons in life.

"I'm not judging her, Mum. I just don't think my imagination is up to the task."

"Well, she might have got a little curly around the edges but she

25

was quite a beauty in those days. And a little dynamo on the field. What work has she given you anyway?"

"You know I can't tell you that, Mum. But thanks for the PR job you did on me. It obviously caused quite an impression."

"I don't remember saying all that much." Kit recognized the ever-so-humble tone in Lillian's voice. It was a dead giveaway that said she'd been caught out at something. Like the way she always said "um" before asking a favor or before admitting that she'd already done something that someone else was bound to consider questionable or premature.

"So tell me about Celia." Kit dragged the phone off the desk so she could reach the fridge to get another Coke.

"I don't have a lot of time, darling, so it will have to be the bare bones. I'm sure you could find out more if you need to by going through my old magazines."

Kit actually shuddered at the thought. Lillian had worked for years as a freelance theatre critic and that, combined with the short stories she used to write for women's magazines, meant her study was effectively insulated against nuclear fallout by twenty years' worth of arty magazines and copies of *Cleo* and *New Idea*. She'd had to buy every issue just in case her latest story was in it and no one had bothered to inform her. At least that had always been her excuse.

"Chel came from somewhere in the Western District, if I remember correctly," Lillian was saying. "Not from one of the moneyed families out that way. I think her father was the manager of someone else's sheep or cows or whatever. Anyway her parents worked like navvies I gather to give her the best they could. And she turned up trumps in a big way. She met Carl Orlando at the Boat Races one year."

'The Boat Races? That's where you met Dad. And didn't Constance and James spy each other across a crowded room on the same day?"

"Well, it was the social event of the year for all of us, girls and boys alike, who'd been imprisoned in separate schools while being trained to be proper young ladies and gentlemen. The Races separated the men from the boys and the women from the wallflowers. They flexed their muscles and we scratched each other's eyes out to be the first to dance with them. I imagine it's all still going on. I'm sure it was the same in your last year at school, darling, though knowing you I don't suppose you noticed."

"Obviously not," Kit said.

"Where was I? Oh yes, Carl Orlando. He was the cousin, I think, of Suzie Goodall. A splendid-looking boy—well, young man really. He'd been sent out from England by one of the publishing houses to do whatever it was the Poms regularly did to their colonial outposts. They're still doing it, from what I hear from Charlie Hindstead. Anyway it was apparently love at first sight, though Chel still had a year of school to get through. They were married the day after final exams. He was already well-off but I heard he came into an inheritance from his Spanish grandfather or someone. That's when they started Orlando House and, as they say, the rest is history."

"What about the rest of her story?" Kit asked, standing up to thump the side of the air-conditioner to remind it that its thermostat was lying again about having cooled the room down.

"Well, she had a daughter a few years later. When we had lunch that day I remember Chel being so proud of her, of what she was doing for herself, although she seemed sad that they'd drifted apart a little. I gather the girl's been quite a handful over the years. She's doing journalism or some such thing in London and here and there. I got the feeling Chel was a little jealous too, in a way. The daughter, now what's her name . . .?"

"Elizabeth," Kit said.

"Yes, Elizabeth, she virtually ran away at the first opportunity. It obviously hurt Chel but I suspect the problem lay with the girl's relationship with the stepfather not with Chel herself. At least I inferred that much."

"So what happened to Carl?"

"He was killed in a car accident. Such a tragedy. Chel loved him so much I would have thought she'd have stayed in widow's weeds till her turn came. But I suppose some people just can't take being on their own. Though god knows why she married that Robinson fellow. Katherine, I have to go now. I can hear Connie hoo-hooing up the side path and I'm not nearly ready to go."

"OK, Mum. Thanks for all the goss. Give me a ring when you get home and try not to lose the farm on the roulette table. I love you."

"Love you too, Katherine," Lillian said before the line went dead.

Kit picked up the file on Geoffrey Robinson again and stared long and hard at the photo of the man who was giving Chel Everton such a hard time. Bastard! Kit was developing quite a soft spot for her new client.

"Been to see the bank manager, have we?"

"Jesus, Del! You frightened the life out of me," Kit said, bending to pick up the scattered contents of the file that had taken flight when she'd leapt to her feet. "And what, pray tell, has the bank manager to do with anything?"

"Your gorgeous legs have come out of hiding, sweetheart. The only time a sensible woman wears a skirt these days is to get money that's not already hers from a stingy man in a bad suit who behaves as if the cash comes from his own private superannuation fund."

"Very funny. *I've* been working, unlike some people I know."

"Well, that's one way of making sure you can pay the rent next week," said Del, bending over the sink to splash cold water on her tanned face and long long neck. She undid another couple of buttons on her lavender blouse and leant her statuesque body into the breeze from the air-conditioner.

Despite the fact that much of Del Fielding's daily banter consisted of smart one-liners this handsome gray-haired woman was one of Kit's best friends. She often wondered why, seeing the most insulting wise-cracks were usually aimed in her direction. But Del was smiling now so Kit stopped wondering, as usual, and pulled a face instead.

They had been firm friends since the day, twelve years ago, when Kit and her partner Marek had been called to a disturbance outside Aurora Press. Del was standing in the doorway, all six foot of her, with arms folded, hurling abuse at three drunken yobbos who'd decided that a window belonging to a bunch of feminists was an appropriate place to take a piss. They had also been accosting every female passer-by, whether they had business at Aurora or not. Kit was still a uniformed cop then but that hadn't deterred one of the offenders from taking a swing at her as she tried to book him for indecent behavior. Del had caught hold of Kit before she hit the ground and later, after a second divisional van had taken the three drunks away, Del had treated Kit's cut lip while Marek took the necessary statements.

"Where's Brigit?" Kit asked.

"Hanging round the knicker department of Dimmey's. There's another sale on and our Brigie does so love a bargain," Del said, rubbing her hands together. "I swear I don't know what the woman does with all that underwear."

"Are you two going to Angie's tonight?" Kit asked.

"Probably. It is Friday after all. Will you be joining us, or is sultry Sam still in town?"

"No and yes. We're going out for dinner."

"That should be exciting," Del said flatly. "I don't know what you see in that airhead."

"There seems to be a lot of things you don't know today, Ms. Fielding," Kit snarled. "I'll thank you to keep your uncharitable remarks to yourself."

"Oh, excuse me! I'm sorry for living in hope that one day you'll take up with someone who's at least *half* as smart as you are."

"I don't want to hear this, Del," Kit said, picking up her shoes.

"Of course not, sweetheart."

"And don't be patronizing. Just because it's been centuries since you were in lust."

Del shook her head slowly as she watched Kit stuff several manila folders and the shoes into her briefcase. "That remark couldn't be further from the truth," she said with a smile. "It does, however, show how little you know about long-term *meaningful* relationships, Katherine. With you it's only ever lust, which may be exciting, orgasmic, weight-reducing and the best way to spend a spare hour or two, but is also superficial, empty and above all transitory."

"Thank you for the analysis, Dr. Freud," Kit said, one hand on her hip in a gesture of standing her ground. That was impossible to do for too long under that know-it-all gaze, and she really hated it when Del was having one of her "it's time to get serious and settle down, Kit" days. Unable to think of a clever parting shot she shrugged her shoulders, grabbed her briefcase and, opening the office door, said, "My love life, *Delbridge*, is none of your business."

29

"Sure. Until next week when you don't have one and are in desperate need of company," Del called after her.

"That's what friends are for," Kit said, closing the door behind her. She took the stairs two at a time and dumped her briefcase on the small landing at the top while she unlocked the door to her apartment. As she stepped inside she heard a faint rustling sound above her and, expecting a surprise attack, quickly removed her pantihose before ascending the five steps from the inside landing. She was right. She only made it halfway past the sitting room before a deranged black commando launched itself from behind the begonia and grabbed hold of her leg.

"Let go, you lunatic!" she shouted as she tried to walk Quasimodo-like into the kitchen with The Cat clinging tenaciously to her right ankle. When she bent to pick it up it darted maniacally off in several directions at once before leaping onto the kitchen bench to sit demurely as if butter wouldn't melt in its mouth.

"I heard you this time, you feral feline. You're getting careless, Thistle," Kit said, leaning in for the customary head-butt hello.

She turned the kettle on, threw some coffee into a mug and stared absently at the collage of photographs on the wall. There was a polaroid shot of herself sprawled on the couch with The Cat from Hell perched on her shoulder. It was only the two bright satanic eyes which distinguished the tiny black ball of fur from the shoulder-length curls of Kit's worst-ever haircut. The Cat was a lot bigger and Kit's hair a lot shorter now than when that shot had been taken two years ago, about the same time as the one of her brother Michael above it. He was poised in front of one of his cosmic landscapes, waiting for a reaction from Lillian who looked as though she was suffering severe indigestion. Amongst the collection there was also Detective Sergeant Jon Marek peering over the top of a *Phantom* comic; Nick and Phil grinning lasciviously at each other at last year's Christmas party; Genevieve looking totally ravishing outside a café in Firenze; and Del at Angie's, mouth open as usual, haranguing someone else for a change, while Brigit overflowed a bar stool in the background.

Kit had never been able to figure out why Del was so disdainful of her personal relationships. That wasn't entirely true; of course she'd figured it out. She was just reluctant to acknowledge there was a certain amount of truth in what her friend was saying. It really riled Kit that it had reached the stage where the moment she met someone new she realized she was also anticipating Del's reaction. There would always be some unsolicited remark about her choice of partner, and when the affair didn't work out it would undoubtedly be because of Kit's cavalier attitude towards any sort of commitment. Though why Del would want Kit to commit herself to someone she'd called an airhead, or worse, was something Kit couldn't fathom, but that was Del.

Kit placed the coffee on her desk and was about to turn on her computer to tackle chapter five of her novel when she noticed the light flashing on the answering machine. There was a message from her mother about going to Adelaide, a reminder from Marek about a barbecue on Sunday, then the dulcet tones of Sam Hellier.

"Um, this is me. I'm really sorry Kit but we'll have to postpone dinner. Dominic wants me in Sydney this afternoon for a re-shoot of that Callio thing. Got to go. Sorry. See you next week."

"Shit! Shit, shit, shit." There was no way Kit was going to break down and join Del and Brigit at Angie's after being stood up by sultry Sam. She switched on her PC, typed three pages of murder and mayhem into chapter five of her novel, then went out and hired three action movies and settled in for a night of vicarious body thumping, alone—again.

Chapter 3

The worst thing about any surveillance job is the sheer boredom. And the cramps. You can't take along a good book in case you get too involved in it and forget why you're sitting in the front seat of a car in a dead-end alley on a Saturday night suffering periodic muscle spasms. Besides, you can't turn on the interior light to read by as the whole idea is to be inconspicuous. For the same reason you can't have the car radio on, at least not too loud, and you can't get out of the car too often to stretch your legs because that would look a bit sus too. So Kit sat with her feet up on the dashboard trying to do a cryptic crossword by streetlight. She had a clear view of the Patrician Club's main entrance which, despite the address, was not in Collins Street proper but in the narrow lane which ran beside the featureless two-storey bluestone building. The lane, unlike the alley piled with rubbish in which Kit was parked, was about fifty meters long and ended in a small car park, sentry box and all, reserved for Patrician members.

Kit had witnessed the drivers of several cars, on their third or fourth circuit of the block in the impossible quest for a legal car park in the center of Melbourne, finally take a punt on parking illegally in the vacant lane. Each time the mountain disguised as a balding moustached doorman, employed to prevent such liberties, had waited till the driver and any passengers were out of the car before sauntering over to inform them that in actual fact parking there was just not on.

It was only eleven p.m. but Kit felt as if she'd been sitting in her car for a week. It was damn hot and the stinking alley, bordered on three sides by buildings which blocked out all but a tiny patch of night sky, offered no respite from the heat.

Just in case the seven-thirty appointment at the Patrician was a cover for something else Kit had begun her surveillance of Geoffrey Robinson at six o'clock. Parked three sweeping drives away from the Robinson residence she had watched Celia and Geoffrey return from their afternoon of tennis at six-fifteen. He had emerged again, in a dark green Bentley, at seven and driven from Toorak to the Patrician with only one stop—at the South Yarra Post Office where he checked a private postbox. He'd entered the Patrician a little after seven-thirty after exchanging a few brief words in the doorway with an elderly gent who was on his way out.

"God, this is so boring," Kit complained to the brick wall beside her. The radio was caught in a time warp, playing the same songs over and over and over, and if she heard one more rap tune she was going to shoot the bloody thing. The huge door in the lane opposite swung open and Kit caught sight of Geoffrey amongst the group of Patricians who seemed to tumble from the club as if they'd been regurgitated. Several minutes later she was following the green Bentley down St. Kilda Road. Her renewed hopes of a reasonably early night, however, were dashed as Geoffrey ignored the last possible turn-off for home, took a right turn at the junction and a left into Gray Street, slowing down as he got to the sexual hub of downtown St. Kilda.

"Oh great, Geoffrey! So this is what you do with your spare change," Kit said as she too had to slow to cruising speed to maintain a sensible distance behind OHP's business manager as he perved at the short-skirted red-lipped scenery. He pulled into the curb four or five times and, though apparently hard to please, was caught for posterity in full color by Kit's motor-driven Nikon. She was confident she'd managed to get at least one profile, his unmistakable ears fairly flapping in the breeze as a charming blond put her best tit forward in her bid to bonk in the back seat of his Bentley.

"No deal, sweetheart," Kit said aloud. "Our Geoffrey seems to be looking for something special tonight."

Geoffrey turned down the next street on the left and Kit had to slam on her brakes to avoid ending up in his boot as she rounded the corner. The Bentley was curbside again and this time Geoffrey was consulting with a young punk whose black jeans were so tight he must have sprayed them on. Kit had no choice but to drive on. She pulled in a little further up the street and looked back to see Geoffrey parking the car on her side of a large elm tree, out of the full glare of the streetlight on the corner.

In her struggle to get into the back seat Kit missed the shot of Master Snake-hips opening the passenger door of the Bentley and getting in. The telephoto lens couldn't pick up any detail from that distance but Kit could make out that the young man did not remain in view for long, and that for some reason Geoffrey had tilted his seat back—just a little.

"I wonder if this is the kind of floozy Celia had in mind," Kit thought. She was quick off the mark when the Bentley's interior light came on a few minutes later as the passenger door opened. She got a couple of good shots of man giving boy money before Geoffrey's hand shot up to cover the light.

"Bourke Street, Monday night. Eleven p.m. to be exact. Twenty-six degrees and no breeze." Kit switched the walkperson's record button off while she argued with the top of the esky sitting on the passenger seat beside her. "For god's sake I just want a drink, let me in!" She thumped the lid with one hand at the same time as her jiggling of the handle with the other released the catch. The lid leapt out the open window and landed in the gutter. "Oh fine, if that's the way you feel," she said, getting out of the car to retrieve it.

"Right now, where was I?" She settled back into the driver's seat, twisted the top off a bottle of mineral water and switched the record button back on. "Monday night, eleven-oh-five. Still no breeze. Geoffrey Robinson, the portly Miles Denning and Mr. Zaber Ink himself were the first to arrive for what appeared to be a purely social evening. They were joined over the next fifteen minutes by Marjorie Finlay, the power-dressed marketing director desperately in need of sensible shoes; Greg the blimp Fulton, desperately enamored of Marjorie Finlay; a tall elegantly dressed gray-eyed woman who was obviously desperately interested in everything that went on around her despite her detached manner; and a petite blond who, although

34

obviously desperate about her life in general, made only a few half-hearted attempts to distract Fulton's attention from the impressive Marjorie F, who in actual fact was directing all her attention towards Geoffrey. Here they come. End transmission!"

Kit turned her attention to the doorway across the street. The Stone Garden was one of those first-floor city restaurants accessed by a long flight of stairs from an inconspicuous door at street level. Staking out such an establishment was next to impossible, unless all you wanted to do was record the comings and goings and not the goings-on. So Kit had reserved a table for two and after convincing her brother Michael that getting a free meal would be worth the effort of finding a clean shirt she had arrived a good fifteen minutes before the group from OHP. While Michael had pushed sushi around his plate and discussed his ideas of light, color and the cosmic inspiration of his latest painting, Kit had kept her eyes and half her mind focused on the Robinson entourage. Apart from giving her a chance to see the public, or rather socially acceptable, side of Geoffrey it had also made it easier to know who to photograph leaving the restaurant. Which was what she was doing now, a good hour after sending Michael home in a taxi.

The first to leave was the gray-eyed woman who strolled up the street alone and climbed into a Stag. Next to emerge was Greg Fulton and the little blond, followed shortly afterwards by the rest of the group. There was a lot of laughing and shaking of hands in the street before Marjorie Finlay and William Zaber set off in one direction and Geoffrey and Miles Denning in the other.

Kit started her car but waited till they had walked round the corner before making a U-turn to follow Geoffrey. Denning was standing beside the Bentley, waiting for Geoffrey to unlock the doors. Next stop the Patrician. The alley Kit had used on Saturday was occupied by a beat-up old Holden so she had to park down the street a little in a No Standing Zone.

Half an hour later Kit grabbed her camera to get a shot of one of the city's new breed of boy wonders leaving one of the city's oldest boys' clubs. Kit recognized Ian Dalkeith from two photographs she'd seen in the weekend papers. One had shown him hobnobbing with all the right people at a recent polo match, obviously trying to polish off a few of his rough edges. The other had accompanied a short article describing in typically vague terms the redevelopment plans for Dalkeith's latest acquisition. Several hectares of disused docklands would eventually be transformed into "a state-of-the-art integrated business and residential district worthy of Melbourne's position in the international market place"—whatever the hell that meant.

It appeared the young property developer was cultivating a public persona. Two years ago the press would have said "Ian Who?" But now there were two things about the boy from Nowhere, that mythical place not found on any map, that the social pages at least could not ignore: he was very very rich and very very handsome. For the life of her Kit couldn't work out how a forty-year-old parvenu from the world of real estate had become friends with a fifty-four-year-old wanker from the publishing industry. Unless of course they had first met in the front seat of Geoffrey's Bentley! But that would be too weird.

Kit was beginning to wonder just what went on amongst the Patricians that prompted Geoffrey to follow a couple of hours at his club with a few quick thrills in St. Kilda. For here he was again, cruising along the gutter, checking out the local merchandise. The punk from Saturday night—or at least it looked like the same guy—stuck his head through the open window of the Bentley but was obviously not the desired flavor for the night. He stepped back from the car and pointed down the street, whereupon Geoffrey pulled out into the traffic again then parked one block further down.

Kit watched as Geoffrey just sat there, waving off the approaches of a couple of perfectly acceptable sex workers, until a tall redhead sashayed past his car, expertly ignoring him. "Hooked you, you jerk-off," Kit said with a laugh as she saw Geoffrey lean across the passenger seat. The woman, dressed in *very* long black stockings and what was probably a skirt but looked more like a crimson leather belt topped off, literally, with an almost-but-not-quite transparent black singlet, turned on her professional heels with a casual "what, who me?" look. She approached the car and, with one finely muscled arm resting on the roof, she bent from the hips with a perfectly straight back to find out how she could possibly help the gentleman.

Whatever it was he needed was apparently within her field of expertise. Kit followed the car down a couple of backstreets then photographed the woman escorting Geoffrey towards the wide concrete steps of a nondescript two-storey house. St. Kilda was full of these once-grand old buildings, many of which had been divided up into self-contained apartments. Kit grabbed her leather jacket, chucked a blanket over her camera gear, leapt out of and locked her car and sprinted across the street. She struggled into her jacket, zipped it up to the throat and pulled a black baseball cap from the pocket. She slowed down to a brisk walk but was level with the gate before she realized Geoffrey was still standing in the building's well-lit lobby. Pulling the cap down over her eyes she kept on walking till she'd gained the cover of a large tangled bush on the other side of the front garden, then vaulted the low fence and made a dash for the wide veranda and the bed of hydrangeas directly in front. She pulled herself up and from a crouching position peered through the tall narrow window beside the front door in time to see Geoffrey and the crimson tart ascend the carpeted stairs.

Kit tried the door before she noticed the numbered keypad recessed into the wall. Pretty posh for a cathouse, she thought. Now what?

The only access to the rear of the house was a narrow garden down the right-hand side of the building, overgrown but not exactly unkempt. Kit noticed a light go on above her on the first floor but could only assume it was Geoffrey. She pushed her way through the bushes till she found the bottom of the fire escape. It was unlikely, however, that the rickety wooden stairs would provide a safe escape in the event of fire and absolutely no way was Kit going to test their ability to carry anything heavier than a woodworm.

She figured the building, in its heyday, had been one of those charming seaside guesthouses specializing in a touch of gracious living for middle-class holiday-makers. Or perhaps it had been an annual retreat for a collection of crusty old bachelors and spinsters, à la Deborah Kerr and David Niven in *Separate Tables*. Whatever it had been before the veneer of seediness had taken root in this part of the city, before drugs and prostitution had taken over from Luna Park and the beach as the main tourist attractions, it was now only the stuff of memory. The muffled sound of grunting and groaning followed by a clearly audible, "Oh yes! Yes, Mr. Bond. Give me both barrels," escaped from the window just above Kit's head to confirm the fact.

Kit climbed the fence, just under where she'd seen the light go on and tried to work out if there was higher ground on the other side. Next door was a derelict building, similar to the one Geoffrey was ensconced in but missing most of its windows on this side. Derelict did not necessarily mean empty so she gave up on the idea of trying to get a better view and went back to her car.

An hour later Kit was having serious problems with a dead body. She had just watched it fall forty feet from a South Melbourne warehouse roof into a conveniently placed dump bin. Too convenient! It needed to be found fairly soon. She dragged it out of the bin and back up to the roof. This time it landed on the roof of a car. That should attract some attention!

She saved the file, closed it and opened a new one. A new empty one. She got up and walked away from the very blank screen, then wandered into the kitchen, removed the cotton scarf she'd tied around her neck, soaked it under the cold tap again and put it back on. How could she be creative when even the weather was against her? She was sure the heat was turning her brain to mush.

Excuses, excuses, O'Malley! Kit knew she was doing everything she could think of to avoid the issue at hand. Which was . . . what?

"Come on, you know," she said to herself.

"OK. It's love. Or is it romance?" herself answered.

"Either one, O'Malley. Just get on with it."

"All right already!" She went back to her desk and flopped into her chair a safe distance from the unhelpful keyboard. Everything was ripe, the set-up was perfect, it had to happen sooner or later.

"Later," she said. "I'll think about it tomorrow."

I've heard that one before, Scarlett, a little voice from nowhere said. She eyed the blinking cursor suspiciously, as if it had been going through her garbage or reading her personal diary.

"You've forgotten what it's like, O'Malley, that's your problem," Kit said dismally as she downed the last of the iced coffee in her mug and escaped to the kitchen to pour some more from the jug.

"Oh no I haven't," she argued. "I know it's been a while but it's not something you forget. My problem is I don't have the faintest idea how to write about it." She made a piece of toast and Vegemite to put it off a little longer.

How do you make someone fall in love—on paper? How do you do it in real life, for god's sake? That one you can answer, Katherine O'Malley.

No I can't, Kit argued silently. I've no idea how that happened. I just opened my eyes one day and I was right in the middle of it. These things are not planned, so how the hell do you put it on paper so that it doesn't look contrived?

"It's going to be contrived no matter what you do," she shouted at the empty room.

The Cat, which was sensibly maintaining a safe distance, mewed loudly as if she agreed wholeheartedly.

"Oh be quiet, Thistle. What the hell would you know? All you ever do with that handsome Mr. Rufus next door is flirt."

Kit returned to her computer to see if it had written a page or two of erotic fiction while she'd been in the kitchen. The cursor winked on, off, on, off—taunting her from the otherwise empty screen.

So far she had a fine cast of characters in a workable plot which actually had a beginning, a middle and an end—well, at least the synopsis did. She had four-and-a-bit chapters of a well-paced (she hoped) storyline, with carefully placed victims, several viable suspects and one decidedly nasty piece of work who was motivated by lust—lust for lust, lust for power and lust for money. So, she thought, the bad guy is suitably motivated—or is that typically motivated? Whatever. The bad guy is not the center of the piece though. He is merely the thing which makes the good guy . . . what? Which *makes* the good guy, of course. There would be no need for a hero if there was no bad guy.

The thing here is that the bad guy doesn't even have to make it to the last page. The hero does, however. And what's more the reader has to care enough about the hero to want to make it to the last page with her.

"Oh my god. What have I taken on here? I must be mad. Am I mad, Thistle honey?" The Cat's meow was definitely in the affirmative.

So, where was I? Oh yes. The bad guy has to be suitably motivated but the hero has to have depth. So what motivates the good guy? Or in this case the good girl. Why on earth would anyone want to be a detective? There's nothing terribly glamorous about it, that's for sure. I should know. And it's certainly not the money. Clients like dear old Celia do not grow on trees. So what then? Ask yourself Kit. As you say, you should know.

"Yes," she said, "but we know I'm only doing it for the purpose of research and for pocket money so I can afford to torture myself with this computer every other night."

Kit got up and paced the lounge room floor several times just to waste time, and then did it again just to make sure. She ventured out onto the patio to see if the cool change was hiding out there. It wasn't.

Perhaps I should forget about in-depth characterization and just shuffle a few more bodies and suspects around my hard disk, she thought. On the other hand I could rewrite this as a science fiction detective story, then Flynn Carter could be an android and wouldn't need a past, or a life philosophy, or any depth at all—just a prime directive to make sure that good always wins out over evil. No. I suppose that's a cop out. In order for the reader, or even me the author, to believe in the notion of "Flynn Carter to the rescue" she has to have hopes and dreams and flaws. It might seem like a great achievement to have her solve the case in hand quite brilliantly, but she has to have another life. She can't exist solely to rescue Sweet Charlotte from the villain and push Dastardly Derek under the train thereby saving the townsfolk from a fate worse than aerobics. She's got to have a mother, or a dog, or some friends even if they're just waiting in the wings. She's got to eat, go shopping, get angry about something, or at least think about something other than the case, even if it's just about what she's going to eat, or buy or get angry about. She has got to be real.

"No dummy, not real. This is fiction, O'Malley," Kit corrected herself. "She has to be believable. But what the hell does that mean? Half my friends aren't believable. Start again."

She returned to her computer and typed, tentatively, the words: "Depth—asparagus, toilet paper, the ozone layer."

"Smart arse," she said aloud and then added: "Beliefs, dreams, wants, needs, desires; I need, I want, I ache . . ."

"Whoa, Katherine. Who are we talking about here? This is getting personal." She saved the tiny file and went into the kitchen. She filled the sink, unloaded the dishwasher and did three days' worth of dishes by hand. Now she knew for sure that she would do anything to avoid the issue. She felt that all she'd managed to do was set the scene, get the plot going, introduce the heroic Flynn Carter (she had a memorable name if nothing else) and the love interest. Now what? Flynn had managed to get from one side of a room or two to the other without it reading like it had taken Kit three hours to work out how to get her to walk. She knew "depth" was not the issue here; love was. Flynn had a past, and a social life, she even had a dog and a passion for Italian food. But how did she feel about falling in love? How would she feel as she fell?

"Pretty bloody silly," Kit said to the saucepan. With her hands in the sink, however, there were suddenly plenty of viable thoughts floating around with the bubbles. She started to get excited, wanted the chore to be over so she could write them down. She knew in her bones though that when the time came—even if she stopped right now to record them—that these perfect ideas, these pearls of wisdom, these unutterably romantic notions would disappear down the plughole with the dirty dishwater.

She wondered what on earth it was she was trying to achieve. This unavoidable untamable urge to write was doing serious damage to her psyche. God, how many nights had she lain awake with the pure poetry of brilliant dialogue and unforgettable descriptions rattling around her brain? In the dark she would concoct a magic potion of verbs, nouns, adjectives and startling metaphors that would raise raw emotion and the pangs of love to new and incredible heights (E. B. Browning eat your heart out!) only to have it all evaporate the moment she turned on the light to find a pen. She often imagined there was a whole novel skulking around the ceiling or hiding in the back of her closet. But perhaps she was only a literary genius in the dead of night when the lights were off. Unforgettable descriptions indeed! The cold light of day was all it ever took to turn those raw emotions and her beautifully composed, nerve-jangling, gut-wrenching love pangs into mushy romantic fiction.

"So what's wrong with that, O'Malley? Romantic fiction is what this is all about," Kit said as she pulled the plug and watched her inspiration go down the gurgler with three peas and a sodden piece of cabbage.

She'd set out to write a romantic detective novel, or was it a detective novel with a romance? Perhaps she should forget the romance and just write a detective novel; after all it was the love business that was stretching the bounds of credibility.

"I think I'm depressed, Thistle." Kit wiped down the bench while The Cat flung her head around trying to capture the cloth every time it swept past.

Kit returned to her computer and started typing: "How do you develop a sexual attraction on paper, using a machine? How do you convey feeling of any sort with words?"

OK, she thought, I might—just—be able to write how *I* feel using words that aren't vomitously sentimental but how do you convey someone *else's* feelings, especially when that someone is a figment of your imagination, a complete work of fiction? There has to be a tension, a tingling, a full orchestra in the background, a feeling of association like: "Oh yes, woo, I've been there" or "Oh god wouldn't it be wonderful to *feel* like that."

Kit read what she had just written then abandoned the file, sending it into that parallel universe which accommodates randomly discarded pieces of information, left socks, lost biros and all those numbers with lots of zeros that governments the world over claim is the real money they've saved their taxpayers. Kit was getting desperate. Maybe she *had* forgotten what it was like.

"How do you make love real?" she asked, scratching Thistle's head. Hadn't someone already asked that? No, that was "How do you make love stay?" or something like that. It was Tom Robbins in *Still Life With Woodpecker,* that's right. Now if he could write a love story that took place inside a packet of Camel cigarettes surely Kit could write one that takes place in a detective novel. She remembered finding quite a few answers in that book—way back when she was barely a quarter of a century old, backing her pack around the world, believing in the romance of pyramids and the certainty that real love once found would last forever. That, of course, had been when she was still looking for herself, before she found love and then lost it again in a rain-soaked Italian village. If there was only one true love in every lifetime then Kit had had hers—and carelessly misplaced it.

She contemplated clearing the towels off the top shelf in the linen cupboard and crawling in there with the moth balls. Instead she went and stood in front of the stereo, trying to decide what kind of music might quell the rising angst that was taking control of her reason. She was feeling quite seasick, which was pretty disconcerting considering she was standing in a well-anchored and totally landlocked lounge room. Taking several deep breaths she decided Beethoven's fifth piano concerto might just soothe the savage breast and help her locate her sense of proportion, which appeared to have gone into hiding to avoid being roughed up by the nasty seeds of doubt germinating in her mind.

Lillian always said Kit's irrational moods were the result of having been born in the eye of a hurricane; it made her calm in the center and decidedly ragged around the edges. Kit on the other hand knew these moods were hereditary, the result of having a mother who had spent too much time in high altitudes.

She went back to her computer and typed in "Life's a Bitch—and then you bleed" before switching it off. She grabbed a tub of chocolate ice-cream from the freezer, a spoon from the drawer, The Cat from the bench and escaped to the lounge. Ludwig wasn't helping at all so she switched him off too, turned on the TV and VCR, selected her favorite movie and threw her melting body into her armchair.

"That's better," she said to Thistle as the deep space salvage team began their rescue of Ripley and Jones the cat for the forty-third time.

Chapter 4

"Thistle, please come out. Now, damn you!" Kit was down on her hands and knees opening one kitchen cupboard after another, trying to coax out the creature playing percussion with the pots and pans. "If you don't come out right now I shall shut all the doors and go on holiday for a week. I'm sure what's left of you when I return will make a fine calpac."

"That's no way to talk to that beautiful feline," Del said from the doorway.

"You get her out then," Kit said, crossing her arms and slouching back against the cupboard with her legs splayed out before her.

Del strolled over, her gaze travelling from the wild black hair down the slender neck and body till it was arrested with what seemed to be admiration by the naked tautly muscled thigh revealed by a strategic slit in Kit's tight black skirt. "That's a most unattractive way to sit," she said and knelt down to peer into the open cupboard. "Come on baby," she cooed. "Come on out, precious, or your mean mother will turn you into a hat."

Thistle came bounding out, her tail flicking irreverently at Kit while she rubbed around Del's ankles as if greeting a long-lost friend.

"Brazen hussy," Kit snarled as she got to her feet and pulled her skirt down to straighten it just above her knees.

"Stockings would be a nice touch, Katherine," Del said, adjusting the collar of Kit's turquoise silk shirt.

"I do believe you're right, Ms. Fielding. But I shall put them on in the car because Mad Manx here can't resist my ankles at the best of times and stockings send her wild with desire."

"I don't know how you sleep in here with all these people watching you," Del said from the doorway of the huge bedroom, across which Kit was throwing shoes in her search for the pair to the one she was holding.

"They help me dream," Kit said with a wave at the gallery of beautifully framed prints adorning the walls. Amongst them Katherine Hepburn stared with barely contained excitement from the stern of the *African Queen*; Ingrid Bergman stood on a rocky crag wearing her shining partisan's face while the bells tolled for someone or other; and Audrey Hepburn's Eliza Doolittle made her grand entrance at Ascot, while Deborah Kerr and Yul Brynner reined in their sexual attraction during one of the most famous dancing lessons on celluloid. And that was just one wall.

Above Kit's queen-sized futon, which rested on a carpeted platform two steps up from floor level, an exquisite Catherine Deneuve lounged in a chair, offering her shirt to an unsuspecting Susan Sarandon; while over by the window the stunning and silent Louise Brooks contemplated the ramifications of opening Pandora's Box.

"Well I hate to rush you, Ms. Make-believe, but this thing starts in half an hour and as you know I'm only going so you've got a reason to be there."

"I know, I know. I'm ready already."

"Hair," said Del simply.

Kit stomped back to the full-length mirror by the window. "What's wrong with it?" she asked, offering her customary palms-up gesture.

"It looks like a bird's nest."

"It is. I've got a whole flock of finches in here somewhere," she said, running her hands through her short hair to quieten it down a bit.

Ten minutes later they were in the thick of a traffic jam en route to the Hilton Hotel. At least *they* were en route to the Hilton. The rest of the jam was going to a night cricket match at the MCG. Kit was trying to struggle into her pantihose in the confined space of Del's Volkswagen while Del was swearing out the window at no one in particular.

"My god I'm melting," Kit complained. "I need another cold shower already."

"We could go to Angie's instead," Del suggested hopefully. "It would be cool there."

"It wouldn't help my case but," Kit stated, finally managing to get her skirt down again.

"Don't call me but or I'll keep driving till we run out of petrol. I really hate these things, you realize," Del added for the tenth time.

"I know already. But you're such a martyr, *Saint* Delbridge."

Kit had discovered quite by accident that Del had shelved an official invitation to the very same publishing function that Geoffrey and Celia were due to attend at the Hilton. Del had a great many connections in a lot of surprising places and it never ceased to amaze Kit who her friend knew and why. In this case the cap she wore was that of literary critic, highly regarded for both her regular contributions to weekend newspaper supplements and the reviews of less mainstream fiction published in her own Aurora Press. Despite her reputation she rarely attended publishing or media industry soirees unless the guest speaker was an author she particularly wanted to meet. She'd had no desire to get within three suburbs of tonight's special guest but Kit had finally managed to talk her into attending after agreeing that Del could join any stakeout of Geoffrey afterwards. Kit had warned her that it would probably just be hot and boring—but that was the deal. Kit was to be Del's assistant editor for the duration of the Hilton affair, then Del would get to play detective for a night if Geoffrey decided he needed stimulation of something other than his brain.

The cocktail party was the last event on the agenda for Week One before Kit met with Celia Robinson again the next day. Although, knowing Geoffrey, it would be just the first part of the last thing. She thought back over the events of the last couple of days while Del raged at the traffic. Kit had followed Geoffrey on Tuesday to his luncheon rendezvous with Ian Dalkeith at a pub bistro in South Melbourne. She'd had to drink a glass of water for every beer she ordered so as not to get drunk sitting at the bar for two-and-a-half hours. Her subjects ate a casual lunch then gave their undivided attention to a collection of neatly bound reports of some kind. There seemed to be nothing furtive in their discussion and they had taken a table by the window rather than a booth at the back so whatever they were up to appeared to be above board. There was, however, something about the immaculately dressed Ian Dalkeith that made Kit's skin crawl so when their meeting was over she'd followed him instead of Geoffrey.

She'd tailed him to an expanse of desolate weedy riverfront land, littered with twisted metal and huge dislocated cranes and bordered in parts by the battered remains of a corrugated iron fence. Totally incongruous in this vision of post-nuclear devastation was the shiny new cyclone wire fencing about twenty meters in from the street which cordoned off a row of dilapidated wooden warehouses and a sagging wharf. Dalkeith had obviously not visited this wasteland to revel in his dream of transforming it into a "state-of-the-art integrated district." All he did was drive along the fenceline, stopping only to get out and check the gate.

Kit had picked up her tail on Geoffrey again when he'd turned up at the Patrician at eight that night. A long and stiflingly hot two hours later he emerged and Kit once again followed him to the house in St. Kilda. This time he'd picked up a woman of similar build, and no doubt disposition, to the crimson tart of Monday night, although this floozy was a blond, and together they selected a matching blond boy to play with. It was on that occasion that Kit wondered whether the apartment or maybe even the whole house belonged to Geoffrey as it was he who punched in the combination to unlock the door. Or perhaps he was part-owner in what Kit's ex-partner Marek called an Accordion Conglomerate, where a bunch of so-called respectable businessmen buy into such an establishment so they can decorate their own "squeeze boxes" to carry out private takeovers of the body corporeal.

On Wednesday morning she'd called in a favor from a friend at the local council to find out just who did own the house. Geoffrey's scheduled lunch with Miles Denning and Marjorie Finlay that day— yesterday—had been cancelled by accident, or rather by *an* accident, the witnessing of which was a sight indeed for Kit's sore eyes.

Guessing that Geoffrey and his companions might do lunch locally Kit had been sitting as nonchalantly as possible on the brick wall in front of OHP's terraced and landscaped front garden, trying to blend in with the clutch of desperate smokers who were obviously banned from doing so inside their place of employment. Just after the second wave of midday lunch-takers—those who actually took lunch rather than a smoko—had passed through OHP's double glass doors Geoffrey had emerged from his imaginary empire followed closely by Ms. Finlay and Mr. Denning. Geoffrey had taken a deep breath, surveyed the world at his feet and promptly fallen arse over tit down the front stairs, all six of them.

Kit had resisted both the automatic reflex of leaping up to help a fellow human being and the much stronger urge to roll about laughing. Which was more than could be said for Miles Denning who, once it had been ascertained that his colleague had not had a heart attack or been taken out by a sniper, assumed an expression that basically said Geoffrey's novel way of getting to the front street had made his day. Marjorie Finlay on the other hand had sounded somewhat like a fish-wife, screaming Geoffrey's name in apparent horror as she watched him tumble to the footpath below. She'd rushed down to help him, realized he wasn't dead or seriously injured and, after regaining her obviously much-practiced Lauren Bacall voice, assumed full executive control of the situation by ordering everybody about.

Geoffrey's sprained left ankle and his consequent reliance on a pair of crutches had not, unfortunately, put the kibosh on his mystery six p.m. appointment that day, which turned out to be a meeting in the cocktail bar of the Regent Hotel with Ian Dalkeith and two other men, one of whom was of the American persuasion. Kit had not been able to photograph them together as it would no doubt have drawn atten-tion to her leisurely drink at the bar, but had managed to snap each of them afterwards from her car across the street as they left the hotel. Geoffrey had then gone home, and stayed there for a change.

"There's only one thing worse than a horde of stuffy publishing types getting pissed on free champagne," Del stated as she parked the car in Clarendon Street near the Hilton, "and that's a horde of scruffy journalists doing the same. And tonight we have both."

"Ah, but it will be much more fun for me to keep an eye on the roving randy Robbo if I am *also* getting pissed on free champagne," Kit said. "After all, Celia didn't really want me skulking around the streets—it's so tacky, you know."

"Hi. Katherine, isn't it? My name's Julie," said the ungainly bespectacled young woman who approached Kit with a glass of champagne in each hand.

"Er, yes," said Kit, a little taken aback. She'd been feeling like a shag on a rock since Del had deserted her after the first five minutes, which was only ten minutes ago. She'd gone to get them another drink and forgotten to come back. Using the cover of looking for a place to set down her empty glass, she glanced around the room till she spotted Del grinning at her from the midst of a clutch of semi-inebriated journalist types. Her reluctant escort, suddenly the life of the party, was probably setting her up for something. Kit accepted the champagne from Julie, who'd barely drawn breath after introducing herself.

"Your boss said you might be feeling a bit desperate, not knowing anyone else here."

"Well, not exactly desperate. Del tends to exaggerate a bit," Kit said. I'll kill her, she thought.

"Really? I only know her by reputation. She was chatting to one of my colleagues who does—know her I mean—and she just mentioned that you were standing over here all alone so to speak."

"So to speak," Kit said, wanting to crawl under the smorgasbord and hide. "So, are you a journo?"

"Good gracious no!" Julie exclaimed with the same surprise Kit would have felt had she said yes. "I'm an editorial assistant. Well, more a general dogsbody really. I work for Sandy Everett at Orlando House."

Kit nearly snorted her champagne all over the general dogsbody. Oh Del, you're beautiful. You've earned a reprieve, she thought, as she coughed out a politely interested, "Really?"

"Oh yes. That's *my* boss over there," she said, pointing in the general direction of about fifty people.

"I actually applied for a job at OHP some time back," Kit lied. "What did I miss out on?"

"It's a great place really. Everyone's so friendly. I have to deal with

49

most people there in one way or another in my capacity as Mr. Everett's, Sandy's, assistant. He's a commissioning editor, quite high up."

"What's the big boss like?"

"Mr. Denning? A lovely man. Probably quite experienced, I'd say, and friendly."

Kit was reconsidering the pardon she'd given Del. This woman was a dipstick of the first order. "What about the other top brass? I always find that if the chairman of the Board is a regular human being, for instance, that it sort of flows right on down through the ranks, so to speak," Kit said, quite at a loss at how to get useful information from someone who felt that a man of Miles Denning's calibre and reputation was "probably" quite experienced.

"Well, our chairman is a woman. Mrs. Robinson. We don't see much of her though. She was married to our founder, Mr. Carl Orlando, before he was killed in a car accident a few years back. That was before my time of course. I think she's expected here tonight; she usually attends these sort of functions. Rumor has it she drinks a bit, and there's certainly a bit to drink here," Julie said with a conspiratorial nudge to Kit's elbow.

"She obviously married again after her husband's death," Kit said, realizing she could probably ask this woman anything she liked and it wouldn't appear strange. A ditzy gossipmonger would be unlikely to realize she was being pumped for information.

"Oh yes. She married Geoffrey Robinson, our business manager. They're quite an odd couple really, when you see them together, I mean. She's sort of all roly-poly and jolly and he's stiff and conservative, a real cold fish."

"Well, I suppose even the most mismatched couples must have something in common," Kit said.

"Money probably," Julie said. "And power, I suppose. Being the boss's husband makes you more than just a business manager, doesn't it?"

"I suppose it does," Kit said with a smile. "I wouldn't imagine you'd have a lot to do with him though."

"No, not really. But he does do his rounds regularly. You know, sort of wanders about the office like a prison warden with his hands behind his back, making sure that everyone's in their right place doing what they should be doing. If he's looking in on someone who has their own office, like my boss, then he stands around in the doorway making inane conversation about publishing deadlines, or book covers, or the cricket. He always loiters longer than necessary because he doesn't really have anything to say and he never remembers people's names. It drives Sandy mad, but at least he's got an office. The rest of us suddenly find Mr. Robinson looking over our shoulder."

"I gather you don't like him much," Kit said, emptying her glass and wondering how soon she'd be able to get another.

"It's not a matter of like or dislike. I mean, he's never done anything to me to make me dislike him. It's just that he's sort of sleazy, in a rich sort of way. Like if he thought you had something to offer him then he'd take the trouble to remember your name; if not, then he's polite enough to keep his options open. It's creepy really. Speak of the devil. See what I mean?"

"Absolutely," Kit said, in no doubt that Julie was referring to the very peculiar sight indeed that marked the arrival of Celia and Geoffrey. Odd was an understatement. Geoffrey swung along on his crutches, his ears making him look like a businesslike radar dish in a soft gray suit, while Celia and her hair rolled in like a beach ball in a flurry of flame-red silk. "I think another drink is definitely in order."

Julie, who it seemed was also all alone "so to speak," followed Kit to the bar like a good little general dogsbody. As they stood waiting for the barman to open a fresh bottle of champagne, an elegant hand with fingers ringed in gold brushed Kit's arm as its owner reached for the ashtray on the bar. There was a throaty "excuse me" as the woman took a very deliberate look at Kit, gave Julie a cursory nod, then interrupted one of the men beside her to disagree with some point he was trying to make about promotional schedules. Kit recognized her as the gray-eyed woman from Geoffrey's outing to the Japanese restaurant on Monday night. At such close quarters, however, the angular face revealed a certain calculated fierceness Kit had not noticed then. Her general demeanor shouted "approach with caution," and her not unattractive features were made almost severe by a bun which pulled her brown hair back so tightly it looked painful. The deep voice, however, had an unforgettable tone and the intensity of the woman's gaze had quite surprised Kit.

"Who *was* that?" she asked Julie when they got out of earshot.

"You mean Miss Enigma? That's Adele Armstrong, Mr. Robinson's secretary."

"Miss Enigma?" Kit said, taking a long look over Julie's shoulder at yet another player in Geoffrey's little theater of surprises. Kit watched intrigued as the woman reveled in the power of holding three men at bay with an oh-so-subtle barrage of contradictory body language. Yes. No. Yes. No. No chance fellas, thought Kit.

"Yeah, Miss Enigma or the Dragon Lady. She is not generally well-liked. Not that she gives anyone the chance. She is just *so* superior. She thinks that because her boss is one of *the* bosses that makes her more important than the rest of us. We're all expected to call her *Ms.* Armstrong—can you believe it? Mostly we call her Miss H and M; you know, high and mighty. After all it doesn't matter who she makes coffee for, she's still only a secretary."

Kit guessed that Julie's venom was born of envy not dislike. Adele Armstrong was quite obviously a manipulator, someone who always knew exactly what she was doing and what she wanted or, more to the point, what she had to do to score the extra points. Kit knew the type. She *was* important because she made sure she was. Someone like Julie would always have a Ms. Armstrong above her because she saw the importance in the position rather than the power in the person.

"How long has she worked for Mr. Robinson?" Kit asked, trying to drag her attention back to the scowling Julie.

"Only about two years. She didn't even go up through the ranks like most of the other secretarial staff at OHP. She came right on in from nowhere and sat at Mr. Robinson's right hand, so to speak. God, look at her now. All those men hanging off her every word. She's not even attractive or anything."

"I think she's quite striking," Kit said.

Julie looked at Kit as if she'd just arrived from Planet 10. "You think so? It's probably the air of masculinity that surrounds her that makes you think that. Most of the women at work think she's actually a transvestite," she said in all seriousness.

"Really?" said Kit with astonishment, for there was nothing at all masculine about Adele Armstrong. Standing at the bar Kit had practically been bowled over by the almost tactile look Adele had cast over her. From head to foot it had been fleeting, penetrating, overtly sexual and unmistakably female.

"Mind you," said Julie, leaning close and dropping her voice to a whisper, "most of the men, at least those who've tried to crack on to her, say she's a . . . you know, a lesbian."

Kit looked suitably surprised while she tried not to laugh. Oh dear, you poor thing, she thought. Julie could obviously accept the notion that Adele Armstrong was a man in drag more easily than the possibility that she was a woman who chose to love women. Julie had rolled the "L" word round her mouth as if trying out a new swear word on her best friend at primary school. She was still nodding at Kit with a raised eyebrow and a knowing look, as if this was her most valuable piece of gossip, when the cavalry arrived in the form of Del, two strange men and a whole bottle of icy cold champers.

"That was great fun," said Del as she sloshed port into a couple of glasses while Kit made coffee.

"Yeah well, he's not usually that quick. I was sitting outside that place till two a.m. on Tuesday."

"Do you suppose the guy in that other car was watching us or the house?" Del asked.

"What guy?" Kit set the mugs down on the coffee table and threw herself on the couch.

"The guy in the car down the street."

"Why didn't you say something at the time?"

"What, and wake you from your beauty sleep? Besides, you're the detective. I thought you'd noticed him."

"When did he turn up?" Kit asked.

"He was there already."

"He probably just lives there then. In his car, I mean. Could you see what he looked like?"

"Interested are we?"

"Of course I'm bloody interested, Del," Kit snapped. Her friend had the most annoying habit of playing games with useful bits of information. She was at her most exasperating when she prefaced juicy gossip with "you'll never guess who."

"OK. No, I couldn't see what he looked like even through the telephoto, it was too dark. I can tell you that he's a chain smoker with a moustache and possibly a beard. That much I could see every time he struck a match. And I did take a photo of the car for you."

"Thank you, Dr. Watson," Kit said with a grin. She reached over with the port bottle and refilled Del's glass. "The thing I can't figure is the part Ian Dalkeith plays in all of this—whatever this is."

"Maybe your Mr. Robinson is investing in Dalkeith's property development."

"Maybe. But if it's above board why would he be dodging questions about it? It's more likely tied up in that little salon of sin."

"So perhaps that's all there is to it. A couple of wealthy guys with a mutual interest in sex with anything on two legs set up their own private whorehouse. What else would you expect from all that male bonding at the Patrician Club? That *was* Ian Dalkeith with Robinson in the lobby of that house tonight and they were obviously providing that Yank with a bit of local culture. So where's the mystery?"

"Who is that American though?"

"I don't know, darling. You seem to have more questions about this case than your client does. I'd like to remind you, before you lose any sleep over this randy band of men, that Celia hired you just to follow her husband not to solve every mystery in town."

"Ah, but I do love a mystery, Del. I can't help myself. I have to develop that last film. Do you want to stick around?"

"Sure, why not. I doubt that Brigie will be waiting up for me." Del followed Kit down the short hallway that opened off the landing which surrounded her sunken lounge room. Kit had turned the smallest of her apartment's three bedrooms into a darkroom. Her friend Angie, who was particularly handy with a monkey wrench, had done a bit of creative plumbing on the pipes in the adjacent bathroom so the new darkroom had running water.

"A photographer you ain't," Kit said an hour later as she collected the prints from where she'd pegged them to a piece of string hung across her open lounge-room window.

"But thank you for your time and assistance," Del said snidely. "I warned you I was only used to a totally automatic camera."

Kit dropped the prints on the coffee table beside the orderly piles of photos she and Del had been selecting to present to Celia the next day. She sat down next to Del and gave her an apologetic grin. "OK, let's see what we've got."

She extracted some of the prints and put them to one side then sorted the remainder into chronological order before choosing the clearest shots.

"Why are you leaving those out?" Del asked, picking up the discarded pile which included a photo of Del and Thistle and several of Ian Dalkeith surveying his wasteland property.

"As you say, Del, Celia hired me to follow Geoffrey. I doubt she'd be interested in how Mr. Dalkeith spends his afternoons."

Kit selected the shots of Geoffrey's Wednesday meeting at the Regent Hotel with Dalkeith, the American and the other mystery man. She wrote the date, time and place on the back of each. The last photos were the seven Del had taken that evening. They were blurred but the identities of the three men standing in the foyer of the St. Kilda house were still unmistakable. Geoffrey and Dalkeith stood to one side as the American leered in response to the attention being lavished on him by the same crimson tart Kit had seen Geoffrey with the first night she'd staked out the house.

"She looks familiar," Del said, looking over Kit's shoulder.

"She's in the earlier pics. She's also of a type," Kit said, indicating the top photo on one of the other piles. "Our Geoffrey is obviously a legs man, although a well-endowed crutch seems to attract his attention too."

"She's side-on, you can't see her face properly. And you criticize my photography." Del picked up the photo of the two blonds Geoffrey had played with on Tuesday.

"I gather this is the mysterious car that was lurking in the street with us tonight," Kit said. She turned the photo around several times, pretending she couldn't work out which way it went.

"Oh you're such a card, O'Malley. You're . . ." Del was about to say

55

something truly smart when something in the photos of Dalkeith she still had in her lap caught her attention. Kit didn't notice Del had stopped talking. She was too busy staring open-mouthed at the photograph of the car.

"I've seen this somewhere before, Del," she said, reaching for the magnifying glass.

"Quite possibly, it's a fairly common make," Del said absently, taking the magnifying glass from Kit's hand.

"No, I mean I've seen this one before. It was parked in the lane opposite the Patrician the other night."

"Yeah? Well I think maybe it *is* following you then. Take a look at this." It was the last photo Kit had taken of Dalkeith on Tuesday as he was leaving his riverfront investment. She'd snapped him as he turned his car left out through the old broken gateway heading away from where she had parked a short distance down the street. There in the background, parked an equal distance from the gate on the other side, was the same beat-up brown station wagon.

"Shit! What's going on? Who the hell would be following me?"

"Beats me," Del said. "But I'd brush up on your observation techniques if I were you, sweetheart. Fancy not noticing that old heap tailing you everywhere."

Kit felt a chill up her spine. Maybe Celia had hired someone else to make sure she got the job done properly. That was unlikely.

"It could be Douglas," she said aloud.

"Who the hell is Douglas?" Del asked.

"Celia's solicitor. I don't mean it's him. But maybe he hired someone else to dig into Geoffrey's financial dealings while I'm running around sorting out Celia's suspicions of adultery."

"Seems like a waste of money to hire two detectives for the same case."

Kit stared at the two photos for a long time. She picked up the other piles and flipped through them.

"There it is again!" Kit said horrified. "How the hell could I have missed this?"

"That's Dalkeith with that Yank again," Del said. "Who are you investigating here? Robinson or Dalkeith?"

"That was the day Geoffrey had the meeting with Dalkeith, the

American and this bloke," Kit said, pointing to the next photo. "But this is the shot with that bloody car in it."

"So what's the common denominator here, O'Malley?" Del said, as if the answer was sitting right in front of them, sharing the port.

"Geoffrey . . . or me," Kit said.

"Or Dalkeith. Come on, Miss Marple, this is your area of expertise not mine."

"God, I think I need a holiday," Kit groaned. "Somewhere cold. I think this hot weather is making me stupid. The night I saw that car opposite the Patrician was the first time I saw Dalkeith, in the flesh, I mean. You said you think the driver has a moustache?"

"Yeah, either a big bushy one or a beard as well. I only glimpsed him by match light remember."

"Well, maybe Douglas did hire him. If Geoffrey's involved in some sort of shonky business deal with Dalkeith it would be logical to have someone follow Dalkeith. Obviously I can't do everything. I'm sure Celia would have mentioned it to me though. This is very curious."

"Curious indeed, my love. But I don't intend to lose any sleep over it. And neither should you. Speaking of which, I am going home and you should go to bed. You can ask your client all about it tomorrow."

Chapter 5

"So what is he doing here?" Celia asked in a tone that conveyed amused disbelief rather than disgust. She had flipped quickly through the photographs of the women her husband had picked up on the streets, saying nothing more than "They're all tall. Typical!" before putting them to one side.

"At the time I thought he was paying the boy," Kit answered. "But when I developed the film I realized that it's an envelope he's handing over. It probably contains money but it could be anything, I suppose."

"And this house?" Celia asked, tapping the photograph with the stem of her champagne glass.

"According to the records the council rates are being paid by a company called Wellborn Enterprises which appears to be a subsidiary of another called Freyling Imports."

"Wellborn indeed," Celia snorted. "That bastard's got delusions of grandeur."

"Your husband may not have any involvement with Wellborn, Celia. I know that doesn't mean much when he obviously has such an interest in the place but, short of asking him outright, I doubt if you'd be able to trace the money he's been spending to that particular house. On the other hand Douglas Scott may be in a better position than I am to get more detailed information on Wellborn, Freyling Imports and any other related companies. I am certain that Mr. Robinson is involved in some sort of deal with Ian Dalkeith, so even if your

58

husband's name doesn't turn up on someone else's books Dalkeith's name probably will. With all this evidence, though, you could just confront your husband and ask him."

"Oh no. Not yet," Celia said adamantly. "I want to get the whole picture first. I plan to give him almost enough rope to hang himself before I throttle him with it. So I shall pass the gist of what you have discovered on to Douglas so he can do a little digging within his field of expertise while you continue on in yours. You have done an excellent job so far, Katherine, though I rather knew you would."

"Thank you, Celia, but it hasn't been a difficult task."

"Only because my husband is so busy thinking with his you-know-what that there's no chance of his few remaining brain cells being able to draw his attention to the fact that he has lost all sense of propriety."

Kit controlled the urge to laugh by making a fuss of moving her chair further into the shade of the umbrella they were sitting under on the patio. It was still blisteringly hot but the hint of a southerly breeze brought some relief and was certainly a welcome change from the north wind which had been raging around the city for the last two days.

"Speaking of Mr. Scott's field of expertise, do you know if he has hired anyone to investigate your husband's dealings with Ian Dalkeith?"

Celia looked quite taken aback. "You mean another detective? I most certainly hope not. You know my ideas on the matter of hiring . . . er . . . outsiders. No, I feel sure he wouldn't have. Not without telling me. Why do you ask?"

Kit took a deep breath. She had already considered the possibility that the tail on Dalkeith had absolutely nothing to do with her case on Geoffrey Robinson. But she had to be sure. "I wouldn't worry about it, Celia. It's just that on a couple of occasions while keeping an eye on your husband I've noticed an old Holden station wagon hanging around as well."

"What, following Geoffrey?" Celia sounded quite appalled.

"Not necessarily. Each time it turned up Geoffrey was meeting with Ian Dalkeith. It's more likely the person in the car is following Dalkeith. He may even be a minder. But I had to ask."

"Yes, of course. I shall ask Douglas if this has anything to do with him, but I doubt it. Ah, Byron, perhaps you'd like to pour Miss O'Malley another champagne. Or would you prefer coffee, Katherine?"

The Ghost Who Walks, Kit thought, as once again Celia's ghoulish personal secretary appeared behind her without a sound. She had no idea how long he'd been there. She glanced up at him, almost nervously, acutely aware of how exposed her neck was in the white T-shirt she was wearing with her linen trousers. She requested a coffee before returning her gaze to Celia, to find her client's attention was momentarily distracted by the commotion going on in the Forum.

Kit couldn't help smiling. Celia was certainly one out of the box. She had insisted that they enjoy their luncheon on the patio before getting down to the real reason for Kit's visit. Discussing sex, sin, power and the merits of appropriate social behavior over a quiet glass of champagne and plate of fresh asparagus while a deaf gardener lowered a Greek nymph onto her new pedestal in the fish pond was diverting to say the least.

Celia had first taken Kit on a guided tour of the Forum, which was far more extensive than Kit had originally thought. They had strolled barefoot along a maze of grassy paths past tiny groves of tangled vines revealing garden seats or trickling waterfalls, and through an arch of climbing roses to a group of finely sculpted women in flowing marble robes, looking for all the world as though they were passing the day in serious conversation. Celia talked earnestly and warmly about her garden, describing each statue and its provenance, and explaining why she had chosen a particular plant for this rockery or that setting. Although Kit admired Celia's imagination and obvious hard work she still felt the concept itself was a little too bizarre. All the statues and sculptures were originals, not a plaster cast reproduction or painted garden gnome in sight, and many were intricate and quite exquisite, but Kit couldn't help feeling that Celia's meticulous attention to detail placed her somewhere between pathologically obsessive and totally whacko.

The slight rattle of an empty cup on a saucer as he was just about to place it in front of Kit was the only thing that announced Byron's reappearance with the coffee. Kit nearly jumped out of her skin. This time it was Celia's turn to cover a smile.

"Byron, be a dear and help those two out with the thingy before they do any more damage than is necessary," she said, waving her free hand in the direction of Burke the gardener and his incredibly clumsy assistant who was flailing about in the fish pond. She finished the champagne in her glass and reached for the bottle to refill it. "Quiet isn't he?" she said.

"That's an understatement," Kit replied with a grin. "Where did you find him? I mean, how did you come to employ him?"

"I found him a long time ago," Celia said quietly, stealing an affectionate glance in the direction of the pond where Byron, a look of undisguised distaste on his face, was doing his best to render assistance without getting wet. Celia quite obviously collected herself from thoughts far from the business at hand and returned her gaze to Kit. "He came to me about three years ago with impeccable credentials. I was in need of a personal assistant for secretarial duties, as a chauffeur, butler, you name it. He was perfect and has proven to be invaluable. I trust him more than just about anyone I know, except perhaps Douglas."

"An extraordinary job description in this day and age," Kit said, immediately regretting it.

Celia flashed a wicked smile. "Yes. Lucky aren't I?" She laughed. "And I would say that my money is put to better use than my husband's. Wouldn't you agree?"

"You have a point, Celia. Speaking of which there are just a couple more photographs I'd like you to see."

Kit reached for the envelope labeled "Wednesday/Thursday" and removed the contents. "Do you know this man?" she asked, presenting one of the photos she had taken after Geoffrey's Regent Hotel rendezvous.

"No. I've never seen him before. Quite handsome for such a big man, isn't he?" Celia said, studying the picture of the silver-haired broad-chested American.

"He's a Yank, if that makes any difference."

Celia shook her head. "Geoffrey is acquainted with many Americans through the company. This one I'm sure I don't know."

"How about this guy?" Kit held out the photo of the other mystery man from Wednesday's meeting.

"Of course. That's Gerald Grainger. He's an old colleague and friend of Geoffrey's. He's an entrepreneur of sorts, though in what I have no idea. I find him quite repulsive, which possibly explains why Geoffrey didn't mention seeing him this week. He lives in Point Piper or Potts Point or one of those other posh pointy places in Sydney. Dreadful man." Celia threw the photo down in disgust.

"What's wrong with him?" Kit asked, picking up the photo to take another look now that she had a name to go with the face. Grainger was a tall angular man with large hands and bony wrists which stuck out awkwardly from the cuffs of his white business shirt. His face was plain and instantly forgettable, although his nose had obviously been broken more than once which might serve as a reminder if someone had to identify him in a police line-up.

"He is one of those men, not unlike my husband as all this proves," Celia sneered, pushing the photos away from her, "who cannot keep his mind above his belt. He and my husband used to spend a great deal of time together when Geoffrey and I were first married, before Gerald returned to Sydney to live. He is a crass and uncouth man. It was bad enough that he saw nothing wrong in propositioning most of my friends, but when he tried it on my daughter I decided enough was enough. I told him what he could do with his disgusting intentions and made it quite clear to Geoffrey that his friend was never to cross our threshold again."

Celia was quite shaken by the memory and Kit had absolutely no idea what to say. What an arsehole was her immediate thought, but she doubted whether that particular choice of words was an appropriate response to a disclosure that had nothing to do with her case and was none of her business. Celia filled the awkward silence by changing the subject completely. "So, we carry on according to the schedule, Katherine. Unless you have any suggestions about how we should proceed?"

"No, Celia. I think the way we are going is the most effective. Judging by the calendar of appointments for next week though I think we'll just get more of the same. Even his sprain is not . . . um . . . slowing him down."

"Well, of course not. He only uses his feet for walking on after all,"

Celia snorted. "He'd have to sprain the other thing to even consider taking time off from anything."

"Do you think it's worth carrying on?" Kit laughed.

"Oh yes, my dear," Celia said adamantly. "I'd like to know exactly what Geoffrey is up to while Douglas is still investigating his side of things. Another week at least, but that will probably be enough." She rummaged amongst the pile of photographs for the black leather filofax she had placed on the table earlier. She opened it and after handing Kit an envelope began leafing through the pages.

"Next week, next week," she muttered. "Ah. Friday is quite full and I have an appointment with Douglas at nine. Perhaps you could come at ten, in the evening?"

"Er, yes, of course," Kit said, a little taken aback.

"I realize it's a late hour but Geoffrey will be dining out that evening. And, as I said the rest of the day is a busy one. I do hope that I'm not completely ruining your social life, Katherine."

"No, Celia, it's fine. My social life is rather dormant at the moment. Believe me there's nothing to ruin."

"Good. Then Friday ten p.m. it is. The last appointment, unless of course you discover something completely new. In that case we shall review the situation. That check," she said, indicating the envelope Kit was still clutching in her hand, "should cover your time for the week. If you make up an account of anything that's outstanding we can finish everything up nicely next week."

Kit nodded and reaching for her briefcase dropped the envelope in. Celia gathered up the photographs carefully, as if she might catch something from them, and stuffed them back into one of the large envelopes. "If you could hold these for me please, Katherine, until such time as they're needed," Celia said, thrusting the package at Kit. "I'd rather they were out of my sight."

"Should I bring them back next week?"

Celia sighed deeply before struggling to her feet. "What I would really like you to do is burn them. They make my stomach turn. But burning the evidence would not change what Geoffrey has done. Is doing. You'd better have them with you."

❖ ❖ ❖ ❖ ❖

The weather, which simmered on the hot side of unbearable for the next seven days, was broken briefly by a violent wind storm on Wednesday that ripped roofs from houses in three suburbs and dribbled a cupful of rain on Mount Dandenong to the east. The city was like hell's kitchen, there were bush fires throughout north-east Victoria, and some of the toughest water restrictions in years were enforced throughout the state.

It was Friday again—they seemed to be coming around with monotonous regularity—and Kit was on her way back to Celia's for the last time. During Week Two, apart from finding out that the Yank —who'd been registered at the Regent Hotel under the name of David Watts before departing for Sydney on Tuesday—was apparently a businessman on holiday, she had indeed only managed to uncover more of the same. Although she was heartily sick of following Geoffrey on his nightly forays, she was a little regretful that after tonight she'd have no reason to call on Celia.

The fact that the last seven days had been all work and no play, all sultry weather and no sultry Sam made the smell of change in the thick air tonight feel distinctly ominous. It seemed that more than her work for Celia was coming to an end. Sam had called from Sydney postponing yet another weekend in favor of a possible new job, and after nearly a month of no contact Kit was beginning to lose the lust. She had spent most of the week, when she wasn't tailing the libidinous Geoffrey Robinson or working on her novel late at night, sitting in a cold bath with a bottle of bourbon and a good book or three, trying to escape the heat and ignore the fact that her social life was more than dormant—it was virtually extinct. Telling Celia, of all people, about it was the closest she'd come to admitting, even to herself, that she was seriously lacking something serious.

She had dragged herself to Marek's on Sunday to catch up with a few old friends from the force but the seemingly endless conversations over the coleslaw about children or new jacuzzis had only made her more depressed. After a few games of pool at Angie's on one of Geoffrey's few nights at home, Kit finally had to acknowledge that the problem was not her social life—that had always been as active as she cared to make it—the problem was her life in general. Here she was at thirty-two years old with an almost perfect life, and no one to share

64

it with. She was her own boss, doing a job she enjoyed which allowed plenty of time to devote to her writing. On that score she was better off than most people she knew but, on the other hand, most of those same people had someone to talk over their daily triumphs or failures with.

Despite the fact that it was usually her lovers that did the leaving, Kit had somehow earned a reputation as a heartbreaker with a love 'em and leave 'em attitude. It was almost totally unfounded and she knew that the smart-mouthed teasing of her best friend Delbridge had a lot to do with the myth gaining such wide attention. She didn't really mind; after all a notorious reputation was better than no reputation at all (who was she kidding?) but it did make it difficult to be taken seriously. Kit had never been into one-night stands; she'd rather read a book or watch a movie than indulge in sexual aerobics just for the sake of it. But it was six years since she'd been with anyone for longer than four or five months, and eight years since she'd been in love. Eight whole years and she hadn't even come close.

As the first huge dollops of rain struck the windscreen she decided it was time to give it all up and try celibacy. She and Sam were certainly going nowhere fast. She turned into Celia's driveway, expecting it to be deserted as usual, but was greeted by what looked like an emergency services convention. There was an ambulance with lights flashing, two police cars and a Mercedes in front of the house and a plumber's van parked on the lawn.

"Oh shit, don't tell me she really has throttled him," Kit said aloud as she parked her car.

Chapter 6

As Kit made a dash through the pelting rain towards the front door a ruddy-faced man in overalls came barreling out as if shot from a cannon. He excused himself while still on the run and headed straight for the van on the lawn. Kit heard a familiar yet unexpected voice in the hall and walked in through the open doorway to find her friend and ex-partner Detective Sergeant Jon Marek giving his undivided attention to a large uncooperative black umbrella. His mane of tousled gray hair belied the fact that he was only thirty-five years old and was quite at odds with his Adonis-like face and athlete's body. He had always maintained throughout their three-year partnership that it had been the strain of working with Kit that had turned him prematurely gray.

"Don't you know it's bad luck to open an umbrella inside?" she said.

"Eh? Oh, it's you, O'Malley," he said as if he'd been expecting her. "I've been expecting you."

The ruddy-faced man brushed past Kit again, this time lugging an armful of metal poles and a tarpaulin. He was having a great deal of trouble with the latter so rather than lose the lot he dropped the tarp then grabbed one corner and dragged it up the hallway. The metal rivets screeched across the marble tiles sending a fingernails-on-a-blackboard shiver up Kit's spine.

"What the hell is going on?"

"A local citizen has met with an untimely demise," Marek said, thrusting the umbrella at Kit and indicating she should follow him.

"Who killed him?" Kit asked, expecting to see Celia handcuffed to a standard lamp in the lounge room.

"I said demise. What makes you think someone's been murdered?" Marek said, turning to face Kit so suddenly that she ran into him.

"I said killed. And I have no idea what I should be thinking. But your presence suggests something other than death by misadventure, Jonno." Kit struggled with the umbrella which had sprung open during the collision.

"Yeah, well you know that when a ratepayer as rich as this one kicks the golden bucket our lords and masters like to have all the bases covered. But seeing as the only weapon, as such, that we've found is a fish pond I'd say it's a case of accidental death by drowning. And it's a her not a him. Leave that up, you'll probably need it out here," Marek added, opening the door to the patio.

Kit suddenly felt sick to her stomach. She stepped with great trepidation onto the patio overlooking the floodlit Forum. The rain, which slid so silently down the marble torso of the motionless Perseus, thumped with an irritating urgency on the caps of the three officers trying to raise a canvas canopy over the bald-headed body of Celia Robinson.

"Oh shit, what happened?" Kit asked, collapsing into one of the patio chairs. She was unable to take her eyes from the dismal scene before her but couldn't help thinking that it looked like a carefully designed set for a Miss Marple movie. A now sodden blanket covered most of Celia's body, as if someone had put it there to keep her warm, and she lay on her back on the lawn with her arms neatly by her side, looking for all the world as if she was taking a nap. The only things out of place were Celia's extremely hairless pate and the extraordinary amount of water she was lying in. In fact there was far too much water around for it to have come from the rain which was only now getting really serious about drowning them all.

"That umbrella would be far more useful over our heads, O'Malley," Marek said as he dragged a chair up beside Kit.

"Where did all the water come from?" Kit asked. She handed the umbrella to Marek. She didn't care in the least that she was getting soaked to the skin.

"The fish pond. The fountain was gushing like a bloody geyser when we got here and there appears to be something blocking the outlet pipe. That's what that plumber is trying to fix." Marek tried to remove a cigarette from the packet with one hand, while holding the umbrella over them both with the other.

The man in the overalls had just stepped into the pond and was searching around under the water for the cause of the problem. Every time he moved a small tidal wave surged over the edge and lapped ever so gently at the senseless body on the lawn.

"Can't you move her?" Kit said.

"We haven't got all the photographs yet," Marek replied. "Pete had to get more film from his car. Oh, here he is. It's about bloody time, Pete. Get a move on before we all get washed away."

"Yes, sire," said the surly Pete Fowler who always looked as though he had a bad smell up his nose. Considering his job he probably did. He winked at Kit then turned his attention and camera to the task of recording Celia's penultimate resting place.

"How did you know I was going to be here?" Kit asked.

"We found this in her pocket." Marek handed Kit an envelope with her name printed on it. It had already been opened so she removed the contents. There was a check, made out to O'Malley Investigations, for $2000, and a small piece of paper neatly printed in red with the words: "January 19, North 4; 5 p.m.; January 20, FISC, 11 p.m."

"I don't get this. Tonight was our last appointment. This is far too much money and this, whatever it is, is for next week."

"So fill me in, O'Malley. What's the deal here?"

"She hired me to tail her husband. Where is he, by the way?"

"We've sent a car to pick him up. It took us a while to find him."

"I bet it did. Who found her then?"

"Her solicitor, Douglas Scott. He's having a stiff drink while he gives his statement to Nick," Marek said, finally getting his cigarette lit while Kit looked expectantly at him.

"OK. Briefly, he had a nine o'clock appointment with the late Mrs. Robinson but when no one answered the bell he let himself in. The patio door was open and he found his client lying face down on the grass with her head and arms in the water. Naturally he dragged her out but says it was obvious that she'd been there for some time. He rang an ambulance and called us. End of story. Except that, judging by the empty bottle under that statue over there, it looks like she probably had a bit too much and fell down. Maybe she hit her head or maybe she was too pissed to realize it was water she was trying to breathe and not air. "

"You're so crass, Marek. People like Celia Robinson don't get 'pissed,' not on Moët anyway and certainly not when they're expecting company," Kit snapped. "Something is definitely sus here."

"You think so?" Marek said in his best patronizing voice, which Kit chose to ignore. "It looks pretty straightforward to me. Her solicitor said she was a drinker."

"A drinker, yes, but not a rolling drunk."

"You knew her well enough to make that judgement?"

"I think so. Though not well enough, I must admit, to know that she was as bald as a bandicoot. Where's her hair?"

"Good question. And I have another. Why did you assume that a *he* had been killed?"

"Because it's quicker and cheaper than divorcing a priapic husband."

Marek stared at his eyebrows for a few seconds before saying, "I give up. That one hasn't come up in the cryptic crossword yet."

A shout from the fish pond saved Kit from having to detail the licentiousness which accompanied Geoffrey's permanent hard-on, though she knew she may eventually have to. Meanwhile the plumber, triumphantly holding aloft what was left of Celia's yellow wig as if it was the scalp of a conquered foe, was shouting that he'd found the source of the problem.

"I think I'm going to puke," Kit said, making for the patio door before she witnessed any more of the circus going on around the sodden body of her ex-client. She found a bathroom, locked herself in and took off her cotton shirt to wring it out over the hand basin. She shook her head vigorously and ran her hands through her wet hair before putting the shirt back on. Then she went looking for Douglas Scott.

She found him in the lounge, a plushly furnished room full of couches, cushions, potted palms and begonias, heavy curtains drawn against the proceedings in the Forum outside, and the best-stocked bar Kit had ever seen. Nick was diligently recording everything Scott was saying. He looked up when Kit entered, quickly suppressed an inappropriate grin and got to his feet.

"Don't let me interrupt, Detective Jenkins," she said. "I just want a word with Mr. Scott when you're finished."

"I think we're done," Nick said. "Unless you have anything else to add, Mr. Scott?"

A lock of snowy hair fell forwards across a pair of unbelievably tangled eyebrows as Douglas Scott shook his head and turned to face Kit. He was visibly distressed and obviously agitated at the thought of having to go through the details yet again. Nick excused himself and left the room, picking up Kit's cue that he should make himself scarce.

"I'm sorry to bother you right now, Mr. Scott. My name is Katherine O'Malley and . . ."

"I know who you are, Miss O'Malley," he said, reaching for his glass only to find it empty.

"Call me Kit. Can I get you another?" Kit offered, holding out her hand.

"Yes. Please. A whisky, thanks."

He watched Kit with the concentration of someone determinedly trying to ignore everything else that was going on around him as she refilled his glass with the Glenlivet which stood open on the bar, and filled another with Wild Turkey.

"This is a damn tragedy. She was such a fine woman," he said, accepting the drink as he blinked back the tears pricking his pale blue eyes. Kit liked this man already and not simply because he looked remarkably like an Old English sheepdog. She guessed he was about sixty, though his gentle face had scarcely a line except around the eyes where the telltale creases hinted at a disposition more accustomed to deriving great amusement from life. It was easy to understand why Celia had trusted him so, though seeing him sitting there barely able to control his grief Kit suspected his loyalty had a bit to do with the fact that he'd been more than a little in love with their mutual client.

Kit sat down opposite and knocked back her bourbon in one swallow, wondering how, or even whether, she should proceed. She had expected to close the case tonight but not by default. The fact that her client was dead meant, effectively, that she had no client, despite Celia's cryptic note and generous check which suggested she had changed her mind.

"You and I probably have a few things to go over, Miss O'Malley. Kit. But not tonight if you don't mind. And I don't think the police need to know all the details, especially when Geoffrey is likely to turn up at any minute."

"Of course, Mr. Scott," Kit said, relieved. "Do you know where he was expected to be this evening?"

"Douglas, please," he said. "Luckily, he was in acceptable company —for a change. I suggested to that detective in charge that they contact Geoffrey's secretary Adele. She was apparently out shopping, which is why it's taken so long, but she told them that Geoffrey was dining with Miles and two visiting reps from OHP's printers in Hong Kong."

"What about Byron? He seems to know everything that goes on around here."

"He wasn't home." Douglas looked pathetically at his empty glass so Kit went to the bar, refilled her own and brought the bottle of Glenlivet back for him. "God, I'll have to ring Elizabeth and tell her," he was saying. "I don't imagine she'll want to hear of her mother's accident from Geoffrey."

"Um, don't you think this whole 'accident' thing is a little suspicious?" Kit said hesitantly.

Douglas looked pained but not surprised by the suggestion. "A little," he said quietly. Further discussion was put on hold as a commotion in the hall heralded the arrival of Geoffrey Robinson, his breathless voice demanding the whereabouts of his wife.

Kit got to the lounge door in time to see a uniformed officer escorting Geoffrey into the Forum. They had passed Donald Grenville, the coroner, in the hall. "Well, well, well, if it isn't Katherine O'Malley," he said with a warm smile.

"Hi Donald, how goes it?" Kit said, moving away from the lounge and out of Douglas's earshot.

"Couldn't be better, my dear. I wouldn't be dead for quids. And I see you have managed to survive and flourish without Flash Marek to hold your hand. I like the wet look. You look positively ravishing, but then that's nothing new."

"And you haven't changed one bit, you old bastard."

"Flattery will get you nothing but my undying passion, Katherine," Donald said, twirling the thicket of whiskers under his nose.

"How about the lowdown on the task at hand?"

"Well, it's so damn wet out there I could do little more than a rudimentary examination. My guess is the woman drowned somewhere between six and nine p.m. The rest will have to wait till we've both dried out a bit."

"Was it an accident?"

"It seems so. The evidence, as it stands, fits the theory that she stumbled, probably in a state of intoxication, headfirst into the water. There is bruising on the forehead and on the chin, consistent with a fall. Either injury may have rendered her unconscious or in no fit state to extricate herself from the pond. But that is just the theory; I shall know more on the morrow."

"Jesus Christ, what a bloody mess!" bellowed Geoffrey, as he and Marek, followed by the stretcher carrying Celia's shrouded body, crowded in through the patio door.

Kit took her leave of Donald and headed back to the lounge. She wanted to be there when Geoffrey entered. Douglas was in the process of topping up his glass again.

"You'd better have another yourself, Kit," he said. "I think we're in for one hell of a performance."

"God, Douglas, I just don't know what to do next. And what a thing for you to have to go through. She was just so, so . . ." Geoffrey turned aside dramatically to compose himself, or, rather, to decide which of the emotions that were running uncontrolled across his face best suited the present company. He settled on a mournful look complete with an exaggerated and regular blinking-back of an imaginary wellspring of tears. Douglas extracted his hand from Geoffrey's, ushered him to the couch and poured him a whisky. The elegant walking cane which Geoffrey had traded his crutches for sometime on Wednesday provided more than adequate support for his grief and gave him something to do with the hand that wasn't holding the whisky glass.

Kit watched Marek shuffling from one foot to the other, waiting. He hated these scenes. Having to question a grieving individual was an odious task, but Marek had his own emotions so securely locked up in a cupboard somewhere that he had a harder time than most dealing with what he scathingly called the "raw, seething quagmire of self pity."

"I'm sorry to put you through this right now, Mr. Robinson, but I will have to ask you some questions," he said.

"Of course. I understand," Geoffrey said with a sigh which was audibly cut short when he noticed Kit standing there. He looked questioningly at Douglas, while Kit looked earnestly at Marek with a slight shake of her head.

"This is . . . ah, detective, O'Malley," Marek said falteringly.

Geoffrey acknowledged her with a nod while his eyes never left her legs. Douglas swallowed rather too loudly so Kit decided the best place to sit was next to him, putting Marek between herself and Geoffrey. She was sorely tempted to tell Geoffrey just where it was that she'd last seen him.

Geoffrey spent the next fifteen minutes raving about the sheer injustice of human destiny that ends the life of one so gracious, loving and giving in such an undignified and lonely way. If only he had stayed home this evening. If only he'd been able to help her give up the drinking. If only . . . It was a distraught and eloquent performance, greatly deserving of an Oscar, and one that had Marek so convinced of the man's emotional devastation that he kept his questions to a minimum. With each declaration of concern for Celia's drinking habits, of his constant fear of leaving her on her own at any time, Geoffrey built up a picture of himself as a caring loving man in the habit of sacrificing much of his own lifestyle for that of his adoring but dipsomaniacal wife. The fact that he had to be aware that Douglas would know that most of what he claimed was unmitigated garbage did not hinder his performance one bit. Geoffrey obviously felt secure in his assumption that family business was just that; appearances must be maintained, and one certainly does not let the hoi polloi—let alone the local constabulary—think one is anything less than perfect. Except, of course, in his descriptions of Celia's drinking problem, which he could and did labor to death, because the police already

73

knew about that. And, thought Kit, it reinforces the theory of death by misadventure.

"At what time did you leave the house?" Marek asked.

"I think it was a little after six p.m. Miles Denning, our publisher, called for me. We had a drink in this room with . . . with poor Celia . . . before going out for dinner with clients at the Shangri La. That was where your officers found me and broke the news." Geoffrey was overdoing the fidgeting to the point where Kit desperately wanted to scold him into sitting still. "Um, if you'll excuse me for a minute," he finally said, hauling himself to his feet. "I think I ate something that disagreed with me at lunch. I've been up and down all evening."

"Was there anyone else in the house when you left? Your wife has a secretary, I believe," Marek asked when Geoffrey returned ten minutes later.

"Daniels. No, he wasn't here!" Geoffrey stated sharply. "He is no longer in our employ."

"I didn't know this had happened," Douglas said, unable to hide his surprise.

Whoa! Throw the plot another twist, thought Kit.

"No doubt Celia would have told you this evening, Douglas, had she . . ." Geoffrey broke down again.

"When did this Daniels leave your service, Mr. Robinson?" Marek asked.

"He didn't leave. I asked him to go," Geoffrey said. "In fact it was his betrayal of my wife's trust that probably pushed her to drink as much as she seems to have tonight. You see I sacked Mr. Daniels yesterday. He had been stealing, and not just money but valuables from the house. Celia of course was dreadfully upset; she had entrusted him with a great deal of responsibility."

Kit glanced at Douglas who looked totally flabbergasted.

"God, I knew she was upset. She was such a trusting soul. I should have stayed home," Geoffrey was saying.

Trusting soul, indeed! Kit thought. Celia had been a clever, intuitive and sensible woman; one not easily deceived. Sure she'd made the mistake of marrying Geoffrey, but then everyone's entitled to one gross error of judgement in their life, and she had admitted to Kit that though she'd been attracted to him and enjoyed his company she had never trusted him. She *had* trusted Byron, however. If there was any truth in what Geoffrey was saying it would indeed have been a shattering revelation to Celia, but Kit had so little faith in Geoffrey's veracity that she doubted his whole story. It was all so unnecessary, as if he was setting a scene to cover the possibility that Celia's death would prove to be something other than an accident. With Celia conveniently unable to verify or deny Geoffrey's statement, Kit wondered whether her client had actually known anything at all about the alleged reasons for Byron's alleged dismissal. Surely if Byron *had* been stealing it would have been Celia who sacked him, and in that case Douglas would probably have known about it.

"We'll need the address of this Daniels," Marek said, "just in case we need a word with him."

"Of course, I'm sure you may need to do that," Geoffrey said, a little too suggestively. "The only problem is I have no idea where he lives. On Wednesday I went to his flat—well, to the address he had given us—to confront him. I wanted to see him on his own turf so as not to create a scene in front of Celia. The woman who answered the door said she didn't know anyone called Byron Daniels and claimed she'd been living in the place for six months. So I had to wait until he arrived for work yesterday, whereupon I discharged him."

The thick plottens, Kit thought. She was trying very hard to stop herself from thinking the worst about this whole situation but Geoffrey was making it very difficult. Why was he doing his best to cast Byron in a less than favorable light? If Celia's death *was* an accident then this stuff about Byron was pretty irrelevant. Sow the seeds now, just in case. But why? The good old standby of the ex-employee with a grudge doing in the mistress of the manor was about as obvious as the butler doing it. It also implied that something had been done. Geoffrey seemed to be working on two levels here: agonizing over Celia's alcoholism and the tragic nature of the accident, while hammering in the notion of misplaced trust and betrayal. Every second thing Geoffrey said made Celia's death seem even more suspicious. Well it did to Kit. She had no idea what Marek was getting from all of this.

It suddenly dawned on Kit that she was so anxious to disbelieve everything Geoffrey said that she was rather overlooking the obvious. As much as she didn't like to acknowledge it, there had to be some truth in what he was saying; he couldn't just make it up because Byron himself would be able to dispute it. Unless of course Geoffrey had something else on Byron which had convinced him that here was not a good place to work any more. But if he hadn't been sacked for stealing then what would make him leave Celia's employ? And why didn't Douglas know? It was all too weird, too coincidental.

"If he'd been stealing, Mr. Robinson, why didn't you go to the police?" Kit asked.

"That was Celia's decision," Geoffrey replied before returning his attention to Marek. "I was all in favor of it of course, but Celia was anxious to avoid any scandal."

"Excuse me, sir," Nick said from the doorway. "There's a woman out the front to see Mr. Scott."

"That will be my niece. I rang and asked her to collect me. I didn't think it would be a good idea for me to drive myself home," Douglas said. "Do you need me for anything else?"

"No, Mr. Scott. We have your statement," Marek said.

"Geoffrey, will you be all right if I leave now?" Douglas asked.

"Yes, thanks. I asked the officer who brought me home to inform Jane and Colin and ask them to come over. That's my sister and brother-in-law," Geoffrey added, looking at Marek. "I'll be fine, Douglas. You go on home."

"OK, if you're sure. Oh, I've already put in a call to London to inform Elizabeth, but she was out. I'll keep trying. That's if you'd like me to, Geoffrey," Douglas said.

Geoffrey nodded gratefully, saying he didn't think he'd be able to cope with breaking the news himself.

Kit followed Douglas out into the hall and walked with him to the front door. "You didn't know about this business with Byron?" she queried.

"Of course not. It's very strange indeed. I do, however, know where to find him. Kit, I trust your professionalism and your discretion— mostly because Celia seemed to have so much faith in it."

"Likewise, Douglas," Kit said with a smile.

"For the same reason I am a little concerned about the welfare of

Byron Daniels. But I would rather not discuss that here and now. As we have other unfinished business, on Celia's behalf, perhaps we could meet in my office on Monday, say at noon?"

They shook hands and Douglas made a dash out into the storm. Kit caught a glimpse of athletic legs clad in tight black tracksuit pants as the woman lounging against the Mercedes beneath a huge red umbrella rushed forward to give him shelter. They embraced tightly and Douglas, suddenly looking decidedly the worse for wear, allowed his niece to help him down the drive to the car parked behind Kit's.

Chapter 7

It was close to two a.m. by the time Kit got home. She'd given her statement to Nick, Marek had promised to let her know the autopsy results and she'd left Celia's house soon after the arrival of Geoffrey's sister, mostly because she couldn't bear to see him go through his tragic routine again. She'd driven straight to Angie's bar where she found Del and Brigit eating a late supper. A quarter of a bottle of bourbon later they had taken her home and poured her onto the couch.

What had been a straightforward surveillance job for a woman she'd come to respect enormously had turned into something decidedly nasty. Uncovering the tawdry nature of a subject's private life was part and parcel of domestic cases of this kind. After all it rarely transpired that the husband, or wife, was behaving suspiciously because they were organizing a surprise birthday party for their spouse. But despite the level of Geoffrey's infidelity Kit had not expected this case to end in death, anyone's death.

The whole evening had felt like a rerun of a B-grade forties movie, complete with the carefully arranged corpse of a wealthy eccentric placed in the most bizarre surroundings the set decorators could come up with. Enter the trusted solicitor, the unfaithful husband, the disgraced personal secretary, the wayward and absent daughter, the cynical cop and the private eye who knows more than anyone else but still hasn't the faintest idea what's going on.

Kit couldn't get the image of Celia lying there in all that water out of her mind, and while Douglas's honest grief had been touching, Geoffrey's behavior had, as usual, made her want to throw up. And Marek, well, he seemed all too ready to believe the whole thing was an accident; the situation was tidier that way. Oh, he'd done everything that was necessary and asked all the appropriate questions, at least all those appropriate to an investigation where an accidental demise was a foregone conclusion. That was typical of Marek though, Kit knew that. While he didn't believe—like she often did—that suspecting something made it so, he did hold that suspicion always turned a simple case into a complicated mess. Granted, Kit knew a lot more of the background details than Marek did, and as she hadn't enlightened him he had no reason to be as suspicious of Geoffrey as she was. After all the available evidence did suggest it was an accidental death and until, or rather unless, the autopsy proved otherwise Kit had a responsibility to Celia to respect their contract of client confidentiality. Besides, if Celia had carelessly drowned herself then Geoffrey's philandering was immaterial and would be of no interest to the police.

Del pointed out several times during Kit's ravings on the subject that just because she had liked Celia and couldn't stand Geoffrey it didn't mean there had been any foul play at all, at all. But Kit didn't need to be told she was letting her dislike of Geoffrey fuel her suspicions and color her judgement—just a little. She knew she was convinced that Celia's death was *not* an accident simply because she was sure that Geoffrey had something to do with it. Considering his sterling alibi, however, that was next to impossible. But while she kept telling herself, "Don't be silly, of course it was an accident," another little voice in her brain kept saying, "There is something wrong with this picture."

"Accidents do happen," Brigit said, fluffing up extra cushions and putting them behind Kit's back so she could sit up straight to drink her coffee. "That's the thing about accidents, they strike the most unlikely and unsuspecting people when you least expect them to. That's why they're accidents. They just happen. Even so, you'll always have one or five people standing around saying there must be a logical explanation for this, a reason; something or somebody must be at fault. It can't be an act of god or a little performance of kismet without the music because *someone* has to be responsible."

Kit and Del stared open-mouthed at their friend's inebriated grin, trying to work out if this was one of Brigit's serious attempts at profundity or if she was just talking because it was something practical to do with her tongue. Sometimes it was really hard to tell. When Kit had first met Brigit, all those years ago after she had finally accepted Del's repeated dinner invitation, she had wondered what the sharp, intelligent, pragmatic and cynical Del could possibly have in common with such a naive and optimistic fruit cake. Kit had, quite mistakenly, thought Brigit was just a bit thick, until she realized that although she had a totally cockeyed way of looking at most things she was far from stupid.

"I mean, if you were to fall down right now, Katherine," she continued, "that's assuming you could get up in order to fall down, I seriously doubt you would be in any fit state to get yourself out of a puddle let alone a fish pond without assistance. It would be gravity and alcohol that holds you down, not the water—after all the pond is actually incapable of helping or hindering you. You would drown and it would be an accident."

Kit tried to remonstrate but Del put her hand over her mouth and said, "No buts. Brigit's right. Now go to bed."

It was another hour though before Del and Brigit finally went home, having decided that the evening's tragedy, coupled with overwork and a shitty love life, was having a detrimental effect on Kit's good humor. They took their leave, promising to return at lunchtime to take her away to the beach for the rest of the weekend—even if they had to kidnap her. Kit didn't need much convincing however. There was no way she was going to turn down an offer to escape the city, the oppressive heat, the mystery of poor Celia's death and the likelihood that Marek would pester her with more questions. Not to mention another case of writer's block which meant that her hero Flynn Carter and the new love of her life had probably starved to death in the cellar they'd been locked in for the last two days. And "shitty" was such an accurate description of her own love life that Kit decided that not being home on the weekend would be an ideal way of starting her new life of celibacy. If she wasn't there she wouldn't be waiting around for Sam to ring and organize when their next date wasn't going to be.

As she struggled out of her clothes and crawled into bed it occurred to her that she was spending far too much of her life just waiting around. Waiting for someone like Sam to turn up, or just ring, and then eventually just waiting till she was so bored with someone like Sam that she'd go out searching again—only to find someone else like Sam. Despite what Del thought about her questionable taste in partners or, more to the point, the frequency with which she traded in one inappropriate lover for another, Kit knew it was the only emotional response she'd been capable of these last few years.

"So who has it hurt that I've made a hobby out of lustful relationships with no future?" she asked of Thistle as she dragged her out from under the doona. After all she'd had to do something with her time while she was biding it.

Time out, she decided. Enough is enough is enough. She knew she wouldn't find what she was looking for while she was actively looking for it because nothing is ever that simple. "Love is much too clever for that." Oh god. Who said that? she thought, horrified.

But, as she finally drifted off to sleep, she realized, or dreamt that she realized, that love was not going to even bother to try and catch her while she was breaking the land speed record in an effort to avoid it. Even though it was obviously what she was looking for. No, it didn't work that way. Real love worked like a name you can't quite remember. It's there all the time, right on the tip of your tongue, but there's no way you'll remember it while you're thinking so hard. Then suddenly, three days later while you're making spaghetti and trying to recall when you last went to the dentist, the name suddenly pops right into your mind like one of Brigit's accidents. When you least expect it. Yep, love's just like that—an accident waiting to happen.

Swan Street, Richmond on a steamy Monday morning was not a pleasant place to be. Kit emerged from the bakery with a bag of coffee scrolls and a slight hangover and cursed Del and Brigit for dropping her off on the way to the office on the assumption that she was actually capable of functioning properly before her second cup of coffee. She desperately searched the pockets of her shorts for her sunglasses as she squinted into the offending brightness of the day, and groaned at the thick pall of smog that hung over the city, almost obscuring the construction cranes which had become permanent fixtures on every building in the central business district.

The collective noise and smell of several thousand cars, driven by lone office workers en route to the city center where they would eventually find a car park next to their neighbor from the outer-outer suburbs, seemed to be concentrated into the relatively small area just in front of where Kit was standing. The driver of a tram which was stuck in the middle of the Church Street intersection was madly ding-dinging her bell at the car that was hindering her progress, even though the rest of the bumper-to-bumper traffic in the city-bound lane was going nowhere either. An overheated Valiant was having an altercation with its owner who was beating the bonnet viciously with his briefcase and three pedestrians were abusing the shit out of a motorist who had almost kneecapped them when he suddenly decided to reduce the gap between his car and the next for no other reason than it moved him six inches closer to work.

As Kit stood rooted to the footpath, marvelling at the sheer stupidity of the vast majority of the motoring public, she realized that nothing short of a small nuclear device would put an end to peak-hour madness of this kind. A passing sparrow left a sloppy deposit on the soft-top roof of a parked MG, the weight of which set off the car's alarm. Kit wanted to run for the hills. This was not a good way to start the day, let alone the working week.

She stared up at the clock on the ball-topped tower of Dimmey's department store and realized why everyone was so grumpy. Apart from the temperature, which was already well into the high twenties, it wasn't even nine o'clock. There was not a single sensible person about in the world yet; all civilized human beings would still be in bed dreaming of waterfalls and honeydew melons. Which was exactly where Kit would still be if Del and Brigit hadn't dragged her out of bed at such an ungodly hour to leave the beach and drive back to the city.

Brigit's quiet house among the tea trees right on the beach was always the perfect place to iron out a frazzled mind. The restorative effect on a jaded spirit of even a couple of days of clean sea air and raucous afternoon thunderstorms was almost immeasurable. High bright sun in a crystal clear sky, wet sand and rolling surf, good food, great wine and lazy midnight strolls on the beach. What more could a body ask for? More, thought Kit, as she felt that all the good had been completely undone by Del's vicious attack on her senses at six this morning. She wandered back to the office trying to work out a way of getting revenge.

She soon gave up on the idea because, although she felt she had been robbed of the physical benefits of all those hours of rest and relaxation, she realized that psychologically speaking (or was it emotionally?) she did feel a lot more together. She knew that once she actually woke up properly, yesterday's burgeoning desire to lie gasping and attentive at the feet of her Muse would still be there, as would the notion that it would be far more profitable to stop and think things through carefully, clearly and logically than to go jumping to conclusions and generally carrying on like a drain. Thus it had slowly dawned on her over the weekend that there was no reason why Celia's death could not have been an accident. In drinking a toast or two to the woman who would now never be her friend, she'd realized she was suffering from what Brigit had said was the need for someone, anyone, to be at fault. Not having a faith to provide a reliable and comforting escape in situations like this, she had resorted to the need to place blame. In Kit's life there was no he with a capital H by whose will this sort of tragedy could occur; there was only a he by the name of Geoffrey who Kit had wanted to believe had a motive for offing his good lady wife. But, she finally acknowledged, that was the stuff of late-night movies and other works of fiction, like her own novel, not the way of the real world.

Thinking of her book brightened Kit's mood considerably. The brief respite from home and work had cleared a lot of things in her mind, not least of which was how to get Flynn Carter out of that damn cellar. She was so looking forward to getting back to her book that she thought of her noon appointment with Douglas Scott as something of an irritation. She intended to give Douglas the final report she'd prepared for Celia, hand over everything else she had and close the case very securely.

Del met her in the hallway outside the door of Aurora Press and taking her gently by the elbow escorted her back outside.

"Before you go into your office I have two things to ask you," she said seriously.

"What, for goodness' sake? Why are we standing in the street?"

"Patience, Katherine. First of all I wish to know if you were serious last night when you said you were giving up lust?"

"Del, it's much too early for this. I'm usually asleep at this time of the day, not thinking about lust."

"Good, good. But did you mean it?"

"Yes. No. That's not what I meant. What I said was I'm going to give up doing anything *about* lust."

"Oh. Oh well, that will have to do."

"What's the other question?" Kit asked.

"It was just a back-up really, in case you weren't serious about the lust bit."

"Well, I am serious, not that it's any of your business in the hot and sober light of day in the middle of the bloody street. But I am as serious as anyone can be when they have nothing whatsoever to lust after." Kit was getting annoyed. She desperately wanted a cup of coffee and a cold shower but her deranged friend was holding her captive on the footpath in the middle of peak hour.

"Shit," Del said. "You get question number two in that case. Is there a rule in your private detective's code of ethics or whatever about not getting involved with your clients?"

"Del, you have to get involved or you can't do for them whatever it is they want done."

"No, I mean *involved* involved. You know."

Kit pulled her sunglasses down her nose just far enough to take a good unfiltered look at Del's eyes. She was beginning to think Brigit may have accidentally put some funny herbs into their morning pot of hippy-piss. "I think you should give up that camomile shit and get back on the caffeine, Del. What on earth has gotten into you?" She turned to enter the building.

"Look, I'm only doing this for your own good. Is there a rule about it or not?"

"Not that I'm aware of. It would, however, be pretty unprofessional not to mention plain silly in most cases. But I would say that a rule like that would depend on the individual PI or on the policy of the agency he or she works for. It would also depend greatly on the client of course."

"Oh dear," Del said. "I think I'll go to Greece."

Kit laughed at Del's universal solution to everything she didn't want to face. "I assume, Ms. Fielding, that there is someone waiting in my office," she said with a grin.

"Very astute, Miss Marple," Del said, following Kit inside. "Just watch yourself, Katherine O'Malley, and remember your vow. That's all I ask. This one is just your type—a Gucci waif."

"Whatever that means," Kit said, shoving the paper bag into Del's hands. "Here, take these with you. I think you might be faint with hunger." She headed down the hall and stopped to take a serious breath and compose her face. There was little she could do about the fact that she looked like an extra from a beach party movie, but then the person waiting in her office had no appointment and Kit didn't really want a new client this week anyway.

Startled sky-blue eyes looked up from a copy of *A Study in Scarlet* as Kit opened the door. The top half of the slender body that jumped to attention as the black-booted feet hit the floor was clad in a loose white T-shirt and an open red vest. The legs were wearing a pair of those jeans which have been washed fifty times in a cement mixer then laid out to dry for three weeks on an old tin roof before being strategically ripped just over the right knee and under one back pocket and sold for $150 to idiots who couldn't wait for their own clothes to wear out.

The young woman replaced the book on Kit's desk and ran a delicate finger through her short blond-tipped hair to put a stray curl back in its place behind her right ear. Obviously waiting for me to tell her whether I'm the detective or the cleaning lady, Kit thought as she shut the door behind her, suddenly wishing she wasn't dressed like a beach bum.

"Sorry," the woman said softly. "I'm waiting for Katherine O'Malley."

"Wait no more," Kit said, immediately wanting to cut her tongue out.

"Oh," the woman said and unabashedly looked Kit up and down as if she was up for auction in a slave market. Kit wanted to do the same back to her but couldn't actually make her eyes move from the astonishingly attractive face.

She tripped around the corner of her desk, collected herself expertly and calmly indicated to the woman that she should sit down again. With her jungle shorts hidden by the desk and all its clutter, Kit felt a little more like she was ready to do business, or at least fake it that she was a professional.

"My name is Quinn. Quinn Orlando," the woman said, screwing up those piercing eyes for the most fleeting of moments as if that action and the mere pronouncement of her name would provide Kit with the answers to every question she had ever asked. The name did ring a vague bell but Kit wished the woman could find something more interesting in the room to look at apart from her.

"What can I do for you?" Kit asked. Just name it; anything, she thought. Just stop looking at me.

"I want to hire you to find out who murdered my mother," the woman replied.

Kit was suddenly wide awake. Quinn Orlando! Elizabeth Quinn Orlando Robinson.

"Murdered?" she said, collapsing into her chair.

Chapter 8

Celia Robinson's wayward daughter sank with obvious relief into the deep cushions of the couch as Kit escaped to her kitchen, accompanied by the ominous bass-line of the *Jaws* theme pounding at her brain. Just when you thought it was safe to go back in the water, Kit thought.

She grabbed the ice-cream and milk from the fridge and stole another glance at Quinn Orlando as she dumped everything on the bench. The blond tips in her hair suited her well and Quinn resembled her mother just enough for Kit finally to be able to reconcile Lillian's description of the young Celia breaking hearts on the hockey field. But the cheekbones and the almost arrogant way she carried herself, not to mention those incredible blue eyes, could only have resulted from the genetic input of Carl Orlando. And what a result!

Stop it, O'Malley! she thought sternly. She really hated it when Del was right, and Gucci waif was a very apt description. And here she was, upsetting Kit's hard-won conviction that Celia's death was an accident. What was it you were going to do? Kit reprimanded herself. Remember? Think things through to their logical, I repeat logical not emotional, conclusions. No jumping any guns and going off half-cocked. She growled audibly as she fought with the lid of the ice-cream container.

"Do you need some help with that?" Quinn asked.

"No, thanks. I'm accustomed to spending most of my waking hours doing battle with inanimate objects. It will surrender in a minute." It did. The lid flipped off spraying Kit with ice as the container skidded across the island bench at warp speed. Having suggested they discuss Quinn's suspicions over a cold drink in the comfort of her apartment, Kit was now wishing they'd gone to the pub. She always felt at a disadvantage in kitchens. Even her own appliances hated her. And trying to make iced coffee under the gaze of this perfect stranger, delightful as she may be, did nothing whatsoever for her confidence.

"I love your apartment," Quinn said. "Can I look around?"

"Go ahead," Kit said, realizing that her guest was trying, quite unsuccessfully, not to laugh at what was going on in the kitchen. She grinned broadly to cover her exasperation. Quinn dazzled her back then got up to wander as nonchalantly as possible around the room.

It still gave Kit a thrill when other people seemed to like her place. She had certainly put a lot of time and effort into transforming it. The open-plan design was a far cry from the claustrophobic rooms Kit had first encountered when she rented the apartment from Del. After going stir crazy within the first month she'd talked Del into making some minor changes, beginning with the removal of three walls. The renovations had turned a dingy hallway, two small rooms and a cramped kitchen into a bright and breezy living area. Polished boards and floor rugs gave the space warmth while Kit's odd collection of furniture gave it character.

The south wall of what had been the hallway, which ran from the stairwell by the front door to the galley kitchen, was adorned with old movie posters and a selection of Kit's own photographs. It overlooked the sunken sitting room and dining area, which in turn opened onto a large enclosed patio which ran the width of the building. Opposite the kitchen was Kit's study, furnished with two huge desks, one of which was a work station for her PC and printer. A notice board on the wall behind was cluttered with black-and-white photos of Melbourne and numerous pieces of paper held in place by multi-colored drawing pins.

"That's a great picture," Quinn said, pointing to the larger-than-life Sigourney Weaver shouldering her grenade launcher as she prepared to do battle with the Mother of all Aliens.

"It's my affirmative action poster," Kit said. "I hung it by the front door to remind me each morning that nothing is impossible." Except getting the vitamiser to work, she thought, flicking the on-off switch several times before she realized she didn't have it plugged into the power point.

Kit watched Quinn run her fingers appreciatively along the edge of the small cedar dining table at the far end of the room as she took in the wall of shelves stuffed with books. Moving towards the French doors opposite the entrance stairwell the young woman smiled as she peered at the crowd of pot plants which bordered the sheltered patio. Kit realized, with a certain amount of satisfaction, that for a change Del was only half right. While Quinn was someone that Kit (or just about anybody, for that matter) would definitely notice across a crowded room she was not, however, her type. She was too young for a start.

"This is just great," Quinn exclaimed as she turned back to the sitting room where her attention was arrested by Kit's substantial movie library. Against the wall between the French doors and a tall narrow window that shed light on Kit's study was a large-screen TV and entertainment system. Two speakers hung suspended on the wall on either side above shelves that held a huge collection of movies and CDs.

"I gather you're a bit of a film buff," Quinn said, stating the obvious.

"Addict would be a better description," Kit replied. She deposited two empty glasses and a small plate of biscuits on the coffee table before returning to the kitchen.

"You obviously spend a lot of time here," Quinn said. "I've never lived anywhere I cared enough about to make it as homely as this." She shrugged off Kit's surprised look. "Well, you've seen my mother's house," she added, returning to her seat on the couch. "I haven't been home yet. I stayed with Uncle Douglas last night after he picked me up from the airport."

"I guess you know I have an appointment with him at twelve then?" Kit said.

"Yes. I . . . Oh, you beautiful thing!" Quinn exclaimed.

Kit should have known, before she looked up in surprise, that the compliment was meant for the show-off who shared her apartment. Thistle was putting on her best "pat me, I'm adorable" performance by wrapping herself joyfully around Quinn's legs.

"That little hellcat believes I bring people into our home for the express purpose of making a fuss of her," Kit said, placing the jug of iced coffee on the table.

"I'm sure she deserves every bit of attention she gets too," said Quinn as she picked up the purring cat.

Kit sat down in her armchair and poured the coffee while she tried to work out how to broach the subject of Celia being murdered by a fish pond. The sudden silence was made more awkward as the smile of delight that had been animating Quinn's face while she played with Thistle slowly gave way to an expression of pain and confusion.

"Do you believe my mother's death was an accident, Kit?" she asked quietly.

"I honestly don't know," Kit said. "On Friday night I was convinced the circumstances were too strange for it to have been an accident. It didn't *look* right. Now I think that reaction was mostly shock and disbelief. What have the police told you?"

"Nothing much. They don't have the autopsy report yet. Apparently it was a busy weekend at the morgue. I spoke to the officer in charge of the case last night and he seems to believe it was an accident. He's a homicide cop though. Why would the homicide squad be involved if it was an accident?"

"Well, it is standard procedure. It's like the arson squad always attending a serious fire. As Marek says, in a case like this it's best to have all the bases covered."

"Marek. That was his name. Do you know him? He's a pretty weird guy."

Kit laughed. "That's an understatement. Jon Marek and I were partners for a while. And he's a friend. But, like a lot of cops, he doesn't have much of a life outside the force. Got a heart of gold though."

Quinn looked surprised. "He doesn't seem to have his heart in getting to the bottom of what happened to my mother. He wasn't rude or anything but he seems to have accepted that it was an accident. He refused to consider any other possibilities."

"Sounds like Marek. Don't let him fool you, Quinn. Or upset you. If all the facts gathered so far indicate your mother's death was an accident then that will be the line he takes. It doesn't mean his mind is closed to other possibilities, it just means that he'd rather it was an accident. It's less work for him and his staff; it's certainly less harrowing for the deceased's friends and relatives."

"Well, that's a fine attitude," Quinn said sarcastically. "What if he misses vital clues while he's avoiding all this work?"

"He won't. If there's anything at all suspicious about your mother's death he'll find it. Marek and I used to make quite a good team. I would react to things the way you have about your mother. I always believe that nothing is ever what it seems. Marek, on the other hand, would take the whole scene or situation at face value and then he'd pull it apart bit by bit so that all the pieces could be seen. When he put it back together he'd make damn sure all the pieces fitted properly. Sometimes he was right, sometimes I was, but mostly we ended up in the same place even though we came at it from opposite directions."

Quinn looked unconvinced as she leant forward and poured herself another drink. "Does that mean you'll help me?"

"If there's something to investigate, yes. But I have to warn you I have my doubts. As I said, on Friday I was convinced that there had to be foul play—of some sort. But think about it, Quinn. Who would want to murder your mother?"

"My stepfather," Quinn said simply.

Kit ran her hands through her hair and took a deep breath. "OK. I have to admit he was my first choice. But why? What's his motive?"

"He's a prick."

"Yes, well that's true," Kit agreed, "but it's hardly a motive."

"Hell, I don't know." Quinn shrugged in frustration. "Maybe it's money. Maybe he was going to run off with one of those whores. Maybe he and Mum just had an argument."

"That's a lot of maybes, Quinn, and I've already considered them all, believe me. But I've had a couple of days to think this through and I've had to acknowledge that just because I don't like Geoffrey it doesn't mean he's capable of murder. That's assuming there *was* a murder.

Besides, he's got an alibi. He left home with Miles Denning and spent the rest of the evening, until the police called for him, dining with Denning and two other people."

"I realize that, Kit. But did you know the restaurant where they had dinner is only five minutes from our house?"

Kit reached up and massaged the back of her neck to dampen the familiar tremor of excitement she always felt when an unfounded suspicion became a vague possibility.

"Does Marek know this?" she asked as she stood up and walked restlessly to the window.

"He didn't seem to until I pointed it out to him. He wasn't nearly as interested in the information as you are however."

"Oh god, I don't know, Quinn," Kit sighed. "The idea of Geoffrey sneaking away from the restaurant without his dinner companions noticing is interesting to say the least, but it sounds like an episode of *Columbo*."

"So? That doesn't mean it's not possible."

"But it's not likely, is it? From what your mother told me about him I don't believe he'd be anywhere near clever enough to think it up let alone carry it out."

"My mother!" Quinn almost snorted then continued more calmly. "My mother, I believe, was constantly underestimating that bastard. You only have to consider these curious financial dealings Uncle Douglas has been investigating, not to mention the disgusting stuff you uncovered. What on earth was she thinking about? I can't understand why she didn't confront him with it all and throw him out into the gutter where he belongs."

"Yeah, well, I wondered that a few times myself. But she obviously had her reasons. She told me last week she had to find out everything she could before she confronted him. She wanted me to stay on the case for the second week while Douglas continued his financial investigations, even though we acknowledged I probably wouldn't get anything new. Which I didn't. I just got more of the same. I don't know about Douglas though. He may have discovered something, and maybe your mother *did* confront Geoffrey with it. But if that was the case I'm sure Douglas would have informed the police. Has he found anything?"

"No," said Quinn quietly. "But that doesn't mean a thing. They may have had an argument and Mum could have let it slip that she knew something was going on."

"So, what then? You think that Geoffrey keeps his dinner appointment, slips out during the meal, drowns your mother in the pond and then slips back in time for dessert?" Kit said a little too dramatically. Quinn looked understandably stunned as she fought back angry tears and tried to control herself enough to speak. Kit sat down beside her on the couch. "I'm sorry, Quinn. But it does sound a little like you're looking for someone to blame here. If your mother did confront Geoffrey with any of the stuff we've found out he'd be crazy to do anything until he knew how much was known and who else knew it. Would you agree with that?"

Quinn nodded and burst into tears. Kit hesitated for a moment before putting a comforting arm around the young woman's shoulders.

"Maybe he already had it planned," she said between sobs. "He mightn't have known she was having him investigated."

"That would be *some* coincidence," Kit said. She leant forward and rummaged around on the shelf under the coffee table for a box of tissues and pulled out a handful. Quinn blew her nose noisily and tried to smile.

"I guess it would be," Quinn said. "But Uncle Douglas told me everything Geoffrey said on Friday night. That stuff about Byron just didn't make any sense, and all those lies about my mother's drinking. OK, so she drank a bit, but she wasn't an alcoholic. I probably drink more than she does. I just don't think it was an accident."

Kit looked seriously at Quinn for several seconds before shaking her head. "Neither do I. I guess you've hired yourself a detective."

A look of relief came over Quinn's face, it was probably the first time she'd been able to relax since Douglas had phoned her in London with the news. She took a deep breath and managed a fairly wan smile as she straightened her slight frame and shut away the grief for another time and place. "Great. Thanks," she said. "So what do we do now?"

"*We* don't do anything. I do," said Kit. "I've got a few things I can follow up, not the least of which is a cryptic note your mother left me.

I'll have to talk to Marek, and of course I have the appointment with Douglas at twelve. I've also got to find Byron Daniels."

Kit got up and jogged the three steps up to her study where she began rummaging around in the chaos for the envelope Marek had given her on Friday night. She noticed the winking light on her answering machine but decided to ignore it for the time being.

"Uncle Douglas knows how to find Byron. He's been calling him all weekend but he must have gone away somewhere," Quinn was saying. "But what's this about a cryptic note?"

Kit returned to her chair and emptied the contents of the envelope into her lap. "I nearly forgot about this. Last Friday was supposed to be my last appointment with your mother. Celia and I had agreed at our previous meeting that unless I came up with something new any further effort would be a waste of my time and her money. So I went to your home on Friday with everything I needed to close the case. But Marek gave this to me. It's a check for $2000, which is far more than what Celia owed me for expenses. She'd been paying my fee in advance so I can only assume that she wanted me to check something else out. But I have no idea what this means." Kit handed the small piece of paper with the red writing to Quinn. "Is that your mother's handwriting?"

Quinn nodded as she read aloud, "January 19, North 4; 5 p.m.; January 20, FISC, 11 p.m." She looked questioningly at Kit who threw up her palms in a "search me" gesture.

"The nineteenth. That's tomorrow," Quinn said. "What do we do with this? It could mean anything."

"It is probably one of Geoffrey's mystery appointments," Kit said. "It would be easy enough to keep an eye on him tomorrow to find out what he does at five o'clock. That's assuming, of course, that your mother's death hasn't caused him to cancel all his appointments. But even if he does keep this one we still may not learn anything. If it's a meeting of some sort at his club, or the house in St. Kilda, then we'll know where he is but not why. That's one reason I need to speak to Byron. He prepared the lists of Geoffrey's known appointments and any other details Celia thought would be useful to me. He's probably the only person who can explain what it means. Unless Douglas knows something about it. In all the confusion on Friday night I neglected to show it to him."

"So if Uncle Douglas doesn't know what it means, and we can't find Byron in time, then we'll just have to follow Geoffrey," Quinn said.

"Whoa, hang on a second, Quinn," Kit exclaimed in surprise. "If there's any following to be done, I'll do it. None of this 'we' business, it doesn't work that way. You hire me. I do the work."

"But I want to help. I can't just sit around waiting for written reports. I'll go crazy."

"I'm sure I can come up with lots of things you can do to help. But not that. Besides, I imagine you'll have a certain amount of family business to attend to."

"But I *want* to be involved, Kit. Uncle Douglas will take care of the business stuff," Quinn pouted.

"No doubt Douglas will do all he can to help you through this as easily as possible," Kit said, guessing that Quinn was accustomed to getting her own way without actually accepting responsibility for anything. What was it Celia had said about her "stubborn, selfish and wayward daughter"? Oh yes. Elizabeth was trying to find herself, away from family interference. Kit wagered that Quinn's search wasn't making her stray too far from the family money or the power and privileges that went with it.

"There'll be some things, however, that only you can do, Quinn," she said. "And Douglas was pretty cut-up on Friday. This is hard on him too, you know."

Quinn looked as though she was about to do a "how dare you" number on Kit but then thought better of it. "I guess you're right," she said sweetly. "But if Uncle Douglas doesn't need me tomorrow I would like to come with you. No, don't shrug me off," she said, closing her hand gently around Kit's forearm. "I'm the one who's paying so I want to be involved with you as much as I can."

"Actually your mother has already paid me for this week," Kit said, waving the check and trying to ignore the almost seductive tone in Quinn's voice. "And it's not my policy to have my clients tagging along on the job. I work alone."

"You sound like one of those hard-boiled detectives." Quinn let go of Kit's arm.

95

"I *am* a hard-boiled detective, Quinn," Kit laughed. "So let's drop the subject for now, OK?" And for god's sake stop flirting with me, she thought irritably.

"OK," Quinn said demurely. "For now."

Kit rolled her eyes in frustration but managed a smile. She had a strong feeling that Quinn Orlando would be dogging her every move until this case was over. Oh well, she thought, as long as she pays for the privilege who am I to complain about a little company on a long and lonely stakeout?

"I have to make myself a little more presentable before I meet with Douglas," she said abruptly. "Do you want to wait?"

"Sure. I was thinking we could go together," Quinn said. "I'll drive you into the city if you like."

It took Kit no time at all to shower and change into a pair of tailored black trousers and a soft white shirt. As she gathered up all the files related to the case, Quinn made a sly comment about the transformation from beachcomber to executive being at odds with Kit's image as a hard-boiled anything.

Chapter 9

Money, money, money, Kit hummed quietly to herself an hour later as she followed Quinn through wide glass doors into the plush foyer of Douglas Scott's suite of offices in William Street. The legal firm of Jenkins, Cazenove, Scott and Harris occupied the entire third floor and Kit guessed the money paid for the interior decor of the reception area alone would have kept her and Thistle in top-shelf bourbon and imported Scottish salmon for a decade and then some.

The luxurious lilac carpet was positively begging to be rolled in, the antiques strategically placed on the five occasional tables between the waiting chairs were exquisite, the paintings were originals and the Abigail Trellini lithograph was numbered 1/100.

Bourbon, salmon *and* Grange Hermitage, Kit amended.

Margaret Richards told them to have a seat while she informed Mr. Scott they had arrived. Kit knew the receptionist's name was Margaret Richards because her gilt-edged name plate was nearly as big as her mahogany desk, which was nearly as big as Kit's entire office.

"It's just as well Ms. Richards is such an imposing woman," Kit whispered to Quinn as they were swallowed up by the cushions on the couch, "or she'd be lost amongst the furniture."

"It's a bit over the top, isn't it," Quinn agreed. "I've always suspected the old boys were on the receiving end of a major practical joke. I'm sure the decorator was a rabid feminist. I can't see them choosing all this purple without a lot of encouragement."

Kit laughed but immediately slapped her hand over her mouth as Margaret Richards turned her disapproving gaze in their direction. Such raucous behavior was obviously not acceptable.

"None of this seems to fit with the man I met at your mother's on Friday. He surely can't be responsible for this pretentious atmosphere?" Kit said quietly.

"Good heavens, no," Quinn laughed. "Uncle Douglas, believe it nor not, is one of the younger partners. Hugh Jenkins is the old fuddy-duddy of the firm, though the name on the door now belongs to his son Harry and he's at least sixty. Alexander Cazenove, last time I heard, was semi-retired. He's Uncle Douglas's brother-in-law. And Stuart Harris is quite possibly the stuffiest man I've ever met." She was about to say something else but was silenced by the sight of Margaret Richards rising up from behind her desk like a schoolmistress about to discipline a rowdy student.

"Mr. Scott will see you now. If you will follow me, please."

Quinn had already leapt to mock attention.

"Walk this way," said Kit under her breath as she took Quinn's offered hands and struggled ungracefully to her feet.

"She scares the shit out of me," Quinn whispered, then said more loudly, "It's OK Margaret, I know the way."

"We do not go in unannounced, Elizabeth," Margaret said.

"No. Of course we don't. Sorry." Quinn obediently fell in behind the titanic receptionist as she rolled her way down the hall and opened the door at the end. It was all Kit could do to retain her composure as Quinn turned and winked at her.

"Miss O'Malley and Miss Robinson," Margaret announced.

"Orlando," Quinn said curtly as she slipped past Margaret into the spacious office.

"Ms.," Kit said because the word was out before she could stop herself.

"Hmph," grunted Margaret as she left, closing the door behind her.

Douglas Scott, one arm still around Quinn's waist in an affectionate embrace, offered Kit his hand and a warm smile. His adorable eyebrows were still totally out of control but the rest of him was far more together than when she'd last seen him. He was a picture of gentlemanly charm and elegance, his white hair softening the businesslike effect of his superbly tailored gray suit. "Sit down, please. I'll organize some coffee while we wait for Alex, who's been doing most of the investigative work for me," he said. "Oh, unless you'd rather have tea, Kit."

"I never say no to coffee," Kit said, sitting down in one of the four leather club chairs arranged around a small glass-topped coffee table by the floor-to-ceiling window which overlooked William Street. She propped her briefcase against the leg of the table and stared vaguely at the gray stone building across the street until her attention was commandeered by Quinn who flung herself into the opposite chair.

"Kit has agreed to help us, Uncle Douglas."

"Us?" Kit said in surprise.

Douglas smiled as he took the chair next to Kit's. "I would have asked you myself," he said, "but Elizabeth wanted to meet you first and she, after all, is the one doing the hiring."

"Look," said Kit, suddenly wondering what on earth it was she'd gotten herself into, "I am willing to do everything I can to help but I don't want to take anyone's money under false pretenses. It's in my nature to be suspicious, especially of people like Geoffrey Robinson, but, as I said to Quinn, in this particular instance I also have my doubts. Until we have the results of the autopsy and know one way or the other we have to face the possibility that Celia's death *was* an accident."

"But you don't believe it was, do you?"

"It doesn't really matter what I believe, Douglas. The police will only be interested in the facts. You know that. We could present Marek with our suspicions but the police would have to have hard evidence that a crime was actually committed before they took us seriously. And even if the autopsy results are inconclusive we'd still have a difficult time proving Geoffrey had anything to do with Celia's death, let alone that he actually killed her. I'm afraid that if it does become a murder investigation Marek's prime suspect won't be Geoffrey at all."

"Who else could they possibly suspect?" Quinn asked in surprise.

"Byron Daniels."

"But that's ridiculous," Douglas said. "Byron would never do anything to harm Celia."

"So where is he? And how much of what Geoffrey told the police on Friday night is true?"

"I don't know where he is. But Geoffrey's story about Byron stealing from Celia is totally unbelievable. He would have no need to steal from her."

"How can you be so sure? And why on earth would Geoffrey lie about it?" Kit asked.

"To cover up for himself," Quinn snarled.

"Now that *is* ridiculous. Sooner or later Byron would be in a position to deny it all."

"We think something has happened to him," Quinn said.

"Like what? You're not suggesting he's met with a mysterious accident as well?"

"It would explain a lot," Douglas said.

"If it comes down to it, the police will think Geoffrey's story explains a whole lot more," Kit stated, looking from Quinn to Douglas as she wondered why she was playing the devil's advocate when she totally agreed with their suspicions.

"That is why it worries me that Byron hasn't turned up," Douglas stated quietly. "I know the man often spends the weekend with friends in the country somewhere. If he hasn't seen the television news or read a newspaper in the last two days it could explain why he didn't rush home. He simply may not know. But . . ."

"But now it's Monday," Kit said. "He should be at work, surely."

"Not necessarily," Douglas said, almost desperately. "But it is curious."

"Curious?" said Kit, raising an eyebrow. Douglas Scott was a master of understatement. There's something you're not telling me, she thought.

The conversation was interrupted by Margaret Richards ushering in a young girl carrying a silver tray, a coffee pot and fine china cups. The coffee was poured and handed out nervously then the girl, responding immediately to a slight toss of drill-sergeant Richards's head, backed away and followed the receptionist out the door again.

Kit was about to pick up her cup when Quinn leant forward and reached for her hand.

100

Oh god, Kit thought as she was forced to give those blue eyes her undivided attention.

"You *are* going to help us, aren't you, Kit?" she queried. "You haven't changed your mind?"

"No, of course I haven't. I'll do what I can, but we have to consider all the possibilities here. And at the moment we can't rule out Geoffrey's story about Byron." She withdrew her hand so she could pick up her cup and sit back in the chair. She was sure Quinn's smile was more one of self-satisfaction than relief. What the hell is going on here? she asked herself. I don't need to be seduced into this. I've already agreed to do it. *You and your hormones are simply feeling flattered by this sweet young thing* said a sarcastic voice in the back of her head. We are not, she argued back.

Kit looked over at Douglas who apparently hadn't noticed anything untoward in Quinn's behavior. Perhaps he's used to it, she thought. Perhaps I'm imagining things and this is just the way she is—with everyone. She glanced back at Quinn who was still watching her intently, a half smile hanging around the corners of her mouth. Nope. She knows exactly what she's doing, Kit thought. And it's definitely not my imagination.

"The police haven't even asked me if I might know where to find Byron," Douglas was saying. "That suggests to me that they're not interested in locating him."

"I gather that means you haven't volunteered the information either," Kit said dryly.

"There didn't seem to be any need," Douglas returned.

"Of course not," Kit said, unable to keep the sarcasm out of her voice. This was crazy! Even if Marek was going with the death by misadventure theory he still wouldn't have ignored Geoffrey's story about having to sack one of his late wife's most trusted employees. "I'm a little confused about this," she said. "If you really are worried that something has happened to Byron I don't understand why you haven't told the police where he lives so they can start looking for him."

"We were rather hoping you would find him for us," Douglas said.

"Why? That doesn't make sense. Unless you believe what Geoffrey said about having to fire him."

"I don't believe Geoffrey's reasons," Douglas admitted cautiously, "but that doesn't mean I disbelieve everything he claimed in his statement to the police."

"Are you saying that Geoffrey did sack him but for reasons other than those he gave on Friday night?" Kit asked, leaning forward to rest her elbows on her knees.

"We can't discount that possibility."

Kit stared at Douglas in astonishment for several seconds before dropping her head into her hands and raking her fingers through her hair in exasperation. "Why would Geoffrey tell half the truth? What other reason could there possibly be?"

"I have no idea," Douglas stated.

"Oh great!" She threw her hands up in a gesture of defeat. Kit had no idea whether Douglas was telling the truth or not. She was getting to the stage where she didn't care. I should just get up and walk out. I don't need this shit, she thought, and then wondered why she never listened to a thing she thought as she heard herself say, "Quinn told me you've been calling him all weekend, Douglas. Did you make any other attempts to find him?"

"I went to his house on Saturday morning. There was no car in the garage and no one answered the door, which is why I assumed he'd gone away for the weekend. He often worked long hours for Celia so it was not unusual for him to take one or two extra days off when she didn't need his services."

"So it is vaguely possible that he's been incommunicado for the past two and a half days," Kit said, wishing she was also still in hiding, lounging on the sundeck at Brigit's beach house. There was too much going unsaid in this room for her liking. And why the hell were they so determined to protect Byron? And protect him from what? Unless everything they were doing was simply aimed at protecting the family from scandal. God, how boring!

"Excuse me," she finally said, filling the silence that had followed her last statement, "but I'd really like to know what's going on here."

Quinn looked surprised but Douglas's expression was totally unreadable. Kit had no option but to press the point. "OK. We all agree that there's something not quite right about Celia's death. Given

Geoffrey's somewhat questionable behavior of late he has to be our prime suspect—that is, if our suspicions have any basis in fact. But Geoffrey won't even figure in the police's reckoning unless we give Marek everything we have on him. And it's obvious that idea is not on the agenda here—at least not yet."

"You're right, Kit. That is not an option at this time," Douglas confirmed.

"Throw the bastard to the wolves," Quinn said through clenched teeth. "Let the cops and the gutter press have him. Who gives a shit?"

"*You* will Quinn, if it turns out to be unnecessary," Kit replied quietly.

"So that leaves Byron. Only he can confirm or refute Geoffrey's story, unless he *has* met with an accident. Personally speaking, the guy gave me the creeps but you two seem to have the utmost faith in his loyalty. I don't know him from Adam so I have no real reason to doubt what Geoffrey said about having to sack him, whatever the reasons, and neither will the police. The very fact that he seems to have vanished into thin air makes Geoffrey's story believable."

"Maybe Kit is right, Uncle Douglas. We don't really know for sure." Quinn was looking uncertain, and not for the first time Kit realized.

"Byron would not steal from Celia," Douglas stated sharply.

"Says you," Kit snapped. She was getting sick of this. "The lord of the manor says otherwise."

Douglas took a deep breath as if he was making a monumental decision. He looked at Kit as he spoke but it was obvious he was wary of Quinn's reaction. "Celia paid Byron an annual salary of $67,000. He lives in a house bought for him by Celia and he has sole use of one of her cars. He did not need to steal from her."

Kit's jaw had dropped at the mention of the salary but Quinn's voice exploded in anger before Douglas had even finished speaking. "She bought him a house? What the hell did she buy him a house for? If she was paying him that much money he could buy his own bloody house!"

This was some turnaround. Kit looked from one to the other: Quinn was absolutely livid, while Douglas looked like he wanted the floor to open up and swallow him.

"Well," Kit said, trying to restore some balance to the proceedings, "it's obvious that Quinn didn't know about this. I assume that means that Geoffrey doesn't either."

"Exactly," Douglas said, managing to compose his features enough to face Quinn. "Elizabeth, I'm sorry. I should have told you."

"*You* should have told me? Why the hell didn't my mother tell me? He's just a secretary for god's sake. Who on earth pays a secretary that much money? And why the big secret?" A thought obviously occurred to Quinn at that moment; it was written in horror all over her face. "Uncle Douglas. They weren't? Oh god—Byron and my mother weren't . . ."

"No, Elizabeth. They weren't lovers."

"Then what the hell was going on?"

"Byron didn't just perform secretarial duties, Elizabeth. He was Celia's personal assistant, butler, chauffeur, even confidant. He kept her life organized and was at her beck and call. But most of all he was her friend. She got none of that from Geoffrey, and you haven't been home much in the last few years. Byron was always there for her. So she paid him what he was worth to her, though she didn't believe even that was enough."

Quinn looked as though she'd been slapped in the face. Her chin was quivering as she blinked back the tears. Hugging her knees to her chest she wiped angrily at her eyes. Douglas reluctantly got up to attend to the insistent beeping of the phone on his desk.

Kit fished around in the pocket of her trousers as she moved across and crouched beside Quinn's chair. Quinn took the offered handkerchief and forced a small smile. Her voice when she spoke was even smaller. "Quite a revelation, huh? To find out your mother had to pay for her friends."

"Quinn, I don't think . . ."

"Don't look at me like that, I didn't mean it," Quinn said, reaching to wipe the frown from Kit's face. She withdrew her hand quickly and actually blushed. "I'm sorry, but it's pretty scary to find out that maybe your mother needed you as much as you needed her. Especially if you find out when it's too late."

Kit didn't know what to say; she never did in moments like this. It frustrated the hell out of her, even though she knew that nothing she could say would make Quinn hurt any less. And her grieving would be that much more painful now it included a strong dose of the what-might-have-beens. There was nothing worse than realizing you'd missed all the opportunities you were ever going to get to put something right.

"If there's anything I can do," she offered, covering Quinn's hand with her own to give it a comforting squeeze. She realized she was voluntarily digging herself far deeper into this family's mess than she knew was good for her. But she also knew it was too late to back out. Quinn's fingers closed around Kit's as if she were hanging on for dear life. "I'm OK now, Kit, really. Thanks."

The sound of Douglas's polite "ahem," designed to inform them that there was someone else in the room, got a reaction from Quinn that sent Kit tumbling backwards off her haunches. Quinn squealed with delight and leapt out of the chair, allowing Kit just enough time before she ended up on her arse to catch a glimpse of a tall slender woman dressed in a gray suit, a white collarless shirt and . . .

Who *cares* what she's wearing! thought Kit desperately. She was more embarrassed than she could ever remember being, but then who the hell wouldn't be when they're lying sprawled on the floor three feet from quite possibly the most beautiful woman they'd ever seen in their entire life? OK, she conceded, so the circumstances aren't exactly conducive to being able to form an objective opinion here, O'Malley. You've got to admit that things tend to get a little out of perspective when the goddess of decorum has totally deserted you and you'd rather die than have to stand up. *Now* would be a really good time, Scotty. Beam me up. Please!

"I thought we were waiting for your father," Quinn was saying, so excited she could barely contain herself. "Oh wow, this is great. How long have you been back? Why didn't you tell me, Uncle Douglas? Oh, where are my manners?" The words were positively tumbling out as Quinn turned back to face Kit. "Kit, this is . . . What are you doing down there?"

"Resting," said Katherine Frances O'Malley, without doubt the coolest private eye in Melbourne. She got up, brushed herself off and waited nonchalantly to be formally introduced while she tried not to stare at . . .

"Alexis Cazenove," Quinn said. "This is Katherine O'Malley. Kit, Alex."

Somebody stuck her hand out to shake the long-fingered one that belonged to Alex Cazenove. Kit didn't realize it was her until she felt the woman's firm grip.

"Katherine," Alex acknowledged in a voice that was like a molten version of the gun-metal gray she was wearing. She had managed to control the smile twitching at the corner of her wide mouth but, Kit noticed self-consciously, she couldn't quite hide the amusement in her gray eyes.

Laugh at me and get it over with, Kit thought wretchedly. "Pleased to meet you, Alex," she said quite calmly considering that under normal circumstances this woman would have made her go positively weak at the knees. Given that her idiotic hormones had already been woken up by the number Quinn had been doing on her all morning, it was amazing that she was actually capable of standing.

"I haven't seen her for three years, Kit," Quinn said, grabbing Kit excitedly by the arm only to let go and do the same to Alex. "This is such a surprise!"

Alex Cazenove smiled and Kit *did* go weak at the knees. Oh dear! Pull yourself together, woman, she told herself sternly. Retreat. Sit down. *Calm* down. Move, dammit!

Kit noticed that Douglas had returned to his chair. She did likewise, managing to get there without falling over or otherwise making a fool of herself. She rummaged around in her briefcase to give her cover while she checked out Douglas Scott's niece, who of course wasn't taking any notice of her because she was far too busy giving Quinn a warm embrace before stepping back to wipe tears from the younger woman's face.

Now that Kit was safely sitting down (on a chair instead of the floor) she felt much more in control and therefore capable of forming a reasonable opinion. And she had to admit that Alexis Cazenove was not exactly beautiful—well, not in any traditional sense. In fact some people might not even give her a second look. They'd have to be brain dead though, she thought. Alex's mouth, glossed with a subtle shade of red lipstick, was perhaps a touch too large for the narrow face but complemented the fine line of her jaw and the hint of high cheek-bones which were only truly noticeable when she smiled. Her thick shoulder-length auburn hair, more red than brown, fell in waves so that it appeared neither straight nor exactly curly. It was pushed back behind her left ear revealing a drop earring with a single pearl that matched the string around her slender throat.

Kit guessed she was in her mid-thirties and estimated, from the memory of standing almost level with those perfect smoky-gray eyes, that she was about five foot eight. Everything about her was straight, slender and well proportioned, from her shoulders to her long legs which were clad in stockings just a shade lighter than the short straight skirt and long jacket. To cap it off the woman was sublimely self-confident and apparently completely oblivious to the fact that she was drop-dead gorgeous.

Kit let her gaze travel back from Alex's legs to Alex's face, only to find Alex's eyes staring directly into hers. She was listening to Quinn but looking at Kit.

There is nothing for it but to keep right on staring, O'Malley, anything else would be too obvious, Kit thought. She was just starting to feel truly uncomfortable when Alex, with that amused smile dancing round the corner of her mouth, finally turned back to answer Quinn's question.

Chapter 10

Kit's show-and-tell part of the meeting was a fairly traumatic experience, all things considered. A little way into her presentation of the case so far Douglas had to rise to her defense when Alex, apropos of nothing in particular, questioned the usefulness ("no offense intended, O'Malley") of her continued involvement when they had their own competent team of regular investigators. "If we have to use these *professionals*, shouldn't we keep it in the family," she had said. Again, "no offense, O'Malley."

"None taken," Kit had replied through clenched teeth, wondering what on earth she'd done wrong to be suddenly reduced in this woman's opinion to one of those "professionals" (such a dirty word) who have nothing but a surname to answer to.

Quinn, obviously surprised at Alex's barely disguised disapproval, pointed out that it was she and not the firm who was employing Kit, whereon Douglas attempted to defuse the ensuing awkwardness by making a fuss of organizing another pot of coffee.

Ten minutes later Kit tried again. Concentrating on the business at hand enabled her to get control of herself, if not the situation, and a fresh cup of coffee gave her something to do with her hands when she wasn't using them to spread out the photographs of Geoffrey's extra-marital activities. The atmosphere in the room by this time, however, was so thick with emotions of one sort or another it could have been buttered and spread with Vegemite.

Where Celia's reaction to the evidence of Geoffrey's perfidious behavior had been disappointment and annoyance, Quinn's was pure unadulterated rage and disgust. Despite the seriousness of the situation Kit was highly impressed by the sheer variety and inventiveness of Quinn's invective. Douglas's expression registered the same reaction as Quinn, but while he sat there in tight-lipped silence Quinn raged and cursed her stepfather for the low-life cheating whip-dicked bastard he was.

The only calm person in the room was Alex, who sat surveying the proceedings in a manner so detached as to seem downright uninterested. She barely glanced at the photos, relying instead on Kit's verbal report of the surveillance job, and the only time she showed any emotion other than super-cool indifference was when she responded to Quinn's distress with genuine concern and affection.

Douglas obviously knew a little more than Celia did about Gerald Grainger but as Quinn had paled at the sight of the person her mother had described as "a repulsive, crass and uncouth man" Kit thought it was time to divert the discussion away from the subject of sex. "Douglas, did you hire someone else to follow Geoffrey?" she asked before dropping the photos of the mystery man in the station wagon on top of the one of Gerald Grainger.

"No. Celia mentioned this man but it has nothing to do with me, I assure you," he stated, glancing at the three pictures before handing them to Alex.

"You don't recognize him, I gather," Alex said. When Kit shook her head Alex peered at the photos more closely then tossed them back onto the table dismissively. "It could be anyone. They're not very clear shots."

"Well, as you can see, it wasn't him I was photographing in these two," Kit said, a little too defensively. She shrank inwardly as Alex raised an eyebrow in surprise.

"What makes you think he's an investigator?" Alex asked.

"He could be anything," Kit said. "That was just my first thought. He may not be following Geoffrey at all. In fact each time this guy has turned up Geoffrey has been with Ian Dalkeith."

"Where was this shot taken?" Douglas asked, indicating the photograph of Dalkeith leaving his riverfront property.

"That's a most unattractive piece of land Dalkeith plans to turn into a 'state of the art integrated business and residential district.' At the moment there's nothing there but a warehouse, a rotting wharf and a brand new fence," Kit said.

"He's not going to last long as an entrepreneur if he doesn't know the property boom is over. Nobody with any sense is investing in this sort of thing at the moment," Douglas said.

"In that case that's probably just where my stepfather put his money," said Quinn.

"Not even Geoffrey is that stupid, Elizabeth," Douglas responded with a half-smile.

"What was he doing there then?"

"He wasn't there," Kit said. "I followed Dalkeith after he had lunch with Geoffrey a couple of weeks ago."

"But this car *was* there," Alex stated, tapping the photograph. "It seems to be quite obvious that this person is following Ian Dalkeith not Geoffrey."

"Maybe," Kit said with a shrug. "And maybe he was following Dalkeith just on that particular occasion—like I was."

Alex gave a short humorless laugh before sitting back in her chair. "Maybe this man is following *you*, O'Malley," she suggested as she swung her left leg over her right knee, which meant, effectively, that she was no longer facing Kit. God, this woman uses body language like punctuation, Kit thought, still wondering what she'd done to deserve this antagonism.

"Why on earth would anyone be following Kit?" Quinn was saying. She reached out, put her hand over Kit's which was resting on the arm of the chair and squeezed it reassuringly, as if she too was puzzled by Alex's attitude.

"I have absolutely no idea, Quinn," Alex responded. "But I'm sure you're not Ms. O'Malley's only client. This might have nothing to do with us whatsoever."

"Alex may be right," Kit said to Quinn, making a point of using Alex's first name. "Someone *may* be following me, though I can't imagine why as you *are* in fact my only client at the moment." She acknowledged Quinn's gesture by turning her hand over and clasping

Quinn's. Quinn smiled, as if she and Kit shared a great secret, then gave Alex a look that was almost defiant, as if she was daring Alex to say something else that she considered inappropriate. Alex, for her part, was wearing an expression of undisguised . . . something. Kit couldn't quite work out what it was but the woman seemed to be trying very hard *not* to speak.

"We don't seem to be getting very far on this matter," Douglas said, looking from Kit to Quinn to Alex and back to Kit again. "Shall we go on to the next point?"

"Perhaps we should use the registration to find out who owns the vehicle—or am I suggesting the obvious?" Alex said, ignoring her uncle's remark.

"I've done that. It's a rent-a-wreck, hired for a three-month period, paid in advance eight weeks ago by a Mike Finnigan who doesn't live at the address he gave. No one does—it's a park. So I can only assume that his name is as phony as his place of residence," Kit said. "Though I *had* already guessed that," she added before Alex could suggest the obvious again.

"Very strange," Douglas said.

"Indeed," Kit agreed as she gathered the photos together in a neat pile. "Celia's accident aside, we have a great many unanswered questions. Geoffrey is carrying out some sort of business, we assume, with Dalkeith, possibly Grainger and maybe even that American, Watts, though he seems to have left town. There's some guy in an old car tailing Dalkeith or Geoffrey, or me, and Byron Daniels is missing. Did you look into Wellborn Enterprises, Douglas?"

"I did," said Alex, reaching into the briefcase propped against her chair. She pulled out a folder and from it several sheets of paper. "Wellborn Enterprises is a subsidiary of Freyling Imports and has four directors."

"I'll wager Geoffrey isn't one of them," Kit said.

"Well, that's a winning bet," Alex said with what was almost a smile. "Ian Dalkeith, however, is. He, Edwina Baynes and Malcolm Smith own thirty per cent each and Shirley Smith holds the other ten per cent. You're frowning, O'Malley. Do you know the Smiths?"

"No. But the name Edwina Baynes rings a bell. I just can't place it though," Kit said standing up. She walked the few paces to the window to stretch her legs and stared down at the William Street traffic while Alex continued with her report.

"Wellborn Enterprises owns several properties in Melbourne, Sydney and Coolangatta. In Melbourne these include two sites in South Melbourne and one each in Footscray, Frankston and Port Melbourne, as well as the house that Geoffrey frequents in St. Kilda and others in East Melbourne, Windsor and Gardenvale. It also owns a modeling agency called *Skintone,* as well as a couple of those instant printing places and three video stores."

"That's quite a mixed bag," Quinn said.

"From these addresses I'd guess that the Footscray site is the one where O'Malley photographed Dalkeith. Was that on the Maribyrnong River?" Alex asked. "O'Malley! Are you still with us?"

"What? Oh sorry." Kit turned away from the window. She'd been miles away, searching her memory for Edwina Baynes, and now realized her three companions were waiting expectantly for something. She had to blink a couple of times and when her vision had reacquainted itself with the softer light of the office Kit found that her gaze was focused quite firmly on Alex Cazenove. Again she felt almost incapable of looking anywhere else. Holy shit! she thought, taking a sharp breath. She reached out to steady herself against the rush that started somewhere around her knees, raced right up her body and then trickled deliciously back down again. It's just as well you were already sprawled on the floor the first time you saw her, O'Malley, because that's certainly where you would have ended up, she said to herself. Shaking her head she blinked hard again, hoping she appeared disoriented from the light rather than just plain disoriented.

"Are you OK, Kit?" Quinn asked.

"Yes, of course. Did I miss something?" she asked, returning to her seat.

Alex, wearing a completely unreadable expression, handed her the piece of paper she was holding and pointed to a line about halfway down the page. "Is Dalkeith's building site on the Maribyrnong?" she asked.

"Ah, yes. It wasn't too far up from where it meets the Yarra," Kit said, scanning the page. "That's it!" she exclaimed.

"That's what I was asking you, O'Malley," Alex said.

"No, no. Not that—this," Kit pushed Alex's finger down the page.

"The *Skintone Agency?*" Alex said, awkwardly withdrawing her hand.

"Yeah. And the name. Look, it's a typo. I knew the name was familiar. But it's *Barnes* not Baynes. Edwina Barnes. Well, I'll be damned!"

"Don't keep us in suspense, Kit. Who the hell is she?" Quinn asked.

"Well, she's not just one *she* exactly. At least not any more. Edwina Barnes is, or rather was, a call girl. A high-class high-priced call girl. But Edwina Barnes is also a name, like Chanel or Disney. The real Edwina, if she's even still alive, would be about seventy years old but her name is still on the door of the 'service organization' she started back in the forties or fifties. At least it was the last time I had anything to do with it, which was about eight years ago. Edwina's organization has serviced a lot of very important and influential men in Melbourne over the years. Local businessmen and politicians employ Edwina's girls for their own enjoyment or to entertain clients or visiting dignitaries. Edwina herself retired, a very wealthy woman, about ten or twelve years ago."

"You're assuming this is the same Edwina Barnes," Alex said. "And this business is registered as a modeling agency."

"Modeling agency, my foot!" Kit laughed. "The *Skintone Agency* has to be an escort service. Edwina doesn't *do* anything else."

"But you said she'd retired," Quinn said.

"Well, at seventy she could hardly front up for active duty but, as I said, Edwina Barnes is also a name. One or more of her girls could be managing this so-called modeling agency."

"You seem to know an awful lot about this prostitute," Alex said, raising an eyebrow.

"Yeah, well, it's a long story. About eight years ago four of Edwina's girls were brutalized by a client, a really sick bastard who had a thing for blindfolds, handcuffs and beer bottles. One of the women died from her injuries. The investigation was a fairly delicate operation because so many of Edwina's clients were such *important* men. Few of them ever used their real names and the unimportant ones rarely used the same name twice. We had no idea who the perpetrator was so another police officer and I went undercover. Anyway, although I never met Edwina herself, I spent a bit of time with her colleagues."

"You worked with them?" Quinn seemed quite astonished.

"In a manner of speaking. I was undercover, Quinn. I had to make it look good."

"Did you get the guy?" she asked.

Kit sighed. "Yes and no. We caught him but he jumped from a fifth-floor hotel balcony."

"I suppose that's justice of a sort," Douglas stated.

"It was much too quick to be called justice," Kit said, shaking her head. "But this isn't getting us very far. What about Freyling Imports?"

Alex, who had been watching Kit quite intently, dragged her attention back to the papers in her lap. "The directors of Freyling Imports are the aforementioned Edwina Barnes, Malcolm Smith, Shirley Smith and one Davis Whitten."

"Not Dalkeith this time?"

"No. But, as with Wellborn, Ms. Barnes, Malcolm Smith and in this case Davis Whitten hold thirty per cent each, and Shirley Smith again holds the remaining ten per cent."

"Have you found out who the Smiths are yet?" Douglas queried.

"No. I'm assuming they are husband and wife but I haven't been able to trace them in Melbourne. I contacted Michael in Sydney on Friday. I expect to hear something from him today. Ditto for Davis Whitten."

"What does Freyling Imports import exactly?" Kit asked.

"Just about anything, I gather," Alex replied. "It has a large client base of companies and customers which, as far as I can ascertain, have no other connection with Freyling, Wellborn or any of the people involved with them. Freyling imports everything from computer hardware and electronic security systems to cosmetics, videotapes, truck parts and hydraulic mechanisms—for building cranes of all things. Their head office is in Port Melbourne."

"Curiouser and curiouser," mused Kit.

"And curiouser," Alex added. "I discovered this morning that Freyling Imports is an irregular customer of Orlan Carriers."

"What?" said Douglas sharply.

"Orlan Carriers? What's that?"

"It's part of Orlando House, Kit," Douglas replied. "It's a transport company that Carl started in 1969, with a single vehicle, to aid OHP's local distribution. In the mid-seventies OHP had some spare cash so it was injected into Orlan Carriers which became moderately successful in its own right."

"Well, it seems we have found a connection between Geoffrey and Dalkeith," Kit said, "albeit an indirect one."

"What about that brothel or whatever it is that Geoffrey goes to in St. Kilda? Dalkeith is one of the owners," Quinn said.

"That merely indicates a shared interest, not necessarily a business connection."

"So, what happens next, O'Malley? The ball seems to be in your court," Alex said.

"I suppose it is. Could you get me a rundown of this irregular transport that Orlan Carriers has done for Freyling Imports?"

"Of course," Alex said. "Do you think it's important?"

"I've no idea," Kit shrugged, "but it's a place to start. I'll also need Byron's address, Douglas, and any other details about him which might help us locate him."

Kit reached into her briefcase, took out the envelope with Celia's cryptic note and handed it to Douglas. She poured herself another cup of now lukewarm coffee while she explained how she'd come by it.

"What does it mean?" Douglas asked, passing the slip of paper to Alex.

"I was hoping you could tell me. I assume it's one of Geoffrey's mysterious appointments. That's one reason I really need to talk to Byron. I figured he might have some idea of where to start, seeing as he prepared the other lists for me."

"January 19. That's tomorrow," Douglas stated.

"If we can't find Byron, Kit and I are going to follow Geoffrey," Quinn said matter-of-factly.

"*You* are?" Alex said. "O'Malley, I don't think that's a good idea."

"It wasn't my idea," Kit said. "And besides, *Quinn*, I said I didn't want you tagging along."

"No, Kit. What you said was, if Uncle Douglas didn't need me for anything then I could go with you."

Kit was quite sure she hadn't said any such thing but decided not to argue. Alex, however, seemed to be a little on the annoyed side. "What on earth are you thinking about? What do you want to go traipsing around town with O'Malley for? I'm sure she doesn't need any help."

"I thought it would be fun," Quinn said testily.

"Fun? Quinn, you don't need to get involved."

"Alex, I *am* involved!" Quinn snapped. "Or have you forgotten what this is all about?"

Alex reached out and, with a resigned sigh, put her hand gently on Quinn's forearm. "Of course I haven't forgotten. It might be dangerous, that's all. This is O'Malley's *job*. You might get in the way of her working properly."

I'll say, thought Kit. Although, as much of a distraction as Quinn would no doubt be, Kit was just grateful that it wasn't Alex who was insisting on coming along with her.

"Well, it seems we have covered everything and it's nearly two o'clock." Douglas was on his feet, signaling the end of the meeting. "Perhaps we should call it a day and get together again when Kit has more information, unless we hear from the police first."

"I plan to drop in on them and see what Marek has come up with," Kit said. "I want to check out Byron's place first though."

"I'll get his address for you," Douglas said, walking over to his desk.

"Douglas," said Kit, following him, "do you know anything about his family or friends?"

Douglas shook his head and handed Kit a piece of paper on which he'd written an address. "As far as I know his parents are dead, and I know nothing of his friends. He's a fairly introverted fellow."

"Kit, I'll meet you in the foyer in a couple of minutes," Quinn said as she followed Alex out the door.

"So, tell me about Gerald Grainger," Kit said to Douglas when they were alone.

"I can't tell you anything good about him," Douglas replied. "He's a self-made millionaire with no manners and very little taste. He made a small fortune from a debt collection agency which he reportedly won in a poker game. I don't know how much truth there is in that story though. He earned a certain amount of notoriety for his rather questionable methods of collecting moneys owed before trying to clean up his image by investing in all sorts of comparatively respectable ventures. He owns five or six nightclubs in Sydney and on the Gold Coast, a recording studio and several racehorses. Grainger is a boastful, conceited and thoroughly obnoxious man."

"Celia said he made a pass at Quinn."

Douglas gave a humorless laugh. "Celia always did have a knack for understatement. Grainger tried to molest Elizabeth. She was only fifteen years old at the time."

"Oh, Jesus!"

Douglas shrugged and reached for the phone which had been beeping for a few seconds. Kit crossed the room to get her briefcase while Douglas told Margaret Richards to hold his next client for a couple more minutes.

"Kit, do you think you could talk to Elizabeth about not confronting Geoffrey with any of this yet," Douglas said. "I know it's not your concern, but she seems to like you and she might listen to you. She's too upset about her mother to be able to separate Geoffrey's rather significant indiscretions from her conviction that he had something to do with her death."

"I'll have a word with her, Douglas, though I don't see why she should listen to me any more than you or Alex," Kit said. *Down, down, deeper and down* she sang to herself, wondering just how far she was going to let herself be dragged into this family's mess.

Kit passed Margaret Richards, escorting Douglas's next client, in the hallway and as she approached the foyer she saw Quinn dancing excitedly from one foot to the other.

"Oh Alex, really? I'd love to. This is so exciting!" Quinn exclaimed with delight as she threw her arms around Alex's neck and kissed her on the mouth. Alex smiled that devastating smile but when she noticed Kit standing there she suddenly looked *almost* uncomfortable.

"I'm so excited, Kit," Quinn said unnecessarily.

"I can see that," Kit said with a grin.

"Can I tell her, Alex?"

Alex ran her left hand through her hair, pushing it back behind her ear, as she glanced at Kit, gave a slight shrug and nodded to Quinn.

"Alex has just asked me to be her bridesmaid," Quinn said. "She's getting married next month."

"Married?" Kit said, more than a little taken aback.

"You sound surprised, O'Malley," Alex said, a look of amusement in her gray eyes.

"Surprised? Do I?" Kit asked. Flabbergasted is more like it, she thought. Married! My god, what a waste. "Congratulations, Alex," she managed to say.

Chapter 11

"Should we be doing this?" Quinn asked, looking around nervously.

Kit pulled the plastic card out of the door she'd just managed to unlock and looked at her partner in crime over the top of her sunglasses. "You wanted to come with me. You could wait in the car if you don't like it."

"No way. I've always wanted to know what it felt like to be a burglar."

"You are a *very* strange person," Kit whispered with a grin. She pushed open the glass door from the deck at the rear of Byron Daniels's house in Prahran, parted the heavy curtains that were drawn against the summer heat and stepped inside. As Byron had answered neither his phone nor the front door bell, Kit had decided there was nothing else to do but break in and search for anything that might give a clue as to his whereabouts. Quinn was close behind, hanging on to the waistband of Kit's trousers and looking over her shoulder.

"What's with you?"

"Nothing! This is really exciting."

"You idiot," Kit laughed. "Do you think you could let go of me and find a light switch so I can shut this curtain?"

"Right. OK. Sorry," Quinn babbled as she made her way to the closed door on the other side of the room and flicked the switch beside it. They were standing in what was obviously a sunroom, furnished with cane armchairs, a couch and a large coffee table. There was a bar in the corner, the floor was gray slate and the walls were decorated with large black-and-white photographs of men in various stages of undress.

"Well, there's not much in this room," Kit said. "We'd better check the rest of the house."

"What are we looking for?"

"Something that might tell us where Byron is," Kit replied. "Look for an address book or a diary. Anything."

The sunroom door opened into a long wide hall which ran towards the front of the house. Kit tried the first door on the left, glanced around the sparsely furnished bedroom and closed the door again. "A guest bedroom by the looks of it," she said to Quinn who had opened the door to the bathroom opposite. They continued down the hall towards the patch of bright sunlight streaming through an open door.

"Oh my god! What is that smell?" Quinn complained from behind her hand which was covering her nose and mouth. She grabbed Kit by the elbow. "You don't think . . ."

"I don't think so, but wait here," Kit ordered and walked hesitantly into the room. She was holding her nose but the nauseating stench still made her gag.

The kitchen appeared to be empty. Protruding from an alcove at the other end of the large room was one end of a table covered with a cloth. Kit walked towards it, leaning to her right so she could see the other end of the table without having to get too close. She was so convinced she was going to find Byron Daniels's dead body slumped over his corn flakes that she nearly stepped in the source of the smell.

"Oh, yuk!" she exclaimed.

"What is it?" asked Quinn from the hallway.

"Half the ant population of Melbourne trying to carry away a huge bowl of extremely putrid cat food," Kit answered. She stepped back and stamped her feet to get rid of the ants that were crawling all over her shoes. The bowl of what several days ago was probably a tasty seafood surprise was now literally alive with ants. It was sitting in direct sunlight next to another bowl full to the brim with sour milk.

"I wouldn't come in here if you don't want to lose your breakfast, Quinn." Kit glanced quickly around the kitchen, picked up a notepad lying on the bench near the wall-phone and escaped back into the hallway.

"Judging by the amount of food left for the cat it looks like Byron *was* going somewhere for the weekend," Kit said, leading Quinn down the hall to the next room. "I wonder where the cat is. It certainly didn't eat much of its dinner before the ants invaded."

The next door opened into a study. It was an inviting room, lined on the left-hand side with bookshelves and occupied by an armchair, a large oak desk and a computer work station. Kit sat down in the sensible ergonomic chair and flicked the switch on the desk lamp. The notepad she'd taken from the kitchen didn't tell her much. It was full of doodles, a few phone numbers with no indication of who they belonged to, and reminders to do things like pick up the dry cleaning and pay the gas.

"This man is obsessive," Quinn stated. She was standing in front of the wall of shelves. "These books are actually in alphabetical order, by author and then title."

"Well, this is certainly the tidiest desk I've ever seen in my life," Kit said as she opened one drawer after another. "Aha, a teledex. Oh dear! I think he's paranoid as well as obsessive. There's not a single surname in this thing. It's all first names or initials."

"Maybe this will tell us something," Quinn said, punching the message button on the answering machine by the phone.

"Byron, darling," began an extremely camp male voice, "this is just to remind you, if you haven't already left, not to forget the CD player. I know how forgetful you are when you're in a highly emotional state. I'm sure your good lady will sort out that bastard husband of hers and everything will be peachy again. So stop worrying and get your gorgeous bod up here ASAP."

"Gorgeous bod?" Kit almost laughed. "I assume that Byron's good lady is your mother."

"Sounds like it. It doesn't tell us anything though," Quinn said.

The next message was left by the same man. "It's me again. Can you bring some extra deck chairs. I've just heard from Paul, and he and Brucey are going to come. This is going to be the party of the year."

"Brucey?" Kit and Quinn said at the same time.

The machine beeped again and a familiar voice said, "Byron, I just wanted to reassure you that there is nothing to worry about."

"Oh my god," Quinn cried, hugging herself as she collapsed into the armchair at the sound of her mother's voice. Kit was at Quinn's side in a moment, feeling helpless because all she could really do was clasp her hand as Celia's voice continued.

"You know I couldn't care less what you did before you came to me. Just ignore him. Nothing you have done could compare with his deceitful and disgusting behavior. I shall wait until Katherine has investigated this shipment or whatever it is next week and then I will confront him with everything we know. And that will be the end of the matter. So I will see you on Thursday. Enjoy your holiday and come back to me refreshed and relaxed, my dear friend."

"Oh god, oh god, oh shit. Shit!" Quinn was rocking back and forth in Kit's arms, taking short sharp breaths. "It's like hearing a ghost," she said softly.

"It's OK to cry, Quinn. Let it out."

"I *can't*," she stated desperately. Her gentle blue eyes were filled with an expression of such utter sadness that Kit could almost feel her pain, but there was nothing she could do to help, except hold her.

After a few minutes Quinn straightened up and smiled wanly. "I'm fine now. I'll be fine."

"You probably need a good stiff drink," Kit said standing up. "Why don't you raid Byron's bar while I check out the rest of the house." She punched the eject button on the answering machine, took out the tape and slipped it into the pocket of her trousers as she walked back into the hall.

"No. I'm OK, really. I'd rather come with you."

"Either Byron is the neatest person I've ever met or he's found the world's most fastidious housekeeper," Kit said from the center of the large and immaculate living room. Not that it looked like any living had ever been done in it. "This looks like my Great Aunt Clare's lounge room, the one she used only when the Anglican minister came for afternoon tea or when her card girls came to play bridge. The rest of the time it was closed up to keep the dust off the antiques. But Aunt Clare would never have lowered the tone of her best room with a television."

"I bet her taste in reading material was a little more, um, temperate too," Quinn said, flicking through the pile of magazines that had been stacked neatly in the center of the ornately carved coffee table. "Oh my goodness," she added, affecting a prim and highly offended great aunt voice, "they're full of naked men!"

"They're probably to keep the card girls entertained during afternoon tea," Kit said with a grin. "Well, there's nothing in here. Let's check the last room and get the hell out of here."

The master bedroom, opposite the living room at the front of the house, was spacious, despite the canopied four-poster bed. Apart from a monstrous gilt-framed mirror bolted to the wall opposite the bed the walls were undecorated. The seat in the bay window was strewn with clothes and books, and the floor was littered with what looked like half the contents of the walk-though dressing room which led to the ensuite.

"Does this strike you as running contrary to expectation?" Kit asked as she stepped over the mess of clothes and shoes and pushed at the slightly ajar door. The bathroom was in the same state of disarray, with several towels, used condoms and three empty champagne bottles scattered over the floor. The tiled edge of the large spa bath held a selection of bath salts and bubbles, two champagne glasses and an ashtray containing several butts and a half-smoked joint.

"This must have been some party," Quinn said, gingerly picking up one corner of the bedclothes from the floor as if she half expected to find a comatose Byron or his party guest underneath. "Do you suppose this is Byron's mess, or someone else has been in here looking for something?"

"I'd say it's all his mess," Kit replied as she rifled through the contents of the open top drawer in Byron's dressing room. "But if someone *has* been here they obviously found what they were looking for in this room because the rest of the house is untouched."

"Maybe we disturbed them and they ran off," Quinn suggested.

"Maybe. It's more likely this is the only room in the house where he ever lets his hair down. I can't imagine him going off for a holiday and leaving the place in this condition though. But I'm not one to judge. My bedroom always looks like this."

She shut the top drawer and opened the next one down. It was full of socks. The drawer below it held neatly folded T-shirts and the one under that was partly open but stuck fast with something which had been jammed into it. Kit got down on her knees and slipped her fingers into the drawer to try to pry it loose.

"Have you found something?" Quinn whispered in her ear.

"I don't know yet. Why are you whispering?" Kit asked, yanking at the drawer. She tumbled backwards as it came all the way out emptying the contents on the floor.

Quinn laughed before she could control the impulse. "Sorry, Kit. Do you have a problem with your balance or something?"

"It's just a small problem. I'm also afraid of heights and not particularly fond of spiders, real estate agents, fat people who insist on wearing pink or rap music. If there's nothing else you need to know about me right now do you think you could help me up?" Kit said in mock indignation as she held out her hand. When Quinn reached out to assist her Kit pulled her down onto the floor.

"Oh yu-uck," Quinn laughed. "Just what I need, to be rolling around the floor with Byron's jocks."

"Serves you right for laughing at me." Kit picked up the large brown envelope which had been wedged in the drawer. "The way this was jammed in there with Byron's intimate apparel, I'd make a guess it was shoved away quite hastily," she said, tipping the contents onto the floor.

"It's nothing. Just another one of his stick magazines," Quinn said sounding quite disappointed. "And it's ten years old at that." She took the envelope off Kit's lap and peered inside to make sure it was empty.

Kit gave a short laugh. "A highly informative edition, however, Ms. Orlando. Just look what the young Byron Daniels was doing ten years ago." Kit turned the magazine around and held it up in front of herself so Quinn could see the double-page spread which had been flagged with a yellow post-it note. There was Byron, as naked as the day he was born, posing in various stages of erectness with a bevy of beautiful and muscular football players in a variety of steamy locker room and shower scenes.

"Do you suppose they're real footballers?" Quinn asked, leaning in to get a better view.

"I doubt it, Quinn. Do you suppose this is what Geoffrey really had on Byron? Your mother did say on that answering-machine message that she couldn't care less what Byron had done before he worked for her."

"And that nothing could compare with my stepfather's behavior," Quinn added. "But why would Geoffrey want to fire Byron in the first place? I mean, we know, given *his* tastes, that this sort of thing is hardly likely to offend him."

Kit turned the magazine around and looked at it more closely. "Perhaps someone found this old magazine and sent it to Geoffrey in an attempt to blackmail your family by threatening to create a scandal about the sordid past of Celia's personal secretary. Maybe that's where Geoffrey's money has been going. To a blackmailer."

"Don't be ridiculous, Kit. Why would he pay good money to avoid a scandal that's much less damning than anything he's been into and then turn around and fire Byron anyway? This has probably got nothing to do with . . . with anything. What's that?"

Quinn tugged at something protruding from the bottom of the magazine and pulled out a glossy black-and-white photograph. It was an enlargement of Byron and one of the equally naked footballers. The words "*Everyone has a secret life*" were scrawled in thick black text across the bottom.

Kit raised an eyebrow. "Nothing to do with anything, you think? This is a very new print." She turned it over and read, "Factor Four. Does that mean anything to you, Quinn?"

"No. What is it?"

"Beats me. That's all it says. It's been rubber stamped right against the edge though so there may or may not be more to the name." She slipped the photo and the magazine back into the envelope and struggled to her feet. "Come on, I've seen enough. And I don't know about you but I am starving."

An hour and a half later Kit sat cooling her heels, while the rest of her body dripped with perspiration, outside Marek's office waiting for him to finish a telephone call. The station's air-conditioner had broken down again, and quite some time ago judging by the number of electric fans positioned strategically and ineffectively on several desks in the virtually deserted squad room.

Kit had left Quinn drinking coffee in the café across the road where they'd had a very late and very awful lunch, although at nearly four o'clock it was more like an early dinner. Kit was grumpy. She hated bad food, she was sick to death of the heat and she'd practically had to tie Quinn to the table to prevent her from tagging along. She knew Marek would be really pissed off that she'd been out of touch for nearly three days. She also didn't know how many of the Robinson family secrets she was going to have to reveal to satisfy his case without hurting hers, so she didn't want Quinn there.

On top of all that, the subject of Alex Cazenove's antagonism in Douglas Scott's office had come up over the limp salad and the poor excuse for pasta when Quinn had expressed her puzzlement over her friend's behavior. "I've never known her to be so . . . so . . ."

"Rude?" Kit had suggested.

"No. Well, yes, she was, but that's not the word I was looking for. Disagreeable—that's it. It's not like her at all."

"Well, it has been—what did you say?—three years since you've seen her. She's obviously changed. Where's she been anyway?"

"Perth mostly. She went over there with . . ." Quinn had deliberately stopped herself from saying with whom by stuffing a piece of garlic bread in her mouth. "She had a job there, but I guess it didn't work out. And now she's back."

"And about to get married," Kit said. "Not to the person from Perth, I gather."

"Ah, no," Quinn had said, quite emphatically. "She's marrying Enzo. They've known each other for years. He's just divine. You'll probably get to meet him."

Kit couldn't imagine why she would ever have a reason to meet the gorgeous Alex Cazenove's divine fiancé Enzo, but she hadn't said that to Quinn. She glanced over her shoulder to see if Marek was off the phone yet. He glowered at her again so she got up and walked over to one of the fans to try and cool off.

Oh goody, she thought. Marek's fuming at me from in there and Quinn's probably still seething in the café across the road. Things could be worse, I suppose. No, they couldn't! Look at the cast you're playing with, O'Malley. You've got one dead client who may or may

126

not have been murdered; one new client who's a delightful but spoilt little rich girl; one chief suspect who's a lying, cheating, sex-mad possible murderer; one extremely beautiful lawyer who hates your guts for no apparent reason; one obliging lawyer who, nonetheless, doesn't seem to be telling you the truth, the whole truth and nothing but the truth; a missing personal secretary who turns out to be a gay ex-porno star; and an angry homicide cop who'd have your balls for breakfast if you had any.

"Where the hell have you been, O'Malley?"

"Hi, honey," Kit said sweetly. "Having a bad day?"

"Don't 'hi, honey' me. Get your arse in here before I arrest you."

"Oh yeah? What for?" Kit asked as she strutted past Marek, threw herself onto the old leather couch by the wall and dropped her brief-case on the floor.

"I'll think of something."

"Where is everybody anyway?" Kit asked waving at the empty squad room.

"Out looking for you."

"Oh, of course. Where else would they be?"

Marek poured two coffees from the percolator on his filing cabinet, handed one to Kit and stood there staring at her, waiting for something. Jon Marek was one of the few cops Kit had ever met who refused to drink the sump oil that passed for coffee in most stations. He'd carried his own thermos of the real stuff when they'd been on patrol together, and as soon as he got his own office there was always a brew on the boil.

He was still waiting.

"What?" she asked, throwing out her hand palm up to show she had nothing whatsoever up her sleeve.

"Good question."

"I thought so. OK, Jonno, I give up. You have obviously been looking for me for some reason. Here I am."

Marek smiled almost benignly. Kit hated it when he did that. "I had a few questions to ask you, Ms. O'Malley, in connection with a possible homicide that occurred on Friday evening last, sometime between six and nine."

"Possible homicide? You said it was an accident."

"I may have been mistaken. Anyway, *you* seemed to think there had been a murder."

"*I* thought Celia had knocked off her shit of a husband."

"Where have you been since Friday anyway?"

"At the beach."

"At the beach. I see. You have—make that had—a client who was quite possibly murdered and you go off to play surfie chick for the weekend. That's a novel way to run a business."

"Was there something in particular you wanted to ask me, or did you just need someone to abuse for half an hour?" Kit asked.

"Tell me more about Geoffrey Robinson," Marek said, sitting on the corner of his desk.

"Like what?"

Marek sighed heavily. "C'mon, Kitty, help me out here. I've got a possible homicide on my hands and no one is giving me diddly. The husband broke down in tears both times I talked to him on the weekend and practically had to be sedated. The daughter turned up here this morning doing a song and dance about how her mother must have been murdered and that her stepfather must have done it. The family lawyer withheld the fact that he knew the address of the missing secretary until two hours ago when *I* thought to ask *him* for the information. You're not going to do a Sam Spade on me and quote client confidentiality, are you? And stop smiling!"

Kit obediently put on a straight face. "You know I'll tell you anything I can that's relevant. In exchange for everything you have, of course," she said. "You say it's only a possible homicide. Hasn't Donald completed the autopsy yet?"

"It was a busy weekend," Marek said glumly, relocating himself in his own chair behind the desk.

"So I've heard."

"Oh yeah, who from? You been talking to Grenville and not me?"

"No, the daughter told me. She's hired me to find out how her stepfather killed her mother. She said you gave her the busy-weekend excuse this morning," Kit said.

"Excuse be buggered! The heat seems to have driven the whole city completely barmy. We had one domestic murder, a service station attendant got killed during a bungled hold-up on Saturday night, some kids found an as yet unidentified woman floating in the Yarra with the back of her head blown off, and we've got two other unnamed and unclaimed bodies who departed this world under circumstances which can only be described as suspicious. And as for Robinson killing his wife, the man has an alibi, for Christ's sake. I'd appreciate it if you would remind your *new* client of that fact and try not encourage her in this little fantasy."

"But if Geoffrey's not a suspect in this possible homicide why do you want to know more about him?"

"Because I can't get a handle on the man. Grenville's preliminary report states that your deceased client was probably unconscious before she ended up face down in the fish pond. He is not certain of this as yet, but suggests the bruising on the *back* of Mrs. Robinson's neck would suggest that she was struck heavily from behind. Either that or she fell backwards and struck her head on the edge of the pond before rolling over and accidentally drowning. When I put the former possibility to the grieving widower and asked if he knew of anyone who might want to harm his wife he went completely to pieces. That was yesterday."

"He didn't, by any chance, suggest that Byron Daniels might have a grudge against Celia?" Kit asked.

"Why do you think we're looking for him?"

Kit shrugged and ran her hands through her hair. "Marek, don't you think a recently fired, now missing employee fits a little too conveniently into the 'most obvious suspect' box? I mean, Geoffrey was pretty determined to cast Byron in an unsavory light on Friday night when Celia's death was simply an accident not a possible homicide."

"I can't help the facts, O'Malley. Robinson fired him for stealing on Thursday."

"Says Geoffrey Robinson. Celia's lawyer, on the other hand, knew nothing about it, which is unusual in itself. On top of that Douglas Scott claims that even if there *had* been cause to sack Byron—and it would *not* have been for stealing—Geoffrey would have had no say in the matter at all. Whatever the reason."

"Interesting," Marek stated.

"I'm glad you think so."

129

"Why wouldn't it have been for stealing?"

"Because Celia paid the man a salary of $67,000. And she'd bought him a house. Two 'facts' that Mr. Robinson knew nothing about."

"So? Doesn't mean he's not a thief. $67,000, huh? I guess I'm in the wrong business. What'd he have to do for that?"

"Just about everything, I gather," Kit answered. "Except what's on your filthy mind, Marek," she added when he raised his eyebrows suggestively.

"You know that for sure, like you also know for sure he's not a thief?"

"I know that because Celia told me. And because I've since discovered that Byron is, more than likely, gay."

"More than likely? I'm sorry, Kit, but none of this adds up to anything much at all. Whether the guy was sacked or not sacked, for stealing or not stealing, the one fact remains that he is mysteriously missing and his ex-employer is mysteriously dead. Did you find anything at his house?"

Kit looked up in surprise to find Marek smiling that bloody annoying smile again.

"You *were* going to tell me you'd been there, weren't you?"

"Me? Of course I was, Jonno," Kit said, looking around herself before leaning forward to look under Marek's desk for the spies, bugs or hidden cameras. "Douglas told you, right?"

"Nick Jenkins saw you driving off just as he was turning into the street. So what did you find? Nick said it looked like there'd been some kind of wild party."

"Only in one room, or two if you count the bathroom. What did Nick find?"

"O'Malley!"

"All right, already. I'm just fishing. Here," Kit smiled, took the tape from her pocket and threw it across to him. "Everything *we* found confirms our theory that Geoffrey Robinson was lying through his teeth about the reasons for allegedly sacking Byron. There were messages on his answering machine from some friend about a party he was supposed to be attending on the weekend, which could explain his absence . . ."

"But only for the weekend," Marek interrupted.

"And one from Celia telling him there was nothing to worry about, that she couldn't care less what he did *before* he worked for her, and that nothing could be as bad as what her husband had been up to."

"That still doesn't explain where he is now."

"She also told him to have a good holiday and that she'd see him on Thursday."

"And you're trying to tell me that this highly paid completely loyal employee is still lazing about somewhere having a jolly good holiday even though his employer was found dead nearly three days ago? I mean, it's not like she was one of those unidentified stiffs we've got in the morgue, for Christ's sake. Celia Robinson was a well-known person. The Sunday paper had a huge article about her, her company, her charities, her garden, her bloody weird statues and her god knows what else!"

"Really?" said Kit. "I didn't see it, but then I haven't read a paper since Thursday, or turned on the radio or TV since Saturday morning. Maybe Byron hasn't either. Look, Marek, all we know is that he's on holiday. I don't know where he is or why he hasn't turned up. Douglas seems to think he has friends in the country somewhere so he may have gone there for this party. On the other hand he could have gone to Bali for the week or Uluru, he could be on a religious retreat or off white water rafting or bloody mountain climbing for all I know. Do you think they deliver the Sunday paper at the summit of Mount Kosciusko?"

"Don't be a smartarse. What else did you find there?"

"Nothing," Kit lied. "What did Nick find?"

"Nothing, except that a neighbor said she'd last seen Daniels on Friday morning, leaving the house with a young blond guy who he'd introduced to her as his nephew."

"I'll bet he was," Kit said. "You really don't have a whole lot then."

"Just one odd fingerprint that we haven't got a match on as yet."

"*One* fingerprint? That's it? Where was it?"

"On the champagne bottle that was found near the body. It's the only clear print on it, all the others are partials. It was in the sticky-up bit in the bottom."

"You mean the punt," Kit said.

"Yeah, whatever. Trouble is, being in that spot it could belong to a drive-in bottle shop attendant or anybody!"

"Somehow I just can't picture Celia pulling into a bottle shop for a bottle of Moët, Marek. It's more likely it was delivered to the house, probably in a box with eleven others just like it. Why don't you check the cellar and see if there are any more with matching prints?"

"We've done that. Still no match. We do know it doesn't belong to the deceased, her husband, Daniels, Scott the lawyer, Denning the publisher, or the only other person we know of who has been at the house in the last fortnight."

"Who's that?" Kit asked.

"You," Marek replied, getting up to pour himself another coffee.

"That's a relief," Kit said. "I was so careful about wiping my prints off the rest of the bottle but I completely overlooked the punt."

"Very funny. Now we've dispensed with the small talk, tell me about Robinson."

Chapter 12

"So how much did *you* tell him?" Quinn asked after Kit had related what Marek had told her.

"Just the bare bones. I've got beer, mineral water, Coke and a cask of Riesling," she offered, standing in front of her open fridge.

"Oh, a beer, please. It's so damn hot I might just take it outside and pour it all over me," Quinn said, wandering aimlessly around the lounge room. "Can I put some music on?"

"Sure. Could you let that mad cat in too, please? She suffers from chronic recurring amnesia. Whenever she's outside and sees me inside she suddenly forgets she has her own private entrance through the laundry and sits at the patio door and shouts at me until I open it for her."

As soon as the door opened Thistle bounded in, wrapped herself affectionately around Quinn's ankles, and then affected an air of extreme self-importance as she strutted across the lounge, up the stairs and out of the room.

"Now *that* is a cat with a mission," Quinn stated.

"Yeah, she's probably gone straight out the laundry window again," Kit said flatly, pouring two glasses of beer. She left one on the coffee table for Quinn and carried the other into her study. The counter on the answering machine recorded that there were ten messages so she pushed the play button and sat on the corner of her desk.

Marek: "Kit, I need to get a few things straight. Can you give me a ring?"

Sam: "This is me. Just rang to say hi."

Just hi, Kit thought. That'd be right, though I suppose there's not much else to say.

Marek: "There's no point having one of these machines if you never listen to your messages."

Lillian: "Hi, darling. I'm home again if you're still out of coffee."

Sam: "Ah, it's eleven p.m. on Saturday. It's me, Sam. Where are you?"

Where am I? Kit exclaimed. You should talk!

Marek: "Where the hell are you, O'Malley? If you're home now, pick up the bloody phone!"

Lillian: "I . . . Oh, dear."

Sam: "Kit. We need to talk. I'll be back in town on Tuesday. I'll see you then."

Marek: "Jeez, O'Malley!"

Lillian: ". . . and the plumber tells me it's going to cost $700 to fix the hoojah on the thingy. Could you come and check it out for me? I think the man is trying to diddle me. I knew I should have encouraged you to get an apprenticeship in some useful trade, Katherine. By the way Michael has broken his wrist. Honestly that boy is so clumsy. He was trying to . . ." The line went dead.

"My mother," Kit said in response to Quinn's amused expression. "She probably told the whole gory story before she realized her recording time had run out. On the other hand she may have thought she was actually talking to me."

Quinn laughed and then they both nearly jumped out of their skins as the first song on k.d. lang's *Ingénue* blared out of the speakers at full volume just as the phone started ringing. "Sorry," Quinn shouted as she fumbled with the knobs trying to find the volume while Kit stabbed the answering-machine button to interrupt the recorded message cutting in. At that moment the doorbell rang.

"My god, it's like Spencer Street Station around here," Kit said.

"Hello, Kit? It's Douglas Scott. I was wondering if you might know where Elizabeth is?"

"She's here, Douglas. Just a sec and I'll get her for you," Kit said.

She put the receiver down on the desk. "Quinn, it's for you. I'll get the door."

The bell had rung for the third time by the time Kit swung the door open.

"Ah, Katherine, you *are* here. You look very nice, dear. What are you all dressed up for?"

Kit looked down at her extremely creased black trousers and tired white shirt then back at her mother who, as usual, looked sparklingly fresh and pressed. She was wearing a loose-fitting multi-colored blouse over cream linen slacks, and had a pair of spotless white runners on her feet and the world's largest sunglasses on her face. She also held a bottle of champagne in one hand and a jar of what looked suspiciously like the seventy-third offering of zucchini pickle for the season in the other.

"Love the shades, Mum. Come in."

"They are most definitely *not* mine."

"I suppose someone mugged you and forced you to put them on."

"They're Connie's," Lillian said, handing the bottle and jar to Kit so she could remove the bizarre eyewear. "Mine were totally demolished on the plane back from Adelaide on Saturday by an extremely boring man with a very large bottom." Lillian headed up the stairs to the landing overlooking the sitting room but stopped short when she realized Kit wasn't alone.

"I didn't realize you had company, Katherine. Is this one of your friends?" Lillian whispered, emphasizing the last word. "I'm not interrupting anything, am I? I can come back later."

"No, it's OK, Mum. She's not one of my friends. Well, I suppose she is a friend but not . . ." Kit threw her hands up before draping an arm round her mother's shoulders and saying quietly, "She's Quinn Orlando, Celia's daughter. Besides, you know you're always welcome, no matter who's here."

"I was just being polite, Katherine. I wouldn't really have left. Bring the bottle," Lillian ordered, heading for the kitchen. "Speaking of Celia, I do hope you're not going to make a habit of losing people to whom I recommend your services."

"I'll try not to, Mum. Not that I had anything to do with it personally." Kit removed the cork from the bottle and filled the champagne flute Lillian had taken from the cupboard. "Which hoojah on what thingy did you need a plumber for?"

"Oh god, don't remind me! It was so embarrassing and it completely ruined my luncheon today. I had Tanya Baily, you know the new editor of *Backdrop*, as well as Jocelyn Miro and Adam Burgess from my theater group, Malcolm Tunstall and of course Connie over for quiche and champagne when all of a sudden the sink just blew up! I had a geyser in the kitchen, we all got thoroughly drenched and the cold tap nearly took Malcolm's ear off when it shot across the room."

"Pity it didn't knock him out cold and save us from his appalling movie reviews," Kit said.

"I had Lake Hume in my family room and that's the only reaction you have?"

"Sorry, Mum. Do you need help cleaning it up?"

"Oh no. My guests were very helpful. Malcolm turned the water off at the mains and everyone pitched in to stem the tide while we waited for the plumber. Honestly, that man was such a crook. He put a cap on the thingy so I could at least have water, spent two hours investigating the problem and then told me the job was going to cost at least $700. When I queried the amount he said house calls were always costly. House calls indeed! How else could a plumber fix your plumbing? It's not like you can take your taps and pipes along to a service station. The man must think I'm a senile old lady."

Kit laughed. "I can ask Angie to take a look if you like. She'll at least be able to tell you if the guy's trying to rip you off."

"Angie? You mean Angie the ex-lawyer who runs that pub? Don't tell me she's a plumber too. Is there anything she doesn't do?"

"She just happens to be able to tell the difference between a down-pipe and a tap washer, which is more than you or I could do. So if you want me to I'll drop in to the Terpsichore, which is not a pub by the way, and ask her to make a house call—that's if you can wait till tomorrow to get it fixed."

"Well, it's after six now. I'm not going to let that conman in over-alls charge me overtime rates," Lillian said as she refilled her glass.

"Is everything OK, Quinn?" Kit realized Quinn had finished her phone call and was hovering politely in the background.

"Oh, yeah. Uncle Douglas just wanted to make sure I didn't make any plans for tomorrow morning. There's a whole lot of family business we have to attend to apparently." She shrugged, obviously uncomfortable with the thought of having to deal with such matters.

Kit introduced Quinn to her mother and vice versa then left them to it while she went to change into a pair of jeans and black T-shirt. She was searching high and low for the pair to the blue canvas shoe she'd found in the bathroom when the doorbell rang again and Lillian called out that the doorbell had been rung.

"You could have answered it, Mum," she said, coming back into the living room to find her mother was much too busy giving Quinn a there-there hug to play butler.

The last person in the world Kit expected to find standing on her landing when she opened the door was doing just that—standing on her landing as if she'd done it hundreds of times before.

"Alex?" Kit was unable to do anything about the surprised tone in her voice.

"Your friend who was just leaving Aurora Press said I might find you up here," Alex said.

"That must have been Del," Kit said, thinking that there was no way Brigit would have been able to resist personally escorting Alex up the stairs, if only to see Kit's reaction when she opened the door.

"I was just on my way home and I thought I'd drop off that stuff you wanted on Orlan Carriers. I've also finally got some information on the Smiths."

"Great. Come in. Quinn is still here."

"Yes, I noticed her car parked in the side street. By the way there was a man loitering with no apparent intent in the hallway downstairs."

"What does he look like?"

"Thirtyish, dark hair, moustache, neatly dressed. Do you know him?"

"It sounds like several people I know but I'd better check it out. Go on up. Quinn can fix you a drink if you want one. I'll be back in a minute."

Kit left the front door open, clasped the railing and made her way down the stairs to the landing. There was indeed a man loitering in the hallway, in fact he was loitering right outside the door of O'Malley Investigations and Kit had no idea who he was.

"Can I help you?" she asked. "Up here," she added when the guy jumped and glanced about, uncertain where the voice had come from. Looking at his precisely cut short hair and Freddy Mercury moustache Kit rejected her first thought that he might be the man who'd been tailing Geoffrey or Dalkeith—or her—around town lately. He was wearing beige trousers and a black short-sleeved shirt but looked like he'd be just as comfy in a nice tight silk jumpsuit or black leathers.

"You're Katherine O'Malley."

"Is that a question or a statement?" Kit asked, heading down the rest of the stairs. She felt only mildly silly in her bare feet with one blue shoe in her hand.

"I know this might seem weird," he said, "but I've been following you. I need to talk about . . ."

"Following me?" Kit interrupted. "For the last two weeks, right?"

"No!" he said, surprised. "Just today, since you left Byron's place. I'm a friend of his. He told me about you, though I didn't realize until I followed you here that you were you, if you know what I mean." He smiled and shrugged. He was an extremely handsome man though Kit guessed he was closer to twenty-five than Alex's estimate of thirtyish.

"Do you want a drink?" she asked him.

"Excuse me, everyone," Kit said to the three women who appeared to be having quite a jolly party in her kitchen. "This is Damien Beatty. Damien, this is my mother Lillian, Celia's daughter Quinn and her lawyer Alexis. Damien is a friend of Byron's. He followed us from Byron's house today, Quinn."

"Followed you?" Lillian exclaimed.

"He doesn't look like the man in the photograph," Alex said. "I gather you didn't know this one was following you either."

"This one? You have more than one person following you, Katherine?"

Kit glared at Alex but otherwise ignored the dig. "It's OK, Mum, really."

Lillian rolled her eyes and reached for her glass. "If you say so, dear."

"Why did you follow us?" Quinn asked.

Damien picked up the glass of beer Kit had poured for him and took a thirsty gulp. "I was looking for Byron. I'd already been into his house, I have a key, and had just got back into my car across the road when I saw you two arrive. I watched you try the front door then go around the back. When you didn't come out again I figured you either had a key, which was unlikely seeing Byron doesn't exactly have many women friends, or had broken in. I had no idea who you were so I followed you. I don't really know why, I've never done anything like it before."

"Byron was supposed to have gone to a party on the weekend," Kit said.

"I know," Damien said. "It was my friend's, my lover's birthday. We were all, about eight of us, spending the weekend at his farmhouse outside Castlemaine. Byron had a few extra days off so he was planning to stay on, only he never showed up. He didn't ring to say he wasn't coming and we haven't been able to contact him. It's not like him. So I drove down this afternoon to see what was up."

"What about other friends? Maybe he's staying with someone else," Alex suggested.

"I rang everyone I could think of. Most of his friends were at the party." Damien turned to Quinn. "The first number I rang, after I'd heard the news on the radio on the drive down, was your mother's. Your father told me to bugger off."

"He's *not* my father," Quinn spat.

"Geoffrey Robinson is Quinn's stepfather," Kit said. "He claims he sacked Byron last Thursday because he'd been stealing from Celia."

"That is bullshit!" Damien exclaimed. "Excuse me," he added, glancing at Lillian.

"Did Byron tell you what really happened?" Kit asked.

"He came to my place late on Wednesday night. He was really upset. Robinson had rung him at work asking if Byron would meet him at nine p.m. at the Prince of Wales Hotel in Fitzroy Street and not to say anything to Celia about the phone call or the meeting."

"Did Byron agree to that?" Kit asked.

"Sure. But he told her anyway. Byron went to the pub where Robinson bought him a drink, sat him down and then accused him of following him. Robinson was apparently under the impression that Byron was gathering information to blackmail him with."

"*Was* Byron following Geoffrey?" Kit asked, suddenly wondering if the man in the beat-up old Holden was Mr. Daniels in disguise.

"No, *you* were," Damien said, obviously puzzled by the question. "Byron didn't tell Robinson that of course, even after the guy threatened to tell his wife about . . ." Damien hesitated, looking from Kit to Lillian and back again.

"Don't mind me," Lillian stated.

"Don't mind her," Kit agreed. "It was photos, right?"

"Yes. How did you know?"

"We found the magazine in his bedroom. So Geoffrey thought Byron was going to blackmail him so he tried to do it to Byron first. Did he actually fire him?"

"No. He just threatened to show Mrs. Robinson the photographs if Byron didn't mind his own business. Byron was distraught by the time he got to my place. He really loves, loved, his job and thought the world of Mrs. Robinson. He doesn't give a damn about those photos himself, but he didn't want her to see them. He couldn't save himself by telling Robinson that yes, he was being followed but not by him, that his own wife had hired a private investigator to keep an eye on him."

"Did he go to work on Thursday?" Alex asked.

"Yes. He wasn't going to but I suggested the best thing to do would be to tell Mrs. Robinson himself. So he rang to say he was going to be late and waited till Mr. Robinson had left for the office before fronting up for work."

"So Geoffrey didn't see Byron on Thursday, in the morning," Kit stated.

"No." Damien pulled out one of the breakfast bar stools and sat down heavily.

"You're sure?"

"We had lunch together after he spoke to Mrs. Robinson. He

hadn't seen her husband since the night before," he said, standing up then sitting down again.

"Why would Geoffrey tell the police that he sacked Byron on Thursday morning when he didn't even see him then?" Alex asked, taking her jacket off and draping it over the back of a stool.

"Why would he claim he had sacked him at all?" Kit asked, only mildly distracted by the sight of Alex's tanned arms. A really bad feeling in the pit of her stomach warned her that the likelihood of Byron himself turning up to straighten any of this out was becoming as remote as the Voyager space probe.

"And why say it was for stealing?" Quinn added.

"Who is Byron anyway?" Lillian asked.

"Celia's secretary," Alex said. She held her glass out for Quinn to refill with champagne.

Kit took a deep breath. They were so finely muscled and they went *all* the way up to the capped sleeves of her white silk shirt.

"Something has happened to Byron, hasn't it." It was a statement more than a question. Damien looked absolutely miserable.

"We don't know that," Kit said, trying to convince herself as much as Damien. "There might still be a logical explanation for all this. Did Byron tell you about what happened with Celia on Thursday morning?"

"He said Mrs. Robinson was livid. She told Byron she didn't give a damn about some stupid photos that had been taken ten years ago, no matter what was in them. She was so angry about her husband's blackmail attempt that she was all for getting you to rush over with some photos I gather you have of him, Kit. Her husband, I mean. She wanted to march into his office and throw them at him—just before she shot him, I think. Byron talked her out of that."

"So Thursday lunch was the last time you saw him," Kit said, absently noting that Alex's left wrist was decorated with a fine gold bracelet. Quit it, O'Malley, for goodness' sake! she reprimanded herself.

Damien nodded. "Mrs. Robinson suggested that as he had this week off anyway he may as well start his holidays straightaway and stay out of her husband's way. She said she would ask you to find out where her husband got the photos from, but Byron told her he'd

141

rather do that himself. That's what he was intending to do after we had lunch. I haven't heard from him since."

"When was he expected to turn up for this party?"

"Friday night. He said he'd come up earlier if he could track down the source of the photos."

"How on earth was he going to do that?" Alex asked.

"He knew the guy who took them," Damien replied. "I'm sorry, I can't remember his name, only that he used to work full-time for the magazine the pictures were in. Byron had already discovered that the magazine had been bought out by someone about three years ago." Damien looked apologetic again. "I can't remember who, sorry."

"Factor Four?" Kit suggested.

"Yeah," he said hesitantly then shrugged. "Maybe."

"Does Byron have a blond nephew?" Kit asked.

"Byron's got one grandfather, in Brisbane, and no other family. Why?"

"The police said he was seen leaving his house on Friday morning with a young blond guy who he introduced to a neighbor as his nephew."

"A blond, huh? That would explain the state of his bedroom. It must be someone very new too or he would have told me about him." Damien shook his head then did a double-take and stared at Kit. "The police said? What have the police got to do with this?"

"Byron has been missing, as far as we can all figure out, since Friday morning. His employer died on Friday night. They just need to talk to him, Damien, that's all."

"Why? It was an accident, right?"

"Possibly," Kit replied.

"We don't think so," Quinn stated. "We think my step–"

"We think," Kit interjected "that Celia's death is a little suspicious."

"What? You don't think Byron . . ." Damien stared at everyone in disbelief. "The police don't think . . . Oh no. No way!" He turned to Quinn. "There is no way that he would have harmed a hair on your mother's head. He . . . well, he was really, really fond of her."

"It's all right, Damien," Kit said placing her hand on his forearm. "We don't think Byron has done anything, except go missing. So let's see if we can work out where he might have gone missing to. OK?"

Chapter 13

By day the Lord Rochester Hotel—located in the back streets of Collingwood amidst car repair shops, storage warehouses, a few run-down turn-of-the-century workers' cottages, and factories that specialized in making small metal doodads for larger metal doodads that were made elsewhere—served cold beer and cheap counter meals to a subspecies of overalled and tattooed men in desperate need of social reconditioning who still called their girlfriends chicks and wouldn't be seen dead talking to a poofter. By night the Lord Rochester became Route 69, one of the longest-running and most popular gay bars in Melbourne which served cold beer and top-shelf liquor to a subspecies of gay and straight party animals who didn't care that they had to front up for work the next day as long as they could dance all night. And stuff the hangover!

Kit was rammed up against the bar with a drag queen's elbow in her left ear and Alex's arm pressed across the small of her back so she could grip the counter on the other side to avoid being crushed any further forward. Apart from being nearly seven feet tall, the guy beside Kit was an almost perfect reconstruction of Barbra Streisand. He kept apologizing for the behavior of his elbow but as he had nowhere else to put it Kit just smiled and told him to forget it. Besides, if he put *his* arm down Alex would have to release her grip on the bar and move *her* arm and that was the last thing Kit wanted.

The barman slammed a vodka and lemonade, two double Jack

Daniels and a pot of mineral water down in front of Kit and she handed him half her life savings. She mouthed a thank you, as there was no point ruining her vocal cords by trying to compete with the retro-techno-punk post-apocalyptic version of *O Fortuna*, and turned on the spot into the waiting arms of Alex Cazenove. Kit handed two glasses to the woman who had insisted on helping her carry the drinks but who suddenly looked extremely awkward about being pressed up against the person she'd spent the whole day being completely and deliberately disagreeable to. Alex smiled and although Kit couldn't work out whether it was genuine, forced, apologetic, embarrassed or just an ordinary everyday no-hidden-meaning devastating Alex Cazenove smile, she was awfully glad that Barbra Streisand still had his elbow in her ear or she would have swooned pathetically to the floor and been trampled by half of Route 69's mixed Monday night crowd who were determined to get a drink from the bar whatever the cost.

Alex had managed to escape backwards and was trying to make her way through the hot, sweaty and desperately thirsty throng and Kit, close on her heels, was thinking how apt the music was, it being all about Fate barging in and ruining all chance of triumphant love and happy-ever-afters. Once famous solely for being the opening and closing numbers of *Carmina Burana*, before it was shanghaied by the PR people at Nescafé to promote the most stirring cup of coffee ever made, this version was so loud it was bouncing off all the walls at once and making Kit's teeth rattle. Despite the volume, however, she could still hear the warning bells going off in her head. After all there was nothing as ridiculous as someone whose nerve endings were going completely gah-gah over a person who didn't particularly like that someone at all, at all. And there was also absolutely *no* point in allowing herself to become interested in a person whose interests lay elsewhere. And Kit was *not* thinking about Alex's impending marriage. In fact the way Alex was watching over Quinn—correction, make that "watching" full stop—Kit was beginning to wonder if Alex knew whether she was on the right path by intending to plight her troth to the divine Enzo.

She pushed her way through the crowd, trying not to spill the over-priced drinks down the back of the 501s and blue silk shirt that Alex had insisted on going home to change into. That detour was only part of the rebellion that had taken place in Kit's kitchen four hours before when she had announced she would check out Route 69, Byron's regular Thursday night hangout, to see if anyone remembered seeing him there last week.

The other rebels had miraculously managed to find a table in one of Route 69's back rooms. It was stuck in a corner behind a thick concrete column, a huge plastic potted plant and about fifty people but it was, nonetheless, a table and it even had four chairs around it. Kit was glad Lillian hadn't insisted on coming along with everyone else who was suddenly making it their business to see she was doing her job properly—there just wouldn't have been enough seats.

Kit sat down heavily next to Damien and handed him the mineral water before taking a swig of bourbon. She had to concede that it was sensible to have enlisted Damien's help in tracing Byron's movements last Thursday night. After all it was only in the movies that the barman just happened to remember the nondescript customer who had ordered three nondescript beers and a packet of nondescript nuts one night last week because he, the barman, remembered thinking to himself at the time that he'd better remember this particular nondescript customer just in case someone came round asking questions about him next week. Looking at the wall-to-wall humanity—and Monday was a quiet night at the Route—Kit realized it would have been next to impossible for her to work out who to ask. She had actually tried the barman but after repeating the question three times to be heard over the music he'd asked her if she was crazy.

Damien, on the other hand, was at least able to pick specific people out of the crowd who might actually remember having seen Byron five nights ago, hopefully in the company of a blond boy who had his name, address and telephone number tattooed on his forehead. While Damien's company was logical, the presence of Quinn and Alex was not; nor was it particularly helpful. Kit took another sip, wishing she'd given the barman the rest of her money for the whole bottle, as she watched Alex casually drape her arm across the back of Quinn's chair and lean in close to say something to her.

To say what? Kit wondered as Alex looked deliberately at Kit while she was saying whatever it was, and Quinn glanced at Kit then made

145

a "don't be ridiculous" face at Alex. Shit! Kit thought. What are you doing here, O'Malley? Get a life, for god's sake. So what if Sam's "we have to talk" message had sounded particularly ominous. You were losing interest anyway, remember? But there's no point going completely masochistic by transferring that interest to an unattainable someone who doesn't even like you. Got that? She doesn't like you! On top of that she's getting married to the divine Enzo and she's obviously got the hots, whether she knows it or not, for the incredibly wealthy Gucci waif to your right.

Kit finished the rest of her bourbon in one swallow and forced herself to give her undivided attention to Damien, who had been shouting in her ear that he'd already spoken to five people, two of whom had stayed home last Thursday night and three who could not recall seeing Byron.

"Damien, are you sure, with everything that happened to Byron last week, that he would still go out partying as usual on Thursday night?" Kit shouted.

"You saw his bedroom, Kit. I can't think of anywhere else he would have picked someone up for the night. Besides, you don't know him like I do. Sure he was upset about that prick Robinson, but Byron's a resilient guy. He's bounced back quickly from even the worst disasters in his life, and there have been a few of them. He probably found the information he'd gone looking for and was out celebrating."

"I have to admit," Kit said, "that I can't reconcile the Byron I met at Celia's with the Byron in those photographs. I mean it was obviously him but . . ."

"But he had a body back then, right?" Damien said. "He used to be into that whole scene. You know, ray-lamp tans and body building. Byron did it for shape not bulk—he was no beefcake. But then he got really sick about four years ago with some kidney thing and it just wasted him. When he got well he started back at the gym but found he'd lost interest in the body beautiful—unless it belonged to someone else of course. And speaking of bodies I suppose I'd better mingle or we'll be here all night."

Kit had to stand up to let Damien get out, then she shuffled across into his chair, tilted it back against the wall and put her feet up on the one she'd been sitting on. Closing her eyes she smiled as the

146

booming rhythm of *I Am What I Am* coursed through her body. A wave of exhaustion hit her when she realized it was still Monday, that she'd been up since six a.m., and that her body did not like her very much at the moment.

A hand slid up her right arm. She opened her eyes to find Quinn smiling at her.

"What?" Kit asked.

"Alex thinks you're a bad influence on me," Quinn repeated, leaning in close to speak directly into Kit's ear.

"Really?" Kit said sarcastically. "It must be some record to have that kind of effect on someone you've only known for fourteen hours. What's her problem, for god's sake?"

Quinn grinned. "It's a long story," she said.

"I'll bet it is," Kit laughed, glancing at Alex and then away in a hurry because those stunning gray eyes had reflected, for just a second, the same friendly amusement they'd held when they'd first looked down at Kit lying sprawled on the floor of Douglas's office. Get a grip, O'Malley! Kit thought as she was nearly knocked her off her chair by a sudden and exhilarating body rush. Again? Had she been standing up, she would have fallen down.

Hey, I don't need this shit, Kit thought. Please, please let this ridiculous and inappropriate case of lust wear off! Bad influence, huh? "Do you want to dance Quinn?" she asked, standing up.

"You bet." Quinn leapt to her feet. "Back in a minute," she said to Alex as she clasped Kit's outstretched hand and maneuvered herself out from behind the table. Alex looked suitably stunned.

Good, thought Kit, then walked smack into a very large stationary object.

When Kit had finished apologizing for spilling the guy's drink, and Quinn had finished laughing and apologizing for laughing, Damien introduced them to John Baxter—known to his friends as Tooly. Kit didn't dare ask why.

"He saw Byron here about midnight last Thursday," Damien shouted.

"He was looking awfully pleased with himself," Tooly explained in a voice that was as thin as he was fat. "He wouldn't tell me why, the spoilsport."

"Tell Kit about the guy," Damien said.

"What a dish!" Tooly exclaimed. "He was mighty persistent. Kept hovering around us—me and Byron and that delicious Timmy Denton—trying to join in on the goss. He shouted at least three rounds. I tell you, I would have gone anywhere with him but he was definitely putting the moves on Byron."

"Had you ever seen him before?" Kit asked.

"No sweetie, none of us had," Tooly replied.

"Was Byron interested?"

"Not at first, he had something real big on his mind, I could tell. But then he mellowed out and—well, what can I say?"

"What did this guy look like?"

"As I said, really dishy. A bod a bit like Damien here, only even thinner, same height though. Blond hair. It looked natural but it's hard to tell these days until you . . . well, we won't go into that one. Blue eyes. Let me see, probably nineteen or twenty years old."

"Name?" Kit asked.

Tooly looked thoughtful for a few seconds, then shook his head. "No idea. I don't believe we introduced ourselves."

"Do you know if they left together?"

"Honey, they could barely keep their hands off each other when they came by to say ciao to me around two a.m. I assume they shuffled off together but I didn't actually see them go."

"This dish didn't happen to mention what he did for a living?"

"I doubt it, honey. If I remember correctly we were talking about the Midsumma Ball and a new band that Poppy Curtiz has started. It's called the Screaming Queens—if you don't mind! No one was talking about boring things. No wait, now that I think on it he may have mentioned something about being an entrepreneur. That can't be right, he was just a baby. Maybe he said he worked for an entrepreneur." Tooly shrugged his more than generous shoulders. "Doesn't mean much in this day and age though, does it, honey? He was probably just big-noting himself. I guess an entrepreneur's assistant sounds better than a plumber's apprentice."

"I guess so," Kit agreed. "Well, thanks for your time, Tooly."

"Any time, dearie."

Kit waited till Tooly had disappeared into the crowd before screwing up her face. For some reason being called dearie by a male of the screaming queen variety was considerably less offensive than being called dearie—or honey, love, babe or girlie—by any other male-type person whose acquaintance she'd just made, but it still made Kit's skin crawl.

"Now what?" Quinn asked.

"It depends. Is the other guy who was with Byron and Tooly here tonight, Damien?"

"Tim Denton? No, he went to Darwin on Saturday."

"In that case I'm outta here. I can't stand the noise anymore and a body could die of thirst before it got a drink at this bar," Kit stated.

"Are you going home then?" Quinn asked, disappointed.

Oh dear! "No, I'm going to the Terpsichore. I've got to see a woman about a busted pipe," Kit said.

"What is the Terpsichore?" came Alex's voice from directly behind Kit.

"A club, piano bar, pool parlor, disco, coffee lounge, you name it," Kit said. "For women," she added, looking at Damien.

"I know, Kit," he said with a grin. "I thought I'd stick around here anyway. I'll let you know if I find out anything else." He fished around in his pocket for his wallet and pulled out a business card. "Will you do the same?"

"Of course," she replied, slipping the card into her back pocket. "Do you two want to share my taxi?"

The Terpsichore—or Angie's as it was more commonly known—had been running for three years which was somewhat of a record for a women's club in Melbourne. One reason was that the whole kit and caboodle was privately owned, unlike most other women's venues which tended to last only as long as a hotel took enough money over the bar to justify lending one or two back rooms for what were euphemistically known as "private functions."

The Terpsichore's main success, however, lay in the fact that it wasn't just a weekly late-night dance venue. It was open from midday until two a.m. Sunday to Thursday and till four a.m. on Fridays and Saturdays. It had a pool room, which guaranteed a regular clientele, and the soundproofed Red Room at the back meant the loud dance music or live bands did not drown out the conversation or soft music in the piano bar. The bistro, run by Angie's lover Julia, also served some of the best food north of the city which, considering how close it was to Brunswick and Lygon Streets, was an achievement in itself.

Kit gazed at the Terpsichore through the windscreen of the taxi while she waited for the driver to give her change. Angie Nichols had bought the former church manse from an elderly Italian gent who'd been using it to store the overflow from his used-furniture shop further up the street. The church itself, since its de-consecration, had been used for a variety of activities including an illegal betting shop (busted in 1979) and a progressive community school (closed in 1986). In its current incarnation it hosted adult education classes in karate, carpentry and migrant English. Little or no maintenance had been carried out on the church since it stopped being one so it looked rather sore and sorry for itself beside the bluestone manse which had been lovingly restored by Angie and her three semi-silent partners. They had gutted the interior and injected a considerable fortune and twelve months' work into its renovation and redecoration.

Angie's provided a welcoming respite from just about anything that could be bothering a person and for this reason alone it had become Kit's home away from home, which was why she was now questioning her sanity. Why on earth did you bring them here, O'Malley? she thought morosely. Are you mad? You're supposed to leave your work at the office, or out on the streets. You should have sent them home!

Quinn and Alex, who had slipped out of the back seat of the taxi as soon as it pulled up—no doubt to escape the stench of citrus air-freshner which did little to cover the lingering smell of body odor most of which rose in a fug from the driver himself—were standing on the footpath carrying on an animated conversation. Well, Quinn was, Alex was just laughing a lot.

Kit raked her fingers through her hair and took a deep breath before clambering out of the taxi. Despite her annoyance with herself at allowing her young client to latch on and follow her absolutely everywhere, she *was* worried about Quinn. Celia's daughter was enduring a serious case of denial and Kit wondered when the crash was going to happen. Kit remembered how, when her father had died, Lillian had set her jaw and straightened her back just long enough to inform everyone and then had gone completely to pieces. Kit had never seen her mother like that before. It was more heartbreaking than her own immediate sense of loss. She'd pushed her feelings into the background to cope with having to take charge of all the arrangements, which was quite a task for a sixteen-year-old. Lillian had recovered her equilibrium right in the middle of the wild Irish wake that Patrick Francis O'Malley's rowdy and lovable friends had helped Kit organize, but it had taken Kit herself a month to dismantle her defenses enough to face her own grief. And then, of course, there'd been Hannah two years ago.

"Are you coming, O'Malley, or are we going to spend the rest of the night on the footpath?" Alex demanded.

Kit had no energy left even to try and think of a smart retort so she led the way up the path to the entrance at the side of the building. Opening the door she could hear the incomparable Ella Fitzgerald singing *It's Only A Paper Moon*, and as she stepped inside her sour mood immediately began to dissipate. The *what on earth have I gotten myself into?* expression on Alex's face, as she stared open-mouthed at the four life-size caryatids that supported the cupola over the fountain in the middle of the slate-tiled foyer, made her feel even better.

"Far out!" exclaimed Quinn. "My mother's been here, hasn't she?"

Kit explained that Angie had become a born-again new age hippie around the time she'd bought the building, and that of the other three partners one was a witch and another ran an assertiveness training program for "wimmin" so, all things considered, she felt they'd been fairly restrained in their decorative references to the cult of the goddess. They had at least confined it to the foyer. "Wait till you see the rest though," she added.

Alex looked as though she'd rather go home right about then, but asked where the toilet was instead. Kit pointed to the door to their left then escorted Quinn into the piano bar/bistro.

"Far out," Quinn said again, this time with delight as she looked around the lacquered walls, every square inch of which had first been wallpapered with articles, paintings and photos of real, down-to-earth, flesh and blood women who had led, influenced or taken part in just about every field of human endeavor ever invented. "I'm going to like this place. Lead me to the bar," she said.

151

"Close your mouth, Katy darling, it's quite unbecoming," said Angie, who had interrupted her conversation with two women at the other end of the bar to serve Kit and Quinn. Angie had a trim figure but was big boned, with large gentle hands and the biggest feet Kit had ever seen on a woman. Right now though she looked somewhat like a crazed Amazon warrior dressed in black and red tie-dyed pants and a white T-shirt emblazoned with the words Right On Fairies!

"What's with the hair, Angie?" Kit asked, reaching out to touch her friend's crazy mass of curls which, since she'd last seen them, had been dyed an extremely violent shade of red.

"Carol is on holiday. I asked her offsider Chantelle to give me a color that looked as though she'd spilt a good bottle of shiraz in my hair."

"I don't think Chantelle's a wine drinker," Kit said unnecessarily.

"Tell me about it. What can I get you? And your friend?"

"Quinn Orlando, this is Angie Nichols. Angie, Quinn. Quinn, Angie. We'll have a couple of cleansing ales, please. Had a busy night?"

"So-so. The pool comp finished about an hour ago. It's been pretty quiet since then," Angie said as she placed fresh coasters on the bar and pulled two pots of beer.

"Where's Julia?"

"The love of my life went completely pre-menstrual at about ten o'clock eastern standard time. She was dropping glasses and spilling stuff all over the place. I couldn't do a thing with her and when she threw a perfectly good plate of lasagna across the kitchen I sent her home." Angie was about to lounge against the bar when something over Kit's shoulder caught her attention and made her stand bolt upright.

"Well, I'll be damned!" she exclaimed. "Of all the gin joints in all the world I *never* thought you'd walk into mine."

Kit turned around to find Alex standing there, arms akimbo, looking like her life had just flashed before her eyes. Either that or she thought the crazy red-headed hippy behind the bar was delivering the most bizarre pick-up line she'd ever heard.

"I might have known you'd end up running a gin joint like this," Alex said, quite calmly considering her face had changed from the deathly white of the just-seen-a-ghost variety to the color of rhubarb in a matter of seconds. She took a seat next to Quinn.

"Do you two know each other?" Kit asked, realizing it was a completely ridiculous question.

"We shared a house back in . . . Oh god, Alex, it was seventeen years ago," Angie said.

"Time certainly flies, when you're . . . er . . ." Alex said.

"When you're getting old," Quinn said with a grin. "Let me see, seventeen years ago I was eight years old."

"Who brought *her*?" Angie asked, looking accusingly at Kit.

"Don't look at me," Kit said. "I don't know either of them. They've just been following me around all night. Your old housemate looks like she could do with a drink though. I think the shock has been too much for her."

Alex, who had just managed to regain her composure, cast a grateful look at Kit and took another swig of Quinn's beer before putting it back on the bar.

"Too much for *her*?" Angie said. "I had the most enormous crush on this woman way back then. A serious case of unrequited lust that lasted nigh on two years—the memory of which still stirs the old loins, I might add—before she took off to finish her degree in Vancouver or wherever it was."

"Toronto," said Alex softly. She was blushing again but she was also smiling.

"Please don't tell me you came back from Canada and married that Peter, Peter, oh what was his name?"

"Hindmarsh," Alex said. "And no, I didn't."

"Thank god for that," Angie said as she placed a pot of beer in front of Alex. "That guy was terminally boring."

"But she is getting married next month," Kit threw in.

"Oh no. What a shame. I thought you would have seen the light by now," Angie said.

Alex laughed an uncomfortable laugh and Quinn looked as though she was going to say something then thought better of it.

"Damn. The last minute rush," Angie said as she went off to serve a group of five women who had just walked in.

"I need a more comfortable chair," Kit said. She got up and carried her drink over to one of the leather booth seats in the piano bar. Alex and Quinn followed her. Kit realized she was starting to get used to it.

"You can stay at the bar if you want, Alex. You and Angie could talk about the good old days at uni," she said.

"Some other time maybe," Alex said. "What I really want to do is tell you about the Smiths so I can go home to bed."

"The Smiths? Who are the Smiths? Oh, I remember, that's why you came to my apartment in the first place," Kit said.

"Exactly. We all sort of got sidetracked, what with Damien turning up and your mother insisting on ordering home-delivered pizza for everyone," Alex said.

"And you insisting on going home to change," Kit added.

"I really like your mum," Quinn stated, trying to change the subject.

"Thanks, Quinn. I really like my mum too. So, tell me about the Smiths," Kit said to change the subject back again. She had a feeling that now was not a good time to let Quinn dwell on the subject of mothers.

"All the specific details are in the folder I left on your desk, along with the info on Orlan Carriers and Freyling Imports. Which reminds me, I left my briefcase at your place too so, if it's not inconvenient, I'll drop by in the morning and pick it up. And my car. Now, the Smiths."

Alex pushed her hair behind her left ear with her index finger while she gathered her thoughts on the subject. The action had the opposite effect on Kit whose thoughts became progressively ungathered as she watched Alex's finger trace a line along her jaw. When Alex rested her chin between her thumb and index finger and looked directly at her, Kit just wanted to die, right then and there. She had a vision of herself in seventeen years' time sounding just like Angie, bemoaning a serious case of unrequited lust—and for the same woman, for god's sake! Kit simply could not remember being this attracted to anyone. Ever. And she was *not* having a good time.

"Kit? Are you OK?" Quinn asked gently.

Kit dragged her gaze from Alex's. She looked at Quinn with a half-smile. "I'm fine," she lied. "I think I've just been awake too long today. I'm absolutely stuffed." Not to mention absolutely, irretrievably and ridiculously smitten, she thought.

"Right. I think we're all tired," Alex said. "Michael Dixon, an ex-colleague and old friend of mine, tracked down the Smiths in Sydney. Correction, he tracked down Malcolm Smith in Sydney. Shirley Smith, who is his sister and not his wife as I surmised, lives here in Melbourne somewhere and owns something called the Endicott Center in the Dandenongs."

"What made you think you'd find him in Sydney?" Kit asked.

"Well, if you remember, Wellborn Enterprises owns several properties in Sydney and Coolangatta. I thought it was a good place to start. Anyway, the Smiths, Dalkeith, Edwina Barnes, Grainger and Whitten, in various combinations, seem to have their fingers in a great many pies. Michael is still trying to untangle the paper trail. They have companies within companies, some of which seem to do nothing but front for other companies which own businesses and properties up and down the east coast."

"What businesses?" Kit asked.

"All sorts it seems, from a construction company in Wollongong and a real estate business in Paddington to video stores all over town and a restaurant in Double Bay. One of Gerald Grainger's nightclubs is owned by another subsidiary of Wellborn. About the only thing, from memory, that belongs solely to the Smiths is a small fleet of luxury pleasure boats. Oh, and the Endicott Center of which Shirley Smith is a director. It appears the total revenue from her ten per cent shares in Freyling, Wellborn and the other companies goes directly to the Endicott Center. It's the only straight line Michael has been able to uncover."

"And Geoffrey's name still hasn't turned up on anything?"

"Not yet. But Michael loves this sort of stuff. He says it's like trying to solve a Rubik's cube. If Geoffrey has any connection he'll find it."

"What is this Endicott Center?" Quinn asked.

"I gather it's some sort of sanatorium or health farm. The other board members include two doctors and a psychiatrist."

"Mmm. Are you busy tomorrow, Alex?" Kit asked.

"Why?"

"Well, I was going to check out the Skintone Agency and then drop into the *St. Kilda Star* to see if a journo friend of mine has anything recent on Edwina Barnes. I'm also hoping she might have heard of Factor Four seeing it's not listed in the phone book. And I'll have to pick up Geoffrey's tail to find out what the mystery appointment is at five p.m."

"So?"

"So I was wondering if you'd have time to check out the Endicott Center. In person," Kit said. That way there's no chance of you following me around all day, she thought.

"Ah, sure. I'll take a drive out there in the morning after I pick up my car."

"What about me?" Quinn asked, almost petulantly.

"Is Geoffrey included in the family business Douglas needs you for in the morning?"

"Yeah. The pig," Quinn sneered.

"Good. You get to keep an eye on the pig. Just don't lose control, OK? We don't want Geoffrey knowing that we know anything at all. When he leaves you follow him wherever he goes—at a distance. You can call me at the *Star* or on my mobile to tell me where to meet you when I've finished."

"Neat," Quinn said excitedly.

"I don't think it's neat," Alex stated.

"Give it a rest, Alex," Quinn snapped.

Chapter 14

"Yes, you're very beautiful, Thistle, and I love you to death, but I don't need your tail in my coffee, if you don't mind," Kit said, dragging The Cat from the breakfast bar onto her lap. She picked up her mug and stared blankly at the newspaper in front of her. "This is not a good way to start the day," she moaned. "There's nothing in here but bad news and more bad news." She pushed the paper away and squinted at the digital clock on the kitchen bench. It said 9:43 . . . 9:44—only five minutes had elapsed since the last time she'd looked yet it felt like she'd been sitting there for three hours.

"I hate mornings!" Kit shouted at the wall. "Especially when that woman turns up here looking refreshed and positively ravishing. Did you see her, Thistle? Nobody should look that good before noon."

"Manuel," yowled The Cat.

"Manuel indeed, Thistle, and don't bite me, you little maniac." Kit stood up, dumped The Cat unceremoniously on the stool and wandered vaguely into her bedroom to finish getting dressed. She stared at herself in the mirror, ran her hands through her wet hair and wondered what on earth she must have looked like when she'd answered the door an hour before. The bell had woken her so she'd thrown on a white singlet and a pair of black tracksuit pants which were more holes than pants. Her hair was in its usual sleep-induced state—squashed flat on one side and sticking straight up like a cocky's crest on the other—and for a moment she thought her eyes must have been totally bloodshot until she realized it was Alex's red silk shirt she was staring at. Ms. Cazenove had declined an offer of coffee, picked up her briefcase and left again before Kit was even fully conscious.

"She probably had much more sleep than you," Kit said to her reflection as she buttoned up her jeans. Although right now she regretted the sleep she'd missed out on, she still felt mighty pleased with the work she'd done last night. By the time she'd got home, after organizing for Angie to check out Lillian's plumbing and taking a taxi via Albert Park to drop Alex and Quinn at Alex's place, it had been close to two a.m. She had gotten her second or third wind by then, it was still too hot to sleep and instead of being sensible and going to bed anyway she'd decided to write Flynn Carter and her lover out of the cold cellar and into a nice hot bath, thereby completing chapter six. She'd finally thrown herself into bed at four a.m. thinking she was now ready to let someone else read her work-in-progress seeing it actually felt like it was progressing.

Kit tucked a blue and white cotton shirt into her jeans and went looking for her shoes. She found one where she'd left it under her desk and the other where Thistle had put it under the couch. She checked that her wallet, keys and sunglasses were in her leather pouch before buckling it round her hips, pulled her manuscript out of the top drawer of the filing cabinet where she had to hide it so The Cat wouldn't kill it like she had the first print-out of chapter one, poured herself a fresh cup of coffee and headed out into the real world in search of a literary critic.

Despite feeling confident that Del would give her honest opinion and nothing but constructive criticism Kit wondered, momentarily, whether her fledgling artistic sensibility was really ready for that kind of honesty—from her best friend. Still, someone had to read her book sometime; that was the whole idea after all. She stopped on the landing outside her front door, trying to organize all the things she was carrying to leave one hand free for the railing, and waited for the wonky sensors in her brain to stop reeling so she could tackle the stupid wooden planks without feeling she was going to fall through the spaces between them. She reached the bottom and managed to get her office door open without spilling a drop of coffee. Dumping everything on the desk she leaned round the partition to see if there was anyone else alive at this ungodly hour.

"Jeez, you look like shit," Del said, peering over the top of her half-moon glasses.

"That's probably because I died during the night. And this *must* be Hell. What happened? Were you burgled or something?"

"Very funny. I've been looking for a lost love and I thought I might have filed her away here somewhere." Del made a show of shuffling the thousand and one papers strewn across what she called her creative bench into some kind of order.

Kit went back for her coffee then slumped into a chair just as the front door swung open and Brigit flashed in, as bright as sunlight and just as painful to Kit's tired eyes.

"Morning," she sang.

"Shut up!" Kit and Del said in unison.

"Well, excuse me. If you don't mind I'll just sit at my desk and breathe to myself," Brigit said as she flounced her generously proportioned frame into the only decent chair in the office and started opening the mail. Her smug smile was a dead giveaway that she was pleased that, for a change, she was the only person in the building who wasn't sporting a hangover.

"Do you still want to read my book?" Kit asked nervously.

"Don't tell me you've finished it," Del said.

"Good heavens no. But I finished chapter six last night and I think it's at the stage now where you'd be able to, um, you know, see how it's going and tell me what you think."

"Oh, OK. If you like," Del said, as if she couldn't care less.

"You don't have to if you don't want to, Del," Kit said sulkily.

"If I don't want to? I've only been waiting for nearly five months."

"Six chapters! I think that's so exciting," Brigit exclaimed.

"I'm sure that makes Kit feel a whole lot better about being so damned secretive," Del said.

"It does, thank you, Brigit. And I wasn't being secretive, Del, you know that. I just didn't want to jinx myself. I wanted to get it moving before letting anyone read it. I mean, let's face it, even *if* I find a publisher it'll probably only be my friends who buy it. And if they've already read it why would they bother? Besides, Del, you laughed at the idea of me writing in the first place."

"No I didn't, sweetheart. What I had trouble with, if you remember, was your hero. I mean how realistic a character is an ex-cop turned private investigator who writes bestselling detective novels on the side? It's just not real."

"It's not supposed to be real, Del. It's fiction."

"Yes, but it's been done to death on television. It sounds like Jessica Fletcher meets Charlie's Angels in an episode of Hill Street Blues. Who would believe it?" Del asked.

The unmistakable sounds of Brigit thinking came from the other side of the room as she settled her chair into its best meditative position. "I would," she said. "Kit's hero sounds just like Kit."

"My point exactly," Del stated. "And you think Kit is real? Look at her. She looks like something the cat dragged home last night. She's just a figment of someone else's imagination—like we all are."

"Oh, please, don't go all extential on me, it's too early," Brigit said.

"Ex-I-stential, Brigit," Del corrected.

"Whatever," Brigit said, getting to her feet. "I'm going out to get some coffee before you blame me for your appalling childhood."

"What was wrong with my childhood?" Del demanded.

"Whatever my imagination can conjure up as I take my fictitious fat body down to Irene's for sustenance," Brigit said. She closed the door soundly behind her.

"So, do you want to read it or not?' Kit asked, trying not to laugh at Del who hated it when Brigit had the last word.

"Of course I do. I'm just jealous that you've actually done what I've only talked about doing for the last twenty years, *and* that you did it without my invaluable advice. Hand it over before you change your mind."

A larger-than-life poster of a borderline anorexic in a g-string and wet singlet kept Kit company while she waited for someone to acknowledge the button she'd pressed beside the "please ring" sticker on the desk. The grainy black-and-white nature of the photograph no doubt enabled the photographer to class the picture as erotic art rather than pornography, but it didn't fool Kit one bit. Neither did the Skintone

Agency's glossy reception area with its luxurious leather couch, slate floor tiles and rented pot plants. Piles of shiny folders, thick with mugshots of model-type women and men, were scattered over a large chrome and glass coffee table. They made it appear that Skintone was exactly what it purported to be, but Kit had never been one to trust appearances.

There were only two doors in the room. A metal one, directly behind the tidy but unattended desk, and the glass one through which she had entered the second-floor premises from Chapel Street. The metal door was flush with the wall and had no handle. The desk had no drawers for her to rifle while she waited, and there was no convenient teledex or appointment book to flick through. How the hell was she supposed to gather information if the bad guys didn't help out just a bit by leaving valuable clues lying around the place?

Kit pressed the button again as she gazed nonchalantly around looking for evidence of the peephole or hidden camera she felt sure somebody was watching her through. The metal door made a soft whooshing sound as it opened and a middle-aged woman with an extraordinary amount of hair piled on top of her head stepped into the room. There was no time from where Kit was standing to see what lay beyond the door before it closed again.

"Sorry to keep you waiting. I'm Delvene Sharp, the manager of Skintone," the woman said in a nasal voice filtered through the clenched Macleans smile she had pasted on her face.

"Hi, I'm Gloria Weaver, pleased to meet ya," Kit said, limply shaking the woman's offered hand.

"How may I help you, Gloria?" Delvene asked, with forced politeness.

"Well," Kit said, crossing her arms awkwardly, "I thought I'd like to be a model. I seen your sign on the door downstairs and I was wondering if youse, I mean your agency, would be able to help." She uncrossed her arms, made a show of straightening her shirt then thrust her hands in her back pockets.

"Our books are full at the moment. Skintone is not taking on any new girls. Sorry."

"Oh. I understand," Kit said dejectedly as she shuffled from one foot to the other. "It's only that I thought maybe youse could gimme some advice, ya know. I've had some experience. I done some fashion parades for our department store at home. In Morwell. I was pretty good at it, so I just thought, well, ya know."

"Morwell," Delvene stated, barely able to keep the snigger out of her voice. "That's a little town down in Gippsland, isn't it?"

"It's not that little," Kit said defensively.

"Of course not, dear." Delvene tried to inject a motherly tone into her voice but it just made her sound patronizing. She came out from behind the desk and walked around Kit, looking her up and down. "Well, you've certainly got good bones. And lovely long legs, dear. I'll bet you were the star of the catwalk at home. Ah, and green eyes. They're definitely in at the moment."

Oh goody, Kit thought. My eyes are "in." She felt like lot number four at a horse auction and was sorely tempted to stamp one foot and open her mouth so Delvene could check her teeth.

"The thing is, you're really a bit old for Skintone, even if we were looking for new girls at the moment."

"Too old? I'm only thirty-two. And I was sure I could get work in Melbourne doing this sort of thing. What am I gunna do?" Kit looked miserably at Delvene and sat down heavily on the couch. "I really need the money, ya see. Me husband threw me out when he took up with his secretary. She was me best friend too—would ya believe it?" Kit dropped her head in her hands but peered through her fingers at Skintone's manager.

Delvene shook her head and rolled her eyes, obviously trying to think of a quick way to get rid of this small-town hick without being completely rude. "Perhaps if you show me your folio, Gloria, I could recommend another agency," she suggested.

"Folio?" Kit queried innocently.

"You don't have a folio? Oh, dear, you simply must have a folio. Now that is something I *can* help you out with."

Delvene was about to say something else when the front door opened and two men walked in. Kit was awfully glad her hands were already covering her face because that's no doubt where they would have ended up—in surprise at being caught out. Don't be ridiculous, O'Malley, she thought. He has no idea who you are. You've been

162

watching him through a camera lens, you idiot. Nonetheless she kept her hand over her mouth and nose as she looked abjectly from Delvene to Ian Dalkeith and then nowhere in particular. Out of the corner of her eye she caught Delvene gesturing to Dalkeith that he could ignore the tearful Gloria on the couch.

"Is she here?" he asked in a handsome voice that perfectly matched the handsome features and handsome clothes.

"Yes. She's waiting out the back. I'll buzz you in."

Kit glanced at Dalkeith again, this time noticing that his face was slightly pockmarked, in a rugged Robert Redford sort of way, and that he wore a small diamond stud in his left ear. He cast an uninterested look in her direction so she sniffed loudly and made a fuss of trying to find a tissue in her pocket. She realized she felt slightly unsettled. Dalkeith's look had been more than just uninterested. Or was it less than just uninterested? Whichever way she analyzed it there was no doubt that his were the most emotionless and dishonest eyes she had ever come across.

When Dalkeith stepped forward to follow Delvene, Kit got her first look at the young man who had arrived with him. Had they been real tears she was sniffing back she would have choked on them. Clink, clink, she thought as a couple of little cogs in the grand scheme of things slipped into place. Just how they fitted, and why, was another thing altogether but Kit felt sure that finding Dalkeith in the company of this particular young man was, to say the least, fairly significant. The fact that he was a dishy blond about twenty years old, "with a bod like Damien's only thinner," simply made the fact that he was also the same Master Snakehips she'd seen getting into Geoffrey Robinson's Bentley two weeks ago even more interesting.

Delvene slid her hand underneath the reception desk and the metal door whooshed open again. Kit caught sight of a pre-fab metal bench, a laptop computer and a couple of wooden crates. A pair of shapely legs clad in black stockings, the left foot on the rung of a stool and the right one crossed and swinging free, was all Kit could see of the "she" who was apparently waiting for Dalkeith.

"You're late, Ian. Everything else is on time. They've been unloading for hours." The woman's voice, laced with irritation, had a

163

dull echo to it which led Kit to guess that the area on the other side of the reception area was spacious or empty or both. She also had the feeling this was not the first time she'd heard that voice.

"Christo!" Dalkeith snapped. "Stop perving and get a move on."

Kit looked up at Master Christo Snakehips and realized it was her he'd been perving at. He shrugged one shoulder and dropped his head to the right, as if he had a crick in his neck, and followed Dalkeith into the back room without a word.

"Who rang the bell?" the woman's voice asked.

"A wannabee," Delvene replied. "I'll deal with her."

As the door closed again Delvene opened the top drawer of the desk, pulled something out and approached Kit with an expression that implied she was going to deal with her in a hurry. "Now, Gloria. Getting a folio together can be quite expensive. Stand up, dear."

Whoa. This wasn't just being dealt with. This was the bum's rush and then some, Kit thought as Delvene took her by the elbow and escorted her towards the front door. "Here are the names of a couple of local studios that don't charge too much. These people do a lot of work for us, so they're reliable. And maybe, if they like what you can do, they may even be able to get you some work. OK, Gloria?"

"Gee, thanks, Delvene. I dunno what to say," Kit said, grinning like the Cheshire cat as she wiped her nose with the back of her hand.

"Don't say anything, dear. I wish you luck." Delvene thrust some business cards into Kit's hand as she pushed her body into the hallway outside and shut the door in her face.

"Well!" Kit said huffily on behalf of Gloria Weaver the wannabee model from Morwell as she shoved the cards in her back pocket and traipsed down the two flights of stairs and out into Chapel Street. She weaved her way through the tide of grumpy-looking shoppers, so many of whom were going in the opposite direction that Kit wondered if they knew something she didn't, and took a left into Greville Street and a right a couple of blocks down.

By the time she reached the car park behind Coles her shirt was sticking to her in all the wrong places and the last thing she wanted to do was get into her car and drive anywhere. She opened the door, clambered across the seats to wind down the passenger window to let the hot air out, then stood in the ribbon of shade cast by the six-foot twig she'd parked in front of.

She looked at her watch: it was only one-thirty.

She looked at the sky: it was a blinding shimmering blue studded with huge chunky black clouds. Their hovering presence agreed with the forecast for afternoon storms but right now all they were doing was holding the heat in.

She pulled out the three business cards Delvene had given her and looked at the first one. It said: Thomas De Silva of Toorak. The next one said: Fine Form Photography, J. P. Findlay & Don Ambrose— Photographic Artists. The third one should have shouted Bingo! What it said instead was: Foremost Factor Four, Video and Photographic Studios, Fitzroy Street, St. Kilda.

"Gee thanks, Delvene, you little beauty," Kit whooped as she climbed into her car and set the auto-pilot for St. Kilda. She was spending so much time down that way lately she wondered whether she should take the hint and just move there to save on petrol. Factor Four, now that Kit had an address for it, was not foremost on her list. It could wait. Her next stop was the Acland Street office of the *St. Kilda Star* where an old college friend, Penny Reed, worked as a reporter or rather, as Pen herself said, where she wrote the guff that filled the gaps between the ads.

Kit managed to find a car park in the shade only two blocks from the office of the *St. Kilda Star*. She took a deep breath and walked around the corner into Acland Street, trying desperately to put her mind into resistance mode. Her stomach however ignored her best intentions and started grumbling as soon she came abreast of the first cake shop. By the time she'd got to the third window full of baked cheese cakes, black forest cakes and pastries filled with fruit and custard and dripping with chocolate her taste buds took control of her body and dragged her inside. She emerged half an hour later feeling totally disgusted with herself having consumed two cappuccinos and a torte that went by the name of A Decadent Chocolate Desire.

Kit pushed open the door of the *Star,* took one look at the stairs and cursed her weakness at not being able to control herself at least until after she'd made this call. The office was on the first floor above a café and as she hauled her weak-willed body up and up she realized it had been at least a year since she'd seen Penny.

The office was in exactly the same state of disarray it had been in on her last visit. It still looked like every edition published since the newspaper set up shop in the forties was lying around in easy reach—just in case someone wanted to check a page three article from March 1953 or do a follow-up on a story first printed in 1977. About the only change Kit could see amidst the clutter was the PCs, their blinking cursors indicating that the latter half of the twentieth century had finally caught up with the journos at the *Star*. The last time Kit had been here the elderly social columnist was still using an antiquated Remington typewriter that had a pound symbol and no dollar sign.

"Can I help you?" asked a voice from behind a mountain of paper just inside the door. Kit vaguely recalled the lanky balding guy who owned the voice but couldn't remember his name. "Yeah. I'd like to see Penny Reed if she's around."

"Penny doesn't work here anymore," he said. "She's been gone about six months."

"Oh? Where did she go?"

"Peru, last I heard. No wait," he said, getting up to amble over to a notice board which was a veritable forest of drawing pins, paper scraps, postcards and photos. "Easter Island. That's where this card came from last month. Then she was going to Tierra del Fuego it says here." He pinned the postcard back on the board then peered at Kit as if he was trying to find a place for her in the chaos that surrounded him.

"Are you a friend of Penny's? I mean, did you need to see her in particular or can someone else help?"

"She is a friend, but I guess anyone will do. I'm after some information on Edwina Barnes."

"I remember now," he said triumphantly. "You're that cop, aren't you?"

Kit laughed. "I used to be that cop. I'm someone else now."

"No kidding?" he said, as if Kit had said something sensible. "Edwina Barnes, eh? I reckon the best person to talk to would be Erin

Carmody. She took over from Penny and might have some idea of how to find something in her filing system."

"You have filing systems here?" Kit asked incredulously.

"Of course," he said, placing one hand on his hip. "We know where everything is located." He waved his hand around the room and grinned. "It's here. Somewhere."

"So, is Erin around?" Kit asked.

"Nope. Oops, I tell a lie. Here she comes now."

Kit turned as a flushed and flustered woman burst through the door swearing at the top of her voice. "That bloody little shit Terry Jones. I could strangle him. Just look at these, will you, Simon? I asked for a nice clear close-up shot of what those vandals did to the town hall last night and he takes it upon himself to find the ugliest councillor available and make him stand three miles away from the fucking building and point to it. He knows I hate pointing photographs." She thrust a handful of photos at Simon then stood there with her hands on her hips.

Going solely by appearances Kit thought the whole tirade should have been delivered in a thick Irish accent, but Erin Carmody's Emerald Isle ancestry was probably about as remote as her own. She was a little taller than Kit with long auburn hair and fiery green eyes. At least they were fiery right now. She was dressed in loose pants that matched the color of her hair, a soft white cotton shirt with a lace-up front and a multi-colored crushed velvet waistcoat.

"What do you expect me to do about this?" Simon was asking.

"You could lend me a thousand bucks so I could take a contract out on Terry. I mean, who would miss him?"

"You probably shouldn't be saying things like that in front of a cop who's been waiting to talk to you," Simon stated, indicating Kit with a nod of his head.

"A cop? She looks less like a cop than Terry does a photographer, Simon. Who are you trying to kid?"

"I used to be a cop, now I'm a private investigator," Kit said, offering Erin her business card.

"O'Malley Investigations," Erin read aloud. "Are you O'Malley?"

"You can call me Kit."

"OK, Kit O'Malley. What can I do for you?"

"I actually came to see Penny Reed but Simon here tells me she ran off to South America. I need some information on Edwina Barnes."

"Edwina Barnes the person or Edwina Barnes the multi-million-dollar industry?"

"Both," Kit replied.

"This could take a while. Simon, did you say you were going downstairs to get some coffee?" Erin asked sweetly.

"Erin darling, if I were a woman that would probably be classed as discrimination or exploitation," Simon said flatly.

"Simon darling, if you were a woman you would have been courteous enough to make the offer yourself. I mean, it's not every day we have a visitor who hasn't come to complain about something."

"You have a point. I'll go get some coffee."

Erin led the way to the other end of the room, shifted a box off a chair and motioned for Kit to sit down. She made a show of clearing some space on her desk but gave up when she realized it was a futile exercise.

Chapter 15

"Edwina Barnes. Barnes, Edwina," Erin muttered to herself. She hauled out the third of several cardboard boxes which constituted Penny Reed's filing system although, judging by the countless others just like it that were stacked in corners and stuffed into shelves or under furniture all around the newsroom, boxing things up seemed to be the office policy on file management.

"We haven't done anything on Edwina that I can recall for quite some time," Erin was saying as she dumped three thick and dusty manila folders on her desk. "Let's see, the last article was an open day at the Arena. That was June last year."

"What's the Arena?" Kit asked.

"One of Edwina's more upmarket establishments. Mind you, none of her joints are downmarket, some are just smaller than others," Erin replied. "This is basically just a couple of paragraphs to go with the photos of the Arena's snazzy new foyer, cocktail bar and refurbished bathroom. And we are talking *bath* room here!" She handed Kit the clipping.

"Forget the room, there is none. This must be the biggest bath in Australia," Kit laughed. "Where is the Arena?"

"Beaconsfield Parade," Erin said, consulting a list taped to the inside of the folder. "No doubt it has great views overlooking the bay."

"Probably from the bath," Kit said. She leant over to cast her eyes down the list of establishments that made up the Barnes empire. Geoffrey's favorite retreat was listed, as was the Skintone Agency, but there was no mention of Foremost Factor Four. Edwina operated at least four other brothels apart from the Arena and owned a couple of beauty parlors. The Trueheart Escort Service, which was the one Kit had gone undercover with eight years before, was still going strong.

"In April last year we have one Herbert Frank Smith threatening to sue for damages after falling down the Arena's front stairs. That was obviously his allocated fifteen minutes of fame because it went no further than that," Erin said, replacing one clipping and picking up another. "In January the police raided the Purple Harem, but only because they had a tip-off that some escaped con was there. There's not a lot here, Kit. What exactly are you after?"

Kit shook her head slowly and picked up one of the styrofoam cups of coffee that the poor exploited Simon had fetched for them. "I'm not sure really. Something, anything, to connect Edwina more closely with someone else I'm investigating."

"Well, I doubt you'll connect Edwina herself with anything much at all. Apart from the fact that her girls have been managing her places ever since she retired, Edwina doesn't get out much since her charming son stuck her in a loony bin."

"A what?"

"A loony bin. You know nut house, sanatorium, health farm— whatever you want to call it. But a health farm that employs shrinks and psych nurses is a loony bin as far as I'm concerned. Sorry I didn't mention it before but I thought you must have known that already," Erin said.

"I had no idea," Kit said. "But it would make my day if you told me this loony bin goes by the name of the Endicott Center."

"I can't remember off hand. But what a challenge—I haven't made anyone's day for ages." Erin laughed and opened the other folder and pulled out a sheet of blue paper. "The potted history of Edwina Barnes," she explained. "Simon calls them Penny's bonsai biographies. Let's see. Edwina Adelaide Barnes, born and bred in Collingwood in the 1920s. Twice married, twice divorced. Three children, born in the late forties and early fifties—a son to Nigel Fenton, husband number one, and two daughters to Frank Easton, hubby number two. The first-born daughter, Angela Adelaide Easton, died at age six; the other daughter, Margaret Adelaide Easton, is presumed living but her whereabouts are unknown. The son, Charles Edward Fenton, took a redundancy package from the Education Department in '92 and retired to Phillip Island. Edwina laid the foundations of her escort empire during the forties by hosting a series of so-called tea dances where her girls provided pleasant company for Australian and visiting American officers. After the war those same girls formed the first intake for the Trueheart Escort Service."

"And the rest, as they say, is history," Kit stated.

"Precisely," Erin agreed. "Edwina retired in about 1980 and took herself off for the no doubt well-earned grand tour of Europe and America, leaving her empire in the capable hands of her longest-serving girls. She was gone three years. Two years ago—for reasons apparently unknown, to Penny at least—she was admitted to—you're going to love this—the Endicott Center, an exclusive and très expensive sanatorium in the Dandenongs."

"Yes!" Kit exclaimed. "Now, make my day perfect, Erin, and tell me you know the life story of Ian Dalkeith, the yuppie real estate agent."

Erin's eyebrows shot up in surprise and she tried not to choke on the mouthful of coffee she'd just taken. "Is he the someone else you're investigating?" she asked.

"No, but he or his name keeps popping up just like Edwina's does."

"I feel a serious case of déjà vu creeping up on me," Erin said as she flicked her long hair back over her left shoulder. "This is weird. Twenty-four hours ago Ian Dalkeith was just a name to me. I'd seen his face in the paper a couple of times but that was it. I didn't even realize until yesterday afternoon, when I had cause to do a little digging, that he'd been involved in the fight between the local residents and the developers—on the wrong side of course. He was only a bit player really, just a footnote in the history of the ongoing struggle of Action St. Kilda and other local residents' groups to stop the money spinners from turning the Esplanade into the Gold Coast of Melbourne. He was in there nonetheless, doing his bit to further the gentrification and overall ruin of St. Kilda. I don't know what made

171

him pull out but he and his money were in the news for about nine weeks, nearly two years ago, then he just bowed out."

"So what happened yesterday?" Kit asked. "I mean, what made you look for background stuff on him?"

"That's the weird part. A guy came in here asking for anything we had on Ian Dalkeith. Now here you are, asking for the same. Is this something I should know about?"

"I don't know yet. Who was the guy?"

"A writer from Sydney. He's doing a book on the battles that Action St. Kilda and the Sydney groups have fought against the developers. He said he was down for a couple of weeks to do some research. For some reason though he was particularly interested in Dalkeith and, um, some other guys I'd never heard of." Erin opened her top desk drawer and took out a notebook.

"What other guys?"

"I have to check my notes. We didn't have anything on them. Ah, Davis Whitten and . . ."

"Gerald Grainger and Malcolm Smith?" Kit suggested.

"Grainger, yes, Malcolm Smith, no," Erin stated.

"What else can you tell me about this writer? What did he look like?" Kit asked.

"He was a big freckle-faced guy with a huge red moustache, short hair and eyes like a basset hound. He . . ."

"A moustache?" Kit interrupted.

"Yeah, a long one, and he had a funny accent. It was almost non-descript, as if he was Irish or American but had been living somewhere else for a long time. I suppose it was Sydney seeing he's writing this book. His name was Mike Finnigan," Erin said as she picked up her coffee. "I have the impression you know this guy," she added when she noticed the expression on Kit's face.

"Not really, but I think I may have seen him around here and there." Kit looked at Erin thoughtfully. "If he comes back I suggest you be a little cautious. I might be quite wrong but I don't think he's a writer and I seriously doubt his name is really Mike Finnigan."

"Is *this* something I should know about?" Erin asked hopefully.

"You know more about him than I do," Kit said.

Whether or not his story was the truth was another matter completely, Kit thought. All she knew was that he'd used that name and a phony address to hire a car so he could follow Geoffrey, or maybe Dalkeith. Or me, she added nervously to herself.

Kit couldn't think of a single reason why anybody would be tailing her but that didn't stop her from looking cautiously up and down Acland Street as she closed the front door of the *Star* office behind her. There seemed to be a great many suspicious-looking characters milling about on the footpath but none of them, she was relieved to notice, looked like a big moustachioed basset-eyed writer from Sydney.

The sun's glare, reflected off the window of a car on the other side of the street, stabbed into Kit's eyes reminding her that she hadn't had nearly enough sleep. Get a grip, O'Malley, she told herself as she pulled her sunglasses out of her pouch. So what if this Mike Finnigan is lurking in the background nearly everywhere you go, that does not mean that he, or anybody at all for that matter, is following you. The feeling that she might be completely wrong started as a creepy sensation on the back of her neck then tap danced all the way down her spine. She wouldn't swear to it in court but, in the split second before her eyes had adjusted to the filtered light of her sunglasses, she was sure she'd seen an all-too familiar face.

Kit turned abruptly and headed back towards her car, stopping every now and then to glance casually around or make use of a shop window to see if he was behind her in the crowd. It eventually dawned on her, however, that Tuesday must be official "Dishy Blond Boy Day" in Acland Street. The crowd was littered with variations on the theme and not one of them appeared to be at all interested in her. "Now you really are getting paranoid," she muttered to herself as she unlocked her stuffy car. "The mysterious Mr. Finnigan is one thing but there's no reason why Christo Snakehips would be on your tail, you idiot!"

Kit swung out into the traffic on Fitzroy Street and, as she headed back towards the junction, started scanning the buildings for numbers, looking for the one that belonged to Factor Four. She rolled her shoulders a few times to relieve the tension in her back. After a taste of what it must feel like to have someone following you, even if it had just been her imagination, Kit could almost understand Geoffrey Robinson's attempt to stop Byron from doing it, even though he hadn't been. It was definitely not a nice feeling. Of course in Geoffrey's case the belief that he was being watched was not his imagination. He'd just picked completely the wrong person to blackmail.

Kit laughed out loud. The idea that someone had her under surveillance was ludicrous. Unlike Geoffrey, who was being watched, and followed and photographed, because he had lots of things to hide and was generally up to no good, Kit had nothing to hide and wasn't up to anything much at all. All she did was watch people, and follow them and photograph them, then reveal their secrets to a third party who paid her for the service. What a life!

She pulled into a parking spot and walked across the road to the building that was located at the address on the business card Delvene had given her. The front window was emblazoned with the name Nostalgia Incorporated and in it was arranged a mannequin tableau of a turn-of-the-century wedding party. Listed in gold lettering on the front door were the names of businesses or photographers which Kit assumed were either part of Nostalgia Incorporated or used the premises. Foremost Factor Four was third on the list. The only other thing on the door was a curtain on the inside, which prevented anyone from seeing in, and a big white sign that said "Back in one hour."

"Oh great, what does that mean? One hour from an hour ago or have they only just left?" Kit looked at her watch. It was three o'clock. There was still time to kill before Geoffrey's appointment, whatever and wherever it was. Kit hadn't heard from Quinn so she had no idea whether the "family" was still meeting with Douglas or whether Quinn was traipsing around town after her stepfather.

There was also the possibility, of course, that Celia's cryptic note had not referred to one of Geoffrey's mystery rendezvous at all. Maybe she had wanted Kit to check out something else. But what? Celia had said something about a shipment in the message she'd left on Byron's answering machine, but that had been as light on details as her note.

Celia, Celia, Kit thought. I don't seem to be getting anywhere with this. And where the hell is Byron? Why didn't you at least ring and tell me about what your no-good husband tried to do to him? Realizing that the answers to those questions were not going to materialize out of thin air, Kit decided the sensible thing to do was to ring Douglas's office from her mobil to find out if Quinn and Geoffrey were still there. If they weren't, there was nothing she could do but go home and wait for Quinn to call.

As she stepped off the curb in front of a parked car she heard some-one yell: "Look out, lady!" Look out, lady? What the hell does that mean? Kit wondered. Does it mean "hey you in the polka dot dress, look out, there's a man pointing a gun at you," or "look out you with the pram, there's a big hole in the ground?" It was a pretty stupid thing to yell really when it would make most women wonder who, in this day and age, had the nerve to call anyone "lady."

While these thoughts passed through Kit's mind at warp speed she looked frantically about, just in case the yeller was in fact referring to her, until she noticed the blue Torana swerving across the road. Actually it wasn't so much swerving as bearing down on her with seri-ous intent. The driver, whose face she couldn't see, was not fighting to regain control of a runaway vehicle. He/she was definitely heading straight towards her with what could only be described as malice aforethought.

Kit threw herself backwards across the bonnet next to her and rolled off onto the footpath just as the Torana sideswiped the parked car then squealed off up the street.

"Holy shit!" Kit exclaimed as she struggled to her feet. The heels of her hands had absorbed most of her body's impact with the concrete but she'd also ripped the left knee of her jeans and grazed her elbow. "Ow, fuck! What the hell was that all about?" She rubbed her palms up and down on her thighs to get rid of the jagged pins and needles running from her fingertips to her elbows.

"Hey? Are you OK?" came a voice from behind her.

"Yeah, I'm fine. Sort of. Well, I'll be damned! If it isn't Hector . . . um . . ." Kit said in astonishment, trying to remember the guy's surname. She snapped her fingers a few times to help jog her memory till she realized the movement was hurting her hand. She was actually more surprised by the way Hector was dressed than she was by the fact that it was him.

"Chase. Hector Chase," he said. "If I'd known it was you, *Officer* O'Malley, I'da kept me mouth shut."

175

"Thanks a lot."

"Got to do my bit to keep the cop plague from getting out of control," he said with a grin.

"What's all this then?" Kit asked, reaching out to touch the fine silk of his short-sleeved shirt which was tucked neatly into a pair of black trousers. The last time she'd seen Hector he'd been wearing filthy jeans and a holey singlet and was having the crap beaten out of him by two skinheads after helping them rob a bottle shop. They had apparently decided they didn't want to share the spoils. He'd been sixteen then, which would make him about twenty-two now.

"You knocking off clothing stores now?"

"No!" he said indignantly. "I don't do that shit no more. I'm into computers now."

"What, stealing them or operating them?"

"Programming them, *Officer*, not that it's any of your business. I shoulda let the bastard run you down."

"Did you see the bastard?"

Hector rolled his blue eyes as if he was thinking hard. He removed a rubber band from his wrist, gathered his shoulder-length brown hair back into a ponytail, then thrust his hands into his pockets and just stood there as if he was waiting for a bus.

"Give me a break, Shintaro," Kit said. "Would it make any difference if I told you I was no longer a cop?"

"It might. What happened? Were they too slow in promoting you to Police Commissioner?"

"Something like that. So, did you see his face or not?"

"Nup, the sun was right on the windscreen. I got the rego number though, if you're interested. Got a pen?"

"If I'm interested?" Kit said taking a biro from her pouch.

While Hector pulled out his wallet and removed a business card to write the registration number down, Kit took the time to do a body check. She turned her left hand over and picked out a tiny piece of gravel that was embedded in the skin then inspected her leg through the hole in her jeans. Her knee was grazed and bloody.

"At least your jeans are fashionable now," Hector said.

"Nah, that was last week. I'd have to sew a piece of hippy batik over the hole to be in this week. So who do you work for?" Kit asked, studying the card which had Hector's name and a phone number on it under the word Graffico.

"Me, myself and I. I'm a freelance computer whiz."

"Really? Do you get enough work to support yourself?" Kit asked.

"What are you trying to say?"

"Nothing. I'm just asking."

"Well, yeah, I do. Most of the time. Some weeks are better than others. But I can pay the rent and I'm not starving and I have time to do my own stuff, inventing programs and games."

"I'm impressed," Kit said.

"Yeah sure. Bad boy done good, right?"

"No, not that at all. Although I must admit that is also impressive. I just happen to be in awe of anyone who can do more with a computer than turn it on, tap away for a while and turn it off again without losing everything into a black hole."

"I can manage a bit more than that," Hector grinned.

"I don't suppose you'd be interested in helping me upgrade my antique, would you? I'd like to get one of those modem things and have no idea what I need," Kit said.

"Sure. I don't sell the stuff but I can help you buy it and I'll set it up for you."

"Great, I'll give you a ring. On second thoughts, here, take my card," Kit said. "If you don't hear from me in the next week just ring and remind me. I have a system failure every time I think about my computer. The idea of actually giving it more things to do is a truly frightening concept. I'll pay you for your time."

"You *are* still a cop," Hector exclaimed, holding her business card at arm's length.

"No, I'm not. I'm a freelance inquiry whiz. It pays the rent, I'm not starving and it gives me time to do my own stuff."

"Did that guy try to run you down because of your own stuff or because of this?" Hector asked waving the card.

"I have absolutely no idea why he tried to run me down, but thanks to you I'm at least still alive enough to be able to try and find out. Which is what I'm going to do right now. Thanks again, Hector. I'm serious about that modem stuff, so call me, OK?"

"Sure. Catch you later then," he said.

This time Kit did all the things a sensible person should do before stepping out onto a main road. She looked right, looked left, looked right again and, most importantly, looked out for a homicidal Torana. The coast appeared to be clear.

"Hey, O'Malley," Hector called out. "If you ever need any help with your freelance inquiries give me a call. You know I'm good at getting into places."

"Shit!" Kit exclaimed as she turned to make a smart remark and an arrow of pain shot through her knee. Hector hadn't stuck around for her response anyway; he was already swaggering up the street.

Kit took a look at the car whose bonnet she'd rolled across. The driver's door was stoved in and the side mirror was mangled. The injuries caused by the Torana were actually quite minor, however, compared with the broken panels and scars of past collisions. Either the car was habitually parked in the wrong place at the wrong time or the driver should never have been given a license. Kit pulled a scrap of paper from her pocket, wrote the Torana's rego down and stuck it under the windscreen wiper.

She checked the traffic again then limped across the road to her car. She dialled the number of Jenkins, Cazenove, Scott and Harris and drummed her fingers on the steering wheel in time to Jimmy Barnes's rendition of *River Deep, Mountain High* blaring from her radio while she waited for the jolly Margaret Richards to put her through to Douglas.

"Ah, Kit," he said when he came on the line. "Where are you?"

"Fitzroy Street, Douglas. I gather your meeting is over."

"Geoffrey left here about half an hour ago. He said he had to get back to the office. Elizabeth followed him. I must say I don't really approve of that."

"She'll be fine, Douglas. It's keeping her occupied, you know. Have you heard from Alex by any chance?"

"Not yet. But she only left here at one-thirty."

"Could you tell her that Quinn and I will be at Angie's this evening if she needs to find us? Unless of course we're still following Geoffrey all over town."

"I'll leave that message with Margaret. I was just about to leave for the airport. I have to be in Sydney tomorrow so I'm taking a flight this evening."

Kit hung up and dialled directory assistance to get the number for Orlando House, feeling pretty stupid when she thanked the tinny computer voice that came back on-line with the number.

"No, I'm sorry, Mr. Robinson is not in at the moment," OHP's receptionist stated a few seconds later. "Could I take a message?"

"Perhaps his secretary could help," Kit suggested, wondering if Ms. Enigma, the transvestite-lesbian, would divulge Geoffrey's whereabouts to a total stranger. It was such a pity that the motor-mouth general dogsbody Julie What's-her-name wasn't Geoffrey's personal assistant.

"No, I'm sorry, Ms. Armstrong is not in today," the receptionist was saying. "Oh, Mr. Robinson has just returned. Would you like to hold? It could be some time, perhaps you could give me your name and number and I'll have him return your call when he can."

"Of course. My name is Ellen Ripley and he can reach me on 555-2343," Kit replied, giving the standard Hollywood prefix for movie phone numbers.

Kit started up the car and pulled out into the traffic. She thought about heading to Orlando House in the hope of catching up with Quinn there but decided it could be a waste of time. Geoffrey might be in and out of the office in five minutes and she'd miss them anyway.

She headed through the junction and left up Punt Road, deciding to go back to the office and pick up the photo of Christo Snakehips. If she had time she'd drop it off with Damien and ask him to show it to Tooly. When she stopped for a red light at the Domain Road intersection she called Marek and asked him to trace the Torana's rego.

"This is masochistic. I've got to get air-conditioning," she growled. She glanced up at the clock on the Nylex silo as she coasted down the hill and across the Yarra. It was thirty-nine degrees! No wonder she was melting. If Quinn didn't ring in the next ten minutes she might at least have time to change out of her ripped and sweaty clothes and tend her wounded knee.

Chapter 16

"Have you been out street fighting again, Katherine?" Brigit asked, laboring down the street towards the front door of Aurora Press. At least Kit thought it was Brigit. The overall appearance of the body looked familiar, and the woman was laden with shopping bags which was certainly typical, but there was something completely extraterrestrial about the hairdo.

"Chantelle, right?" Kit said, bending down to stop the contents of one of the shopping bags from rolling into the gutter as Brigit dumped her load at Kit's feet.

"Take it from me, Kit, no matter how desperate you are for a hair-cut in the next month do *not* break down and let that deranged woman get anywhere near you with a pair of scissors. Or a bottle of dye. Have you seen Angie? She looks like a fire truck."

"Yours doesn't look too bad, Brigit," Kit lied.

"Please do not attempt to humor me. Some guy up the street just asked me for the name of my hairdresser because he needs someone to cut his front hedge. This is no laughing matter, Kit. And what about you? You look like you've been auditioning for a role in *The Texas Chainsaw Massacre*."

"Someone tried to run me over with their car."

"Whatever for?"

"I have absolutely no idea, but I'm obviously pressing somebody's buttons." Kit leant back on her car to take the weight off her knee which, in the time it had taken her to clean the wound and change into a pair of shorts and a loose cotton shirt, had changed color three times and was now a vibrant purple.

"What are you doing loitering out here in the heat anyway?" Brigit asked, as if the fact that Kit had been attacked by someone wielding a motor vehicle was not in the least unusual.

"I'm waiting for a call," she replied, pointing to her mobile, "so I know which direction to drive."

"Oh. Ah, speaking of cars, Del took off in ours to pick up that dreadful Miranda Prentice from the airport and take her to Brighton, quite overlooking the fact that I have no way to get home with all this stuff. Could you give me a lift?" Brigit asked, gathering up her shopping.

"Maybe. I'm waiting for Quinn to ring and tell me where she is. You might be able to drop me off with her and take my car home, if you like."

"Perfect. I'll just put all this in the back if you'd like to pop the hatch."

The phone started bleating as Kit was helping Brigit load the car. She dived across the passenger seat and picked up the receiver.

"Quinn Orlando to Kit O'Malley. Over."

"It's a telephone, Quinn, not a CB radio," Kit laughed. "It's quarter past four, where the hell have you been? And where are you calling from?"

"Oh god, I have been all over the place in the last hour or so. I followed the pig to Orlando House. I called you from there but your line was engaged. He came out about five minutes later with a briefcase he hadn't gone in with, then he drove back into the city to the Regent Hotel. I rang you from there too 'cause I figured maybe that was where the meeting was, only you didn't answer. I was about to go in after the arsehole when I realized that the valet was watching his car for him rather than parking it. Anyway he came out again about ten minutes ago with that American guy you had the photo of."

"David Watts. I wonder when he came back." Kit motioned to Brigit to get into the car. "Quinn, where are you calling from?" she asked.

"From the car I hired. I'm following the prick down Flinders Street towards Spencer Street at the moment. The traffic is shitty, we sat at the Russell Street intersection for three light changes."

"You hired a car?" Kit said in astonishment as she pulled out into the Swan Street traffic and headed towards the Tennis Center.

"Yeah, well, I didn't want to use Mum's car in case he recognized it."

"Good thinking Ninety-nine," Kit said.

"Well I thought so. Where are you?"

"I've just crossed Punt Road, heading in your general direction. I'll take Alexandra Avenue and then cut across from City Road. Keep me posted in case I have to change my route. Over and out, OK?"

"So what's with you and this Quinn then?" Brigit asked, after a few minutes of what could only be described as studied silence. Her tone implied that, whatever it was, it had to be juicy and definitely worth something on her gossip scale.

"There's nothing with me and this Quinn, Brigit," Kit stated. She planted her foot and took off from the lights on the Swan Street Bridge and swung into Alexandra Avenue.

"Uh huh," Brigit said, sounding unconvinced as she twiddled with the dial of the car radio. "I heard she was with you at Angie's last night."

Kit flashed Brigit an incredulous look. "It amazes me that your grapevine hasn't completely strangled you with useless information."

Brigit raised an eyebrow, put on her best "I must be right if you're getting so defensive" expression and settled back in her seat after finally choosing a radio station.

"Don't give me that look, Brigit Wells. I know what you're thinking and in this case you are quite wrong." Kit jabbed her Melissa Etheridge tape into the cassette player to kill the mind-numbingly banal song by yet another thin-voiced pop bimbo with no surname that was polluting the airwaves.

"And what was wrong with that music, Miss Snooty Britches?"

"It had to have been damaging the ozone layer, Brigit, it was certainly insulting my intelligence. It's probably what Chantelle psychs herself up with before she does a blow wave."

"Oh, ha ha. So anyway, if there's nothing with you and this Quinn what were you doing together at Angie's?"

"Having a drink after a hard day and night's work. And we weren't alone anyway. Don't tell me your grapevine only supplied you with

182

half the gossip." Kit made a right turn along Southbank Boulevard to take Queens Bridge back across the river towards the south-west corner of the Central Business District.

"What? Who? Tell me. Pretty please. I'll stop teasing you, I promise."

"You are hopeless, Brigit."

"I can't help it, it's in my genes. I know, let me guess. It was that woman who turned up to see you when Del was leaving yesterday. Tell me all. Is she the one who's got your knickers in a knot?"

"My knickers are fine, Brigit. You're the one who seems to be having problems sitting still."

"So who was she?"

"Alexis Cazenove. She's Quinn's friend, she's a lawyer and before you get any fresh ideas about me and my underwear the woman is, for the most part, quite disagreeable. And what's more, for some unknown reason, she does not like me."

"Oh," Brigit said, dejected. "That's it?"

"That's it. If you want to know anything else about her, ask Angie," Kit said as she was rescued from further cross-examination by the phone.

"Angie? Why Angie?" Brigit demanded while Kit was asking Quinn where she was.

"You would not believe this traffic," Quinn complained. "It's taken about three days just to go six blocks. I'm still in Flinders Street, just over Spencer near the World Trade Center, sitting in a jam caused by the biggest bloody truck I've ever seen in my life."

"That's good, Quinn. It's given me time to catch you up. I'm a couple of blocks behind you, just waiting to turn into Flinders. Where's Geoffrey?"

"The ugly stepbastard is right behind the truck, luckily, or I would have lost him. Oh joy, we're finally moving."

"What sort of car are you driving?" Kit asked as she took the corner and swerved out onto the tram tracks to overtake a Renault that was moving like a slug.

"It's a black Suzuki Vitara jeep thing. It's so neat to drive. I think I'll buy myself one."

And add it to the Orlando-Robinson motor pool, Kit thought. "Keep the line open, Quinn. My guess is he's going to take Footscray Road. This is the route Dalkeith took the day I followed him to that wasteland on the Maribyrnong."

"I don't think so, Kit, he's not turning. We're going straight across into North Wharf Road. Well, I think we've just found out what North 4 at five p.m. means."

"Careful, Quinn. Don't get too close. We don't want to blow it now."

"Don't worry, there's two vans and a taxi between me and him."

"Well, I seem to have half the truck population of Melbourne between me and you," Kit said as she changed lanes and pulled up for a red light at Footscray Road.

"There she is," Brigit said, pointing to the Vitara which was the last vehicle to cross the tracks of the Webb Dock rail line.

"Who's with you?" Quinn asked.

"Brigit," Kit replied. "She's going to drop me off with you and take my car home."

"Shithead's pulling up at the customs gate."

"OK. Can you pull over, Quinn? They're not likely to let you through the customs gate anyway."

"Sure. There's a parking bay on my left here opposite the . . . ah . . . Australian Customs Service building."

Kit had to slow her car momentarily while the truck in front of her geared down to turn through the gate by the huge triple silos of a cement company. She pulled up behind the Vitara, unhooked her apartment keys from the chain hanging from the ignition and reached over the back to grab her camera bag.

"Thanks, Brigit. You can keep the car till tomorrow. I can get a lift home from Angie's later with Alex or Quinn."

"Fine. We might see you there later then," Brigit said suggestively.

Great, Kit thought as she got out of her car. Brigit had probably been planning a nice quiet night at home till you opened your big mouth. There's no way she'll stay home now.

"Hit it, partner," Kit said as she flung open the door of Quinn's car and leapt in.

"I was contemplating a career change until I realized how much of my young life I'd have to spend in traffic tailing bastards in Bentleys," Quinn said, squeezing the Vitara in between two trucks the size of aircraft carriers.

"And when you're not in traffic you spend hours sitting in deserted alleys just waiting, watching and waiting. At least you've got air-conditioning," Kit said. She shut her eyes and leant over the vents to cool off. The peculiar vision of Quinn in little round sunglasses and a ludicrous orange towelling hat took a few seconds to register in her mind. "What on earth is that thing on your head?"

"It's my disguise. It's Enzo's fishing hat."

"It's disgusting! Let's throw it in the Yarra while we're here and drown it."

"Enzo would kill me."

"Enzo has a problem, I think," Kit said. So does Alex, she thought.

"What now?" Quinn asked as they approached the customs gate.

A scrawny looking port official armed with a clipboard appeared to be giving Geoffrey a hard time.

"Hang a left into the car park," Kit said, pulling her camera out of its bag.

Quinn swung into the parking area and pulled up behind a barrier of knotty trees that separated the lot from the road.

"Looks like they're not going to let *him* in either," Quinn said as they watched Geoffrey back the Bentley away from the customs gate and make an awkward left-hand U-turn. "I think he's coming in here!"

"Don't panic, just pull Enzo's pride and joy down a bit and ignore them. Does this baby come with a street directory?" Kit asked as she slouched down in the seat.

"Glovebox," Quinn replied. She turned to face Kit as she adjusted the rear-view mirror to keep an eye on Geoffrey.

Kit pulled out the *Melways* and, using it to screen her face, looked up the map for Victoria Dock. "Bingo. This couldn't be a better spot," she said softly. "If North 4 means berth or warehouse four on North Wharf, then it's this side of the dock."

"They're getting out," Quinn stated. "God, he's a big man."

The American, dressed in black trousers and a gray leather jacket, was unfolding his tall broad-shouldered body from the passenger seat of the Bentley which had pulled up about fifteen feet away. Geoffrey was already out and pacing, a wild gale playing havoc with his tailored hair.

"David Watts," Kit said as she glanced at him over the top of the directory. "If he's a businessman on holiday then I'm Dame Edna. What's more, I'll lay odds he's actually the elusive Davis Whitten who Alex's pal in Sydney hasn't been able to track down yet."

"Where did that wind come from?" Quinn exclaimed as the jeep was buffeted from several directions at once.

"I don't know," Kit said, "but it looks like we're in for a mighty storm. With any luck it'll pick Geoffrey up by the ears and dump him in the bay."

They watched as Geoffrey and the American approached the customs gate on foot. This time they were allowed access.

"Start her up, Quinn. We can drive along the river side of the wharf."

North Wharf ran westwards from the customs gate forming a small peninsula between the Yarra on one side and the main basin of Victoria Dock on the other. It was divided almost in half down its full length by a cyclone wire fence, the basin side being a restricted area.

"Don't cruise along as if you're following them, Quinn. Just keep going, and park a bit beyond berth four, facing the river," Kit said as she clambered over into the back of the jeep. "OK. This will do. Pull in now."

When the car came to a stop Kit raised her camera. Geoffrey and the American were still making their way up the wharf, struggling against the wind. She swung the lens around to check out the huge corrugated iron warehouse allocated to berth four on the other side of the fence. All the doors were open and she could see through to the water on the other side. One doorway framed a small section of the

Melbourne city skyline, another was half filled by the bow of a huge cargo vessel which was riding high in the water, and another revealed the back end of a truck parked on the wharf.

"The place looks empty," Quinn said, craning her neck to get a better view.

"Except for the section directly in front of us I think it is," Kit replied. "There's a ship's container being loaded onto the back of a truck, a few guys standing around watching and another two having what appears to be a serious disagreement."

Kit began taking photos of Geoffrey and his partner in alleged crime as they approached the warehouse. The wind had picked up even more and the two men were almost blown into the darkness inside the building.

Swollen black clouds were casting a murky pall over the entire city, as if someone had used a dimmer switch to turn down the sunlight, and when Geoffrey reappeared on the other side of the warehouse Kit could barely pick out his features, even with the telephoto lens.

"Kit, what happened to your knee?" Quinn asked. "Oh, and your elbow?"

While they waited for Geoffrey to make his next move Kit filled Quinn in on the events of the day. Quinn suggested that perhaps it was the mysterious Mike Finnigan who had tried to run her down, but Kit doubted he would change cars just to put an end to her involvement in whatever they were involved in. "Besides, I still have a hunch that he's a private detective or something, rather than one of the bad guys," she added.

"So what's the story with your knight in shining armor?" Quinn asked.

"Who? Oh, you mean Hector. I picked him up a few times for minor offenses about seven years ago, the first time for joyriding around Albert Park Lake in a stolen car. He was only fifteen so they put him on a good-behavior bond and placed him in foster care for three months. He'd been in and out of foster homes since he was about ten because his mother was a junkie. The last time I arrested him—for helping a bunch of skinheads break into a bottle shop in the middle of the night and steal a carload of booze—I put in a good word for him during his court case. He got three months at one of the country youth training centers."

"Don't tell me you like kids," Quinn said as if it was a serious character flaw.

"Not particularly. Marek does however. He was always fronting up

187

in court as a character witness, hoping to help keep some kid off the streets. He supported too many lost causes for my liking but every now and then even I came across someone who was worth going the extra yard for, so I guess Marek's attitude sort of rubbed off on me. I figured if these kids were always treated like deadshits with no future then that's probably how they'd turn out. Hector was one of a few where I could see that it actually might do some good to stand up for him. The social workers kept taking him away from his mother but he loved her and there was no one else to look after her so he kept running away and going home. He wasn't a bad kid, just a bit lost. And he was smart. Despite his mother's habit and the trouble he kept getting into, mostly because of his friends, he barely missed a day of school."

"He sounds smarter than me," Quinn said. "I was always skipping school."

"Start the engine, Quinn, the two stooges are on their way out." Kit clicked off a couple more shots as Geoffrey and the American emerged from the warehouse and headed back towards the customs gate.

Quinn pulled up near Geoffrey's car, where they'd been parked before, and Kit struggled back into the passenger seat.

"Orlan Carriers," Quinn stated flatly. "That prick!"

"What?"

"The truck coming out through the gate. It's one of ours. I think we can assume it's the one that was just being loaded. Do we follow it or Geoffrey now?"

"The truck. The info Alex got for me on Orlan Carriers' association with Freyling Imports was a bit light on details. There were twelve jobs in the last eighteen months, mostly carting stuff from Freyling's head office in South Melbourne to either Wellborn's video and instant printing stores or to one of Freyling's otherwise unaffiliated clients. None of the trucks picked up a load from the docks before, so I think that's our best bet. But wait till Geoffrey leaves the car park."

Instead of taking the road Kit and Quinn had come in by, the truck turned left out of the customs gate then pulled over to the side. A couple of minutes later Geoffrey stopped his Bentley beside the truck; when he took off again the truck followed him.

"Interesting. It looks like we can follow both of them. This is Pigott Street. It comes out on Footscray Road," Kit said, as Quinn waved a white van ahead of her then joined the procession. "You're good at this. Maybe you *should* contemplate a career change. What would you be changing from, by the way?"

"Journalism. I've been working for a magazine called *Crash* in London. It used to be a really radical publication back in the seventies, when I was just a baby. It's a bit more mainstream these days but it still tries to fight the good fight and deal with *the* issues, you know. These days it also covers alternative lifestyles, arts and music. It's fun. But, ah, it doesn't look like I'll be going back."

"Why not?"

"Because," Quinn said, turning left onto Footscray Road, "my mother has left me fifty of her seventy per cent of the company. I am now the major shareholder of Orlando House and, as of two p.m. today, chairperson of the board."

"Holy shit! That's great, Quinn. She didn't leave Geoffrey anything?" Kit said gleefully.

"Not a cent. In fact, of the remaining twenty per cent she gave another five to Miles Denning and the rest to Uncle Douglas."

"So with only ten per cent Geoffrey is now the most minor of shareholders," Kit said.

"Precisely. Needless to say he is extremely pissed off. He doesn't know yet that I get the house as well. She cut him right out of everything. Some revenge, eh?"

Kit glanced over at Quinn, whose voice had been completely devoid of emotion. There was certainly no better way to get back at Geoffrey, but Celia had paid too high a price much too soon to exact that revenge. That thought, or something like it, was obviously going through Quinn's mind as well. She was gripping the steering wheel so tightly her knuckles were white.

"Are you OK?" Kit asked gently. "Do you want me to drive?"

"No, I'm fine. I'd rather drive. Oh god, Kit! What the fuck am I going to do with a Toorak mansion and a multi-million-dollar publishing company?"

"You're asking me?" Kit laughed. "I barely make enough money to keep Thistle in the manner to which she thinks she should be accustomed. I rent my apartment at the incredibly low rate I do only because it belongs to Del, and my fifteen-year-old car operates mostly on wishful thinking—its own, I think. It never quite breaks down enough for me to have to take a gun and put it out of my misery."

Quinn grinned and relaxed her grip, then changed lanes to follow Geoffrey and the Orlan Carriers truck as they made a right-hand turn off Footscray Road just over the narrow Maribyrnong River.

"I think I'm way too young to be a tycoon," she said.

"But just think of the thrill you'll get when you fire Geoffrey," Kit stated.

"Yeah, totally orgasmic. I don't suppose *you'd* like a career change? There'll be an opening for a business manager at OHP . . . oh . . . very soon now."

Chapter 17

"This is a charming neighborhood," Quinn said.

"Perhaps we should call the government's Noxious Weeds Department and report the weird vegetation in these parts," Kit said.

"No, no. The Royal Botanic Gardens should know about this. We've probably discovered a new sub-species or genus or something. We might get to name it."

"Sure, Australis rustycarus," Kit suggested.

"Or Holdenbotanicus," Quinn laughed as she slowed the jeep to a crawl. When Geoffrey's Bentley and the truck had taken a turn down a side street towards the river Kit had told Quinn to keep going so they could circle the next block and approach Dalkeith's riverfront property from the other direction to avoid being spotted. They were currently cruising a narrow street with houses on the right-hand side and landscaped parkland running down to the river on their left.

"This is spooky," Kit said. "It's almost like the residents around here have to conform to some kind of warped zoning regulations for front gardens. Every second house is growing car wrecks and mutant dandelions and the ones in between have manicured lawns and a line of rose bushes up against their front fences."

"Do-de-do-do, do-de-do-do," Quinn sang. "We are now entering the Twilight Zone."

"Good heavens. I'd have thought that was well before your time, Ms. Too-young-to-be-a-tycoon."

"The best TV shows always come back," Quinn said. "Or get made into blockbuster movies."

"Please tell me you're a Trekker too," Kit said.

"Next Generation, absolutely! I'd have given my Toorak mansion to spend time on a holodeck with Captain Picard or Tasha Yar."

"I'd rather jump to warp speed with Jadzia Dax or Captain Janeway myself," Kit said. "Whoa, pull over," she added, as the park on their left stopped abruptly at the shiny fence which marked the boundary of the land Ian Dalkeith had such big plans for. It looked even more like a prime location for a movie set in a nuclear-devastated future than it had the first time Kit had seen it. The wind, which had a clear passage through the desolate paddock, was lifting scraps of rubbish in a frenzied dance amongst the derelict machinery while a length of metal cable, whipping furiously like a cut snake, was clanging against a rusty crane carcass.

"It looks like a rubbish tip," Quinn said.

"I think it's actually where obsolete machines come to die," Kit said. "Oh, but I do love it when another mystery bites the dust," she added.

"What?"

"That nice sign wasn't up the last time I was here," Kit replied pointing at the gate.

"Freyling Imports Storage Company," Quinn read. "So?"

"The other rendezvous in your mother's note, remember? It was eleven p.m. on Wednesday at 'FISC'. Now we know the when *and* the where, all I have to do is be here to find out the what and the why."

"What about the what and why of this afternoon though?" Quinn asked.

"Well, we can't get any closer than this," Kit said, clicking off a few shots despite the fact that there wasn't a lot of activity to shoot. Geoffrey and his car had disappeared from view around the other side of the group of warehouses and the driver of the truck, which was parked in plain view in front of a loading platform, had entered through a half-raised cargo bay door.

"Tomorrow night, however," Kit continued, "I'll get here early and try to get inside for a closer look."

"There's a Mercedes going in now," Quinn stated.

"Ian Dalkeith," Kit said. She raised her camera again to catch the white sports car passing through the open gates. The first photo was blurred by another vehicle which came up the street from behind them and flashed through her line of sight as the shutter opened.

"Kit," Quinn said, but Kit was busy lining up the Mercedes again as it crossed the fifty or so meters of gravel and couch grass between the gate and the warehouse.

"Kit, look!" Quinn said more urgently, pointing up the street.

The car which had overtaken them and ruined her shot had slowed to turn into the street opposite the gates of Freyling Imports. It was a battered brown station wagon.

"Got you this time, Mr. Finnigan!" Kit exclaimed. "And there's only one way to find out who you really are. Here, Quinn, take the camera and keep an eye on the bad guys. Photograph anything that moves. I'll be back in a second."

Kit was out of the car before she'd finished speaking. She tried to sprint up the street but between the gale force winds and the invisible daggers that were attacking her left knee it was more like an out-of-control lope. She felt like Quasimodo on the last leg of a marathon. When she got level with the driveway of the house on the corner she stopped and leant on the front gate. It was one of the "you must cut your lawn and grow roses" residences with a high paling fence down the side which bordered the other street. As she edged her way towards the corner Kit could hear the familiar whirr of a motor-driven camera even over the wind that was screaming through all the metal debris on Dalkeith's lot.

K. F. O'Malley continues her mission to boldly go, Kit thought as she took a deep breath, straightened her shoulders and walked as casually as possible around the corner—straight into the personal space of the alleged writer from Sydney.

"What the hell!" he shouted, stooping to pick up his camera bag which had fallen from his shoulder when he stumbled backwards.

"Well, well, well—if it isn't Mike Finnigan. We must stop meeting like this," Kit said cheerily, as if they were long-lost mates.

"Oh, it's you," he said, as if he'd wished they'd stayed lost. "What do you think you're doing, you stupid bitch, you nearly scared the bejesus out of me."

"Charming. With an attitude like that I think your bejesus could do with a little scaring. Who the hell are you anyway?"

"Piss off, woman, you're going to ruin everything!"

"*I'm* going to ruin everything? Half of Melbourne knows that when you're not living in a park in Balwyn you're following Ian Dalkeith all over town in a rent-a-wreck."

He rolled his eyes at her and scratched the back of his head, the combined actions making him look even more like a basset hound. The huge red moustache, which just about covered the whole lower half of his face, was fairly bristling with annoyance.

"Look, Girl Scout, we've got separate business here. I ain't stopping you from doing your job tailing that pissant Robinson, so just get out of my face, will you?"

"Oh sure, fine, Mr. Finnigan-Begin-Again," Kit said. "But what makes you so sure our business is so separate? As I said, we've got to stop meeting like this."

"Great, have it your own way. Just stay out of mine, OK?" Finnigan thrust his camera into its bag. "I am going now, if that's all right with you."

Kit shrugged and waved her arm in the direction of his station wagon. She waited till he'd opened the door before she turned to head back to Quinn.

"Hey, O'Malley," he called out. He was resting his big hairy arms on the car roof. "Take my advice and stay away from Dalkeith. He's a nasty piece of work."

"As you said, Finnigan, separate business," Kit said, throwing her palms up. "But I've got some advice for you. Get a new wreck. That one may as well be wearing a big 'yoohoo, I'm following you' sign."

Halfway back to the Vitara someone unzipped the sky over Kit's head and by the time she threw herself into the passenger seat she was drenched to the skin.

"So who is he?" Quinn asked.

"Beats me," Kit shrugged. "Which is extremely annoying because *he* knows who I am. What's happened in there?"

"Nothing much. They unloaded the container in about ten seconds flat. A forklift took about fifty huge crates inside. I got pics. There's been no movement since then."

"Well, we can't see a thing through this driving rain. Let's get the hell out of here. It's already after seven and I need a drink. Not to mention some dry clothes."

Kit ran her hands through her hair and knocked her forehead on the bar several times.

"You see," Brigit said, "she's totally flipped over this one."

"Brigit, if I'd had even half the sexual encounters you give me credit for I'd be a physical wreck."

"I'm not talking about encounters, Kit darling. I'm merely pointing out the state you get in when you're consumed by lust."

"The state I'm in happens to be one of exhaustion," Kit said.

"Stop teasing her, Brigit. You sound like one of those breathless romance writers from the American Deep South," Del said. "Now hush up. The beautiful blond heiress with the heaving bosom, whose blue eyes light up only for the dashing private detective on my right, is on her way back."

Kit groaned. Quinn didn't have a whole lot of bosom to heave but it didn't help Kit's case one little bit that the beautiful blond heiress clasped her hand, flashed her blue eyes and demanded that Kit dance the next dance with her. And she didn't need to see the look that passed between her two friends to know the type of expression that accompanied Brigit's strangled giggle. It dawned on her, however, that it was possibly to her advantage that Brigit and Del were convinced she was in a state over Quinn, as they might not notice her become completely unglued when Alex turned up. *If* Alex turned up.

Kit slipped off her stool, shrugged at Del's knowing look and led Quinn back into the Red Room where several women were already singing and dancing along to the deafening strains of Gloria Gaynor's *I Will Survive*. As Quinn flung herself around the floor Kit wondered if her too-young-to-be-a-tycoon dance partner realized that this song was something else that had been around since she was just a baby.

Three songs later, just as Kit was lamenting her own dear departed youth and wondering if she was going to be exhausted for the rest of her life, the DJ changed the pace from something that vaguely resembled music, only inasmuch as it had a definite beat, to k. d. lang's *Constant Craving*.

195

"If we don't slow down I'm going to die," Kit said as she slipped her arm around Quinn's waist. "My knee is certainly going to give out for good."

"You poor old thing," Quinn said in her ear, then pulled back a bit and looked at Kit with an expression that was seriously confused. "There must be something dreadfully wrong with me. I'm sure I should feel guilty about having a good time. But I don't. Is that awful?"

"Oh, Quinn. There's nothing wrong with what you're doing, or with you. Believe me, I know what it's like. Everybody deals with loss in their own time. And in their own way," Kit said softly.

"I suppose so," Quinn acknowledged. "Mum's hair turned completely white overnight when my father was killed. A week later it had all fallen out and it never grew back."

"Is that what the problem was? I'd been meaning to ask you," Kit admitted.

Quinn shrugged. "I guess not everyone reacts that dramatically to a personal tragedy, but I should be feeling *something*, apart from disgust with myself for being so unfeeling. I'm sure other people are thinking I don't give a damn."

"What's this other people shit? Look," Kit began, then took a deep breath; she couldn't believe it was still so hard to even bring this subject up. There was nothing she could do about the tremor in her voice. "There was a time when those ubiquitous 'other people' would have thought I was totally insensitive. I lost a very dear friend, Hannah Beaumont, in a stupid accident a couple of years ago. She was killed by a drunk driver when she was walking home from work."

"That's awful. I'm so sorry." Quinn's eyes were tearful. It was obviously easier for her to empathize with Kit's pain than it was to acknowledge her own.

"I just went totally blank," Kit continued. "I refused to accept that she wasn't going to be around any more. I didn't . . . I couldn't even go to her funeral."

"And for that people thought you were insensitive? Seems just the opposite to me," Quinn stated.

"Maybe. But then I went quite troppo afterwards because I hadn't gone. In an attempt to take my mind off what I was trying to pretend hadn't happened anyway Del took me to Flemington Racecourse.

Actually, I think she was hoping to snap me out of my state of nothingness by making me do something normal. It was certainly something that other people would have seen as an—I don't know—maybe inappropriate thing to do on the day of a friend's funeral. Anyway, I got so pissed I could barely stand and spent every cent I had backing horses that couldn't possibly win. Then, in the last event, this bush pony which had run last every start she'd ever had decided to win the one and only race of her career. The horse's name was Flying Hanna. Can you believe it? The trifecta I'd taken paid $1100. I spent the next three nights dancing, in this very room, while I drank that money too." Kit laced her fingers through Quinn's and rested her chin on their clasped hands. "Then I cried for a whole week."

Quinn pressed her lips together in a futile attempt to stop her chin from quivering. "I just feel like I'm still letting her down," she said.

"Oh, Quinn, she may not have understood you very well but she didn't think you'd let her down. Your mother was proud of you."

Quinn gave a short laugh as she wiped away the one tear that had managed to escape down her cheek. "That's what *your* mother said."

"Well, there you go—and take my word for it, it's not a good idea to doubt anything Lillian says," Kit grinned. She gathered Quinn closer into her arms. "Dance while you can," she whispered.

"Thanks, Kit," Quinn said as she buried her face in Kit's shoulder. "For everything."

Kit had no idea whether the shiver that went down her spine a few seconds later was caused by a rush of cool air from the door as it opened and closed or by the unsettling feeling, for the second time that day, that she was under surveillance. Whatever it was that actually made her look up, there was no denying it this time; someone *was* watching her, or them.

Kit kept hold of Quinn, thinking it might be a little too obvious to hastily push her back. But when k.d. lang was mercifully overtaken by Aretha Franklin and Annie Lennox she figured it was reasonable to let go, of both Quinn and the breath she'd been holding. Quinn gave her a bemused look as Kit suddenly danced away from her and back again before releasing her hand.

"Hey, Alex is here," Quinn shouted.

"I know," Kit said, in what she hoped was a careless tone.

Quinn bounced forward and peered at Kit quite intently, her mouth open in what could only be described as a lopsided and thoroughly idiotic smile. Kit wanted to die.

"Oh dear," Quinn said. "Not you too?"

"Don't you dare say a word, Quinn Orlando."

"My lips will be sealed," she said still grinning. "As soon as I can get my mouth shut."

"Oh god!" Kit groaned.

"Trust me, Kit," Quinn said, wiggling her eyebrows up and down. "Can you face going out there yet?"

"Of course I can, don't be ridiculous."

"OK, OK. Just watch where you're walking. I'd hate to see you trip over yourself now." Quinn screwed up her eyes, which were fairly sparkling with amusement, and slipped her arm through Kit's as they left the dance floor.

"Trust you, you say?" Kit queried as they approached Alex who, despite the scowl, looked totally ravishing with her hair pinned up at the back so there were only a few wispy strands on her neck. No one should look this good in old jeans and a T-shirt, Kit thought, wondering if she'd have to spend all her time being held upright by other people whenever she was within cooee of this woman. Life could become quite awkward.

"Hi Alex," Quinn crowed cheerfully, giving Alex a hug.

"Don't you think this is a little inappropriate, O'Malley?"

Oh sure, like I'm responsible, Kit thought. "Not particularly, Alex," she replied.

"Other people?" Quinn asked, looking at Kit.

"Yup," Kit nodded.

"I need a drink," Quinn said over her shoulder as she turned and pulled at the door. She winked knowingly at Kit on her way out.

"Tact is obviously not one of your strong points, Ms. Cazenove," Kit said, catching the door before it swung shut.

"I'm sorry. It's just . . ." Alex stopped herself when Kit kept walking. "O'Malley, wait," she added, clasping Kit's elbow.

That's done it, Kit thought. She stopped dead in her tracks and looked around for something to hang on to. "What?" she asked impatiently.

"I had a visit from Detective-Sergeant Marek. It was Quinn he wanted to see but . . ."

"And?" Kit urged softly, fearing the worst.

"It's been confirmed that Celia's death was *not* an accident. Your friend Marek is now treating it officially as a homicide. Byron is the number one suspect."

"Bloody hell!"

"That's more or less what I said. Can I buy you a drink?"

"Alex, I reckon Quinn is about this far from folding," Kit said, holding her thumb and index finger about a centimeter apart. "I think we should get her out of here before we drop this little bundle in her lap."

"Good idea. Your place?"

"If that suits you. You could follow us."

"But you've been drinking."

"Quinn hasn't. She might need you to drive her home later though. I think she'll be wanting something stronger than mineral water when she gets this news."

"I knew it! I just knew it. Just wait till I get my hands on that fucking bastard. I'm going to rip his lousy stinking heart out!" Quinn cried as she stomped back and forth through the kitchen. Right now they were tears of anger but it was obvious that Quinn was close to breaking point.

Kit stopped her from pacing and thrust a glass of bourbon into her hand. "Drink it, Quinn," she ordered.

Quinn did as she was told. "I don't even like bourbon," she said with a sour expression, holding the empty glass out for a refill. "Is that Thistle making that weird noise?"

"Well, it's either Thistle the Watchcat or the begonia has learnt how to growl," Kit said. "Alex must be on her way up."

"Grangkle," Thistle said as Kit scratched her behind the ears on her way past The Cat's sentry post at the top of the stairs.

"Grangkle? That's a new one, Thistle. What happened to Manuel?"

"I'm glad I didn't have that drink before we left Angie's," Alex said when Kit opened the door. "I got picked up by a booze bus."

Lucky booze bus, Kit thought as she followed Alex up the stairs. "Well, you can have one now, but I'll put some coffee on as well."

Quinn accepted then broke away from Alex's sympathetic hug. "I'm fine, Alex, except that I'm *really* pissed off now. I'm going to put some music on."

Kit shrugged in response to the questioning glance that Alex cast in her direction as she sat down at the breakfast bar.

"You wouldn't have any brandy, would you?"

"Anything your heart desires," Kit said before she could stop herself. She turned away quickly to get the bottle from the cupboard. Shut *up*, O'Malley!

Quinn had chosen *King of Hearts* and as the Big O launched into *You're The One* Kit poured brandy all over the bench because she was watching Alex instead of what she was doing. Alex dragged her concerned gaze from Quinn as Kit swore loudly and grabbed for the dishcloth.

"Um, Kit?" Quinn called out. "Who's Sam?"

"What? Why?" Kit asked, chucking the cloth into the sink.

"I think you've got a Dear Jane letter. I didn't mean to read it. Sorry."

Kit tried to walk nonchalantly over to where Quinn was standing beside the dining table. She pushed her spare front door key off a large piece of paper and read the few words which were written in a quite unfamiliar scrawl. Kit realized she'd never seen Sam's handwriting before.

Kit honey, if you'd bothered to keep our appointment I wouldn't have to do it like this. It's pretty lousy, sorry. I've met someone in Sydney. This one feels right. You and I didn't seem to be going anywhere anyway. Maybe it is better done this way. I've taken my stuff. All the best. Sam.

"Well, that's that then." Kit screwed up the note.

"It was certainly short and to the point," Quinn said taking hold of Kit's hand.

"It's no big deal, Quinn, honestly," Kit said. She led Quinn back to the kitchen where she dropped the note in the bin, spun the lid off the Jack Daniels and refilled their glasses.

"So who is Sam?" Alex asked.

"History now," Kit replied.

"You seem pretty cool about it."

What do you care? Kit thought, feeling anything but cool under the steady gaze of those delicious gray eyes. "We hadn't seen each other for nearly two months," she explained, breaking the eye contact by looking down at her glass. "And seeing we only met three months ago it's not like it was a long-term thing. I suppose Sam pipped me at the post really. If I'd actually remembered she was going to be in town tonight I would have been the one to end it. Now, can we change the subject, please? What did Marek tell you?" She pushed the bottle into Quinn's outstretched hand.

Alex sighed deeply and after taking a sip of brandy turned towards Quinn. "The autopsy revealed that although your mother did in fact drown she was unconscious before she fell, or was pushed, into the pond. Her blood alcohol level was comparatively low. There was a deep scratch, probably made by a fingernail, on her collarbone and a large contusion on the back of her head. Someone hit her very hard with a champagne bottle."

Quinn gripped the bench with both hands and rocked back and forth. Her mouth was working in several directions at once as she tried desperately to swallow her rage. "Geoffrey's a dead man," she managed to say through gritted teeth.

"The police are looking for Byron. I mean seriously looking for him now. They think *he's* responsible."

"What shit!" Quinn snapped. She downed her drink in one mouthful, filled her glass again and drank that too.

"It might be shit, Quinn, but that's the line the police are taking," Alex said softly.

"We'll just have to find a better line," Kit said.

"Yeah. A clothesline—to hang him from," Quinn snarled. "Oh god, I think I'm going to be sick."

"Second door on the right," Kit called after her as Quinn made a dash up the hall. "She can probably throw up by herself," she added, when it looked as though Alex was going to follow her.

"I just thought . . . You're right of course." Alex sat down again, absently twirled a loose curl of hair around her index finger then rested her chin on the back of her hand. "Maybe I should just take her home," she added, in a tone that almost suggested she wasn't quite ready to leave. She gazed at Kit as if she was trying to read her mind.

Don't go yet, don't go yet. Think of something, O'Malley! Kit prompted herself. She had no idea how she'd cope with Alex on her own, she just knew she didn't want her to leave so soon. Sometime between now and the year 2000 she might be able to think of a better reason than work but right now that was all she had.

"We, I mean you and I, still have a few things to discuss, Alex," she began. "Quinn can sleep here, or lie down for a while, if she wants."

Kit put Quinn to bed in her spare room, after which Alex spent half an hour in there with her while Kit paced the lounge room wondering what to do with herself. She finally made a cup of camomile tea and carried it down the hall, stopping short in the doorway when she caught sight of Alex in the mirror. She was sitting on the edge of the bed, talking gently as she ran her hand affectionately through Quinn's hair. There has to be more to this than tea and sympathy, Kit thought. This woman is in serious denial if she really intends to marry the divine Enzo. And as for you, O'Malley, if there's not a psychological term to describe the lunacy of being uncontrollably attracted to an allegedly straight, about-to-be-married woman who's obviously denying her attraction to the beautiful blond heiress in your spare bed, then Brigit could probably invent one.

"Hey Kit," Quinn said softly.

"Hey to you too. I thought you might like a cuppa."

Alex dropped her hand, rather self-consciously Kit thought, and leant back so Kit could place the tea on the bedside table.

Fifteen minutes later, having left Quinn to try and get some sleep, Kit and Alex sat staring at each other over a pot of coffee. Kit's recap of her encounter with Mike Finnigan and his warning about Dalkeith had been followed by a pregnant pause of unbearable duration.

To avoid Alex's gaze, which was both lingering and questioning, Kit busied herself with the coffee pot. It seemed that Alex wanted but couldn't bring herself to ask Kit something personal.

It's more likely she's trying to think of a reason, that's not self-incriminating, to tell you to stay away from Quinn, Kit laughed to herself, as she poured the coffee.

"So you still think he's a private detective?" Alex queried.

"Or maybe an undercover cop." Kit handed a cup to Alex, then forced herself to relax back into her armchair by slinging her legs over one armrest.

"I also found out this morning that Edwina Barnes has been a patient at the Endicott Center for the last two years," Kit said.

"Really? Shirley Smith's been there longer than that," Alex stated.

"That figures, if she's a director."

"She may be on the board, but as a patient I doubt she has much say in how the place is run," Alex said, trying not to smile.

"What?"

"Shirley Smith is a manic depressive. She's been locked up out there for nine years."

"A manic depressive? I thought that could be self-treated with drugs."

Alex shrugged. "It can in many cases. The problem is that some manic depressives stop taking their medication as soon as they feel OK. Apart from being inclined to flush her pills down the toilet whenever she felt good, Shirley is also prone to psychotic episodes during which she is, and I quote, 'a danger to herself and others.' She apparently tried to kill her ex-husband with a garden rake then drove his sports car through the front wall of a neighbor's house. Her brother Malcolm had her committed after that little episode."

"Who was the husband?" Kit asked.

"I don't know. It was a fluke that I found out as much as I did. While I was driving out there I was trying to come up a plausible reason for turning up uninvited to ask vague questions about the center and one of the directors. As it turned out I went to uni with Endicott's assistant medical director. He told me about Shirley but said it wasn't worth his job to divulge anything else. Do you think the identity of the husband is relevant?"

"Probably not, especially if he was already an ex before she was committed, but we should cover all the bases. But I'm wondering why she's hospitalized down here instead of Sydney where her brother lives."

"I would assume being a director of the institution in which you happen to be confined would have some advantages," Alex stated.

"I guess so," Kit agreed. "I don't suppose you got to see Shirley in person?"

"A glimpse through a window across a crowded dining room. Peter pointed her out to me when he was walking me back to my car. I'll see if I can track down who the husband was if you think it might be important."

"That'd be great, thanks. In the meantime I'll keep looking for Byron. I bumped into a blond today who seemed to be at Ian Dalkeith's beck and call. He also happened to be the same guy I'd photographed with Geoffrey during my first night on this job. Quinn and I dropped the photo off with Damien this evening to see if he could get Tooly to identify him as the guy who picked up Byron at Route 69."

"Nothing we've found so far establishes a very good case for Byron's innocence. What do you think he's up to?"

"I suspect he may not be up to much at all," Kit said flatly. "If he *is* responsible, which I doubt, then he's obviously in hiding."

"And if he's not?"

Kit closed her eyes momentarily as she ran her hands through her hair. She was superstitious about voicing her fears, as if simply saying them out loud would make them true. "Then it's my guess that he is as dead as Celia is."

"But why?" Alex asked, although she didn't seem to be surprised by the suggestion.

"Why indeed. That's the sixty-four-dollar question. Why was Celia murdered? If Byron's alive, why has he vanished into thin air?" Kit ran her hands through her hair again.

"If this Christo character is the right blond boy," she continued, "then he is the last person, that we know of, to have seen Byron— dead or alive. And I've got a really bad feeling that the former state is more likely, especially when I see how the few pieces we do have in this jigsaw are starting to fit together. I mean, Byron gets picked up in a bar by someone who works for Dalkeith and is also not averse to performing sexual favors for Geoffrey. This can't be a coincidence. Which suggests that, regardless of whether it was a premeditated murder or the result of an argument that went too far, Celia's death is only part of whatever is really going on."

Chapter 18

Kit was standing on her balcony, the bougainvillea tumbling down to the lawn which stretched quietly towards the beach. Kit felt supremely confident and Alex felt simply glorious. I just need you to hold me, she'd said, slipping her arms around Kit's waist from behind. A far-off trumpet tripped lightly over the notes of a strangely familiar melody.

Kit could see herself being held by Alex as if she was having an out-of-body experience, which was understandable seeing this *had* to be a dream. Never mind that the lawn was purple; Kit knew, as she watched herself turn into Alex's embrace, that she most definitely did not have a balcony.

The music was getting louder and the tune off-key as the trumpeter sounded reveille right in her face to announce that the day had begun. Kit opened her eyes just as Thistle placed a cold pink paw on her cheek. She blew in The Cat's face to get her to move off her arm then realized it wasn't Thistle who had her pinned to the bed.

What the hell? she thought, turning her head. Quinn was snuggled against her back with her arm draped across Kit's waist.

Somewhere in the bourbon-induced fog that had overtaken Kit's mind was a vague recollection of Quinn crawling in with her at about three in the morning saying she just needed a cuddle. Kit squinted at the clock radio; it was now nine a.m. She slid out of bed, picked up Thistle who was about to play pat-a-cake with Quinn's face, and closed the bedroom door behind her on her way to the kitchen. She poured dried food and some milk into Thistle's bowls, and turned on the kettle before yawning her way to the bathroom to get her robe. It was one thing to allow Quinn to snuggle innocently against her naked body in the middle of the night but another thing all together to be caught starkers in her kitchen in the sober light of day.

"Thistle, did you hit me over the head with the Jack Daniels bottle *again*?" Kit asked when she sat down a few minutes later, a cup of coffee clutched to her chest. "The least you could do is chew more quietly," she pleaded.

Kit nearly choked on her coffee when The Cat suddenly leapt in the air, landed ridiculously on four little tippy toes with her back arched, then scooted out of the kitchen as if it was the hounds of hell who had just rung the doorbell. "Very brave, Thistle," Kit laughed. Trying to recall the last time she'd been alone for her first cup of coffee of the day, she tightened the belt on her robe before opening the front door.

"Did I organize a breakfast party or something?" she asked dubiously.

"We're not staying," Del stated.

"I parked your car out the back. Here's the key," Brigit said.

"You weren't answering your phone," Alex said.

"I unplugged it after you left last night," Kit replied.

"Well, we could have a coffee," Brigit suggested, glancing at Alex.

"We're not staying," Del repeated. "I just wanted to give your manuscript back before we went down to the beach house. We won't be back till Friday. I've made a few notes for you."

"Del, I'm not awake yet," Kit complained, taking the envelope.

"That's OK. We really have to go." Del linked her arm through Brigit's as she turned to leave.

"That's it?" She hates it, Kit thought. It's a wonder she didn't post it or just shove it under the mat before leaving the country so she wouldn't have to face me. "Del!"

A smile overtook the serious expression Del was trying to keep in place. She turned on the top step and faced her. "It is *very* good, Kit."

"Really?"

"Really. We can talk about it on the weekend when we get back."

"I loved it," Brigit announced. "Flynn Carter is just so cool."

Kit couldn't think of anything remotely sensible to say so she just stood there in her bathrobe, grinning like an idiot.

Alex on the other hand, who'd been looking from one person to another with her mouth half open as if everyone was speaking Klingon, obviously decided to ignore what she couldn't understand. "Where's Quinn?" she asked.

"She's still in bed." Kit stepped aside and waved her in.

"Are you *sure* we don't have time for a coffee, Del?" Brigit begged.

"We are going *now*," Del insisted.

"Oh all right," Brigit grumbled as she followed Del down the stairs. "Miranda won't melt out there in the car, you know. Unfortunately."

"Can I make a coffee?" Alex asked.

"Make yourself at home," Kit replied. She put her manuscript in the filing cabinet before sitting down at the breakfast bar again. "What are you doing here anyway?" she added, realizing that Alex didn't seem to be her usual sparkling sociable self.

"I tried to ring first," she replied distractedly.

"I gathered that much."

"Your friend Marek tried too. You were right about Byron," she stated flatly.

"Which right? Is he in hiding or . . ."

"He's dead. At least Marek thinks it's Byron. He needs someone to identify the body. When he couldn't get you he tried Douglas, but he's in Sydney so I was next on the list. Or rather Quinn was, but I don't think she needs this right now."

Kit folded her arms on the bench and put her head down for a second before meeting Alex's apologetic gaze.

"I'm sorry, O'Malley, but I told Marek I'd drop in and ask you to do it. I've never met Byron so I can't. But I'll, ah, go with you—if you like."

Kit raised an eyebrow. "Thanks. I'll just give Marek a call and let him know we're coming, then I'll have a shower." She carried her cup over to the desk and plugged the phone back in.

"I'll take this in to Quinn and tell her what's going on. I have to remind her about dinner tonight too," Alex said, picking up the two coffees she'd made.

Uh oh, Kit thought. "Um," she said, as Alex started to head down the hall. "She's in my room, Alex."

To say that the look on Alex's face when she turned around was one of shock described only part of the effect this little announcement seemed to have on her. Kit could also see disappointment, anger and disbelief. Fighting with all this was the trademark Cazenove determination to appear unruffled. It wasn't working. Deflated—that's the best description, Kit thought. She looks as if she just managed to get her space doors shut before all the atmosphere whooshed out into the galaxy.

"Your room?" Alex managed to say.

"Yeah," Kit said, deciding not to offer any explanation. She indicated the closed bedroom door with a nod and pressed the auto-dial button for Marek's office. After all, she reasoned, even though nothing had happened between her and Quinn it was still none of this woman's business. Let Quinn sort it out, if she wanted to.

"Well?" Alex queried when Kit flopped down on the bench beside her.

"It's him. And there's no way he could have had anything to do with Celia's murder. He was dead before she was. His throat was cut sometime late on Friday afternoon."

"Oh god. Are you OK?"

Kit shrugged and met Alex's steady look with one of her own, holding it a little longer than was necessary as she tried to fathom the genuine note of concern in that question. She finally looked away, wondering what on earth Quinn had said to bring about the transformation. Alex had been *almost* pleasant ever since they'd left Kit's place.

"Goddammit. He's been in there since Friday, Alex. While I've been out looking for him, he's been part of the traffic jam in here that held up Celia's autopsy."

"That's hardly your fault, O'Malley."

"We'd better go and see Marek," Kit said getting to her feet. She covered her mouth and nose with her hand. "The disinfectant in this place makes me feel sick. It smells worse than a hospital. And I hate hospitals!"

❖ ❖ ❖ ❖ ❖

Kit slumped into the passenger seat of Alex's car, put on her seatbelt and wound the window down. The weather bureau had forecast a top of only twenty-five degrees so it wasn't hot, but Kit needed to feel the soothing breeze that had accompanied the cool change. Also she didn't particularly want to throw up in Alex's nice red Celica.

As they turned into City Road Alex's mobile started buzzing. She answered in hands-free mode, but it was Kit who sat up straight and stared at the thing in astonishment.

"Yes, hello. Could I speak to Katherine, please."

"Mum?"

"Oh hello, dear. Young Elizabeth gave me this number. I've got an emergency and some newspaper clippings you might be interested in."

"What's the emergency?"

"There's something in my roof."

"What is it?"

"I don't know, darling. That's what I'd like you to find out. Could you pop over? I'll give you and Alexis lunch if you get here in time."

"In time for what?

"Lunch of course. I'll see you about one."

"Mum, I'm kind of busy today," Kit said, but it was too late. Lillian had already hung up. "Fancy some lunch with my mother—*Alexis*?"

"I'm going to have a beeper permanently implanted in your body," Marek growled. "That way I might be able to find you when I need you, Kitty."

"What on earth for? I don't work for you, or even with you any more, Jonno."

"*Kitty*?" Alex breathed in Kit's ear before she sat down on the couch where Marek had cleared a space for her.

Kit ignored the remark. She was too busy watching Marek making a fool of himself. He handed Alex a cup of coffee, asked her if she was comfortable, then fussed about with his tie to make his already presentable self even more so. Then he sat down at his desk and tried not to look at Alex while he opened the file in front of him. My god, do I come across like this? Kit wondered. Alex obviously has this affect on everybody. If Quinn were here she'd be saying "Oh dear, not him too!"

Alex appeared to be quite oblivious to Marek's behavior. In fact when Kit glanced in her direction she discovered that Alex was watching *her*—closely.

"This case is a total mess," Marek was complaining.

"It always was a total mess, Jonno."

"It doesn't help that you seem to be attracting dead people wherever you go."

"It's got nothing to do with me," Kit declared. "Except maybe in Byron's case. Indirectly."

"I trust you're going to explain that statement."

"Geoffrey Robinson didn't even *see* Byron Daniels last Thursday morning let alone fire him. He did, however, attempt to blackmail him on Wednesday night because he thought Byron was following him."

"Was he?"

"No, I was."

"Where did you get this information?" Marek asked.

"From Byron's best friend who last saw him at lunchtime on Thursday just after Byron had been to the Robinson house where he had seen Celia *not* Geoffrey."

"What could Robinson possibly have on Daniels to blackmail him with?" Marek asked skeptically.

"These," Kit announced, opening her briefcase. She sat on the corner of Marek's desk and handed him the magazine and the photo of Byron. Marek glanced in Alex's direction briefly before pushing the photo away from himself as if he was embarrassed to scrutinize it too closely in front of her.

Kit tried not to laugh as she continued. "Apparently Geoffrey believed Byron was spying on him in order to blackmail him. Geoffrey has been up to a lot of no good lately, none of which he would have wanted his wife to know about, so he threatened to give this to Celia if Byron continued to follow him. Byron didn't tell him about me, or that Celia already knew everything anyway because it was she who had hired someone to follow Geoffrey."

"You're not going to suggest that Robinson killed this guy *and* his wife are you? Remember he still has an alibi for Friday night."

"Of course he does. But did you, by any chance, follow up on the possibility that he might have slipped away from the restaurant?"

"Yes, I checked out your far-fetched theory that he popped home to do the deed," Marek stated, rather patronizingly.

"And you still don't think it's possible? Don't you remember he went to the toilet while you were questioning him that first night? He was gone for ages and claimed he'd been up and down all night because he'd eaten something that disagreed with him."

"His dinner companions verified that he did in fact leave the table several times. And yes, on one occasion he was gone for nearly fifteen minutes."

"You see," Kit interrupted. "That's plenty of time."

"Except that one of the waitresses saw him talking to someone out the back in the car park."

"Talking to who, for god's sake?"

"I don't know," Marek said impatiently. "Some woman. And before you ask your next question, the restaurant's toilets are outside in a corner of the car park. They and the parking area are shared by two or three restaurants. The witness said Robinson didn't appear to know her. He was simply lighting the woman's cigarette. This was confirmed by Robinson himself."

"I'll bet it was," Kit stated. "Well, it wouldn't hurt to check his alibi for Friday afternoon, although it's more likely Byron was killed by the so-called nephew the neighbor saw him with that morning."

"Do you have any idea who *this* alleged murderer is?" Marek asked.

"All I've got is a photo and a first name—Christo," Kit replied. She pulled out her case file and handed Marek a copy of the photo of Geoffrey with Christo Snakehips. "I'm waiting to hear if he's the same guy who left a night club with Byron on Thursday night. I'll let you know as soon as I find out."

"Christo?" Marek sounded surprised. He searched the pile of papers on his desk and pulled out a print-out. "Christopher Edwards?" he queried.

"I don't know. Who's Christopher Edwards?"

"The registered owner of the car that tried to run you down."

"What?" Alex exclaimed. "When did that happen?" She was looking at Kit with a worried expression.

"Yesterday," Kit replied. "And no, Quinn wasn't with me," she added dryly.

"I think it's time to give me everything you've got, O'Malley," Marek demanded.

"OK. But first tell me how you came to the conclusion that the body in the morgue was Byron. Donald Grenville said there were no personal effects."

"Last night the St. Kilda CIB found Daniels's car, the Volvo station wagon registered to Mrs. Robinson, in Acland Street where it had been gathering parking tickets for five days. It was just round the corner from the rooming house where the body was found on Friday evening."

"A rooming house? Did anyone see anything?"

Marek shook his head. "Nobody saw Daniels go in or anybody else leave. The guy who runs the place was out the back for several hours during the middle of the day trying to fix a busted pipe. He found the body when he went upstairs to check the fixtures in the bathroom next to the room Daniels was found in. He stepped in the blood which had leaked out from under the door of the room."

"So whose room was it?" Kit asked.

Marek stopped to consult the file in front of him. "The manager said the room was rented on Thursday by a George Ryan who paid for five days in advance. He took two suitcases up to the room, left again five minutes later and hasn't been seen since. The cases were still there but they were empty."

"What did this guy look like?" Kit asked.

"Tall, middle-aged, dressed in a business suit. Apart from a prize fighter's nose Mr. Ryan had no other distinguishing features."

"It sounds like Geoffrey's friend, the one Quinn can't stand," Alex suggested.

"Grainger." Kit nodded at Alex then turned to Marek. "Gerald Grainger. He's a business associate of Geoffrey's from Sydney. I can give you a photo of him too." She opened her file again. "And one of an American businessman who maintains he's on holiday and goes by the name of David Watts, though it's more likely that he's really Davis Whitten."

"Oh dear! It probably is Whitten," Alex said. "Sorry, Kit, I forgot to tell you that Michael rang from Sydney this morning with that piece of the jigsaw."

Kit. She called me Kit! Oh god, get a grip, O'Malley. Although she suspected it was for Marek's benefit, because it sounded less antagonistic, Kit couldn't help feeling ridiculously thrilled that Alex had used her first name. Of the many people who called her O'Malley, Alex was the only one who always managed to make it sound like an insult.

"Davis Whitten has been in the country for about six weeks," Alex was saying. "He lives in Los Angeles but he owns radio and TV stations all over the States, as well as a major software design and manufacturing company in Silicon Valley, and coffee plantations and mines in Brazil, not to mention his share in the, comparatively speaking, small-time enterprises of Freyling. Mr. Whitten is, according to Michael, an obscenely wealthy man."

"Well," Marek said, shooting Alex an admiring glance before facing Kit, "Ms. Cazenove has given more information in one breath than you have all morning, *mate*. So would you care to back-pedal a bit? Who *is* this guy? Why do I want a photo of him? Why do I care?"

"Well, Jonno, you want a photo of David Watts because he's been hanging around with Geoffrey and this Grainger creep. But if he's really Davis Whitten then you want a photo of him because you might need to know what he looks like in order to investigate what connection a business partner of the aforementioned Grainger and one Ian Dalkeith has with Geoffrey Robinson."

"Ian Dalkeith?" Marek repeated. "You mentioned him the other day. What's his connection with all this?"

Kit shrugged. "He's one of the other directors of Wellborn and/or Freyling Imports."

"And? So what?" Marek shrugged. "Fill in *all* the gaps, Kitty. I don't care where you start but I want the whole story."

Kit obligingly told Marek nearly everything she knew while he interrupted every few minutes with questions about her information or reprimands for having withheld it. When he got up to refill their coffee mugs Kit took the opportunity to reach over his desk and pick up the file with Celia's name on it.

"So, in a nutshell," she continued, "if we start with Geoffrey, we have two murder victims—his wife and her secretary. His associates include a Melbourne businessman who has the reputation of being a nasty piece of work; a Sydney businessman who possibly rented the room where Byron's body was found; an American businessman whose involvement is still a mystery; and two women, one of whom is a renowned society madam and the other an apparent nobody, and both of whom are locked up in the same loony bin while all these men make a lot of money in their names. On top of that there's Christo Edwards who is Dalkeith's gofer, Geoffrey's bumboy and probably Byron's killer, or at least the last known person to have seen him alive."

"I think I'll put in an application for long-service leave, starting today," Marek groaned.

"What are these holes?" Kit asked, putting aside a long shot of the crime scene to study a close-up of Celia's body. The photo had been taken before the storm and before the overflow from the pond had begun to lap at her body on the lawn.

"Give me that, O'Malley," Marek demanded but Kit held it out of his reach.

"Come on, Jonno. I was there anyway, remember?"

Marek pinched the bridge of his nose in frustration. "What holes?"

"These holes in the lawn near Celia's head."

"How the hell would I know what they are?" Marek snatched the photo from Kit's hand and peered at it before politely passing it to Alex. "Maybe there are mutant worms in that weird garden of hers," he suggested.

"They might be aeration holes," Alex said. "There's a garden tool designed to poke little holes in the lawn to help the circulation of air or water through the soil."

"Oh," said Kit, disappointed. She accepted the photo back from Alex.

"We could run with the mutant worm theory if you'd prefer, Kitty," Marek offered. "We can add them to your list of possible suspects."

"You're such a card, Marek," Kit said absently. She peered intently at the photo and willed the vague image that was lurking in the back of her mind into sharper focus so she could actually see it. Oh yes! she thought.

"What are you grinning at now?" Marek asked.

"A walking stick!"

"What?"

"Forget the worms and the gardening tools, Jonno, and consider Geoffrey's walking stick."

Marek stared at the ceiling for a few seconds then back at Kit. "OK, done. Now what?"

"Marek," Kit snarled.

"It was pouring, Kitty. I can tell you for a fact the man did not leave the patio."

"Not while we were all there anyway," Kit stated. "Marek, this photo was not only taken before Geoffrey got there but before it started to rain. Take a proper look at it."

"I don't need to, O'Malley. The man has an alibi. End of story. Stick with the worms."

"Fine, have it your way," Kit sighed, and then smiled. "Speaking of suspects though, I assume you'll be talking to Geoffrey again seeing the person against whom he was casting so many aspersions has an even better alibi than he does."

"Run that by me again," Marek requested.

"Byron being dead is a more iron-clad alibi than Geoffrey dining with friends," Kit explained, shaking her head. "Can I go with you?"

"What for?"

"Humor me, OK? Besides, wouldn't you rather I harassed this fine upstanding citizen in your presence than go off on my own and screw up your investigation?"

Marek snorted and took his file from Kit's hand. "Put that way I don't see how I can refuse," he said. "I'll let you know when I pin him down to a time—*if* I can find you when I need you."

Chapter 19

"Don't you know the way to your own mother's house?"

"Take the next left, please," Kit instructed as she referred to the street directory. "We're making a slight detour. It's only a little bit out of our way. Is that OK?"

"I guess so. Where are we going?" Alex asked.

"To have a wee talk with the waitress from the restaurant where Geoffrey dined last Friday. I got her name and address from Marek's file."

"Why?"

"Let's just say I'm having trouble accepting that Geoffrey's alibi hangs on the fact that he was seen lighting a stranger's cigarette in a car park," Kit explained. "Next right and then slow down, it's number four. There, the blue weatherboard on the left," she added, watching Alex closely over the top of her sunglasses.

Alex stopped the car in the shade of a tree and turned to face her. For the briefest of moments she appeared to be taken aback by something, but covered the flinch of surprise by turning her attention to the buckle on her seatbelt.

"Why are you driving me all over town, Alex?" Kit asked. "Don't you have any lawyer-type things to do today?"

"I cancelled all my appointments for the rest of the week, except for one on Friday morning that I couldn't put off," she replied. "For Quinn," she emphasized. "I thought she might need someone around."

Other than me, you mean, Kit thought. She threw up her hands questioningly, to indicate that Alex had not answered the question.

"Well, she said she'd prefer to be left on her own for a while. So I thought I'd fill in some time. Shall we go?" Alex started to get out of the car.

As they walked up the weed-choked path to the front door she said, "I was wondering why you didn't tell Marek about the warehouse you and Quinn followed Geoffrey to yesterday."

"I want to find out what's going on there myself," Kit said, knocking on the door. "I didn't want Marek raiding the place too soon or, more importantly, asking Geoffrey any questions about it. Something's going down there tonight and I'd hate to scare off Geoffrey and his merry band of perverts before I discover what this is all about."

The front door was opened by a dishevelled young man who reeked of alcohol and ten-day-old socks. "We've got no money this week," he rasped.

"We're not after money," Kit stated. "I'd like to speak to Kylie Trent if she's home, please."

"Kylie!" he shouted over his shoulder. "Just a sec," he said to Kit and retreated down the hall.

Kylie Trent's hair, which was all on top and shaved on the sides, was streaked with blond. She had a bluebird tattoo just below her collarbone, was wearing too much make-up for so early in the day, and Kit decided that trying to count her earrings would be like attempting to win a prize for guessing the number of jelly beans in a jar.

"Yeah?" she asked rudely.

"Hi, Kylie. I believe you work at the Shangri La in Toorak," Kit began, aware that Alex had recoiled—probably in horror.

"No, I don't. I work at the Rumble Café next door. Is this about that guy? I've already told you cops everything."

"I'm not a cop," Kit stated, holding up her inquiry agent's license.

"My name is Kit O'Malley and this is my . . ." Kit hesitated. What is she? "This is my associate, Alex Cazenove," she decided quickly. "I'm a private detective."

"No kidding!" Kylie exclaimed. "Just like V. I. Warshawski."

"Ah, yeah," Kit said, unable to hide her surprise.

"Wow. She's my hero. How can I help you?" she asked.

Kit glanced sideways at Alex who looked more confused than amazed by Kylie's sudden amiableness. Kit opened her briefcase and pulled out her file of photos. "Are you sure this is the guy you saw in the car park on Friday?"

"Positive," Kylie stated, handing back the photo of Geoffrey. "I was out the back having a smoko. This woman came up to him, they spoke a few words, he lit her cigarette and then she got in her car and drove off."

"What time was that?" Alex asked.

"Eight o'clock. I was on my break."

Half an hour after the time established for Celia's death, Kit thought. "Did you see which restaurant the woman came out of?"

"She didn't. She walked in off the street, up the drive. I figured she'd parked there while she went shopping or something. I nearly said something to her, 'cause the car park's only s'posed to be for customers, but I didn't."

"What did she look like and what sort of car was she driving?" Kit asked.

"The car I can't be sure of. I'm a bike person myself; got a Virago out the back. It was a blue sports car, that's all I can tell you," Kylie shrugged. "The woman though, well, she was flashy—or trashy, depending on your taste in clothes. Lots of red hair, a miniskirt that looked sprayed on and a white shirt that came just below her boobs."

Bingo! Kit thought, flashing Alex an exultant grin. She flipped through the photos in her file and pulled out the couple she'd taken of Geoffrey's favorite crimson tart. "Could this be her?" she asked. Please say yes. Please say yes.

"It could be," Kylie said hesitantly. "I'm sure about him 'cause he walked right by me when he went back inside, but I only saw her from the other side of the car park. Yeah, it *does* look like her."

❖❖❖❖❖

Kit looked askance at Alex as they waited for Lillian to acknowledge the doorbell.

"What?" Alex demanded. "It was a simple question, O'Malley, how about a simple answer?"

"*Who* is V. I. Warshawski?" Kit repeated.

"What a silly question, Katherine," Lillian commented as she unlocked the security screen-door. "You know very well who she is."

"I don't," Alex declared in a frustrated tone.

"Oh my goodness, Alexis dear, where on earth have you been hiding?" Lillian asked, raising an eyebrow as she waved them inside. "We'll have to do something about this gap in your life. Take her through to the sunroom, Katherine. I'll be right with you."

Kit had just filled two glasses with ice-cold orange juice when Lillian rejoined them and handed Alex a copy of *Tunnel Vision*.

"She's a character in a book?" Alex exclaimed. "I'm impressed. No one has ever said, 'Wow, just like Perry Mason,' and then given *me* instant cooperation."

"You'll also never have anyone say, 'Well I never, a lady dick, haw haw,'" Kit grinned.

"Oh Katherine!"

"Oh Mum!" Kit mimicked Lillian's disapproving tone. "It's true."

"If you say so, darling. Now, I've made some sandwiches for lunch. Do you want them before or after you find out what's in the roof?"

"After. What makes you think there's something up there?"

"Because I can hear it creeping around. Connie and I got the big ladder out for you before she left this morning. It's in the hall near the manhole thingy."

A ladder? Oh shit! Kit's palms started sweating as she made her way up the hall. Alex was right behind her, offering to help. Kit thought about asking Alex to climb up instead but decided she'd rather be scared witless than let this woman know that she was anything less than perfect. Perfect? Standing on a chair makes you nauseous, O'Malley, Kit thought. Face it, when it comes to heights you are a coward of the highest magnitude. Why would Alex care anyway? And why do *you* care what she thinks?

Alex helped her stand the ladder against the wall, taking care not to bump Lillian's gallery of family photos, and Kit took a deep breath to prepare for her ascent into hell.

"Did Angie go up here when she was fixing your geyser yesterday, Mum?" she asked nervously, trying her weight on the first rung. Now this really *is* stupid, she thought desperately. Think about this for a second: confessing will be far less embarrassing than being paralyzed with fear at the top of this contraption, with your head in a manhole thingy of all places!

"Angela didn't, but that extortionist with the monkey wench did the day before. He also crawled all over the roof outside."

"It's a wrench, Mum, not a wench."

"Do all tradesmen think women are idiots?" Lillian continued, choosing to ignore Kit, who in turn was ignoring her own best interests as she hauled herself up the ladder. "I can't even begin to imagine why he thought I'd believe that a clogged gutter would have caused my kitchen taps to leap off and fly around the kitchen. But there he was, trying to include their unblocking as part of his quote for fixing my taps."

"Are you holding this thing?" Kit asked, worried that Alex's laughter meant she wasn't concentrating.

"Of course I am. Are you all right up there?"

Oh god, oh god, Kit thought as she made it safely onto the fourth step. "I'm fine, hunky-dory, A-OK," she muttered, gripping the top of the ladder as if her life depended on it, which, as far as she was concerned right now, it did.

"She's scared of heights," Lillian said matter-of-factly.

"Thanks a lot, Mum," Kit growled sarcastically as she pushed up at the cover, wondering irrelevantly what the non-gender-specific ideologically sound and politically correct term for manhole was these days. "Aaahh!" she screamed, grabbing at the edge of whatever-it-was-called when a startled furry thing stuck its face in hers and nearly sent her backwards off the ladder.

"For heaven's sake, Mum, didn't you even notice the cat was missing?"

"That animal is never where it's supposed to be," Lillian said defensively. "I thought it was a poltergeist or a possum. I couldn't hear her meowing."

"Of course you couldn't. She can't meow."

"Well, there you go," Lillian stated. "You might need to climb up and help her, Alexis. Don't worry, Katherine, I will hold the ladder."

Kit grabbed the cat by the scruff of the neck and awkwardly handed it to Alex who was suddenly behind her, standing comfortably and calmly on the step below, her right arm pressed against Kit's hip.

Think about the ladder, O'Malley! Now is *not* a good time to go weak at the knees.

Getting down was always worse than climbing up but a few agonizing seconds later Kit was sitting on the bottom rung with her feet firmly planted on the floor. She rested her chin in her hands while she tried to regain her composure.

"Oooh, Fargle Bargle, did mummy not notice you were gone?" Lillian cooed as she held and stroked the Persian which was head-butting her face excitedly.

"The cat's name is Fargle Bargle?" Alex queried.

"No, her name is FB—for Fanny Brice," Kit explained. "I did suggest that it wasn't the most appropriate name for a mute cat but Mum thought it would build self-confidence. She defeats the original intention, however, by calling her anything that springs to mind that just happens to start with FB—like Fargle Bargle or Furry Bum. Last month it was Flaffle Baps."

"I understand," said Alex politely, looking around for some way to change the subject.

"You always know who I'm talking to, don't you?" Lillian said to the cat.

"Is this you, Lillian?" Alex asked, peering at a framed photo on the wall beside the ladder.

Kit groaned when she realized Alex was looking at the enlarged copy of the first family snapshot ever taken of her parents and a bawling baby Katherine Frances O'Malley, her mass of black hair standing on end as if she'd just received an electric shock. Lillian was posing between a harassed-looking nurse and Kit's father, who was leaning against the bonnet of his gray Ford Zephyr and holding Kit out at arm's length as if he didn't quite know what to do with her.

"Yes, and Katherine's father. It was taken the day after she was born," Lillian was saying.

"What's wrong with the building in the background? It looks like it was hit by a bomb."

"It was a hurricane," Lillian said as she dumped FB unceremoniously in Kit's lap and stood beside Alex.

"It was a cyclone," Kit corrected. "Cyclone Ethel to be exact."

"Cyclone, hurricane, what's the difference?" Lillian said. "The building was a little bush hospital in Innisfail, south of Cairns."

"I didn't realize you were Queenslanders," Alex said, as if it mattered.

"We're not," Lillian said. "Well, I suppose Katherine is, technically. But we, her father and I, were only there because Francis wanted to avoid the humbug season with my family. So just before Christmas he decided he wanted to explore the Cape York Peninsula."

"While you were pregnant?" Alex looked from Lillian to Kit who just shrugged.

"When we left Melbourne I was only seven months gone. Katherine's father was something of a lunatic, you see. I loved him dearly but he was madder than any hatter I ever met. When he got a notion in his head to go somewhere, which was every other week, that was that. I either went with him or stayed at home and waited for him to come back. Anyway, when we got to Innisfail, a month later, everyone was battening down their proverbial hatches because Ethel was on the way. Francis hurt his hand helping out the locals and I had to drive him to the hospital, which is where we were, luckily, when the cyclone actually hit and Katherine decided it was time to come out and see what all the commotion was about."

"A month early?" Alex asked.

"She's always been a little impatient," Lillian said, casting a fond glance at Kit who rolled her eyes. "So I went into labor while the wind was trying to knock the hospital down and half an hour later, during a brief lull in the storm, there she was—simple as that. Then Ethel started up again and the east wing of the hospital, on the other side from us, collapsed—just as you see in the picture."

Alex was looking at Kit with one of her half-smiling all-knowing looks, as if Lillian's story had answered a hundred unasked questions.

Kit pulled a face. "Can we have some lunch now, please?" she begged. "All this rebirthing is making me hungry."

"I doubt these will be of any use to you now, Katherine, but you may still find them interesting," Lillian said as she deposited a large envelope in front of Kit. "Don't tell me you're on a diet, Alexis," she added.

"I've already had three, Lillian. I didn't want to appear greedy," Alex replied, reaching for another piece of smoked salmon and salad on rye.

"What is all this, Mum?" Kit asked. She emptied the contents of the envelope onto the kitchen table.

"Well, my suggestion that there might be some useful background material on Chel in my reference library seemed to put the fear of god into you so I decided to do the research myself," Lillian stated. "I meant to give these to you the other day."

Kit laughed and turned to Alex. "Mum's so-called reference library is a study packed to the rafters with two or three decades' worth of women's magazines," she said, spreading the clippings out across the end of the table between them.

"How on earth did you know where to start looking?" Kit asked. Several pieces of paper fluttered to the floor and Alex bent to pick them up.

"Unlike you, darling, I am a very organized person," Lillian declared. "On top of which I had Connie's help, and as you know when it comes to society trivia she has perfect recall of dates, occasions and guest lists. She couldn't tell you what she had for lunch yesterday but she can remember whether the food served at Diana Hadley's charity fundraiser in March 1972 was worth the $150 it cost her to be allowed to sit down and eat it."

Kit picked up a page which featured a collage of photos taken in the members' stand on Cup Day in 1970. The main picture, surrounded by snapshots of Melbourne society's fashion plates trying to outdo each other in the hat stakes, showed Celia looking slim, conservatively dressed and positively shining with happiness. It wasn't hard to figure out why. The man on her arm was handsome, suavely dressed and obviously had eyes only for her. The caption read: *Mr. and Mrs. Carl Orlando, already the toast of the publishing world this year, celebrate another success after picking Baghdad Note to win Australia's race of races.*

"Wow, it's hard to believe she's the same woman," Kit said, passing the page to Alex. "Do you remember her like this?"

"Vaguely," she nodded, "though I didn't really see them very often till I was about sixteen. Celia and Carl did a lot of socializing then and I used to babysit Quinn."

Kit nearly said "so what's new?" but thought better of it. She picked up another clipping instead. Celia, looking more like Kit remembered her, was pictured presenting one of her weird statues to a local restaurateur.

"This is a nice trip down memory lane, Mum, but I don't think they're really much use now," Kit said, fingering the rest of the pile.

"I don't know about that." Alex's tone was highly suggestive and she was staring, eyebrows raised, at the page Kit had handed her.

"My goodness, Alexis, you look like you've seen a ghost."

"I think I might have, Lillian. May I use your phone to call Sydney?"

"Yes of course, dear. It's in the lounge, just through there. The one in here hasn't worked since FB wrestled it to the floor on Sunday."

Alex turned the page around, placed it on the table in front of Kit and tapped her finger on the photo in the top right corner. Then she left the room.

"What is it, what is it? What's she found?" Lillian demanded.

"Mr. and Mrs. Geoffrey Robinson share Cup Day cheer with Sydney visitors Mr. Gerald Grainger and Mrs. Daryl Cook," Kit read aloud. "Well, I'll be damned!"

"Why?" queried Lillian. "Is that a clue? It doesn't sound like a clue."

"I would say it's definitely a clue, Mum. You see, *this* Mrs. Robinson is not *our* Mrs. Robinson. In 1970, as the other photo on the same page shows, Celia was still Mrs. Orlando."

Kit peered at the picture of the "original" Mrs. Robinson until something pressed the ridiculous button in her brain and told her not to jump to conclusions. After all, the petite wheyfaced wife who stood beside Geoffrey at the Melbourne Cup more than twenty years ago might turn out to be just one in a long line of ex-Mrs. Robinsons.

"Why didn't you didn't tell me Geoffrey had been married before, Mum?"

"I didn't know, Katherine, that's why I didn't tell you," Lillian stated.

"Anyway, he was a nobody then—before he married Chel," she added, as if that justified this gap in her knowledge.

"In the grand scheme of things he's still a nobody," Kit said flatly, wondering for the umpteenth time where her mother's little bouts of snobbery came from. She began sorting through the rest of the clippings, this time looking for surprises.

"I'm sorry, darling," Lillian said after a couple of minutes' studied silence, "but I don't actually understand. What difference does it make to anything that he was married before? Why was Alexis so excited?"

"I've no idea, Mum. We'll just have to wait till she gets off the phone."

"I'm off the phone," said Alex, who was standing in the kitchen doorway looking as if she'd won Tattslotto. "I've just spoken to Michael in Sydney to see if he'd managed to follow up on a small detail you asked me to check into."

"Which detail?"

"Geoffrey Edward Turner Robinson," Alex said slowly, "was the ex-husband of one Shirley Anne Smith. The same ex-husband she attacked with a rake before totalling his Mercedes nine years ago. It seems our friend Shirley got herself locked up in a round room for actions which, in a better world than this, would simply have been regarded as a service to society."

Alex slumped back in her chair and stared at Kit, whose jaw was still hanging down around her knees somewhere. That was only half the reason why she was unable to speak; the other half was that she was completely dumbstruck.

"Say something, O'Malley."

"I think I'm going to join Marek on his long-service leave," said Kit weakly.

"That's the best you can manage? We've just established another connection between all these people and you want to go on holidays. That's a fine attitude!"

"This case should be getting clearer by now, not murkier by the second. I'd much rather find explanations for the connections we have rather than turn up more of them."

"What are you talking about?" Alex asked impatiently. "This

particular connection is the first direct link we've found between Geoffrey and Freyling Imports, not to mention all the other subsidiary companies that bear Malcolm and Shirley Smith's name."

"What are *you* talking about? All this does is show that Geoffrey is not averse to letting Orlan Carriers do a few seemingly legitimate jobs for a company that happens to be part-owned by his ex-brother-in-law. And, technically speaking, as Geoffrey's name was not on any of the contracts for those jobs, then the actual connection there is still circumstantial. And what's more . . ."

"That's not the direct link," Alex interrupted. "Michael also told me that, even though they've been divorced since 1973, Geoffrey somehow has joint power of attorney over his ex-wife's affairs. Over *everything*, O'Malley. Every last cent that's earned in Shirley Smith's name is controlled by Geoffrey Robinson and Malcolm Smith. A lot goes towards keeping Shirley in the manner to which she has been accustomed these past nine years, and to funding the Endicott Center itself, but the rest is used by Geoffrey and his ex-brother-in-law as they see fit."

Chapter 20

Damn! This must be the longest sixty minutes in history, Kit said to herself, as she stared at the "Back in one hour" sign that still hung on the closed door of Nostalgia Incorporated. It looked as though the only way she was going to find out anything about Factor Four was to break in. But not in broad daylight. She crossed the road, carefully this time, and walked back to the Celica where Alex was still arguing with Quinn on the phone.

"Ah, O'Malley. Will you please tell Quinn you don't need her tagging along with you on this warehouse stakeout tonight?"

"I don't need you tagging along with me on this warehouse stake-out tonight," Kit repeated, settling back into the passenger seat. Alex glared at her.

"But Kit . . ." Quinn started to say.

"But nothing, Quinn. I don't need you there and I really don't want you there. It might be dangerous this time. And besides, you have to go to this dinner tonight."

"Oh, bullshit. If Geoffrey-the-scumbag is still going to the ware-house he'll have to leave early. So can I."

"Quinn, it's one thing for the now-junior partner to make his excuses in the middle of dinner but another thing for the new chair-person of the board to get up and follow him for no apparent reason," Alex said.

"The thing is, I don't think I'll be able to control myself in his company for much longer. I'd much rather kill him and have done with it."

"That's understandable, but please don't do it at dinner in front of the entire upper management of OHP. It's Geoffrey we want to put in jail, not you," Kit said.

"Douglas and I will be there with you," Alex reminded her. "And once Geoffrey leaves you won't have to endure his company any longer, and Kit can do her job without having to worry about you."

"I don't think I want to be chairperson of the bloody board," Quinn complained. "I suppose I have to dress the part as well. Could you bring my black dress, shoes, and a change of underwear from your place when you go home to change, please, Alex?"

"Of course. We should be back at O'Malley's in a couple of hours so have a nice long bath or something while you're waiting." Alex hung up and turned to face Kit. "Do you think she's ready for all this responsibility?"

Kit shrugged. "She'll be fine, I'm sure. Being thrown right into the middle of something is one of the best ways of finding out what you're made of. Which is, I'm sure, what Celia had in mind for her—though obviously not so soon and not under these circumstances. It's my opinion, however, that if becoming a publishing tycoon overnight was the only thing Quinn had on her plate, she'd already be in there strutting her stuff. But she's got all this other shit to deal with as well, so the sooner we solve Celia's murder and expose Geoffrey the better."

"Speak of the devil." Alex was pointing at the Bentley which had pulled up on the other side of the road, in front of Nostalgia Inc. Geoffrey approached the door but didn't knock or try the handle, as Kit had done despite the sign. He just stood there—waiting. A couple of minutes later Ian Dalkeith and his white Mercedes pulled into the parking spot in front of Geoffrey's car. His passengers, Gerald Grainger and Christo "Snakehips" Edwards, waited with Geoffrey on the footpath while Dalkeith unlocked the door of the studio.

"That's the little bastard who tried to run me down," Kit snarled as she watched them all go inside.

"And the guy who picked up Byron," Alex added.

"We think," Kit said.

"We know," Alex said. "Quinn said Damien rang and confirmed he *was* the guy Tooly saw with Byron."

"Good. I suppose I'd better let Marek know," Kit muttered. "Tomorrow."

"What do we do now, O'Malley?"

"I wish I knew. No, actually I wish Geoffrey would have the decency at least to make a show of being the grieving widower instead of running all over town as if it's business as bloody usual. I also wish I was more than one person so I could follow Dalkeith and his cronies as well as Geoffrey."

"Well, you could follow one car and I could follow the other," Alex suggested.

Kit gave Alex a puzzled look. "How come you think it's OK for you to play detective but it's not on for Quinn? No, don't answer that question. Try this one: how are we going to follow two cars when we've only got one car to follow them in?" she asked, holding up two fingers on one hand and one on the other, for emphasis. "You don't need to answer that one either, Alex."

"It was just an idea, O'Malley, there's no need to bite my head off."

"You're right, I'm sorry," Kit apologized. "And actually, it's given me a better idea, or at least a possible solution." She unzipped her pouch, pulled out a business card and started dialling a number.

"Graffico."

"Hector, this is Kit O'Malley."

"Hey, O'Malley. I didn't expect to hear from you so soon. Has your PC blown up or something?"

"No, it's not that. I was just wondering if you were serious about helping me out sometime. Like right now would be good. Unless you're too busy, of course."

"You mean detective stuff?"

"That's just what I mean. Do you have a car?"

"Yeah. Are you serious?" Hector sounded doubtful.

"You'd be doing me an enormous favor and I'd be giving you some pocket money, but only if you can get here in five minutes."

229

"No worries. Where's here?"

"Same place as yesterday, only this time I'm sitting in a red Celica on the other side of the road instead of lying flat on my face on the footpath."

"I'm on my way. I'll be there in three minutes."

Kit put down her cutlery and gave up trying to be couth. After all, hamburgers were designed to be eaten with the hands, not with a knife and fork. This one was lying open on the plate, surrounded by alfalfa and chunky chips, looking almost as pretentious as the waiter who'd served her. She put the thing together properly, took a mouthful and had to admit that, despite appearances, it was delicious. The fact that she was able to eat while on a stakeout, and actually sit at a table to do it, made it taste even better.

Kit glanced out the window at La "exclusive" Maison, the restaurant on the other side of the narrow street, and wondered how much Alex, Quinn et al. were paying for their *French* fries. Geoffrey's presence aside, Kit could understand Quinn's reluctance to be part of what was apparently some kind of social rallying of the troops. She wondered what on earth they would be talking about while, no doubt, consciously trying to avoid the subject of Celia.

The diners at the OHP table included Miles Denning, Greg Fulton and Marjorie Finlay, as well as the managing editor Christine Johnson and the financial controller Bill Harris. Kit couldn't see Geoffrey, Douglas or Miles at all, but she had a clear view of everyone else, especially Alex and Quinn who had taken the window seats.

Quinn's idea of dressing the part had been to squeeze herself into a tight and very short black dress. She didn't look half bad but Alex, dressed in tailored gray trousers and a black silk shirt, looked positively ravishing. Kit knew it was the memory of seeing Alex in *just* the shirt—a sight which had quite literally taken her breath away—that made the view she now had so appealing, but she was, nonetheless, relieved to be sitting in a completely different restaurant. Apart from the fact that khaki army pants and a black T-shirt made her just a trifle underdressed for La Maison, she also knew she couldn't have coped with being at the same table as Alex right now. Or possibly ever again!

She dragged her attention back to her hamburger and tried to force her thoughts to change track by wondering how Hector was coping on his first surveillance job. He had turned up, as he'd said he would, three minutes after Kit had called him. While he was getting acquainted with Alex, Kit had slipped into the milk bar up the street to get him a couple of cans of drink and a sandwich. Half an hour later he'd got back into his own car to follow Dalkeith and his passengers up Fitzroy Street towards the junction, with strict instructions from Kit to do nothing *but* follow them. Kit and Alex had then tailed Geoffrey to his favorite house in St. Kilda, where he'd stayed for an hour before going home.

It was then that Alex had decided that in order for them to get back to Quinn as soon as possible it would be more sensible for her to shower and change at Kit's place as well. So she'd driven to her apartment and dashed inside to pick up two changes of clothes, which was how Kit had come to see her half-dressed. Alex had emerged from the spare room, the silk shirt half-buttoned and her wet hair all over the place, to ask Kit if she had a hair dryer. After Kit had finished choking on the handful of cashews she'd just put in her mouth she pointed mutely towards her bedroom and then went to find Quinn.

"What on earth did you say to Alex this morning?"

"Why?" Quinn had asked, not even trying to hide the wicked tone in her voice.

"Because she's been almost nice to me all day. I don't think I can stand the change."

Quinn shrugged. "She just stood there looking all self-righteous and demanded to know what I thought I was doing in your bed. I told her I hadn't given it much thought, but whatever I was doing was none of her damn business."

"That's it?"

"No. I also told her that if she didn't stop being a right royal pain in the bum and start being civil to you, I'd not only get a new lawyer but I'd cross her off my Christmas list." Quinn was grinning something chronic.

"Well, being on your Christmas list must be worth a lot to her because the transformation is remarkable," Kit had said.

"I wouldn't take her bad mood personally, Kit. I don't. She's still all over the place emotionally after her break-up in Perth."

"But she's getting married next month."

"Yeah," Quinn had agreed hesitantly, "but the relationship had been a long-term thing and the parting was pretty nasty, especially for Alex. She's still a bit fractious and fragile."

"Confused more likely," Kit had commented. "Here, let me do that," she'd added, turning Quinn around to get at the zip in the back of her dress.

"What do you mean confused?"

"Well, how does the divine Enzo cope when the two of you are together?"

"Enzo? What do you mean?" Quinn had asked, holding onto Kit's arm for balance while she put her shoes on.

"Oh, come on, Quinn. Alex's attraction for you is written all over her face, not to mention expressed very loudly through her body language. Are you telling me he wouldn't notice?"

"Attraction for me?" Quinn had said incredulously then added, "Alex, you'd better get a move on or we'll be late . . ."

"I beg your pardon?" Kit asked, staring blankly at the waiter.

"Would you like another drink?" he repeated.

"Yes, please, a Coke," she replied. She glanced over at La Maison, hoping she hadn't missed anything while her thoughts were off with the pixies. Christine Johnson was talking animatedly about something, Quinn was trying hard to appear interested and Alex's chair was empty. A moment later Quinn cast a casual look in Kit's direction, dropped her right hand down and clenched and unclenched her fist a couple of times. There was no doubt it was signal but Kit had absolutely no idea what Quinn was trying to tell her, until her view of the restaurant was impaired by the red Celica which pulled up right in front of her outside.

"What the hell?" Kit muttered to herself, just as the waiter reappeared with her drink. "Thanks, I'll take it with me," she said, throwing twenty dollars on the table to cover the bill. She walked outside and, leaning her arm casually on the roof of the car, bent down to look through the open window.

"What are you doing, Alex?"

"Get in, O'Malley! Geoffrey has left already."

Kit did as she was told. After all, who was she to argue with a fractiously fragile confused and gorgeous lawyer with an attitude? Stuff that for a joke! the private detective with her own attitude objected. "What are you doing, Alex?" she repeated as she fastened her seat belt.

"Trying to catch up with his taxi," she announced, putting the car in gear and taking off down the street.

"Why? We know where he's going."

"But it's only nine o'clock and the rendezvous at the warehouse isn't till eleven," Alex said, as if that explained everything.

"So?"

"I just thought . . . Shit, O'Malley, I'm only trying to help. Geoffrey suddenly announced he wasn't feeling well and was going home. Miles, who had driven him to the restaurant, offered to take him but Geoffrey insisted he'd be fine in a taxi. When he got up to make the call I pretended I had to go to the loo and I listened in on his phone conversation. He ordered a taxi to take him to St. Kilda, not Footscray, so I thought maybe you should know. So here I am."

"I bet Quinn is really pissed off with you."

"Why?"

"Do as I *say*, Ms. Orlando, not as I do. That's hardly a good example to be setting one so young," said Kit.

"She told me to come and get you," Alex said defensively.

"But I didn't ask you to come and get me. You could have used the same phone Geoffrey did to ring me at the café. I don't need you tagging along, any more than I need Quinn. I don't want to be worrying about you."

"You don't need to worry about me, O'Malley. I won't get in your way. I'll just be your chauffeur."

Kit leant her head out the window, hoping the cool breeze rushing through her hair would help to calm her down. "OK, James, spare the horses and stop trying to catch that taxi. Take me to Footscray, please."

Women! Kit thought as she scrambled along the fence line and under the ramp that ran from the warehouse's loading bay over the public bicycle path and down to the small pontoon dock on the river. Damn her, she even had a change of clothes in the car. Face it, O'Malley, you're in desperate need of an assertiveness training course in how to get the desired reaction when you say no, n-o, absolutely not, no way José.

Kit clambered up onto a boulder and grabbed hold of the fence to pull herself up level with the top landing of the ramp. The gate, which provided the only lawful access to Dalkeith's warehouse from the side facing the river, was chained, padlocked and wearing a big sign aimed at discouraging trespassers. Kit would just have to risk prosecution and find an unlawful access point. She climbed down again and continued along the bicycle path until she could see down the south flank of the building. Unlike the other side, there were no cars, no lights showing from inside and no way she could be seen trying to break in by anyone approaching through the front or back gates. Best of all, there was actually a door that she could try breaking in through.

She headed back to the huge callistemon bush where she'd left Alex sitting on a chunk of bluestone, out of sight of both the dock at the back of Dalkeith's warehouse and the parking area on the south side. There were still only the two vehicles parked there: a brown ute and a blue Torana—minus its homicidal driver.

"Any activity?" she asked, sitting down cross-legged on the ground in front of Alex.

"That guard or whatever he is came out, smoked a cigarette and went back inside. What took you so long?"

"Hey, Alex, these things take as long as they take. You could go back to the car if you're bored."

"No way. I'd hate to think you were worrying about me walking back through that reserve. In the dark. All on my own."

"Follow me then." Kit led Alex back along the bike path, then over the rocks underneath the ramp to the point where the new wire fence met the top landing's main support beams. Pulling a pair of cutters from the leg-pocket of her army pants she snipped a three-foot section of wire, bent it back and crawled through into the space under the loading dock on the other side. There was plenty of room to stand up.

Alex followed her through but then grabbed her arm and pulled her close. "You do realize this is breaking and entering, O'Malley," she whispered.

"I know that, Alex," Kit replied quietly, "and this is just the start. We still have to get inside. Now do me a favor and shut up, or go back to the car." Kit pulled the wire back into place, then headed for the far side of the loading dock which was barricaded by loose sheets of rusty corrugated iron. She moved one piece quietly out of the way and stuck her head out to check if the coast was clear. A minute later, with Alex right behind her, she started working on the lock of the side door.

This is crazy, Kit thought, turning to face her semi-willing accomplice who was standing much too close for comfort. Fighting a sudden and *almost* overwhelming urge to grab Alex by the shoulders, push her up against the wall and kiss her on the mouth until she begged for mercy, Kit managed to whisper, "Make yourself useful, Alex. Go and stand near the front corner of the building and play lookout."

Kit took a deep breath to steady her nerves, her hands and her hormones and returned to the task at hand. It was an easy lock to pick, now she wasn't being completely distracted. She opened the door a crack. There was nothing to see and she couldn't hear a sound. She snapped her fingers to get Alex's attention.

"Dalkeith's car and another one just came in the front gate," Alex said softly before they stepped into the dark interior.

"Looks like we're just in time," Kit whispered. She closed the door behind them.

Kit waited till her eyes got accustomed to the lack of light before moving forward. They had entered what appeared to be a lunch room with a long table in the center and a sink and cupboards on one wall. She crossed to the open doorway and looked carefully out into a dim and deserted hallway, intersected at regular intervals by doors, some open and some closed. The hall extended a good thirty feet to her right before coming to a dead end, and about twenty feet to her left where a faint pool of light indicated another passage leading into the building's interior.

"Stay here," Kit murmured to Alex before creeping towards the light at the far end. She cast a quick glance around the corner to make sure there were no guards or other surprises then took a good look. The hall and its low ceiling continued for about fifteen feet before opening out into the warehouse proper, although a row of metal shipping containers at the end formed a wall on the right-hand side. Opposite the containers, at the rear of the warehouse, was a ramp leading up to a large concrete platform, and at the back of that was a huge door which obviously provided access to the loading bay and the dock on the river.

The light was coming from a fluorescent tube set high in the roof over an iron staircase on the far side of the building. The stairs led up to a glass-walled office and from where she stood Kit could just make out Dalkeith, Grainger, Davis Whitten and—surprise, surprise—a red-haired woman. She could also hear voices, but they weren't coming from the office.

The sliding door to the loading bay on the car park side of the warehouse was partially open. The guard they had seen earlier was leaning in the doorway, looking out and smoking another cigarette.

Kit motioned for Alex to follow her just as far as the corner, then she made a quiet dash for the gap between the first and second containers on the right. She found herself at the head of an aisle which ran the length of the building. Formed by stacks of huge old wooden packing crates, it was about five feet wide and a good sixty feet long.

Kit moved carefully down the aisle to where she could see a gap on the left-hand side and peered around the corner. It was another aisle, only much narrower, and it ran between the stacks for about forty feet. She made her way along that to the next aisle which crossed it at right angles. She realized that about two-thirds of the warehouse was filled with crates arranged in a grid that allowed easy access, though, judging by the amount of dust on the floor, no one had accessed them in a long time.

She started to move forward again in the general direction of the muffled voices but a slight noise somewhere behind her made her stop dead in her tracks. She squeezed into the gap between the next two stacks, crouched down and made like she wasn't there. A couple of seconds later she rolled her eyes and clenched her fists in frustration as she saw Alex creep by, one row back.

Kit ducked out, scooted two stacks along and one aisle over. Reaching out she grabbed Alex from behind and pulled her back between the crates. Every muscle in Alex's body had gone rigid with fright. Kit spun her around in the confined space then clamped her hand over the mouth that looked as if it was about to forget where it was and utter something very loud and indignant. Alex's expression was like thunder but she made no attempt to move away. Not that there was anywhere to go.

Oh my god, she even smells good, Kit thought, wishing she was anywhere but almost in this woman's arms. She glared at Alex to let her know, in no uncertain terms, that she deserved to have the living daylights scared out of her. When she felt Alex relax—and at such close quarters it was a sensation she couldn't help feeling—she removed her hand. The several deep breaths Alex took to calm herself down had quite the opposite effect on Kit, as did the embarrassed smile Alex flashed before mouthing the word "sorry."

Kit closed her eyes and shook her head slowly. When she looked back Alex was still smiling. Kit couldn't help herself: she reached out and placed her thumb and index finger on either side of Alex's mouth to indicate that a more serious attitude was appropriate to the circumstances. Alex flinched slightly at her touch, so Kit gave a resigned shrug and a follow-me hand signal, then turned abruptly and headed back the way she'd come.

She stopped every few yards to pinpoint where the voices were coming from, check the corners before crossing between rows of crates, and make sure Alex was still behind her. The light was getting brighter the closer they got to the center of the warehouse, which made it easier to see but also easier to be seen.

Kit pulled up abruptly when she realized that they were not only about to run out of aisles but that the owners of the voices were right round the next corner. She turned on her heels and crashed straight into Alex, who grabbed her by the shoulders to stop her from falling over then dragged her back into the narrow aisle they'd just left.

Chapter 21

A loud cracking sound and its echo reverberated around the warehouse, making both Kit and Alex jump as if they'd been shot.

"Christ almighty, Andy! What are you trying to do, cut your hand off?" It was Geoffrey's voice and it was coming from just the other side of the next, and last, row of crates.

"It wasn't my fault, it slipped," said a voice which undoubtedly belonged to Andy.

"What the hell was that?" came a shout from the office.

"It's OK, Ian, it was just the top of the crate coming off."

"Well, get a move on. The boat will be here any minute to collect tonight's load," Dalkeith ordered.

"Yes, squire," Geoffrey replied, but only loud enough for those in the immediate vicinity to hear. "Here, let me, Andy. Hold this other bit. No, that bit. OK, lift! Oh god, where the fuck is Christo?"

"I'm over here," came a third voice, so close to where Kit and Alex were crouched that Kit held her breath and screwed one eye shut in anticipation of being caught while she calculated their chances of being able to run like hell and get away with it.

"Well, I don't need you over there," Geoffrey snapped. "Get back here and help Andy load these."

"I thought I heard something," Christo explained.

Alex's fingers curled around Kit's arm as she edged back down the aisle to allow Kit to move further away from the corner.

"I don't give a shit, Christo. It was probably a rat, the place is infested with them."

"Boat's here, boss," someone called out from the back of the warehouse. Kit guessed it was probably the guard on the door.

"Wow," Christo uttered. "Look at them all. Top of the line merchandise, right, Geoff?"

"Right, Christo," replied Geoffrey impatiently. "Just get half of them out and onto the forklift."

It frustrated the hell out of Kit that she couldn't see anything, but there was no way she was going to move any closer. She was still trying to make up her mind what she should do next when an ear-splitting screech of metal on metal helped her decide.

"It's the back door," she whispered into Alex's ear, indicating they should make a run for it. Alex took off with Kit close behind, weaving in and out of the aisles as they headed back into the dark. Any noise they may have made was completely drowned out by the sound of the metal door being hauled up. They stopped running when they reached the shipping containers near the hallway they'd entered by. Kit could feel the adrenaline fairly pumping through her so she bent over and grabbed hold of her knees to steady her breathing. Then she made the mistake of looking at Alex who was leaning back against the container, that heart-stopping smile of hers spreading from one ear to the other and a look in her gray eyes that was pure exhilaration.

Whoa, steady! Kit thought desperately, as she felt the whole universe take one step to the right, then leap back again and slam right into her.

"Are you OK?" Alex asked quietly, leaning close.

Kit nodded stupidly, thinking: there is *no way* this is ordinary lust. It has to be food poisoning or a heavy-duty virus of some sort like the ones that get into your hard drive and send little munchkins out onto your screen to steal your cursor. Trying to ignore the peculiar sensation of being knocked for a loop, she squeezed past Alex to finish what she'd come here to do. Which was what? Oh, right. See what the bad guys are up to. Concentrate, O'Malley!

She crouched down and cast a quick glance around the corner to her right before pulling back. Closing her eyes, she put all the images together in her mind: the back door to the loading bay was raised about halfway, Dalkeith and Grainger were standing outside, Geoffrey was strolling in their direction, and Whitten and the redhead were still in the upstairs office. Kit opened her eyes again when she heard the "oh shit" that Alex muttered under her breath. She followed the invisible line from Alex's pointing finger, across the open space between them and the shipping container that was wedged up against the inside loading bay, to the idiot with a ponytail who was hiding amongst a jumble of crates and giving them a cheery royal wave.

Kit stood up slowly, put her hands on her hips and stared at him with her mouth open. She wondered for a moment if she was actually having a nightmare in which she was a tour guide employed to take amateur detectives on some sort of survival course through the underworld, then decided this scenario was too ridiculous to be a dream. She re-checked the relative positions of the bad guys, all of whom would probably shoot first and not even bother to ask questions later, before indicating in no uncertain terms that he should get his arse over here right now, if not sooner.

"I said just follow him," Kit hissed, after Hector had darted across and side-stepped between her and Alex.

"I am. I did," he whispered.

The sound of a small motor starting up was the only thing that saved Hector's nose from having a short sharp introduction to Kit's fist. She glanced around the corner again in time to see Christo hooning up the ramp at the wheel of a large forklift, on the front of which was a pile of boxes and on the back a guy with altogether too much testosterone. The latter was presumably the Andy who Geoffrey had been talking to.

"Computers," Hector muttered in Kit's ear.

"What?" she asked turning back.

"The boxes. They're Toshiba laptops."

Bloody hell, Kit thought. Why on earth are all these people skulking around in the middle of the night loading computers onto a boat? A boat!

Kit raised her hands and placed one on Hector's shoulder and the other on Alex's. "Stay here," she whispered forcefully. "No matter what happens, do not move from this spot until I get back. OK?"

Alex and Hector looked at each other and then back at Kit before nodding.

Although Kit could hear voices coming from the loading bay, Davis Whitten and the redhead appeared to be the only two members of the opposing team left inside the warehouse. They were still in the office. She headed off down the hall towards the lunch room, hoping to god that her own partners in crime would actually do as they were told this time. She turned the snib on the outside door into the unlocked position so she could get back in easily, slipped carefully outside and crept back through the hole under the loading bay.

Through a gap in the corrugated iron in the south-west corner of the bay she had a perfect view of the lower section of the ramp and the front half of a large and luxurious-looking cabin cruiser which was moored alongside the pontoon dock. The boat's name, painted in large letters on the bow, left Kit in no doubt as to the identity of the tall bespectacled man directing the loading operation.

Well, hello, Malcolm Smith! It looks like the gang's all here, Kit thought as she watched the captain, hat and all, of the *Shirley Too* turn to say something to Geoffrey and Dalkeith.

A few minutes later Christo handed the last of the boxes to the musclebound Andy on the deck of the boat, then climbed into the forklift and drove it up the ramp. Kit did a double take as she took in the incongruous sight in the back of the *Shirley Too*. A striped canopy decorated with balloons hung over a table laden with food and surrounded by deck chairs which, in turn, were occupied by three blond women, each holding champagne glasses and wearing nothing but g-strings.

The tock-tock-tock of high-heeled footsteps almost directly overhead made Kit jerk back from the peephole, even though she knew she couldn't be seen from above.

"They've finished," the woman said. "You'd better get on board, Davis."

"Sure thing, babe. I'll see you tomorrow."

"Davis . . ."

"What?"

"Don't call me babe."

241

That voice! Kit thought, trying to place it. There was no doubt in her mind that this redhead and Geoffrey's favorite crimson tart were one and the same person, but it dawned on her that she'd never been close enough to see the woman's face.

She moved slightly to her left, trying to get a better view through the gaps in the decking above, but it was too dark to see anything more than two pairs of legs. Legs! That's it, she thought. The voice belonged to the owner of the legs she'd glimpsed in the back room at the Skintone Agency. Well, of course it does, O'Malley! Now that you know she's in on whatever this is that's hardly a revelation.

Oh shut up, she said to herself, cursing the shortness of her short-term memory. She couldn't remember whether the voice was familiar this time because she'd heard it at Skintone, or whether it had been familiar then as well, which would mean she'd heard it somewhere else. But where?

Kit turned her attention back to the dock. Captain Smith had started the engine and Andy was casting off the mooring line. Dalkeith and Geoffrey shook hands with Whitten who then clambered into the back of the boat where Grainger was already manhandling two sets of naked breasts.

As the *Shirley Too* pulled away from the dock a row of colored lights sprang to life around the edge of the boat's canopy. Kit almost laughed but she had to hand it to them. They'd obviously decided that the best way to camouflage their nefarious nocturnal activities was to make a spectacle of themselves.

Geoffrey, Dalkeith and Andy reached the top of the ramp before the boat was even out of sight. "Right. That's it for tonight," Dalkeith was saying. "Malcolm says Friday night is still OK for the last load, but he wants to change the pick-up time to nine p.m."

"I don't understand why we didn't send it all in one go."

"That's because you don't understand shit, Andy," the woman said.

"Different customers, different delivery schedule, that's all," Dalkeith stated. "Now, go and tell Bruce that you're taking over from him so he can go home. Oh, and Andy, if you duck out for a hamburger like you did last night I will personally cut your balls off and then drown you in the river. You got that?"

"Yes, Mr. Dalkeith."

"Good. Now piss off."

"That cretin is a serious liability," Geoffrey said, obviously after Andy was out of earshot.

"That cretin is too stupid to be a liability, Geoff," said Dalkeith walking away. "I'm going home. You two can lock up tonight. I'll see you on Friday."

Damn, thought Kit. All this conversation and no one has directly addressed the woman yet. A name might be nice. Come on, Geoffrey.

"Let's go back to your place, babe," Geoffrey said.

I don't think she likes being called that, Geoffrey, Kit thought. And it doesn't tell me who she is.

The woman laughed. "I don't think you'll last that long, Tiger."

Wrong, O'Malley, Kit thought. She obviously doesn't mind being called babe by her Tiger.

"It looks like those bare titties got Mr. Big all excited," she was saying. Geoffrey's inarticulate response was accompanied by the unmistakable sound of a zip being undone.

Oh my god! Kit thought. One half of her mind told her to get as far away from this unexpected development as possible, while the other half told her to stay put until she had a name to go with the red hair and the voice.

"You really want to do it here?" Geoffrey asked, somewhat breathlessly.

"I want you to do *me*, right here. Right now."

Kit dropped to her knees and rolled sideways through the dirt when she realized that in their clumsy jostling for position, Geoffrey had rammed his "babe" up against the fence directly above her.

"Take it, babe," Geoffrey was saying.

"Oh yes, all the way," was the response.

An incredible urge to laugh was Kit's reaction. This is *way* beyond the call of duty, she thought.

"Oh, Maggie. Yes . . . Maggie," Geoffrey groaned.

Oh-Maggie-yes-Maggie? Kit decided that was a good enough name and made a run for the side door of the warehouse.

She found Alex and Hector just where she'd left them.

"I think Dalkeith and the guard have gone, and Christo and the other guy are upstairs in the office," Alex whispered. "We heard the boat leave. Where's everyone else?"

"Grainger, Whitten and Malcolm Smith took off with some naked bimbos in Smith's boat. And Geoffrey . . ." Kit hesitated, fixing Alex with what she hoped was a serious look.

"And Geoffrey what?"

"And Geoffrey and the redhead are out on the loading bay screwing each other's brains out."

"You're kidding," Alex said, her disbelieving tone slightly at odds with her amused expression. "You're not kidding. Honestly, that man must be a walking erection."

"Tell me about it," Kit stated. "I've followed his sexual assignations for weeks but getting that close was something I didn't need."

"You're filthy, O'Malley. What were you doing out there?" Alex queried, reaching out to pull a piece of dried grass from Kit's hair.

"I was rolling around in the dirt trying to avoid the fallout," Kit replied, stepping back awkwardly from Alex who was trying to brush the dust off her T-shirt. "I can manage," she added and ran her hands through her hair to get rid of the debris before brushing her own clothes down.

"Christo! Andy!" It was Oh-Maggie-yes-Maggie doing a great impersonation of the wicked witch of the west, while Geoffrey yanked on the chains to pull the door closed.

"This job must be murder on your nerves," muttered Alex, who was clutching her throat.

Kit growled in frustration. She was still too far away from them to get a good look at Maggie's face. Not only had the light over the stairs been turned out so she could barely make out Geoffrey's features, but he was walking on the wrong side of his babe for Kit to get a clear view.

Five minutes later Geoffrey, Maggie and Christo were gone, all the doors they'd thought about were closed and locked, and all the lights were off, except the one in the office where Andy was sitting with his feet up on the desk.

"OK," Kit announced. "It's time to find out what's left in that crate. If we can find it in the dark." She led the way back, she hoped, to where they'd heard Geoffrey and his mates loading the forklift.

The light from the office cast a glow down the stairs and for about twenty feet out from the corner it was in, but beyond that the warehouse was almost in pitch darkness. Kit found the crate by accident, after walking blindly into the forklift parked next to it. The crate was about five feet square. Christo and Andy had put the lid back on but had, quite considerately Kit thought, not nailed it shut again.

"Hector," she whispered. "Give me a hand, please."

Together they lifted the lid and lowered it to the ground. The clack it made when it met the floor echoed around the warehouse. Kit, Alex and Hector dived back into the cover of the stacks as Andy flung open the door to the office.

"Shut up, you bastard rats," he bellowed.

Oh Geoffrey, Kit thought. You should have challenged Dalkeith's opinion that this cretin was too stupid to be a liability.

"And fuck you, Mis-ter Dalkeith," Andy added, pulling a set of keys from his pocket as he stomped down the stairs. He unlocked the side door and slammed it on his way out.

"What do you suppose that was all about?" Alex asked.

"I think Andy's gone to get a hamburger," Kit replied. "Come on, let's get this over with."

She climbed up on the side of the forklift, pulled a small torch from her pocket and shone the light into the crate. It was about half-full with tightly packed boxes bearing the Toshiba logo.

"There's got to be something other than computers in these boxes," she said.

"I could climb in and open one up," Hector suggested.

"In you go then."

Hector clambered over the side of the crate and, dropping to his knees, pulled one of the boxes free. A charming-looking flick knife appeared in his hand as if by magic and he set to work on the sealing tape.

"You could get arrested for carrying one of those things these days," Kit said.

"We could get arrested for just about everything we've done tonight, O'Malley," said Alex.

"Nah, it's more likely we'd get cut into little pieces for everything we've done tonight," Hector stated, grinning into the torch light. "I hope your gun's got a full clip, boss, just in case that guy comes back."

"I don't carry a gun, Hector."

"What? Are you crazy? All private detectives have guns."

"Not in the State of Victoria they don't. It's against the law," Kit explained. She waved her hand to indicate he should stop yacking and get on with things.

"Oh, great. What are you going to do, O'Malley, dazzle him with your little pen light?" Hector folded back the flaps of the box and pulled out the bubble-plastic packing, then a power cord, then a sleek black Toshiba laptop, which he opened.

"Everything seems in order, boss. It looks like a computer to me. What were you hoping for?"

"Oh, I don't know. Something, anything, to justify all their slinking around in the middle of the goddamn night," Kit replied, throwing her hands up and nearly throwing herself off the forklift in the process. "You'd better put all that stuff back then try another box. Please," she added, handing the torch to Hector so she could climb down and get her feet back on level ground.

"I'm going to search the office, Alex. Please stay right here with Hector."

Kit had just crossed the fifty or so feet of empty warehouse and reached the bottom of the staircase when she heard a key sliding into the lock of the side door. Uh oh, she thought, and grabbed the handrail, using it to help her swing into the space under the stairs.

Andy, whistling tunelessly, stepped inside and dumped an esky on the ground so he could lock the door. He was having trouble with that simple task till he realized it would be easier if he also put down the beer he was drinking so he could concentrate on one thing at a time.

Alex, Hector, for goodness' sake pay attention! That's not me whistling, Kit wanted to shout, when she realized she could still see the thin beam of the torch flicking faintly from the other end of the building. Oh shit! Too late, she groaned to herself as she watched Andy turn from the door and freeze, his attention fixed on what was obviously an extremely puzzling phenomenon. It took a few seconds but it finally must have clicked with him that even "bastard" rats don't have headlights. Kit watched in astonishment as the world's oldest Ninja Turtle dropped to a crouch and executed a very neat sideways roll that put him back in the same balanced crouching position, four whole feet from where he'd started.

Well that achieved a lot, Andy, she thought. What's your next move? She immediately wished she hadn't asked that question, even silently, because Andy's idea of a next move was to produce a very large torch from his jacket pocket, which he didn't turn on, and a hand gun from the waistband of his trousers. Still hunched down he began moving in the direction of the mysterious light.

Kit looked about for some kind of weapon. As there were no handy AK-47s just lying around she had to settle for a slim three-foot length of pipe.

Andy, who was still moving rapidly away from her, hadn't checked his back once. After easing out from under the stairs Kit leapt up and down and waved her arms about wildly, hoping that Alex at least was looking in her direction. Then she made a beeline for the nearest aisle, ran like hell down to the other end and skidded to a stop when she heard Andy shouting.

"Get 'em up. Get your hands in the air!"

Kit crept along the cross aisle and peered around the corner, blinking in the backwash of the high beam that was being directed straight into Alex's understandably startled face. With the light in her eyes there was no way that Alex could see Kit standing about six feet behind the maniac who was pointing the gun at her. In fact Alex probably couldn't even see the maniac who was pointing the gun at her. Don't do anything silly, Alex. Please, Kit prayed, wondering vaguely where Hector was.

Alex, with her arms held very sensibly above her head, squinted into the light and smiled ever-so-sweetly. "Would you mind lowering the torch a bit, Andy, you're blinding me. It's OK, really," she said.

"What do you mean, it's OK? What are you doing here? And how do you know my name?" Andy asked, waving the gun around.

"I'm a friend of Geoffrey's, of Mr. Robinson. He left me here to keep you company."

Oh, good one, Alex! Kit thought. This woman must be awesome in court, she is so gorgeously cool.

"What?" Andy stopped shining the torch in Alex's eyes and played the light over the rest of her body instead.

"What do you mean what? Didn't he tell you, Andy?"

"He didn't tell me nothin'. I never saw you with Mr. Robinson. How'd you get here anyway?"

"I came on the boat with the others. He said I should stick around to keep you from getting bored."

"Yeah?"

Andy *really* wanted to believe this but Kit doubted even he was that stupid. She'd also caught the flicker of fear that had crossed Alex's face. She had obviously just noticed the gun.

Kit stared at the pipe in her hand and then looked back at Andy, debating whether or not to race out and belt him over the back of the head with it. He was about the same height as her, but he was built like a brick shithouse and she had no idea how hard she'd have to hit him to do any damage. And the gun might go off accidentally. She looked at the pipe again. It still wasn't an AK-47. But Andy didn't know that.

Edging out of her hiding place, she moved silently up behind him.

"Drop the gun, arsehole," she growled, shoving the open end of the pipe against the back of his neck.

Andy went rigid but apart from that didn't move a muscle.

Kit took a deep breath and in the best Dirty Harry voice she could muster shouted: "Do it! Or I'll splatter your brains all over this nice lady."

That worked. Andy dropped the gun. And the torch.

"Pick them up, Alex," Kit urged, jabbing the pipe hard into Andy's kidneys to talk him out of making a run for it.

Alex did as she was told, then just stood there staring at the gun in her hand and looking more than a little bewildered.

"Alex, honey, point the gun at the bad guy," Kit said softly.

"Oh, right," Alex said, aiming the weapon in the general direction of Andy's head, crutch, chest, knee, crutch.

"Far out!" exclaimed Hector, popping up from his hiding place in the crate like a jack-in-the-box.

"Christ, Hector! You scared the shit out of me!" Kit snapped.

"Sorry, boss."

"And stop calling me boss."

"Who the fuck are you people?" Andy demanded.

"I don't think the answer to that question is really going to help you much while *your* boss, Mis-ter Dalkeith, is cutting your balls off. Do you?" Kit asked.

"I guess not," Andy muttered, as if he'd just recognized the gravity of his situation. "What are you going to do with me?"

"Nothing, Andy. Personally I've yet to come across a good use for balls, so I thought I'd maybe just tie you up and leave you to explain all this mess to you-know-who."

"Hey, O'Malley, I thought you said you didn't carry a gun," Hector said as he swung one leg over the edge of the crate.

"Shut up, Hector," Kit ordered, a split second before Andy, his brain suddenly functioning at almost the same speed as his body, twisted around and said: "What?"

In two swift moves Andy kicked the torch from Alex's hand and slugged Kit in the jaw, sending her flying out of his way as he barged past into the dark.

Kit had just enough time to register an odd smacking sound before she crashed headfirst into the stack of crates. Then the lights went out.

Chapter 22

Kit was lying on her left side, her head on something soft. Correction, her head on something soft and wet. Oh, Thistle, she thought, don't tell me you've knocked the water off the bedside table again. She tried to lift her head off the pillow but decided that was the worst idea she'd had in a long time. She had neither the strength nor the inclination to do anything more than breathe, her tongue felt all thick and furry and some bastard was beating a bass drum inside her skull.

Face it, O'Malley, it's time to give up drinking. You're getting too old for hangovers of this magnitude, she thought slowly, then flinched as the bed lurched under her. Oh great, now you're going to die in an earthquake because you can't move to save yourself.

"Welcome back," someone said.

"Why is the bed moving?" Kit asked. Ow, that hurt! She reached up to touch her jaw.

"It's not a bed, O'Malley. You're in my car."

Kit forced her body to turn on its back before opening her eyes. OK, forget the earthquake, you've already died. And gone to heaven!

This was no pillow. It was a lap. What's more it was Alex's lap. And there was Alex, her hair falling forward across her face, looking down at her. Kit closed her eyes again, trying to shake off the dream.

"O'Malley, stay awake."

Awake? Kit opened her eyes again. Alex was still there. "I thought I was dreaming," she said.

"You've been unconscious for twenty minutes," Alex explained.

"Oh, that's nice," Kit mumbled.

"Keep her talking," someone else said as the movement of the car stopped.

"Alex?"

"Yes, O'Malley."

"We're in your car, right?"

"Yes, O'Malley."

"And we're in the back seat, right?"

"Yes, O'Malley."

"Then who's driving?"

Alex smiled and brushed the hair back from Kit's forehead. "It's a long story."

"I'm not going anywhere," Kit stated, deciding that even if she was suddenly overtaken by a feeling of perfect health and well-being, she still wasn't going anywhere.

"I told you to stay out of this or you'd ruin everything but I didn't think even you could screw things up this badly."

"Oh, hi, Finnigan," Kit drawled, quite calmly considering one of the few unexplained players left in this mystery was staring at her from the driver's seat. "Where did you come from?" she asked. "And where's Hector?"

"I've been hanging around the edges all night. Which is where you should have been," he replied, turning his attention back to the task of driving the car.

"We told Hector to get out of there and go home," Alex added.

"Good thunking, er thinking," Kit stammered and closed her eyes again.

"O'Malley!" Alex said sharply.

Kit reached up and grabbed Alex's hand to stop the cheek-patting nonsense that was starting to annoy the hell out of her. "Stop already," she groaned. She held Alex's hand in front of her and tried to focus properly.

"Alex, you're bleeding!"

"No, O'Malley, *you* are bleeding or at least you were."

"Oh shit." Kit tried to sit up but Alex wouldn't let her.

"Lie still, for goodness' sake," Alex ordered.

"You mean all this wet stuff is my blood?" Kit asked, running her hand awkwardly over Alex's thigh.

"Don't make such a fuss, O'Malley," Finnigan said. "It's only a flesh wound."

"I'm bleeding to death all over this absolutely gorgeous woman and you say it's only a flesh wound," Kit cried. "Sorry, Alex," she added, completely mortified by what she'd just said.

"For what?"

"Nothing. Everything," she replied quickly. "But I'd probably feel a whole lot better if I knew what happened. How can I have a flesh wound when Alex had the gun?" Kit hesitated a moment, "Oh Alex, you didn't shoot me, did you?"

"Of course not, don't be ridiculous. You've cut your eyebrow, that's all. Andy slammed you into the boxes. You hit your head on the corner of one and were knocked out cold."

"Oh," Kit said because she couldn't think of anything better. "What happened to the steroid steamroller anyway?"

"He's in the trunk," Finnigan stated.

"The trunk?" Kit queried, not understanding.

"The boot, O'Malley. Andy's in the boot," Alex translated.

"What, this boot? Your boot? Why, for god's sake?"

"Well, your idea of leaving him tied up to explain the damage had its merits only if you wanted to be a fly on the wall to witness Dalkeith go completely ballistic," Finnigan said. "I convinced Andy it was in his best interests to make a phone call to the other guy they'd had on guard duty, claim he'd come down with a deadly case of food poisoning and ask the guy to cover for him."

"And he agreed to this?"

"He didn't have much choice. *My* gun was real," Finnigan stated.

"Good point," Kit mumbled. A wave of nausea swept over her body. Even her toes felt sick. She reached up and touched her right eyebrow. Nothing. She was about to make a move for the other one when Alex clasped her hand.

"Leave it alone, O'Malley. You'll only start it bleeding again."

"Some hero, huh?" Kit smiled wanly.

"Yeah, my hero, O'Malley, now lie still."

Kit did better than that. She passed out again.

Quinn flung open the front door just as Kit and Alex got to the landing. "It's about time!" she exclaimed. "It's nearly four o'clock. I was starting to get really worried. I almost called the cops to go looking for you."

"Not so loud, please, Quinn," Kit begged.

"Jesus! What happened, Kit? Alex, what happened to her? Oh shit, is that blood? You're covered in blood, Alex."

"I know. It's O'Malley's blood. Now stop the verbal barrage and simmer down. We're both OK but we would like to come in and sit down."

"Yeah, right." Quinn stepped out of the way to let them pass before closing the door.

Kit slumped into the corner of the couch and pulled her legs up. She tried to smile so that Quinn wouldn't look so concerned but it hurt too much.

"You look awful, Kit," Quinn said.

"Thanks, mate, I needed that."

"Do you want something to drink, O'Malley?" Alex asked.

"Bourbon," Kit replied.

"No, I don't think so, you've got concussion. Quinn, would you be an angel and make me a cup of coffee and see if O'Malley has anything in her fridge with no stimulants in it."

"Milk," said Kit. "I'll have some milk, please."

"So where have you been?" Quinn asked from the kitchen. "And why does Kit look like she went three rounds with the Terminator?"

"One round," Kit said. "It was only one round. And it was the Karate Kid. It's not as bad as it looks, Quinn. I didn't even need stitches."

"We spent the last ninety minutes sitting in casualty waiting for a doctor to put a piece of sticky plaster on her head and send us home," Alex said.

"I kept telling you I was all right," said Kit.

"In between passing out."

"Twice. I passed out twice, Alex."

"For goodness' sake! Stop arguing and tell me what happened," Quinn demanded.

"Why would anybody want to smuggle computers?" Quinn asked, half an hour later.

"Beats me," Kit responded. "In fact right at the moment I'm completely flummoxed by just about everything that's going on around me. My head hurts too much to even work out whether I care about what those bastards are doing and why. Maybe I'm just not cut out for this job."

"You're just tired, Kit," Quinn said. "After all, you did save Alex's life."

"Hardly, Quinn," Kit said, glancing at Alex, who raised an eyebrow and smiled.

"She has a point, O'Malley."

"Really? The real point is that you shouldn't have been there in the first place, Alex. I should have locked *you* in the boot. And there's another thing. I was so busy bleeding all over you and your car that I didn't ask Finnigan anything. Like who he really is and what he was doing there and other pertinent and probably important questions of that ilk."

"He's a cop from LA," Alex stated.

Kit just stared at her.

"That's what he told me. He said he was after Whitten but he wouldn't say why. Just before he left in the taxi with Andy, he gave me a phone number to give you in case you need him."

Kit shook her head slowly. "Need him for what?"

"I've no idea, O'Malley. You're the detective."

"I am?"

"That reminds me," Quinn said, "your police-person friend rang. He said if you still want to accompany him when he goes to see Geoffrey tomorrow you have to meet him outside my mother's house at three p.m. And he told me to stress that by outside he meant out in the street."

"Oh goody," Kit groaned. "If only we'd found something concrete at that damn warehouse tonight. It's on record that Freyling Imports deals in computer hardware, and with no evidence they were shifting anything other than laptops I've got no hope of convincing Marek that these people are up to no good. What I would call a gang of smugglers moving their contraband, he'll call a group of legitimate business people working night shift to get their stock cleared. He'd just laugh at me if I suggested we raid the place on Friday."

"Friday? When on Friday?" Quinn interrupted.

"Nine o'clock at night. Why?"

"Oh, that's OK. It's just that I'd really like you, both of you, to be with me on Friday," Quinn explained. "For the funeral," she added when she saw Kit's blank expression. "Didn't you tell her, Alex?"

"Sorry, no. We were a bit preoccupied," Alex said. "It's at three, then everyone's going back to the house."

"And when it's over I'm going to tell that pig he's got a week to clear out," Quinn announced. "So I can go home."

"Speaking of going home, that's an excellent idea," Alex stated, looking pointedly at Quinn.

"I think I'll stay here, Alex. If that's all right, Kit? You probably shouldn't be on your own anyway."

"That's fine by me," Kit replied, trying to ignore the look of disapproval that flashed across Alex's face.

"Fine. Will I see you tomorrow, Quinn?" Alex asked, standing up. "I have an idea," she added, before Quinn could reply. "Why don't we have dinner at my place tomorrow night? You can come too, O'Malley. I'd like you to meet Enzo."

I have no desire to meet Enzo, Kit thought, as she accepted the invitation anyway.

"He's late," Alex said, glancing at her watch for the thirteenth time.

"We've only been here ten minutes. Are you bored already?" Kit was fiddling with the cap on the bottle of water she had wedged between her legs.

"No, I'm not bored, O'Malley, I just believe in being punctual, that's all."

"Marek being late is probably a good sign."

"What sort of good sign could it possibly be?" Alex drummed her fingers on the steering wheel and checked the rear-vision mirror again.

"He's got your mobile number so if he's been held up on other police business he would have called us. Therefore the fact that he's making Geoffrey wait is a good sign."

"What does that mean?" Alex pulled her sunglasses halfway down her nose and gave a look that suggested she thought Kit had lost a few marbles along with her blood the night before.

Holy Mills and Boon! Kit exclaimed silently, as she felt all her insides go absurdly hot and squishy. There are few better sights in this world, she thought, than a gorgeous woman in a pair of Ray-Bans. Except maybe the sight of this particular gorgeous woman's eyes staring at her over the *top* of a pair of Ray-Bans. It didn't matter at all that Alex's expression implied that she thought Kit was completely nicked in the head.

"It's a simple question, O'Malley."

"Marek prides himself on being a punctual person," Kit explained, trying to put out the fire with a mouthful of water. "If he still believed Geoffrey was a fine upstanding pillar of the community there is no way he would be late for an appointment. The fact that he is ten, make that nearly fifteen minutes late suggests that he is deliberately keeping Geoffrey waiting, which suggests to me that he no longer believes in the veracity of the poor grieving widower. He's making him stew."

"I don't suppose it has occurred to you that the appointment was really for three-thirty and your friend Marek is deliberately keeping *you* waiting?"

Kit laughed. "You may have a point. But there's no way he would do that to you," Kit said suggestively.

"And what does *that* mean?"

"You're not going to tell me you didn't notice him falling all over himself in an attempt to cover the fact that the very sight of you woke up all his dormant male juices and made him go completely to pieces," Kit stated. You should talk, she thought.

Alex stared at Kit with her mouth open. "What on earth are you talking about?"

"Lust, Alex. Marek was quite beside himself with it yesterday morning."

"Don't be ridiculous," Alex said and pushed her Ray-Bans back into place as she turned her attention back to the street.

Yes! Kit thought, as she watched Alex actually blush with embarrassment.

After a few minutes silence Alex said: "Speaking of lust . . ."

"Were we?" Kit asked, covering her surprise by putting her own sunglasses on—quickly.

"I wanted to talk to you about Quinn," Alex began.

"What about her?" Kit asked, her tone sharper than she'd intended.

"Well," Alex crossed her arms and tapped the fingers of her left hand lightly on her lips, as if the action would help get the words out. "I need . . . ah . . . I'd like to know . . ."

"Sorry, Alex," Kit interrupted, "this discussion will have to keep. The cavalry's here." Kit almost sighed with relief at Marek's timely arrival. He cruised past, gave a short wave and parked his car on the opposite site of the street.

Kit struggled out of Alex's Celica onto the nature strip as quickly as she could. The inside of her head still felt as if it was being used as an anvil by a highly strung blacksmith, so the sudden movement produced a surge of nausea. On top of that, her sense of balance was not helped by the fact that the elm tree beside her appeared to be doing the hula. She gripped the door to steady herself.

"Are you OK?" Alex queried. She was leaning on the roof of the car, giving her that look again.

"Fine. Fine. I'm just fine," Kit lied, hoping like hell she wouldn't have to throw up in this nice neighborhood. She sat down on the passenger seat again with her feet in the gutter, closed her eyes and took several deep breaths.

"Put your head between your knees." The voice was gentle and the hand on her thigh was no doubt meant to be comforting. Kit opened her eyes to find Alex crouching in front of her holding the bottle of water.

"I'm fine, really, I just stood up too fast," she said, accepting the water with a grateful smile.

"Perhaps I should take you home," Alex suggested. She placed the back of her hand gently on Kit's forehead. "I think you have a temperature."

If I didn't before I have now, Kit thought. She put her arm out so Alex could help her to her feet.

"Don't you say a word," Kit said as Marek stepped from behind Alex's car onto the footpath.

"You mean you already know you look like shit?" Marek asked. "Good afternoon, Ms. Cazenove," he added, straightening his tie.

Alex gave a cautious nod. "Detective Marek," she acknowledged.

Marek put his finger on Kit's chin and turned her face to get a good look at the purple bruise on her jaw. Kit had tried, but no amount of make-up could disguise the fact that she'd been king-hit by a very large fist. She'd also put about half a can of mousse in her hair to force her fringe to at least hover over her left eyebrow so the steri-strips and swelling were less obvious.

"The color suits you, Kitty. Who have you been annoying this time?"

"Sylvester Stallone's mother," Kit replied.

"I thought I warned you about her," Marek stated dryly. "Are you ready? You'll have to wait here, Ms. Cazenove. I don't want a convention in there."

Alex shrugged. "I'm just the chauffeur. She's got a concussion to go with this new color scheme and the doctor said she shouldn't operate any machinery for at least two days."

"That's a relief. Have you seen the way she drives?"

"I am going to talk to Geoffrey now," Kit said curtly. "Are you coming or not?"

"We won't be long," Marek said to Alex as he trailed across the road after Kit.

"Did you bring the photos?" she asked.

"I know I'm forgetful, Kitty, but I'm not that bad. There *was* only a ten-minute delay between you ringing to ask for them and me walking out the door to come here," Marek grumbled, pulling a large envelope from the pocket of his jacket.

"Good, let's get the bastard." Kit strode off up the driveway.

"Jeez! You promised me you'd behave, O'Malley. If you're going to be like that you can go home," Marek threatened, jogging to catch up with her.

"I promise, I promise," Kit insisted. "Look, I may want to see the creep hang, and preferably by his pizzle, but . . ."

"What? By his what?" Marek interrupted, ringing the door bell.

"His dick, Marek," Kit said, rolling her eyes, "but now I want to get Dalkeith and his myrmidons as much as I want Geoffrey."

"Where do you find all these big words?"

"What, pizzle?"

"No, the other big one," Marek said, as the front door opened.

Geoffrey "Tiger" Robinson stood there wearing an open-necked shirt, dark trousers, an appropriately forlorn expression and far too much Old Spice. He shook hands with Marek, looked at Kit as if he'd never seen her before then led the way down the hall.

Chapter 23

"Now, how may I help you?" Geoffrey asked after showing Kit and Marek into the lounge room. He walked over to the bar and spun the top off a bottle of whisky. "I know it's a bit early in the day for this, but it seems to help me through this traumatic time."

You lying bastard, Kit thought, biting her tongue to stop herself from saying it out loud.

"It's hard to believe it's been almost a week since . . ." Geoffrey let his words trail suggestively off into the ether before collecting himself. "I don't suppose you can have one of these if you're on duty."

"No. Thanks, anyway," Marek said. "Perhaps if you could just sit down, Mr. Robinson, and we'll get this over and done with as quickly as possible."

Geoffrey sat down obediently. He cradled the glass in his hands but didn't actually drink anything.

"I need to go over the statement you made last Friday night and get a few other things straight," Marek explained, taking out his notebook.

"Fire away," Geoffrey said.

"You stated you left the house at about six p.m. after having drinks here with Mrs. Robinson and your publisher Miles Denning. Did you take your own car?"

"No, Miles had come to pick me up."

"And your wife was alone in the house when you left."

"That's right," Geoffrey acknowledged.

"Was it unusual for Mrs. Robinson to stay home like that?"

"What?"

"Why didn't your wife go out to dinner with you?"

"Oh. No, it wasn't unusual. She quite often skipped business dinners. She found them tedious. On that last night, however, she also wasn't feeling very well."

"She wasn't feeling well yet she was drinking champagne?" Marek said.

"Well, she was . . . a drinker, and I told you how upset she was about this dreadful business with her secretary. Perhaps when you find Daniels . . ."

"We'll get to Mr. Daniels in a minute," Marek interrupted.

He doesn't know we've found him, Kit thought and smiled to herself.

"Now, what did you do when you left here?" Marek continued.

"As I said on Friday," Geoffrey sighed, "Miles drove me to the Shangri La where we joined some associates for dinner. I'm not sure what time it was when your officers arrived but, as you know, I returned here with them."

"I'd like to ask you about the woman you met in the car park," Kit said.

"What about her?" Geoffrey said, finally taking a swig of his drink to cover either his surprise at the question or the fact that Kit had spoken for the first time.

"You told Detective Marek that you did not know this woman. Is that correct?"

"Yes, of course it is. She was just there, that's all. She asked me for a light then she got in her car and drove off."

"She was just there? The witness said you watched the woman walk in off the street," Kit lied.

"Really? I . . . ah . . . don't remember to be honest."

"Did you happen to notice what sort of car it was?" Kit pressed.

"No. I wasn't paying much attention," Geoffrey said impatiently. He turned back to Marek. "Is this important?"

Marek shrugged. "Since the autopsy revealed that your wife's death was not an accident we have to go over everything very carefully."

"Yes, of course. I understand." Geoffrey forced himself back into reasonable mode.

"There *is* one point in your original statement which was contradicted by the findings of the autopsy," Marek announced.

"And what was that?" Geoffrey asked, pulling himself up in the chair. Kit noticed he was suddenly looking a little green around the gills.

"You said Mrs. Robinson had been drinking heavily, yet her blood alcohol level was in fact quite low. How would you explain that, Mr. Robinson?"

"I don't know, maybe . . . um . . . I have no idea," Geoffrey blustered. "Maybe she was so upset about Byron that I mistook her behavior for . . . Oh dear, poor Celia."

That's right, Tiger, stick to the original story no matter how idiotic it sounds, Kit thought.

"I just hope you find him soon, Detective Marek. He has to pay for what he's done."

"Find who, Mr. Robinson? And pay for what?" Kit asked.

"Daniels, of course. He must be the one who . . . the one who killed my Celia."

Oh, give me a break! Kit thought.

"Let's talk about Byron Daniels," Marek said. "In your statement on Friday night you said that you fired him for stealing. Is that right?"

"That's what I said," Geoffrey agreed.

"You claimed you waited until he arrived for work on Thursday and then discharged him." Geoffrey was about to agree again when Marek continued: "We have a witness, however, who says that Mr. Daniels saw your wife, not you, on Thursday morning. And that when he left this house shortly after that meeting he was still in her employ."

Kit thought it was stretching it a bit, even for Marek, to classify Damien's hearsay evidence as an actual flesh and blood witness but who was she to contradict him?

"Did I say the morning?" Geoffrey was asking, trying to look vague. "It was the afternoon, I saw him after lunch. I can't imagine why I would have said the morning, except that I was of course in rather a state on Friday night. If you recall, Detective, my wife had just been murdered."

262

"Actually, Mr. Robinson, at that stage it was thought your wife had met with an accident," Marek reminded him.

"Oh, you know what I meant," Geoffrey snapped.

"Yes, of course. Getting back to Mr. Daniels," said Marek, tapping his pen lightly but repeatedly on his notebook. Kit recognized this deliberately annoying habit of Marek's as a sure sign that he didn't believe a single word his subject was saying. "According to our witness, the reason for Mr. Daniels's alleged dismissal was not theft, as you claim, but the fact that you believed he was following you for blackmail purposes."

"That is ludicrous!" Geoffrey bellowed.

"So Mr. Daniels was not blackmailing you?" Marek asked.

"Of course not. What possible reason could he have had to blackmail me?"

Where would you like me to start? Kit thought. "Were you blackmailing him?" she asked instead.

"What? How dare you, young lady!" Geoffrey snarled, then obviously remembered he was talking to someone he thought was a police officer. He turned to Marek. "Who is this witness anyway?"

"Just someone helping us with our inquiries," Marek replied.

"I think these questions are starting to get a bit out of line," Geoffrey stated, trying to get back on top of the situation. "Why are you bothering me with these laughable notions? You should be out looking for Daniels. Then this whole mess will be cleared up."

"We have already found Byron Daniels, Mr. Robinson. He's in the morgue," Marek stated.

"The morgue?" Geoffrey exclaimed, with altogether too much mock surprise in his voice. "What did he do? Kill himself in remorse for killing my wife?"

Oh brother! thought Kit.

"No, actually he couldn't have killed your wife, Mr. Robinson," Marek stated quietly. "He died before she did."

"Well . . ." Geoffrey began, looking strangely perplexed as he took another sip of his drink. He gave the impression that he was searching, rather desperately Kit thought, for a way to change tack. "Well, he probably committed suicide because he couldn't bear the shame of being caught red-handed and branded a thief," he finally suggested, apparently deciding that a return to his original story would be his best bet.

Kit tried desperately to keep a straight face as Detective-Sergeant Jon Marek frowned and shook his head ever so seriously. She knew Marek was enjoying watching Geoffrey open his mouth only to change feet nearly as much as she was. For his part, Geoffrey had turned a different shade of green.

"What makes you think Mr. Daniels committed suicide?" Marek asked.

"Isn't that what you said?"

"No, Mr. Robinson. I wouldn't have said that because Byron Daniels did not commit suicide."

"What? What do you mean?" Geoffrey spluttered.

"Well, you see it's not usual for someone to take their own life by slitting their own throat from ear to ear then plunging the same knife into their own back. For that reason we discounted suicide almost immediately," Marek explained, with a completely deadpan expression, "and are treating his death as a murder."

How very interesting! thought Kit. Geoffrey appeared to be genuinely surprised that Byron had *not* committed suicide. That would mean that he either honestly believed that Byron had a reason to kill himself, or the plan had been that his death should *look* like a suicide. Oh shit! If the former was the case, she thought, then a moldy old can of worms had just been opened because one possible reason for that belief was that Geoffrey thought Byron really had murdered Celia—which meant that he, Geoffrey, had not. Nor did he have any idea who really did. No way, O'Malley! The alternative theory is much more logical, which means that one of Geoffrey's cronies has apparently made a very big boo-boo.

"How dreadful," Geoffrey was saying, trying to regain his composure, "although it was probably one of his poofter friends. You know what they're like."

"I'm sure I don't," said Marek. "But perhaps you know better."

"Are you saying you think Mr. Daniels was killed by a friend?" Kit baited.

"I'm not saying anything of the kind. Are you nearly finished? I do have other things to do today."

"Not quite, Mr. Robinson," Marek said. "As you can no doubt appreciate, no matter who killed him, the murder of Byron Daniels presents us with a great many problems. It changes everything."

"Everything? I don't understand," Geoffrey said impatiently.

"I'm talking about our investigation into the murder of your wife, Mr. Robinson. If our number one suspect could not possibly have committed the crime then who did? Do you have any ideas? Did your wife have any enemies perhaps?"

"Not that I know of," Geoffrey stated. "I can't imagine why she would."

"OK. Can I run a few names by you?" Marek asked.

"Certainly," said Geoffrey nervously.

"Do you know a Christopher Edwards?"

"No," Geoffrey replied a little too quickly. "Should I?"

"There's no reason why you should," Marek replied soothingly. "How about George Ryan?"

"No," he said adamantly. "Who are these people anyway?"

"How about Gerald Grainger?" Kit asked, ignoring Geoffrey's question.

"No," he replied automatically, then obviously thought better of it. "I mean yes. Gerald is an old friend."

"And a business associate," Kit stated suggestively.

"Um, yes, we have done business together over the years. Look, what's going on here? Why on earth are you asking me about Gerry? You can't possibly think he had anything to do with this. Or am I the suspect here? Is that what all this is about?"

"Of course not, Mr. Robinson," Marek lied. "In fact I think we've covered just about everything so we'll be on our way."

"There is just one other thing," Kit interrupted, opening the envelope Marek had brought for her. Pulling out the photos taken of Celia's body before the storm broke, she stood up and walked over to Geoffrey. "We were wondering if you would be able to tell us what these holes are," she said, sitting on the edge of the couch next to him.

"Oh, my goodness," Geoffrey gasped, almost convincingly, at the sight of Celia in close-up. "Holes? No, I'm sorry, I haven't a clue what they are."

"It has been suggested that they might be aeration holes for the lawn," Kit said, offering Geoffrey the photo again. "Do you think that's what they might be?"

"As I said, I haven't a clue. That was my wife's domain. I rarely went out the back. You would have to speak to Celia's gardener about that."

"Of course," Kit said. She was about to slide the photos back in the envelope when something caught her attention. This something was so obvious it should have leapt out and bitten her on the nose the first time she'd seen the photos in Marek's office. But she'd been so sidetracked by the stupid holes that she hadn't looked at the whole picture. In fact she should have picked it up last Friday when she was sitting in the rain looking at the real thing. She recalled thinking at the time "there is something wrong with this picture" but the reason hadn't registered because she'd been distracted by the incongruous sight of Celia's body almost covered by a wet blanket. *Almost* being the operative word.

She'd known then that Celia had been murdered, only she didn't know why she knew it. Oh my god, she thought, and now I know who killed her.

"You are completely out of your mind."

"Why?" Kit asked.

"Why?" repeated Marek. "Well, that idiotic question only proves you've lost it."

"It's a perfectly reasonable supposition, Marek," stated Kit, her arms akimbo as she leant back against the high brick fence of the Orlando-Robinson residence. She threw a royal wave at Alex who was still waiting in her car on the other side of the street.

"It's not reasonable at all, Kitty, and what's more it has more holes in it than this so-called piece of evidence," Marek argued, waving the photo of Celia in front of her.

"What do you mean so-called? Look, Jonno, if I'd been in any condition other than one of extreme shock last Friday I could have told you then that Celia's death was not a bloody accident. She still had her shoes on, for Christ's sake. Celia never, and I mean never, went into her Forum wearing heeled shoes. And neither did anyone else—on

266

pain of death! Even the damn gardener had to wear galoshes over his work boots."

"That's all very well, O'Malley, now that the autopsy has proved what you missed six days ago, but it doesn't give me shit to work on. Take a look at the picture again and you'll see that your friend Mrs. R is wearing low, square-heeled sandals—so these stupid holes in the stupid lawn could not have been made by her shoes."

"That is precisely my point, Marek. Honestly, you can be so thick sometimes." Kit grabbed one side of the photo of the long shot that took in the whole crime scene to hold it still. "Now, *you* take another look. Here we have some slight and square indentations in the lawn. The closer these footprints get to the fish pond the deeper they are. They're also more sharply defined at the back of the heel, which indicates that Celia was possibly walking backwards. The other holes," Kit continued, running her finger over the photo, "follow the same path that Celia took to the pond, at which point they appear to be all over the place, which indicates a struggle, except for these ones which trail off in the direction of old Perseus there, where the murder weapon was found."

"But . . ." Marek began, as he pinched the bridge of his nose in consternation.

"But nothing, Jonno. I'd bet you anything you like that those holes were made by high heels."

"And you want me to arrest Geoffrey Robinson's alleged mistress on the grounds of this flimsy load of codswallop?"

"Yes," Kit replied. "I'm positive that if you put this to the forensics team they'll agree that it's the most logical explanation."

"They may well agree," Marek conceded, "but it doesn't give me enough to arrest even a known crim's elbow, let alone the girlfriend of an otherwise respected member of the community. Who is the other woman anyway?"

"Well, I know her first name and I can tell you where you might find her."

"*Might* find her? Jeez, O'Malley!" Marek started to walk back to his car.

"Plus . . ." Marek was still walking away from her. "Plus I can give you a photograph of her and a witness who can identify her as the woman who met Geoffrey in that car park last Friday night," Kit said hurriedly.

Marek turned on his heel and walked back to Kit, wearing one of his what-else-haven't-you-told-me expressions.

"She's a high-class prostitute by the name of Maggie," Kit stated sheepishly.

"Who, the witness?" asked Marek.

"No, the mistress. She works in a St. Kilda brothel that Geoffrey not only frequents regularly but also partly owns—in a roundabout sort of way."

"I feel like I'm *on* a roundabout," Marek complained, clutching at his tie to try and loosen it. "None of this is good enough, Kitty. I need proof—you know, like some kind of real evidence—to get a warrant. You do remember what evidence is, don't you?"

"Evidence? OK, no worries. I happen to know a place where you're guaranteed of finding a fingerprint to match the one on the murder weapon. You might even find the murderer attached to the finger-print—if you go there at the right time."

"The right time?" Marek queried cautiously.

"All you have to do is organize a raid on Ian Dalkeith's warehouse in Footscray at about nine p.m. tomorrow night. You'll not only catch Celia's killer but probably Byron's as well—not to mention a whole bunch of so-called respected members of the community up to a lot of no good."

"Now I know you're mad," Marek stated.

"Well, that was fun," Kit said as she got back in the car.

"What was he so excited about?" Alex asked.

"I wish it was excitement. I told you he'd laugh at me if I asked him to raid Dalkeith's warehouse tomorrow night. Now I know why people complain that you can never find a cop when you need one. Stupid bastard! I just told him who killed Celia and he suggested that doctor should have committed me last night instead of just barring me from driving."

"But you've been telling him for days that Geoffrey's a murderer. Why does he want to put you in a round room now?"

"Ah," Kit said triumphantly, pulling out the photo she'd managed to pocket before she gave the envelope back to Marek. "Geoffrey didn't kill Celia. Oh-Maggie-yes-Maggie killed Celia."

"The mistress? How on earth did you work that out?"

"It's quite ironic actually because, in a sense, Geoffrey just told me." Kit stared at the photo and shook her head slowly. "I sat on that patio in the pouring rain last Friday night with the evidence of murder lying right there in front of me. The whole scene seemed so bizarre though that I couldn't see what was so obvious, yet I knew in my bones that Celia's death was not an accident."

"O'Malley, please stop talking like one of those tabloid television programs and get to the point."

"Sorry. Take another look at this."

"I'm sorry, but I still don't see anything except Marek's mutant worm holes."

"Precisely. I asked Geoffrey if they were aeration holes and he said he didn't have a clue, that he rarely went out the back because it was his wife's domain."

Alex sat silently gazing at Kit, trying unsuccessfully not to reproduce the expression that had been on Marek's face ten minutes before. "What's the punchline, O'Malley?" she managed to ask.

"High heels," Kit replied, raising her uninjured eyebrow as she grinned.

Alex studied the photograph more closely this time. "She's wearing sandals."

"And?" Kit prompted.

"No shoes in the Forum," Alex said, a smile spreading across her face.

"And everywhere Celia's sandals went so did Marek's mutant worm holes. I'm so glad you're not as obtuse as he is, Alex."

"It's a nice theory, O'Malley, but it's a long way from hard evidence."

"But it is a start. And unless Geoffrey is into cross-dressing as well as everything else then the person who killed Celia had to be a woman. And who else but the *other* woman?"

"But why?"

"How the hell should I know? It's possible, though there's no accounting for taste, that she wanted her Tiger all to herself. Maybe it was planned down to the last detail to make sure Geoffrey had an alibi, or maybe it was an accident. On the other hand, it might not be a crime of passion at all. It may have something to do with this shipment of computers—or nothing to do with it. I don't care, I just know it was her."

"So what happens next?" Alex asked. "If Marek won't raid that place what can we do?"

"I'll think of something. In the meantime it might be an idea to follow Geoffrey when he leaves here."

"What? Now? What makes you think he's going somewhere?"

"Just a hunch. Marek and I fairly rattled his cage in there. He had a nice little reaction all lined up for when he received the news that his late wife's personal secretary had killed himself. So he seemed genuinely surprised, in fact one could say almost flabbergasted, by the fact that Byron had been murdered."

"Interesting," Alex said. "So we're just going to hang around here and see what he does?"

Kit shrugged. "If I'm right he'll probably be busting to find out what went wrong with the suicide plan. I'd like to know who he goes to first, or at least what his next move is."

"What if he's doing that right now, on the phone?"

"So we'll give him half an hour. If he doesn't go anywhere we can go home. I forgot, you have a dinner to cook, don't you?"

"No. Enzo's doing the honors."

"Oh, good," Kit said.

"What does that mean?"

"It means oh good," Kit replied.

Chapter 24

Nearly half an hour later Geoffrey Edward Turner Robinson, at the wheel of his trusty green Bentley, drove hoonishly out the front gate of what, unbeknownst to him, would soon no longer be his castle. He sped off down McGill Crescent like a man with a mission.

"The game's afoot!" exclaimed Alex, somewhat uncharacteristically, as she started her car and took off after Geoffrey. "Or something along those lines," she added as she registered Kit's surprised sidelong glance.

"I absolutely refuse to say 'follow that car,'" Kit stated flatly, wishing someone would rescue her from all these amateur sleuths. This one was hot on Geoffrey's tail, cutting in her after-burners to keep up with the Bentley as it was piloted impatiently through the tangle of traffic on Toorak Road.

Contrary to appearances they were driving against what was, technically speaking, the peak-hour homeward rush from the city. But seeing that peak hour lasted all day in these parts it was actually hard to tell where anyone was going, especially when they decided to go there quite suddenly, without so much as a by-your-leave, and as if they were the only Mercedes on the road.

"I will however suggest," Kit offered, testing the inertia reel of her seatbelt to make sure it would stop her before the windscreen did, "that you keep at least one vehicle between us and Mr. Randypants. We don't really need to see what he's got on his back seat."

Alex obediently eased her foot off the accelerator, dropped back into the traffic and allowed an RX7 to slip in behind Geoffrey as he turned down Park Street, then made a left into Domain Road at the Botanic Gardens.

"So, what did your father actually do, for a living I mean, in between all these adventures?" Alex asked.

"He was a doctor," Kit replied, relieved that Alex was interested enough in her family history to pick up their previous conversation. Rather than start a new one, that is. She couldn't care less whether Alex's interest was genuine or just polite small talk. In fact she would have been happy to discuss the weather, water ballet or even welterweight boxing until the cows came home, as long as it kept Ms. Cazenove light years away from her disconcerting interest in the subject of lust and Quinn Orlando.

Kit had diverted the conversation in the first place, while they were waiting for Geoffrey to do something other than skulk around his house, by turning a casual observation of Alex's about Lillian being dragged off to far north Queensland to give birth in the middle of a cyclone into a lengthy travelogue. So far she'd detailed the O'Malleys' pre-parenthood journey around the four corners of the earth, and covered their later expeditions to Egypt, where she (aged two) and Lillian had been locked in a tomb in the Valley of the Kings while their guide demanded more baksheesh for his services, and to Peru, where Patrick Francis had insisted they all camp one night in the Sacred Plaza at Machu Picchu to fully appreciate the significance of the place.

"Did you appreciate it?" Alex had asked.

"I was five years old. Lillian says I wanted to go to the toilet every other five minutes but couldn't because I was scared of the tarantulas that were going to bite me on the bum. I *think* I have a memory of the place but Brigit, quite illogically, says it's more likely to be a past life poking through my subconscious. Apparently everyone who didn't have a previous existence in the court of Nefertiti or Cleopatra had one at Machu Picchu."

Geoffrey took the turn into St. Kilda Road, heading towards the city, like a man possessed; Alex followed, two cars behind, with the relaxed assurance of a rally driver. If Kit hadn't known any better she

272

would have been convinced that Ms. Cazenove was accustomed to tailing high-speed perverts through the streets of Melbourne.

"Do you suppose it was something you said that put the ants in Geoffrey's pants?" Alex asked.

"Oh, I hope so," Kit replied, wincing as Geoffrey narrowly avoided death-by-very-large-truck. He swerved onto the tram tracks, came to a screaming halt opposite the gates of Government House, then took off again. He was no doubt shaken, but not nearly stirred enough for Kit's liking.

"I have to say, I really admire your mother," Alex said, returning to the safest topic this side of the black stump. "I imagine it would have been quite unusual back then for a woman to do so much travelling, let alone traipsing around all those wildly exotic places with a baby in tow."

"I don't think the travelling was that unusual," Kit shrugged, hoping like hell that Geoffrey wasn't just going to his club as that would not be at all helpful. "But I suppose the places she and Dad visited *were* far off the usual track beaten by the grand tourists. By the time I came along, however, half of hippiedom was doing what my parents were doing—kids and all."

"You're *not* going to tell me your mother was a hippy," Alex laughed.

"No," cried Kit, as if it was the most absurd thing she'd ever heard. "Though I suppose if she had spent the decade doped out on the magic weed it might go some way to explaining her current mental state. But Lillian is basically a no-nonsense, down-to-earth country girl who happens to be as vague as a violet because she married a man who regularly deprived her of oxygen by dragging her off to all those high places where the air is always a little on the thin side."

Kit tried to keep her tone serious but Alex's deep rolling laughter made it a little difficult to concentrate. Kit crossed her legs and directed her gaze up at the station clocks as they turned left into Flinders Street.

"Your poor mother, that's a dreadful thing to say," Alex declared, still laughing.

"Hey, if you think I'm joking you should meet my little brother," Kit continued. "He has *always* been weird, but he took a turn for the extremely peculiar about ten years ago when he started painting cosmic landscapes on old bedsheets. He *claims* he is inspired by intergalactic voices which first contacted him when he was still in the womb."

"You're kidding," Alex said hopefully as she pursued the Bentley up Elizabeth Street and into Collins.

Kit shrugged. "Considering Lillian spent the last three months of her pregnancy in Leh, before Michael was born on a houseboat in Kashmir, I suppose his claim is not beyond the realms of possibility. After all, you can't get much closer to the stars than Ladakh, and it's so much nicer to believe that Michael has a sub-space communication link with the Vulcans than it is to admit he's just one step to the right of completely certifiable."

"You *are* kidding!"

"I wish," Kit stated, before slamming her foot down on the invisible brake pedal which was standard issue in all cars that carried the dreaded passenger-who'd-rather-be-driving. It was an efficient braking system: there was a good two centimeters between the front of Alex's Celica and the right-hand tail light of the taxi that had come to a dead stop in front of them.

"Sorry," Alex apologized.

Kit swallowed, removed her white knuckles from the dashboard and pointed out that Geoffrey had just driven into the Regent Hotel. "Just pull up on the left opposite the driveway," she instructed.

As soon as Alex had stopped in a no-standing zone Kit got out and made a dash for the tram stop in the middle of the street. She was about to curse the sudden surge of traffic that blocked her path, not to mention the two converging trams that blocked her view, when she realized that some of life's little obstacles were sent for a reason. There was Geoffrey, on his way out again, and it was only the Great Tram god's intervention that had prevented him from seeing her standing there like a goose in the middle of the road.

She dashed back to Alex's car. "Warp speed, Mr. Sulu," she commanded as she slammed the door and grabbed for the seatbelt. Alex just looked at her. "Don't tell me you need a translation? OK, OK, I'll say it: follow that car, and step on it!"

Alex did as she was told, grinning, and managed to avoid three cars and another tram as she executed an illegal U-turn to head back the way they'd come. "That was a short visit," she said.

"It was just a pick-up. He's got Davis Whitten with him now."

The streetlight outside Geoffrey's house of ill repute was dying a slow death, flickering dimly in the approaching dusk. It was only a little after six p.m. but a canopy of storm clouds and smog had shrouded the lowering sun, casting an odd orange glow over the entire city. It was an end-of-the-world sort of color and it made Kit feel twitchy—a bit like The Cat every time she got the wind up her tail—only with foreboding, as if something quite dire was about to happen.

"If we ever have another date like this we take my car, OK?" she said to Alex. Oh, great, O'Malley, why not jump into the volcano while you're waiting for the earthquake.

"Why?" asked Alex, as if it had been a perfectly ordinary statement.

"Because I've got half a wardrobe of disguises in my car. Look at me," she exclaimed dismally, gesturing at her semi-crisp white blouse and black trousers. "I'm dressed to interview a prime suspect in the comfort of his Toorak mansion. I can't go clambering around in the bushes of a brothel trying to find a back way in dressed in my best clothes. Apart from anything else, if Geoffrey were to spot me, even from afar, he'd recognize me this time."

"I've probably got something you could wear," Alex offered. "In the back," she added when Kit looked her up and down.

"Enzo's fishing hat?" Kit queried.

"Well, you could try it, but I don't think it would cover much." Alex removed the key from the ignition, got out of the car and went to the boot. "Will this do?" she asked, re-appearing suddenly at Kit's open window with a snappy-looking black coat in her hand.

Kit got out of the car, took Alex by the elbow and escorted her behind the very large tree that stood behind them. Although they had parked a sensible distance from where Geoffrey had left his car right outside the house, Kit was fairly certain it would be asking for trouble to use the street as a dressing room.

She was also quite positive that she would not be able to cope with

275

wearing Alex's coat, with having the smell of her so close. She held her breath.

"It's just a raincoat, it won't bite," Alex said, mistaking Kit's reluctance for god-knows-what, as she took her arm and helped her into it.

You've got to breathe again sometime, O'Malley, Kit thought desperately, as she just stood there and allowed Alex to turn her around while she did the buttons up. Please, please, let it be freshly drycleaned, she begged, finally risking an olfactory overload rather than the alternative of turning blue and collapsing in a dead faint from lack of oxygen.

Oh dear, I knew it: Cazenove No. 5! Kit inhaled deeply then took a step back. It didn't help: the coat came too. She glanced apprehensively at Alex who, thank god or somebody, was too busy scowling at the tartan beret in her own hand to notice that Kit was having an attack of the vapors.

"Nice hat," Kit lied, recovering her voice if not her equilibrium. "I bet you and your betrothed go down a treat at the races on Oaks Day."

"It's not mine," Alex stated categorically, fingering the cloth cap with distaste before jamming it on her head.

"I hope not," Kit stated, wondering how a hat, even one that awful, could arouse such negative emotions. "I assume this means you intend to accompany me?"

Alex answered by putting her sunglasses back on and turning up the collar of her navy shirt. "Mata Hari, you ain't," Kit laughed. "Come on." She slipped over the low brick wall at the front of the house and crept in and out between the huge and unruly daisy bushes planted at intervals along the side fence.

A bed of blue hydrangeas growing beneath the veranda, combined with the grevillea bush in the patchy lawn on their side of the front path, provided reasonable cover, but not enough to warrant the casual way Alex was sauntering along behind her. Kit put her arm out and when Alex walked into it she pushed her back against the fence.

"What now?" Alex whispered.

"We're not supposed to be here, Alex. The idea is *not* to be seen."

"There's no one to see us, O'Malley." Alex shrugged off Kit's arm.

"Just because the Cosa Nostra is not having a barbecue on the front porch does not mean we can go running around the garden with gay abandon," Kit hissed.

Oh, *good* choice of words O'Malley!

"I wasn't," Alex said indignantly. "Oh, dear," she added and flattened herself against the fence as Davis Whitten flung open the front door and strode towards the gate. He unlocked Geoffrey's car, removed something from the glove box, slammed it and the car door closed again, and stormed back into the house. Meanwhile Geoffrey, who had appeared in the front lobby, was pacing like a caged animal. Oh-Maggie-yes-Maggie would probably say like a caged tiger, but Kit thought he looked more like a fruit bat on speed.

"Boy, I *wonder* what's eating them?" Kit said. She glanced over her shoulder at Alex who was looking suitably contrite, not to mention ridiculously adorable in that stupid hat.

Oh god, you're beautiful! Stop thinking, goddamn it! she thought as her skin exploded in a blush of tsunami proportions. In a nanosecond, however, she was overtaken by a panic so complete that she wanted to die, right then and there amongst the daisies.

Did I say that, or just think it—very loudly? It doesn't matter, O'Malley. It must be written all over your face. After all it's written all over *her* face that it's all over your face.

"I'm going to make a run for it," Kit whispered hoarsely.

"For what?" Alex asked.

Alaska, Kit thought. "The bushes under the veranda," she said and took off. She was about to scramble in behind the hydrangeas when someone grabbed her around the waist, dragged her into the dark patch beside the house and pinned her to the wall—with her whole body.

That's it. Now I'm in real trouble. Kit tried to push Alex away from her.

"Christo," Alex whispered in her ear.

Right in her ear! Kit actually felt the brush of her lips. "Let me go," she mouthed desperately. Or I will not be responsible for my actions, she thought.

Alex leant back and removed her sunglasses. In the dim light cast from a window above them Kit could see that, although she looked bemused, Alex was doing a great job of pretending she didn't mind slinking around in the dark with the most embarrassing person in the country. Well if she can do it, Kit thought, so can I. Can't I? She decided to pretend that Alex was *not* turning her into a wobbly mass of jelly. But she was really going to have to wing it. She had never felt so impractical, unprofessional, irrational, out of control and more like jelly in her life.

She had to do something, so she slid along the wall to the edge of the veranda and glanced around the corner. Well, at least not all the Luck gods are ganging up to thwart your every move, she thought. Christo had just gone inside and the front door had not shut properly.

I like Aeroplane Jelly; Aeroplane Jelly for me! she hummed to herself as she beckoned Alex—hell, she may as well, the woman was going to follow her anyway—and then eased her way between the veranda and the bushes. She pushed about halfway along until she could hear voices, then she peeked over the edge. The staircase was visible through the partly open door, she had a side view of Christo and could see half of Geoffrey's back through the narrow window beside the door.

"I just know it's going to ruin everything."

"For Christ's sake, Geoff, it is not," Davis Whitten drawled.

Oh, yes it is, Kit thought.

"And as for you, you stupid shit!" Geoffrey whacked Christo in the ear with the back of his hand.

"Ow! What'd I do?"

"Nothing. It was supposed to be a suicide, you little moron."

"Weren't my fault that poof didn't want to die quietly. And it was *your* mate who got carried away. I didn't do nuthin!"

"Nothing my arse!" Geoffrey shouted. "Who was it who tried to run down that reporter in broad bloody daylight? What were you planning to do after you flattened her, Christo, go back and ask her what she knew?"

Christo shuffled from one foot to the other. Lacking the wherewithal to come up with a suitable excuse, let alone a smart retort, he just held his ear and glared at Geoffrey.

"Leave him alone, Geoff," Whitten said.

"And fuck you too," Geoffrey bellowed as he stomped up the staircase. He was obviously *not* a happy man. "And close the fucking door!" he shouted over his shoulder.

Whitten ranged into view, shrugged at Christo then cocked his head to indicate they should also proceed up the stairs. Christo didn't look too pleased about that idea but pushed the door closed with his foot and no doubt followed along anyway.

Kit dropped awkwardly back into a crouching position. She indicated with a nod it was time to move out and then followed Alex who zigzagged in and out between the daisy bushes before pulling up between the last two nearest the street.

"Wow," she whispered, turning to face Kit. "Are all your jobs this nerve-racking?"

"Not usually," Kit replied.

"They seem to think you're one of those nosy reporter types, O'Malley."

"It would appear so, unless Christo's favorite pastime is trying to decorate his car bonnet with pedestrians of various professions," Kit said. "I did go from the Skintone Agency to the *St. Kilda Star* that day, which might explain this case of mistaken profession. I probably should ring my mate Erin though to make sure Christo didn't try to make a trophy out of her too."

"So what now?"

. . . *my love*. It was some seventies crooner in tight satin pants who finished the line in Kit's head, though she did wonder where the music came from. "Home," she replied.

"Didn't you want to get inside?" Alex reminded her. She leant back against the side fence and looked at her watch.

"I don't like the odds," Kit stated, casting a glance back at the house, "and they're all odd in there. Besides, don't you want to go home?"

"Oh, no," said Alex.

Oh, no? Strange answer, ominous tone of voice, Kit thought vaguely as any sense of the impending danger implied by those two words was momentarily hijacked by the sensation of Alex's hand on her shoulder. Alex's eyes were pretty sensational too.

"Oh, no, what?" she asked under her breath, carefully.

"Oh, no, car," Alex explained. "Oh, no, worse, it's Grainger. What do we do?"

"Don't panic and do *not* run," Kit replied, resisting the urge to do just that—and the next one which was to look wildly about for an alternative. She looked at Alex instead.

A diversion, that's what we need, Kit thought. She tackled the ridiculous idea that sprang into her mind and tried to flatten it before it could convince her it was the only alternative. No, O'Malley, she argued with herself, that is *not* a good plan. Hey, the idea urged, a diversion is a diversion is a . . . you know "by any other name." No way! It's a lousy idea.

She was still watching Alex who was looking wide-eyed over her shoulder at what, judging by the look on her face, could only be a worsening situation. Until now she'd always thought that to be a fairly silly notion, but as she watched Alex's expression change from *oh no*, to *oh shit*, to *oh fuck we're dead for sure* she realized that this situation was indeed worsening. While part of Kit's mind marvelled at how many completely useless thoughts can flash through a person's mind in ten seconds, especially when that person is in a situation where it would be more than a little useful to have all one's faculties working together for a change, another part of her mind managed to get her voice working.

"Has he seen us?" she asked.

Alex rolled her eyes, looked at Kit and nodded. "Yes."

"I am really really sorry about this," Kit said. She leant forward and placed her left hand on the fence beside Alex.

"It's not your fault, O'—" Alex started to say.

Kit slipped her right arm around Alex's waist and pulled her close. "Malley. I don't . . ."

Kit put a stop to any possible objections by kissing her on the mouth. Alex's breath caught in her throat, but otherwise she just stood there.

"Hey! What are you doing there?" Grainger shouted.

Oh dear lord! Alex's mouth. It was soft and sweet and everything she'd imagined it would be.

"Hey! I'm talking to you."

Who the hell cares? Kit could barely hear his voice anyway over the hubbub that took over all rational thought as her blood surfed around her body and exploded in her ears.

This was a *bad* idea, Kit thought, as she went right on kissing Alex who went right on just standing there. A very bad idea. Either Grainger's cohorts are going to come pouring out of the house to drag you both kicking and screaming inside, or Alex is going to lay you out with a well-deserved right hook the moment you let go of her. Either way you lose. You'll be dead or *persona non grata*. She was thinking "dead's better," until a long-forgotten and unsettling hunger tried to take over her body. It was sheer astonishment that made her drag her mouth away. She let go of Alex who stumbled forward a step as if she'd fallen off something.

Her high horse probably, Kit thought, realizing those stunning gray eyes were shining with outrage. Or maybe it was fear. Quite possibly it was both, Kit decided, but at least Alex had had the good sense not to push her away and run screaming off into the sunset. Which, for the record, was exactly what Kit wanted to do. She didn't like being overwhelmed by a mysterious force she had no control over. She wondered for a moment whether someone had snuck up from behind and hit her over the head, until she realized she was still conscious— just. No, this thing, this feeling, had come from somewhere deep inside her, as if she'd been overtaken by a peculiar life force. Maybe it was one of her past lives dropping in for a visit.

Whatever! She wanted to run and hide, to take a slow boat to China or the Last Train to Clarkesville; she wanted to talk to Shirley MacLaine or, better still, an exorcist; at the very least she needed a cup of tea, a Bex and a good lie down. But she was rooted to the spot, and it wasn't just the grip Alex still had on her shoulder that was keeping her standing there speechless with her mouth half-open. What the hell was it then?

A Close Encounter, that's it. I've just had a Close Encounter of *The X Files* kind, she thought. But which sort? Demon possession? Alien abduction?

As Kit registered the sound of the front gate being slammed shut, the part of her that was still sensible remembered that she and Alex were in some kind of danger. The gate? That can't be! All my molecules have just danced the complete uncensored can-can while my heart made a light-speed loop around Alpha Centauri, and he's only *just* walking in the gate. This is crazy, she thought. How could it possibly take only a few seconds to realize you're desperately, uncontrollably and inappropriately in love?

With Alex.

Oh shit!

"Hey!" Grainger shouted.

Alex, who until that moment hadn't taken her eyes off Kit's mouth, jumped with fright and opened her own mouth to say something.

"Not now, Alex," Kit whispered and kissed her again, slowly and gently, resisting with all her might the temptation to use her tongue.

"Hey!" Grainger's voice was louder now. Or was it closer? "What do you think you're doing?"

I haven't the faintest idea what I'm doing, Kit thought, but I'm making it look good. This time all her senses, including the one usually labeled "common," began freefalling all around her. It was just as well Alex was holding her up or there'd be nothing but a senseless puddle of jelly for the bad guys to dispose of.

Holding her up? Holding her?

Alex's lips parted beneath hers.

Oh no! What was she doing that for? Kit pulled back quickly.

Was Alex choosing that moment, with Grainger almost upon them, to get back on her high horse and start abusing her?

Was she about to return the kiss?

Oh, sure, O'Malley!

A big hand grabbed her roughly by the elbow and spun her around, which was just as well because Kit didn't dare look at Alex.

"I'm talking to you. Are you deaf, or what?" Grainger's breath was hot on her face.

"What's your problem, Grandpa?" Alex snarled—well, it would have been a snarl if her voice had been working properly.

God, O'Malley, Kit thought, you took her breath away. Don't be idiotic—it's more likely that you frightened the life out of her.

Kit looked from Grainger's rabid, boxer-nosed face to Alex's indignant "who the hell are you anyway" expression. There was definitely an angry edge to the defiant set of Alex's mouth and she was taking short breaths, as if that was the only way she could contain herself. Kit wondered, nervously, which emotion was the dominant one: Alex's anger with her, or Alex's fear of Grainger.

"I asked you what you were doing here," Grainger snapped.

"What does it look like?" Alex asked snidely, looking askance at Grainger before turning to glower at Kit.

Oh my god! I adore this woman and she's going to kill me. *If* we get out of this alive.

"Yeah, well don't do it here. This is private property."

"Come on," Kit said. "Let's go before the old bastard calls the cops."

Alex draped her arm casually around Kit's neck and glared at Grainger who still had hold of Kit's arm. "Are you going to let go of her or not?"

"Stay out of here," Grainger ordered as he released her.

After they'd clambered over the front fence Kit steered Alex away from the car.

"He's still watching us," Alex said after a quick glance over her shoulder, as they strolled as calmly as possible away from deep shit.

When they came abreast of the next street tree Kit stopped, turned nonchalantly and leant back against the trunk. She *did* want to check on Grainger but, more importantly, she had to escape from Alex's arm which was still around her shoulders.

Grainger was nowhere in sight so Kit led the way across the street and part-way up a darkened driveway. She hoped the owners of this house didn't have a whole mass of dirty secrets they'd kill to protect.

"Honestly, O'Malley!" Alex exclaimed.

Here it comes, Kit thought.

"I don't believe it. One minute we're listening to Geoffrey *actually* admit his involvement in Byron's death, and the next we get trapped in the garden by, and escape from, the very man who slit Byron's throat. I have *never* been so scared in my life."

Oh, I don't know, Kit thought, helplessly. Discovering I'm in love with *you* is at least that scary.

Alex was tapping her watch. "The most amazing thing is that it's only been three minutes, *three*, since I first saw Grainger's car. It felt like we were stuck in there for about three hours!"

Alien abduction, Kit finally decided. It's always accompanied by a serious time loss. She took off the coat Alex had lent her, then removed the tartan beret from Alex's head and folded them together under her arm. "Are you coming?"

"Yes, of course." Alex's hair was all over the place and she still had a wild look in her eyes but at least she didn't appear to be homicidal.

After making sure Grainger hadn't posted any lookouts, they walked back to the car, in silence, down the opposite side of the street. Alex leant on the car roof before unlocking the door and gave Kit a searching and serious look. "O'Malley?"

"Yes, Alex?"

"I admire your ability to come up with a strategy or diversion, or whatever that was back there that enabled us to escape unscathed from what could have been a dangerous, perhaps even deadly, situation at the hands of that alleged murderer, but don't *ever* do that again."

"I wouldn't dream of it," Kit promised, swallowing hard.

Liar, that's all you *will* do.

"Can we go home now?"

"Yes, Alex."

Chapter 25

The lift doors opened onto the eighth floor with barely a sound. Kit figured the plush carpeting in the long wide hallway could probably deaden the noise made by a horde of rampaging storm-troopers and wondered if the serviced apartments were also soundproofed against the outside world.

What a way to live, she thought. There seemed to be surveillance cameras covering every nook and cranny of the building and Kit felt as if she'd just been through more security doors than Maxwell Smart on a bad day. It would be easier to rob the Reserve Bank than get into this building without authorization. She grimaced at her reflection in the humongous gilt-edged mirror hanging on the wall opposite the lift and wished, for about the thirteenth time, that she hadn't worn the clothes she'd finally decided on after an hour of excavating her wardrobe for something appropriate. Usually not one to give a damn about what she was wearing as long as she was comfortable—unless she felt she had to impress a new client—she now decided that white jeans and a purple shirt were quite inappropriate.

Alex would probably think the purple was a statement of some kind and Kit usually knew better than to wear white because she was bound to spill a glass of red wine in her lap. Having the jitters didn't help one bit. Ordinarily she didn't even need to be edgy to turn into a prize klutz and end up wearing her food so she knew she had no hope of surviving this dinner unscathed because she couldn't remember the last time she'd been this nervous. She felt as if she was going on her first ever date.

Now that *is* crazy, O'Malley! she thought. This is not a date of any sort. You're about to have dinner with Alex and her betrothed, for heaven's sake! Under, I might add, the additional chaperonage of the capering Quinn.

Kit put her hand on Quinn's shoulder to stop her bouncing along as if she was riding a pogo stick. She had obviously recovered quite nicely from the mess Kit had found her in when she'd returned home. Quinn's emotional dam wall had finally broken shortly after Kit had left to meet Marek, and she'd spent four hours crying on her own—in every room in Kit's apartment if the scattered tissues were any indication—and another one crying with Kit when she'd got back. While Kit was relieved that Quinn had finally let go, this current bouncy bubbly mood was as annoying as all hell; it was making Kit even more apprehensive. What's more, Ms. Orlando seemed extremely pleased with herself, or with something, which was worrying as it made Kit feel like she'd missed the punch line of a joke.

Quinn led the way down the hall to the far end, pressed the doorbell of number 8C then stood on tiptoes to put her face near the peephole.

Kit was totally unprepared for the exclamation of delight that came from the other side of the door, and completely taken aback by the sight of the guy who flung open said door and said dejectedly, "Oh, it's not Barry. I'm going to have to get a new spyhole, this one makes everyone look like Barry."

"Barry who?" Quinn asked.

"Manilow, darling, who do you think?"

This can't be Enzo, Kit thought, not really sure what she thought Enzo was going to be like, but sure this man wasn't even close. He was tall, broad-shouldered and starting to thicken around the waist but, Kit guessed, probably from good food rather than a lack of exercise. His wavy hair, slightly thinning on top but touching his collar at the back, was dark with handsome flashes of gray which also featured in his burnsides and moustache. He looked like Sean Connery in *The Man Who Would Be King*, although it was probably the faint trace of a Scottish accent that contributed to that impression. He was brown-eyed, olive-skinned and, without question, positively divine. Kit realized with a dreadful sinking feeling that this was indeed Enzo.

Who the hell else would it be? she thought, overcome with an acute case of jealousy, as if being finally faced with this man—this fiancé?—made her hopeless case of infatuation even more hopeless.

"It is *such* a pleasure," Enzo was saying. To her. Kit realized Quinn was already halfway through the introductions so she stuck out her hand.

"Kit, this is Enzo McAllister," Quinn finished. Enzo took Kit's hand in both of his and raised it gallantly to his lips in a gesture that wasn't at all affected.

"I'm so glad you could join us for dinner. I've been hearing so much about you all week that I feel as if I know you already," he said.

"You do?" Kit said, raising an eyebrow. "I don't know whether that's good or bad. I suppose it depends on who's been talking about me."

"I have," Quinn said, "non-stop."

"Are you coming in, or would you like your champagne served in the hallway?" Enzo asked, placing his hand affectionately on Quinn's shoulder.

"I don't know, what do you think, Kit?" Quinn asked.

"Out here would be just fine," Kit said, "although we might need a chair or two."

"Perfect, I'll just go and ask Alex to help me move the chaise longue," Enzo said with a warm smile, stepping aside to wave them in.

Damn! Kit thought. I'm going to like this guy, but I am *not* going to enjoy doing it.

"Bathroom and loo are down there, second door on the right, in case you need them later," Enzo said, indicating the short hallway which ran to the left. "And, seeing as how that's where I was going when you rang the bell, I think I'd better finish what I started. I trust you'll be able to show our guest through to the patio, Quinn. Alex is in the kitchen pretending to help. If you see her touching any of the food please chase her out with the largest knife you can find."

"Enzo can't stand anyone in his kitchen when he's cooking," Quinn explained as she took Kit by the elbow and cuddled into her arm.

"Is it his kitchen or Alex's kitchen?" Kit asked.

"Any kitchen is his when he's cooking," Quinn replied. She steered Kit through the archway on their right into a spacious lounge furnished with two armchairs and a three-seater couch. There was also a low coffee table and a TV and stereo system, as well as a huge bookshelf and cupboard arrangement right next to where she was standing, but the lounge suite, upholstered in a rich mahogany-colored fabric, was so big and so invitingly deep and luxurious that Kit decided she'd be too afraid to sit in it in case she was never seen again.

The apparent spaciousness of the room was actually an illusion created partly by the sliding glass doors on the far side which opened onto a patio bordered with plants, and partly by the fact that it continued around to her right in an L-shape. A large dining table, set only with a vase of flowers, stood against the wall beside a breakfast bar which divided the kitchen from the living area.

The kitchen itself was something straight out of a country living magazine or an ad for the perfect Italian or French village holiday, where you actually get to stay in the home of the region's most renowned chef. The shelves which occupied all the available space on the walls were lined with specialty jars full of herbs, spices and curries, flours and rice of different colors, and pastas of all shapes and sizes, as well as preserved plums and peaches, olives and pickled just-about-everything. The well-worn wooden preparation bench in the middle of the room, cluttered with the makings of tonight's dinner, was overhung by dangling pots, pans, utensils and strings of garlic and dried chilies.

This was Kit's ideal kitchen; the one she dreamt of having if she could ever actually develop a passion for cooking. The smell of garlic and basil contributed to that ideal but the scene, Kit had to admit, was made perfect by the fact that Alex was standing in it, wearing a dark green sleeveless shirt, tailored black shorts and flour all over her chin.

"Ah, you're here, great," Alex said to both of them and then, despite a fleeting look of consternation as she registered the hold Quinn still had of Kit's arm, she added, "Welcome, O'Malley."

"Thanks," Kit smiled. She couldn't think of anything else to say.

"I think you'll live longer if you get out of Enzo's space and pour

288

us a drink instead, Alex," Quinn stated, placing the champagne she'd brought on the bench. She wrestled the bottle of port from Kit's stranglehold, rolling her eyes and trying not to smirk as she did so. Kit ignored her.

"You're probably right," Alex was saying as she washed her hands.

"Does it matter that you have incriminating evidence all over your face?" Kit asked, brushing her own chin to indicate the spot before pointing at Alex's.

"Purely circumstantial," Alex grinned after wiping her face and looking at her hand.

"You missed half of it." Quinn stepped forward to help.

"You're not going to spit on a hankie and wipe it off like my grandmother used to, are you?" Alex asked, leaning back away from Quinn.

"I don't own a hankie. Stand still." Quinn wiped the rest of the flour off Alex's chin with her thumb, which she then licked to destroy the evidence.

Oh god, why didn't I think of that? Kit closed her eyes momentarily against the image that popped into her mind. It didn't help. It was more vivid with her eyes shut.

"Drinks then," Alex announced. "We have champers on ice outside, or you can have bourbon or whatever if you'd prefer, O'Malley."

"Champagne's fine, thanks," Kit said as she followed Quinn who followed Alex out onto the patio.

"Oh fu . . . ar out, what a view!" Kit exclaimed from the safety of the doorway as she took in the panoramic sight of the Melbourne skyline. She'd forgotten they were so high up. She wished she hadn't been reminded. She looked around the immediate vicinity while she counted to ten and took a few breaths. The patio, partially covered by a canvas awning, was a good twelve feet square, which was almost big enough to avoid the possibility of accidentally falling off as long as she stayed right in the middle or close to the door. Of course the brick barrier between the patio and oblivion might prevent such carelessness on her part but it *was* only about four feet high so she wasn't going to tempt fate by sitting on one of the cosy-looking benches built into the wall between the planter boxes and giant terracotta pots.

A table, elegantly set for four, was placed on the door side of safety, and the whole setting was illuminated by lights glowing from inside a couple of Japanese stone lanterns and from a Buddhist deity cast in clay and laughing hysterically at some great cosmic joke.

"I didn't realize you had it that bad, O'Malley. Would you rather eat inside?" Alex had materialized in front of her with a glass of champagne.

"No, no, I'll be fine. Just give me a week or two. The drink will help though, thanks."

Alex was smiling and shaking her head. "What happens when you have to chase bad guys up the fire escapes of abandoned buildings?"

"Alex, you watch all together too much television. I've never had to chase any bad guys up anything. Besides, the bad guys always plummet off the top after the shoot-out or fight scene, so why bother chasing them? But if I did have to pursue someone, I'd make sure I chased them into a single-storey abandoned building or, failing that, I'd just wait at the bottom for them to fall or climb back down. After all they can't stay up there forever."

"You have a point. Cheers," Alex said, clinking her champagne flute against Kit's then turning to do the same to Quinn's.

"It would be a pretty boring scene for a movie though, just watching you sit at the bottom until the baddies got hungry or bored enough to surrender," Quinn stated.

"Precisely. Which is why the bad guys nearly always climb *up*, because a high dive from a building is a much more spectacular death scene for the actor, or rather the stuntperson, than getting cornered in the basement. For the same reason, in every thriller which has a psycho stalking the city one of the main characters always parks in an underground car park, just so they can have a narrow escape."

"Or get spooked for no reason, except that they were stupid enough to be there in the first place," added Quinn.

"Yeah, and half an hour later that same person will probably keep right on walking into a house where the lights mysteriously don't work when they hit the switch just inside the door," said Kit.

"And then wonder why they get hit over the back of the head for the second or third time since they've been investigating this mystery where nothing or no one is what it or they seem to be," Quinn finished.

"And you say *I* watch too much television," Alex laughed.

"What about the detective in your book, Kit?" Quinn asked. "Does she avoid the clichés and the car parks and the fire escapes?"

"Of course not. She's not afraid of heights for a start. But she is always in the process of acknowledging, just before she gets whacked over the back of the head, how completely idiotic it is to be wandering through a deserted car park or a house where none of the lights seem to work because she's bound to be whacked over the back of the head."

"Whose lights don't work?" Enzo asked.

"The ones in O'Malley's book. She's writing a detective novel," Alex said.

"Yes, you told me that," Enzo stated. "That *must* be my glass," he added, relieving Alex of the one she'd been drinking from.

When Alex patted his cheek gently before brushing past him into the lounge Kit felt as though all her nerve endings had been given a Chinese burn. She didn't know how much of this familiarity she would be able to take. Get real, O'Malley, between friends or people who have been married for thirty years it's called familiarity; between fiancés it's called intimacy.

Oh, but she's been talking about me, Kit realized. Her delight quickly withered around the edges when she guessed that Alex had probably been tempering anything good Quinn might have had to say with everything bad she could think of.

"Earth to Kit, come in," Quinn was saying.

"What? Oh, sorry." Kit looked around blankly.

"Enzo was asking about your detective," Quinn explained.

"Is she a Miss Marple solving murders in the manor type or one of the new breed who tackle crime on the mean streets and know how to deal out justice without actually having to kill everyone?" he asked.

"Ah, methinks you're a crime buff," Kit said with a grin.

"I am that," Enzo stated. "I devour the stuff. Everything from Conan Doyle to Colin Dexter and Marele Day to Corris, Leonard, Paretsky, Nava and Robert B. Parker."

"Who's this Enzo, your new accounting firm?" Alex asked, returning with an empty glass which she held out for Quinn to fill.

"They're crime writers, Alex dearest," Enzo said.

"She didn't know until yesterday who V. I. was," Kit confided.

"Oh, for heaven's sake! As if that's something I have to live down," Alex exclaimed. "You lot *do* realize of course that the word 'fan' comes from 'fanatic' and that, generally speaking, most fanatics have a screw or two loose."

"Oh, I was wondering what that odd sensation was," Enzo said as he screwed an imaginary bolt back into his neck. Kit's attempt at trying not to react resulted in her snorting half a lungful of champagne. Quinn just laughed out loud.

"So," Enzo continued, "a cosy little mystery or a hard-boiled detective novel?"

"Hard-boiled, I guess," Kit replied. "With a soft core of lust and romance and good old-fashioned adventure."

"Lust and romance?" Alex sounded inexplicably surprised.

"Yeah, sex sells," Kit stated.

"It does?" Alex queried.

"So I'm told," Kit replied.

"So," Enzo said again, trying to reclaim the conversation, "she's one of the new breed of sexy dykes who tackle crime on the mean streets without having to kill everyone."

"Ah, yes," Kit said, her smile broadening as she registered Enzo's raised eyebrow and half shrug.

"Enzo!" Alex snapped.

"Yes, my treasure?"

Alex looked from Enzo to Kit and back to Enzo. "How did you work that out?" she finally asked.

Enzo shrugged again. "Sex sells. Right, Kit?"

"Right, Enzo," Kit agreed.

"Speaking of sex, I'm starving."

Kit, Alex and Enzo turned as one to look at Quinn who grinned and added, "Appetite is appetite."

"You said a mouthful, kiddo," Enzo stated then raised his hands to fend off the collective groan. "The first rule of the evening is that you *must* find me amusing at all times, or I will take your dinner next door and share it with Mrs. Whitaker."

"I don't think she'd be interested this evening, Enzo," Alex said. "Her new toy boy arrived about an hour ago."

"Och, then the poor lad will be needing food by now to give him the energy to keep up with Mrs. W. I'd better hurry," Enzo said with a melodramatic wave of his arms as he retreated inside.

"We should probably sit down," Alex said. "I *think* he's coming back with something."

"God, I hope so. I haven't eaten anything all day," Quinn grumbled as she flung herself into one of the chairs.

"Here, O'Malley, I think this is the safest spot on the patio." Alex pulled back the chair closest to the door.

"Why thank you, Ms. Cazenove, I do declare I feel safer already," Kit said, placing her glass on the table first so she could accidentally-on-purpose brush against Alex's arm as she did so. The action caused the reaction common to all cases of unrequited passion. Kit thought she was going to faint from the sheer thrill of it and Alex moved away and sat down in her own chair as if nothing untoward had happened. Which of course it hadn't.

Oh boy, that was juvenile, Kit thought, trying in vain not to blush. She sat down heavily and glared at the empty space between her cutlery.

"Kit?"

Kit closed her eyes momentarily before looking up at Quinn, whose face held the exact expression she expected it would. "Yes?"

"You look a bit pale, dear. Here, some of Enzo's bread should *whet* your appetite," Quinn said.

Subtle as a sledgehammer, Kit thought as she glowered at Quinn. "Thank you, *Elizabeth*, but the last thing my appetite needs is whetting."

Alex looked as though she was watching a tennis match as her attention snapped from Quinn to Kit and back to Quinn, who was still smirking at Kit. Kit wasn't game to give Alex anything other than a sidelong glance so she picked up her champagne and pretended to be engrossed in the bubbles. *What* am I doing here? she wondered desperately, just as Enzo returned with a flourish and a large platter of antipasto. He set the food in the center of the table and took his place between Kit and Quinn.

"Pay attention, children, I shall go through this only once," he said and waved his hand over the platter. "We have mushrooms, artichokes, carrots, peppers, cauliflower, sundried tomatoes, olives, eggplant, cantaloupe and prosciutto."

"It looks delicious, Enzo," Kit said.

"It ith," Quinn managed to say around the chunk of bread and prosciutto she'd already stuffed in her mouth.

"The best education money can buy and she still talks with her mouth full," Alex noted.

"They didn't teach table manners in my English lit classes, Alex," Quinn said, offering her the basket of bread.

"Thank you. It was obviously a subject neglected in the boarding school dining room too," Alex said.

"What's with you?" Quinn asked. "I didn't realize you'd been hired by the decorum police."

Whoa! Where's this coming from? Kit wondered.

"Kit," Enzo said, placing his hand on Kit's forearm, "what came first, your writing or your career as a private investigator?"

"Well, I've always had this great desire to write," Kit replied, taking his cue to help defuse the tiff that appeared to be developing on the other side of the table, or at least ignore it. As she spoke, however, she was aware that Alex was watching her closely. Well, she was close. And she was watching her.

"I wrote my first novel," she continued, "in my last year of primary school. It was a homework project where everyone had to write an on-going story or radio play to read to the class once a week. Mine was called *Smuggler's Cape* and was basically a cross between the Famous Five and James Bond."

"Do you still have it?" Alex asked.

Kit shrugged. "I'm sure my mother has it tucked away somewhere. Lillian never throws anything out. Anyway, in my teens I gave up writing prose and turned to poetry. I churned out a lot of really weird blank verse that was mostly obscure references to lost opportunities or unrequited love."

"I think we've all been there," Enzo stated.

"I guess so. But even after I acknowledged that I was never going to be a poet I still had this nagging notion that what I was supposed to be was a writer. I tried short stories for a while until I realized they weren't my forté at all. I'd start with a nice neat little idea and end up

294

with a saga of *Gone With The Wind* proportions. Then I tried a straight out Mills and Boon-type adventure romance, only because I'd heard there was buckets of money to be made. But they're hell to write. It didn't help that I couldn't bring myself to read more than two or three to get the style. Mind you, I think it was the straight bit I had the most problems with. I simply could not write seriously about my heroine's breathless attraction to my hero's throbbing manhood."

"That's understandable," Quinn said. "But how on earth did you make the leap from being convinced you were a writer to becoming a policewoman?"

Kit shrugged and helped herself to another selection of antipasto. "The two are not mutually exclusive. I mean, you have to make a living of some sort while you're slaving away over the great Australian novel or whatever it is. It's the same for all those actors out there waiting on tables while they're waiting to be discovered, except that I'd assumed I could do both at the same time. But the job sort of took over my life. I became so engrossed in it that even when I had the time I didn't have the inclination. I didn't write a thing for about six years. While I was busy I was vaguely conscious of the fact that I was missing something but couldn't quite recall what it was. When not preoccupied with work, like when I was on holidays, I would remember what it was I really wanted to do, to be, and then I'd feel guilty because I couldn't motivate myself to do anything about it."

"But why a policewoman?" Alex repeated Quinn's query.

"It was the only *other* thing I'd ever wanted to be. Actually, that's not quite true. What I really wanted to be when I grew up was a spy. Don't laugh, but I guess I figured that joining the police force was as close as I was ever going to get to being Emma Peel."

While Alex and Quinn ignored her request and had a good laugh at her expense, Enzo leant towards her, placed his elbow on the table and rested his chin on his hand. "Ignore them, Mrs. Peel," he said. "I understand completely. I always fancied *myself* as John Steed."

"You mean you fancied John Steed," Quinn laughed.

Enzo pursed his lips and stuck out his chin. "*And* Mrs. Peel *and* the luscious Purdey. But we're not talking about me. Why did you leave the police force? Was it to concentrate on your writing?"

Kit shrugged. "That was the incentive but not the reason. In the end

I guess I resigned because I was disappointed. And burnt out. I got tired of the attitudes. My own being that I hate taking orders from people who enjoy giving them for no other reason than they can. A lot of stupid decisions get made by people who can barely tie their own laces let alone make two decisions in one day that don't contradict each other. I also got sick of the rankism, the homophobia, the sexism, the back-biting, the whole politics of it. It's not endemic—it wasn't even necessarily directed at me. It was just festering under the skin of enough individuals to make it appear more widespread than it actually is."

"Welcome to the real world," Alex stated flatly.

"Hey, I'm not saying it's unusual. I'm sure it's the same in any large organization, but the force is still such a boys-own adventure that it seemed like an even bigger battle to overcome it. I mean, there you are strapping on your six guns every day to fight crime and you spend half your time scoring hollow victories over some of your own colleagues or suffering bitter defeats at their hands. Even more than in the world outside, a woman has to be tougher, stronger, able to leap tall buildings in a single bound with no run-up, and all that crap just to be acknowledged, let alone accepted. We need to be the first to pull our gun in a crisis, not only to demonstrate that we can be relied upon to back up our partner but also to prove we're *capable* of doing it and won't be affected by any girlie misgivings about actually having to use a weapon. On the other hand, just to show how contrary the attitudes are, in that very same crisis we need to be the *last* to pull our gun to demonstrate we're not prone to overreacting because we're scared or because it's that time of the month and we're inclined to just lose it over nothing."

"No wonder there's a cowboy gun culture in our State police force," Alex stated.

"No, no," Kit said shaking her head, "that's another Western altogether. There were extenuating circumstances in many of those shootings."

"Oh sure," Alex scoffed. "What's the tally now? How many citizens have been shot dead by police in the last few years? Please don't say they were necessary."

"Necessary? No, of course not. It's an appalling record. But necessary is a very black-and-white word and there's a lot of gray in this scenario. I'm not defending or condoning anything but I also refuse to make generalizations. Each case, as you well know, has to be looked at separately."

"Half of the victims weren't even criminals, O'Malley."

"True. But that stems from a brilliant government decision to close down the State's psychiatric institutions without considering the impact that would have not only on the general community and an ill-prepared police force but on those people who should be in care instead of out on the streets."

"So now we blame the government," Enzo said.

"Not entirely, but it does bear a great deal of responsibility in this," Kit stated, wishing this subject hadn't come up at all as she climbed reluctantly onto her soapbox.

"You have to understand," she continued, "that after those officers were killed in Walsh Street and the Russell Street bombing things got really scary in this city. And now, thanks to the government, there's the added problem of having all these psychologically disturbed people at large in the community. It's not their fault. But if one of them goes over the proverbial edge and decides to wander up the street taking pot shots at shop windows with an air rifle they have to be treated as hostile, even if it's understood they may just be asking for help in the only way they know how—by drawing attention to themselves. They may be quite harmless and have no intention of hurting anybody *or* they may have completely wigged out in which case they're just plain dangerous. Whatever the reason, the threat is still real, the danger to the community and to the police is still real—at the time. And that's the only time you've got.

"So these days when the cops are faced with an out-of-control person armed with a gun, or an axe or even a butter knife, they have no way of knowing whether they're dealing with someone who's on drugs, or someone who *should* be on drugs, or just some arsehole who'd really like to kill a cop."

"So the police shoot first. And they shoot to kill. Why is that?" Alex asked.

"That's a bit simplistic, Alex," Kit said. "And it's much harder than you might think to wing someone, especially if that someone is coming at you with a weapon."

"Did you ever shoot anyone, Kit?" Quinn asked softly.

"No. In seven years, apart from a few raids, I never had a reason to take my gun out of its holster—except at the firing range. Mind you, that's another reason why I left the force," Kit said, seeing an opportunity to change the subject.

Alex choked on her wine before spluttering, "What, because you didn't get to shoot somebody?"

"No, because it was starting to worry me how often I wanted to. I used to picture myself drawing my gun, taking aim, and blowing the rotten bastards away."

Alex looked totally appalled but Quinn obviously thought it was a delightful notion. "I can understand that," she said. "If I was a cop I'd start by blowing Geoffrey to kingdom come."

"Well, that would be of some benefit to the community," Kit said. "But what worried me most about my little daydreams was that I was usually whacking one of my fellow officers."

"That may have presented a problem or two," Enzo said dryly. "Was there *anything* about the police force you liked?"

"Oh, yeah. But then I suspect I may be a masochist. I even enjoyed the battle of wits, or is it battles of wit, with the wigs-and-suits every time we got an offender into court. It didn't matter whether we'd collared someone in the act, or had spent months collecting enough evidence to make an arrest, we still had to spend an inordinate amount of time cosseting or confronting the legal eagles from both the defense and the bloody DPP. I mean, the police and the prosecutors are *supposed* to be on the same side but half the time you wouldn't know it—unless you knew it. It was quite a challenge. It was also another reason why I left. Too many bad guys, even habitual criminals, would get minimum sentences or skase it completely. Either way they were back on the streets far sooner than they should've been."

"What did they do completely?" Enzo asked.

"Skase it," Kit replied with a grin. "Don't you know the verb to skase? It means to get away with something or, more specifically, to get off scot-free and live a life of luxury in Majorca."

"On that note," Enzo laughed, raising his hands dramatically, "I shall leave to prepare the main course. And I forbid you to get onto any interesting topics until I return."

"Can I help, Enzo?" Alex asked.

"You can, of course, my sweet, but you may not. On second thoughts you may help clear the table and after you've poured me a glass of wine in the kitchen you will return to our guests with the rest of the bottle."

"Yes, master," Alex stated, pressing her palms together and giving an obedient nod.

"So?" Quinn queried, shuffling into Alex's chair as soon as she and Enzo had left the patio.

"So what?" Kit asked.

"So what do you think of Enzo?"

"I like him very much, Quinn. And you were quite right, he *is* positively divine. I've got one question though."

"What?"

"Does Alex *know* that her fiancé is as camp as a row of tents?"

About three hours later when Quinn had stopped laughing she managed to say, "Of course she does."

"Then what's the story here?"

"It's a marriage of convenience," Quinn whispered.

"Convenience for whom? And why are we whispering?"

"Convenience for Enzo. And we're whispering because I've been sworn to secrecy."

"Why? And if it's such a big secret why do they invite people to dinner? I mean, it's not half obvious which side he dresses on, if you know what I mean," Kit said. Which wasn't exactly true because she hadn't really been sure about Enzo until Quinn actually confirmed it.

"The why is because they're getting married so that Enzo can stay in the country and that's not an altogether legal reason for tying the knot." Quinn was still whispering.

"Especially for a lawyer. What does Alex get out of it?" Kit asked then nearly jumped out of her skin as a great burst of noise nearly blew them off the patio.

"Sorry," Alex called out from inside as the volume went down and the noise became a Fats Waller song instead.

"Jesus," Quinn breathed, "that frightened the life out of me."

"You don't say?" Kit said, looking down at Quinn's hand which had a vice-like grip on her upper arm.

"Oh Kit, I'm sorry," Quinn said. She rubbed Kit's arm and leant in to smother it with mock kisses. "That better?"

"Much better, thank you, my sweet," Kit said, fully aware that they were being watched from the doorway.

"Don't mind me," Alex stated, placing a bottle of Chianti Classico on the table as she pulled out Quinn's chair and sat down on it.

Chapter 26

"How did you get a name like Enzo McAllister?" Kit asked as she finished the second helping of her host's superb gnocchi with pesto.

"Scottish father, Italian mother," Enzo replied. "I was born in Firenze, raised in a wee town just north of Edinburgh, spent my early teenage years in Calcutta where my father had an engineering contract, and my later teenage years in Rome where my mother ran a small music school. I went to university in Scotland, got my first real job in New York, and true love brought me to Melbourne. My father named me Lawrence, after his father, and my mother called me Lorenzo, after her grandfather. Most of my friends think I'm confused, and I fear they may be right."

"Confused or confusing?" Kit asked, wondering who the true love was now she knew it wasn't Alex.

"Both probably," Enzo said.

"It's a quarter to ten, Enzo," Quinn interjected.

"Pardon?"

"Are you cooking a soufflé or something?" she queried.

"No, dear. Why do you ask?"

"Well, you keep looking at your watch. It's driving me crazy."

"Och, my profoundest apologies," Enzo cried, throwing up his hands. "But I'm playing tonight and Rick is picking me up at ten-thirty so I have to give myself time to change."

"*What* are you playing tonight?" Kit asked, noticing that Enzo seemed to be becoming camper by the second. "If that's not a personal question," she added.

Enzo cast her a sidelong look and gave his shoulder a mock seductive roll. "In just over two hours I'll be having an intimate encounter with a baby grand. I'm playing the midnight show at Dorothy's Caviar Bar."

"Dorothy's? Oh wow, I haven't been there for ages," Kit exclaimed. "Is that what you do, I mean, are? I mean . . ."

"Yes dear, I'm a piano player," Enzo interrupted helpfully.

"Piano player indeed," Alex laughed. "The man was a concert pianist."

"Yes, that's true, but I gave it all up for a sleazy late-night lounge act. Go figure," Enzo grinned. "During the day I'm also, sometimes, a trained historian and genealogist."

"Well, I don't know about you Enzo but I'm certainly confused," Kit laughed.

"Darling, you don't know the half of it," Enzo sighed, clasping his hands over his heart. "But the whole story requires a lot more time than I have this evening."

"To believe even half of it, however," Quinn said, waving her empty glass, "requires a lot more wine."

"I *can* do something about that," Enzo said, going inside and coming back moments later with another bottle of Chianti.

"So, tell me about your detecting adventures today, Kit," he requested, refilling all the glasses on the table. "And how did Nancy Drew here do on her first time on the job?" he added, patting Alex on the hand.

"It wasn't her first time, Enzo. She's been following me around for days. I'm going to have to start paying her if she keeps it up."

"Very funny, O'Malley," Alex said dryly. "But it *was* quite fun."

Which bit? Kit wondered. She filled in Enzo and Quinn on her interview with Geoffrey then Alex took over the storytelling with a slightly edited version of their exploits in the front garden of a certain St. Kilda brothel. At one stage during the latter Kit placed her hand over Quinn's to stop the angry drumming of fingers on the table.

"I am. I am," Quinn snarled when Alex had finished.

"You am what?" Enzo asked.

302

"I am going to take him apart limb from limb. With a bread knife. No. An electric carving knife."

"We *will* get him," Kit assured her.

"It's taking too long," Quinn complained.

"But he *will* pay," Alex stated categorically.

"Well, you're going to have to bind and gag me to keep me quiet tomorrow." Quinn frowned as she raised her glass and repeated bitterly, "Tomorrow."

Before anyone could think of something to say Quinn turned to Enzo and gave him a dazzling smile as if no dark thoughts had intruded on her evening. "Can I come and watch you play tonight?" she asked.

"Of course."

"Great! Do you want to come, Kit?"

"No, I don't think so. I feel like I haven't slept for days."

"You shouldn't be going out either, Quinn," Alex admonished. "You need a good night's sleep so you can be strong and composed. You've got a big day tomorrow."

Quinn threw her friend a withering look that basically said: No kidding Alex!, or, That's the understatement of the evening!, or, and probably more to the point, If you don't stop stating the obvious I'm going to take *you* apart with a bread knife.

"It's not going to be a *big* day, Alex," Quinn said calmly but patronizingly. "A big day is what you have when you start school for the first time, or when your grandparents take you to Luna Park, or *even* when you have a lavish and romantic wedding ceremony. They're all *big* days. Tomorrow is just going to be a shitty day."

"Alex," Enzo said, as he stood up and started clearing the table, "sometimes I wonder if you're from the same planet as the rest of us."

"Why?"

"Perhaps you'd like some help getting your foot out of your mouth?" Kit asked her.

"I don't know what I said. What did I say?"

"Nothing, dear," Enzo said, shaking his head. "Quinn, would you like to give me a hand?"

"O'Malley, what did I say?" Alex demanded as Enzo and Quinn retreated inside with the empty bowls.

"Quinn is *trying* to take her mind off this bloody awful mess and you persist in reminding her about it. *And* what's worse you keep telling her how she's supposed to be reacting or behaving. You're very lucky she didn't chuck you off the patio. Quite frankly, you're very lucky I didn't."

Alex shook her head slowly and glared at Kit. "Who the hell do you think you are, O'Malley? You come striding into Quinn's life when she's at her most vulnerable and just take over. You've known her two minutes and you're acting like you know everything about her."

"Hey, Alex, longevity doesn't mean diddly if you only know someone from where you're standing."

"What the hell does that mean?"

"It means . . ." Kit hesitated as she ran her hands through her hair before looking into those angry gray eyes, "it means that just because you've known Quinn since she was in nappies doesn't mean you understand her. You have an idea of who she is, or rather who you expect her to be, that's based solely on your own points of reference which—and this is purely from where *I'm* standing—are more than a little skewed."

"And I suppose you think you understand her?" Alex asked.

"No, and I don't pretend to. I also don't judge her."

"What?" Alex said flatly, twirling her wine glass back and forth in her fingers while she deliberately avoided looking at Kit. "And you're saying I do?"

"Constantly. Look, if she wants to spend the night before her mother's funeral getting drunk while she watches Enzo play piano, what difference does it make to you?"

Alex pressed her fingers to her lips for a few silent moments before meeting Kit's eyes. "None, I suppose. It's just that I care about her."

"I know, Alex," Kit said softly, "and she knows it too. But she'll let you know what kind of support she needs. Why don't you go with her to watch Enzo play?"

"Because she didn't ask me," Alex replied, taking a sip of wine. "She asked you."

Oh shit! Kit thought. That's what this is all about. She brushed her fingers across the back of Alex's hand. "I don't think it was a deliberate omission."

"No?" Alex asked, giving her a searching look as she awkwardly shifted positions in her chair to get her hand subtly out of Kit's reach.

"Have we made up yet or are we still arguing?" Enzo asked, making a grand entrance, this time with cups, a coffee pot and a bottle of port on a tray.

"Both," said Kit, giving him a grin before turning back to Alex who was still watching her, this time with a gaze that seemed to be asking a hundred questions at once.

"Good. Then can I assume it's safe to leave you two alone?"

"I didn't hear Rick arrive," Alex said.

"He just buzzed from downstairs. He doesn't want to leave his stuff unattended in the car. So I've made you some coffee, and you can demolish the whole bottle of port by yourselves if you feel so inclined."

"Where's your tux?" Alex asked.

"Rick's early as usual. I'll get changed at Dorothy's."

"Where's Quinn?"

"Loitering in the lounge," Enzo said pointedly.

Kit got the message and stood up to go inside. "Shall we see them off, Alex?"

Quinn was standing near the entrance hall, shuffling from one foot to the other.

Alex walked over and gave her a hug. "I'm sorry for being such a grumpy old tart," she said.

Quinn laughed. "That's OK, Alex. I know you can't help being old."

"Thanks a million."

"Don't wait up," Quinn smiled, embracing her tightly. Then, obviously deciding that it was boring having things back to normal, she turned to Kit, threw one arm around her neck and kissed her on the mouth. "See you tomorrow, Kit."

"Ooh, girl germs," Enzo stated as he opened the front door, took Quinn by the elbow and ushered her out into the hall. "That was naughty," Kit heard him say as the door closed behind them. When Kit turned around she discovered Alex was halfway across the lounge.

If you're at all sensible you'll go home now, O'Malley, she thought as she followed Alex out on to the patio instead.

"Coffee and port?" Alex offered somewhat tersely.

Definitely time to go home. *Now,* O'Malley. "Yes please," she replied, leaning back against the door frame. She forced herself to stop admiring Alex's delicious shoulders only to find herself staring at the most perfect thighs she'd ever seen.

Get a grip, O'Malley! This is dangerous. Go home. When she looked up Alex was holding a port glass out to her—at arm's length. Closing her eyes was all Kit could do to stop herself from running her hand up that arm.

"Are you OK?" Alex asked.

"Fine. Thank you," Kit lied, taking the glass.

Alex moved away and stood much too close to the edge of hell for Kit's liking. She leant on the balcony wall and looked back at Kit. "So, ah, are you working on any other cases at the moment?" she asked.

"No, Alex, but you know that already."

"Yeah." Alex turned her attention to the view.

"Perhaps I should just go home," Kit said.

"No. Don't leave," she said quickly, turning back to face Kit.

"Well, do you think you could move away from the edge? You're making me nervous."

Alex laughed and returned to her chair. "I thought you wanted to throw me off."

"That was before," Kit said. "In reality I'd be too scared to get that close to you. I mean to the edge."

"I'm sorry about before," Alex said, pushing her hair behind her left ear as she studied the contents of her glass. "I'm a bit . . ."

"Fractious?" Kit suggested.

"That's a suitable word."

"It was Quinn's word. She says you're fractious and fragile at the moment."

"Really?" Alex gave a humorless laugh. "What else did she tell you?"

"Nothing much, except that you'd just come out of a relationship."

"Just?" Alex stared at her feet for a minute.

"Do you want to talk about it?"

"No," Alex said curtly. She took a sip of port before finally meeting Kit's eyes. "It's not the . . . I mean, it's not an issue. It's been over for months. It's unimportant to me. Quinn should *not* have told you."

"Yeah, well, don't be angry with her. She only told me the little she did because I asked her what your problem was."

"Problem?" Alex looked quite surprised. She stood up and took a few paces towards the balcony. "Sorry, I keep forgetting," she said and turned on her heel, looking about her for somewhere to stand. She leant back against the nice solid wall opposite Kit, next to the glass door.

"So you think I've got a problem?" she asked defensively.

"I think you have a problem with me." Kit took a deep breath. "I don't really want to get into this. I think I should go home before I say something I regret."

"Oh, that's helpful."

"Look, Alex, I *know* you don't like me. So what's the point in taking this any further?"

Alex frowned. "What makes you think I don't like you?"

"Well, you don't approve of me then."

"I think you're disturbing," Alex said, so softly that Kit almost didn't catch it. "I mean, I think you're a disturbing influence on Quinn."

"Why, for god's sake?"

"Quinn is vulnerable and . . ."

"You said that before, Alex," Kit stated.

"And I'm saying it again, O'Malley," she snapped. "Your reputation does precede you, you know."

"My reputation?" Kit snorted. "Well, that revelation requires another drink. Who the hell have *you* been talking to?" Kit refilled her port glass and handed the bottle to Alex before returning to the relative safety of the doorway. "Let me guess. Angie?"

Alex shrugged and replaced the bottle on the table. "Does it matter?"

"Actually it does, seeing my so-called reputation is mostly a figment of Del and Brigit's fertile imagination. It's become something of a bar-room joke at Angie's. It's getting less funny by the second, however."

"You may think it's a joke, O'Malley, but it's obvious that Quinn is taking *you* seriously. And a reputation usually has some basis in fact. So, what is it with you? Do you get a thrill out of trying to convert someone? Or is one conquest much the same as another?"

"What the hell are you talking about now?" Kit asked in surprise. "What's this convert and conquer bullshit?"

"She's not gay, O'Malley."

"You could have fooled me," Kit said.

"Oh shit," Alex sighed, refilling her glass again. "You mean you have . . . shit."

"Quite frankly, Alex, it is none of your goddamn business whether we have or we haven't."

Alex opened her mouth to say something then apparently thought better of it. Kit noticed her hand was shaking as she tried several times to push her hair back behind her ear again. When she finally looked directly at Kit there were angry tears in her eyes.

"Alex, you don't honestly think I'd do anything to hurt Quinn, do you?"

"No. I just think your timing is inappropriate and your motives are selfish. She is emotional and confused and . . ."

"Look who's talking," Kit interrupted. "Miss Fractious and Fragile herself. You are one fucked-up individual, Ms. Cazenove. Where the hell do you get off judging my motives and Quinn's emotions while you're standing there in a state of complete emotional denial?"

"What?"

"Oh? You don't think you're confused? Here you are recovering from this broken relationship that you say is *un*important, you're about to enter a marriage of convenience with the reincarnation of Liberace, for god's sake, and you have no understanding of your own feelings for Quinn which is why you're being so antagonistic towards me."

"Well, I'm confused now. I have no idea what you're talking about."

"I'm talking about you and Quinn. I'm talking about jealousy, Alex. I've been watching you watching us all week. I've been watching you trying *not* to admit your feelings for Quinn, or more specifically trying *not* to do all the things you're accusing me of doing."

Kit downed her port and stepped up to the table to fill her glass again. When she turned around she bumped into Alex who was pacing back and forth.

"You have *no* idea . . ." Alex began, shaking her head.

"I'm sorry, Alex. I knew I should have gone home before I opened my big mouth."

"It's OK. I asked for it. I guess," she said, sounding a little bewildered as she filled her own glass again.

"You're going to be on your ear if you're not careful," Kit laughed.

Alex smiled sadly and held Kit's gaze just long enough to make them both feel uncomfortable. When Kit put her hand out to stop her turning away Alex recoiled and raised her hands, palms out. "Don't touch me," she said softly. She leant back against the wall again and closed her eyes.

"Alex," Kit said. "Alex, look at me. Thank you. Let's clear the air here once and for all, OK?"

"What now?"

"Nothing has happened between Quinn and me."

"Nothing?"

"Nothing at all. Except plain, ordinary, everyday, common or garden variety friendship."

Alex swallowed hard and actually looked surprised.

"Quinn is not interested in me, at least not sexually."

"What about you though?"

"Quinn is a very attractive young woman," Kit stated, "but I am not attracted to her."

"You're not?" Alex almost smiled. "Good," she added softly.

Kit was suddenly annoyed. "Yeah, it's great. So lighten up, OK. *You* have absolutely no reason to be jealous. And *I* am going home now to leave you to sort out how you *do* feel—in private." While I drown myself in a bath of bourbon—in private, she thought.

"I don't know, O'Malley . . ."

"I know you don't, Alex, that's why you need to be on your own." And why I need to get the hell out of here.

"You just love it when you think you're right, don't you?" Alex said angrily.

"Only if it's something worth being right about. This isn't. I do, however, love having the last word. So I'm going now." Kit placed her glass on the table.

"Well, you were only *half* right about me being jealous," Alex snapped.

"Frankly, Alex, I don't give a shit," Kit snapped back. "Good*night*," she added, not even looking back as she left the patio.

"I was jealous of Quinn."

Kit noted the surprised tone in Alex's voice but was halfway across the lounge room before the words registered. Jealous of Quinn?

When she stepped outside again Alex was still leaning against the wall, her head back and her eyes shut. She was muttering "Shit, shit, shit."

"What did you say?" Kit asked, moving as close as she dared.

"Shit!" Alex repeated, more forcefully.

"No, before that."

"You obviously heard me, O'Malley." Alex opened her eyes but seemed to be having a difficult time deciding where to look. "I didn't mean it."

"You didn't mean it? Or you didn't mean to say it?" Kit asked quietly.

"I thought you were leaving."

"I changed my mind. What's going on here, Alex?"

"I don't have the faintest idea," she said, shaking her head. "Honestly," she added, her gaze finally meeting Kit's for a long moment before she glanced away and stared down at her feet.

"I could probably explain it," Kit said, touching her gently on the chin to lift her face. She traced her finger along Alex's jaw before pressing her open palm lightly against Alex's cheek, her thumb barely touching the corner of her mouth.

Alex's lips parted slightly as she closed her eyes and leant, almost imperceptibly, into Kit's touch before moving her head so that Kit's fingers brushed across her mouth. Then she pulled back abruptly. "Oh god, oh shit. I don't need this," she sighed, throwing her head back against the wall.

"I'm sorry," Kit whispered. "I thought . . ." but her voice faltered as she realized her whole body was vibrating with a desire so strong she could barely breathe. She ran her hand up Alex's upper arm, caressing it softly as she leant closer, brushing her lips against Alex's exposed throat where it met the collar of her shirt.

"I really don't need this," Alex gasped. She pushed Kit back but kept hold of her shoulders while her gaze flicked from Kit's eyes to linger on her mouth.

"You don't need what?" Kit asked, her body swamped by a Catherine wheel of sensations spinning delicious tentacles of heat out from its center which was located, disconcertingly, in the general vicinity of her groin. God almighty! Who turned the temperature up? she wondered, knowing only one thing for sure: Alex's erratic breathing was driving her crazy.

"I don't need *this*," Alex said, her right hand travelling down Kit's arm and back up again. She let go. "Any of this. I don't need *you*, O'Malley."

"Who said anything about need?" Kit raised an eyebrow.

Alex's lips parted but she didn't say anything. Her eyes just kept searching Kit's face.

Sensing no resistance as she closed the gap between them again, Kit reached down and ran her palm up Alex's bare thigh, stopping when she reached her shorts so that only her thumb moved under the fabric to continue the caress.

"You *want* this though, don't you?" Kit breathed against her throat as she pushed her leg between Alex's thighs. "Don't you?" she repeated, moving her hand up under the shorts to cup Alex's buttock and pull her closer.

Alex let go of the breath she'd been holding. "No. Not *just* this," she said, clasping Kit's hand against herself as she raised her leg to ride against Kit's thigh. "I want *you*."

Until those words, although almost helpless with want for this woman, Kit had thought she still had some control over her senses. Then Alex brought her mouth to hers, tantalizingly close but not quite touching, and Kit honestly thought she was going to die from anticipation. She closed her eyes. She felt Alex's tongue flick one corner of her mouth, then the other. She felt Alex's tongue touch her own and, as a great yawning hunger rose up inside her like some wild animal, she felt Alex's open trembling mouth on hers, moving, devouring the beast before it could escape. And then she felt the ground disappear beneath her feet and she was falling, eight storeys to the ground.

"Oh whoa!" she exclaimed breaking the embrace. She pushed Alex's leg down and stumbled backwards, gulping to get enough air. Alex's eyes were shining with arousal. She was breathless and beautiful, and it was almost more than Kit could bear to look at her.

"It's too much," Kit swallowed.

"What?" asked Alex, tightening the grip she still had on Kit's shirt sleeve.

"I'm scared," Kit said, astonished by the truth of it. She reached out to feel the amusement that was playing the corners of Alex's mouth. "Don't laugh."

"I'm not," Alex whispered. She took Kit's hand and studied it closely as she turned it over and caressed the palm with her thumb. "What are you scared of?"

"The . . . the heat," Kit said simply as Alex bent her head to lick Kit's open palm with the tip of her tongue. "I have *never* felt such heat," Kit continued, grabbing hold of the front of Alex's shirt with her other hand as she felt Alex's breath curling round her fingers. "I'm scared . . . of what's going to happen to my body . . ." Alex raised her eyes to meet Kit's as she pressed her open mouth and tongue into Kit's palm. ". . . if we don't stop this." Still without breaking eye contact, Alex's tongue trailed up Kit's middle finger and rolled around it, before her mouth closed on it, sucking.

"Holy shit," Kit groaned, pulling her hand away so she could clasp the back of Alex's neck. She moved her whole body in against Alex's, pushing her back against the wall. Her free hand moved down Alex's throat, lingering over her breasts before continuing down her side to the bare leg which was raised again and wrapped around Kit's waist.

"O'Malley," Alex breathed in her ear, before running her tongue around the lobe, "if you don't kiss me again soon I'm going to scream."

Kit pulled back slightly, smiling. Hell, her whole body was smiling. She raised both hands to place them on either side of Alex's face. "I don't believe this," she said shaking her head in amazement. She brushed her bottom lip against Alex's mouth. She kissed the corners. She ran her tongue around the developing smile then stopped it by kissing her fully, deeply, slowly at first, and with just her mouth.

She was aware of Alex's hands under her shirt, stroking her sides. She moved her own hands down Alex's back, surprised by the firmness in the flexing muscles. Her hands continued down, massaging her arse, back around her hips and up her stomach to her breasts. To Alex's breasts. She could feel the erect nipples under her circling thumbs beneath the fabric of Alex's shirt. She was still kissing her, open-mouthed, not using her own tongue until she felt Alex's in her mouth, searching.

Oh god, oh god, I'm going to melt. She took her mouth away from Alex's but couldn't bring herself to break contact with her skin. Her lips and tongue travelled across Alex's cheek to her neck, just below her ear, then down to the hollow of her throat. She couldn't stay away from that mouth for long though and before she knew it her tongue was entwined with Alex's, thrusting, probing, exploring.

Kit kept kissing her, savoring her tongue, her mouth, as she undid Alex's shirt, pushing it aside to run her hands over her naked breasts. Alex groaned against Kit's mouth before dragging her own away, her body arching back, her head against the wall, as her hips thrust into Kit's.

Kit ran her tongue around one erect nipple, her fingers around the other as her free hand fumbled with the button and zip of the shorts. Alex's breathing was becoming noisier as Kit slipped her hand down inside her pants, her finger sliding in the wetness as she pressed her palm against Alex's crutch, her thumb massaging her groin.

"O'Malley?" Alex murmured questioningly.

Kit rolled her mouth over Alex's breast before looking up. She reached up to push Alex's hair back from her face then slipped the tip of her thumb between Alex's parted lips. Alex opened her mouth, breathing heavily. Kit pushed her thumb against Alex's tongue and then ran it over her lips.

"O'Malley," Alex said again.

"You are *so* beautiful," Kit said. "And *so* wet."

Alex laughed as she moved against the hand Kit had in her pants.

"Well, it's your fault," she gasped. "I've been like this since you kissed me in that damn garden this evening." She bent and kissed Kit on the mouth. "Mind you," she added, "I have been working up to it all week." She kissed her again. "Now stop playing with me," she breathed against Kit's mouth, wrapping her left arm around the small of Kit's back. "Fuck me," she mouthed, at the same moment that Kit slipped one, then two fingers inside her. "Oh god, yes."

313

Kit pushed her thigh higher up between Alex's trembling legs, pushing against the fabric of the shorts which held her own hand captured as she moved her fingers in and almost out, faster and faster.

Alex was breathing in time with the movement as her hand roughly fondled Kit's erect nipple. Alex's mouth was on hers now, moaning between kisses as her tongue thrust in and out, imitating what Kit was doing to her with her fingers. Then she buried her face in Kit's shoulder, her whole body heaving.

"I don't think . . . oh, goddamn!" she cried. "I don't think . . . I can stand up much longer." She took Kit's face between her hands, gazing into her eyes, and her breathing became merely short intakes of air. "On second thoughts . . ." It was all she managed to say before her words became rising moans and her body shuddered, down and down onto Kit's still moving hand.

Alex wrapped both arms around Kit's back and kissed her long and deep and slow, before reaching down to push at her hand. "O'Malley, you have to stop now or I'm going to fall over."

"I'll catch you," Kit said. Forever.

"I'm sure you will." Alex was smiling as she brushed her fingers lightly over Kit's mouth.

"I want you to know, Ms. Cazenove," Kit said, kissing Alex's fingers, "that this was not a spur of the moment thing. I have been wanting to do this—I mean, I wanted you from the moment I first saw you." Kit glanced down, suddenly feeling strangely embarrassed. "Um, what I'm trying to say is that you are not a 'conquest' of any sort."

"I didn't think I *was*. I'm not a convert either, O'Malley."

"I sort of figured that one out for myself," Kit laughed. "Only about ten minutes ago though. I think I'm a bit slow."

"Well, you caught up nicely." Alex kissed her and smiled. "Come with me," she added, and took her by the hand and led the way inside.

"Alex, wait." Kit caught her around the waist. Alex looked highly amused as she turned into Kit's embrace.

"Wherever you're taking me," Kit said, her hands shaking as she removed Alex's shirt and dropped it to the floor, "it's too far."

Alex moved against Kit's caressing hands. "The bedroom is just down the hall, O'Malley."

"I can't wait that long," Kit whispered, pushing Alex's shorts down as she knelt on the floor in front of her. She ran her hands over Alex's hips then round to cup her buttocks and pressed her mouth against the cotton of her pants before pulling them down and out of the way. Alex's fingers were in her hair, pressing against the back of her head.

"O'Malley, no." Kit felt Alex's hands under her arms. "I can't do this standing up again." Kit kissed Alex's thighs, her stomach, each breast, and her throat, all the way up to her mouth as she stood up again. Alex moved backwards towards the couch, pulling Kit with her as she undid the buttons of her shirt, her hands travelling inside and around the back to undo her bra, then they were at the zip of her jeans.

Kit let go just long enough to pull her jeans down and step out of them. She slid her arm around Alex's waist again and, pushing her right thigh between her legs, she knelt on the couch and covered her throat and breasts and lips with kisses as she lowered her down.

"I'm impressed," Alex whispered against Kit's mouth.

"With what?"

"You didn't drop me," she replied.

Kit hovered over Alex for a moment, looking down into those stunning gray eyes; eyes that were finally looking at her, for her.

I love you. She wanted to say it—more than anything—but as Alex smiled up at her she simply bent down and kissed the smile with one of her own.

"I knew it," Alex said breathlessly, cupping Kit's breasts, one in each hand. "I knew they would fit my hands perfectly," she added, in response to Kit's enquiring glance.

Kit was surprised by the tremor of excitement that rippled through her body at those words. She dropped to her knees, between Alex's legs. "This is amazing," she said, shaking her head. "Why?" Alex laughed; a deep sensual laugh that caused all the aroused parts of Kit's body to tingle as if someone had poured warm champagne over her.

"Because I don't believe I'm here, that we're, that . . ." Kit ran her hands up Alex's legs, pushing them apart as she pressed her body forward, "that I'm touching you, tasting you."

Alex laughed again. "You mean because we've both been such complete idiots all week?" she asked, caressing Kit's cheek and running her thumb roughly over her mouth.

"Because I thought you didn't like me at all," Kit replied.

315

"You were mistaken."

"So it would seem," Kit said, moving her thumbs in circles high inside Alex's thighs. "I wouldn't mind being mistaken like this more often."

Kit ran kisses down Alex's body. She replaced her caressing thumb with her open mouth, running her tongue over Alex's skin, inhaling deeply to immerse herself in the scent of her. She moved her hands over Alex's thighs to her hips, pulling her down onto her mouth, her tongue dipping into the wetness.

"Oh, yes!" Alex gasped, as one hand clasped Kit's shoulder, kneading her skin, while the other was flung out trying to grip the couch. She was moving her hips, undulating against Kit's mouth as her breathing became heavier and louder.

Kit thought she was going to come just listening to Alex groan; her own pleasure mounted as the first spasms began to rock Alex's body. She played her tongue back and forth, on and around Alex's clit, waiting till Alex arched into the crest of sensation before thrusting two fingers inside. "Oh, god!" Alex cried out, clutching at Kit's arm to hold the fingers deep inside as her body convulsed in orgasm, lifting off the couch as the tremors shook her.

"I want *you*, Kit," Alex murmured, still trembling as she reached for her. "*Now*," she whispered, more urgently as Kit's reaction to hearing her name was to hold Alex more tightly.

Alex pushed her right hand between Kit's legs as she pulled her onto her lap and onto her fingers. The thrill that raced through her body was so sudden that Kit had to grab the back of the couch to brace herself. She looked down at Alex who was looking up at her as if nothing else in the world mattered more than giving her pleasure, except that the movement of her fingers inside Kit was obviously still part of her own orgasm. Kit couldn't believe how aroused she was just by what was happening to Alex.

She brought her mouth down on Alex's as she moved against those fingers. Alex's thumb found the perfect motion against her clit, from where a tremor of white heat spread through every molecule in her body, then out beyond her body where it dipped and almost dissipated before curling back on itself to make a return rush to the center.

Kit arched backwards but, at the moment when she thought she couldn't get any higher, Alex removed her fingers. "Ah . . ." Kit said by way of objection, but Alex's smile stopped her from speaking. Alex leant forward, kissing her on her mouth, then her throat, then her breasts as she slid her arms around Kit's back and lowered her onto the floor.

And then there was nothing in the world but Alex's hands, seemingly all over her at once, and Alex's mouth between her legs, her tongue flicking, her lips sucking. Kit was lying, exquisitely high, on the very edge of forever. And then she fell, and soared and fell again, and then came like rolling surf, over and over, and over again.

Chapter 27

Damn, I knew I should have gone up the back stairs, Kit thought as she rounded the corner into Swan Street just as Del and Brigit were getting out of their car in front of the office.

"You're up early," Del said. "Or are you home late?"

Kit threw her a non-committal smile and tried to keep walking but Brigit stopped her by waving a bag of hot donuts in her face.

"So where have you been?" Del asked.

"*None* of your business," Kit stated, taking a donut. "Thank you, Brigit."

"Oh, no. You've been out on the tiles, haven't you? I thought you said you were going to give it up."

"Give what up?" Kit asked innocently.

"Lust, Katherine Frances!"

"I believe what I said was, I was going to give up looking for it. This just came my way, quite unexpectedly."

"Oh, happy accident," Brigit chirped.

"Precisely," Kit agreed. "And besides, this is not just lust. This is something altogether more . . . more, um . . . just more. OK?" Kit suddenly felt a little foolish, and the disbelieving look that was occupying all the movable features of Del's face only made her feel worse—as if she was standing naked in the street.

"I knew it, I knew it! Didn't I tell you this would happen? Didn't I say she was just your type?"

"Who, Del?" Kit asked, unlocking the front door since it seemed that neither Del nor Brigit were going to do it.

"That child, that poor little rich girl with the heaving bosom and the monumental crush on you."

"You mean Quinn?" Kit said, trying to keep a straight face. "Del, I'm standing here telling you that I think I'm in love, and you're rabbiting on about Quinn. What's she got to do with this?"

Del stood there with her eyebrows locked in the up position and her mouth half open.

"I think the happy accident is with the *other* one, Del," Brigit said, as if she was stating the obvious. "Alex, yes?" she added, glancing at Kit for confirmation.

Kit took a deep breath and nodded. Brigit looked sublimely pleased with herself.

"I don't believe this," Kit exclaimed. "This is the first time in known history that I've seen Delbridge Fielding at a loss for words."

"She'll get over it," Brigit assured her. "But you must come in for coffee and tell us all the juicy details. I want to hear absolutely everything!"

"I'd love to, Brigit," Kit lied, "but I have to shower and change before I go to see a nice policeman about a gang of nasty murderers."

"That's not fair," Brigit complained. "You can't just leave it like that."

"I'm afraid I have to," Kit said, heading for the stairs followed by an unsettling feeling that she'd spoken too soon anyway. How *she* felt was one thing, but Alex was something else all together.

Kit knew it was probably just morning-after awkwardness, a combination of excitement, wonder and rampant insecurity, but she was more than a little anxious about this particular morning after. Last night had meant more to her than any other first night she could ever remember, but she had no idea where Alex was coming from. She had been affectionate but distant, almost business-like, when she'd woken Kit and given her a cup of coffee at seven o'clock. The fact that she

319

was already dressed for work added to Kit's impression that in the cold sober light of day Alex regretted the fact that Kit was in her bed; that she had never intended the first night to happen at all; or, that now it had, it would also be the last night.

Oh, wow, but what a night, Kit thought, not even worrying about the stairs as she walked slowly up to her apartment. Each mental flashback of one moment or another of the love they had made until five in the morning was accompanied by an actual physical thrill as her body's memory replayed the sensations. But then she remembered waking up, just an hour ago, to find Alex gazing down at her wearing an expression that almost said "What have I done?" before she smiled, just a half-smile, and bent and kissed her goodbye.

Kit stopped on the first landing for a moment and closed her eyes to recall the last moments before she'd fallen asleep: Alex in her arms, already sleeping, her head on Kit's shoulder, her right arm and leg draped across her body.

It *has* to mean something, Kit thought, trying to ignore the fear that the next time she saw her Alex would begin the conversation with: "Um, about last night . . ."

Kit was so preoccupied with the argument going on between her mind and her body that she nearly tripped over the huge bundle of clothing piled on the landing outside her door. "What the heck?" she exclaimed. "Aah, shit," she added when the body inside the bundle moved and sat up.

"Christ, O'Malley! There's no need to walk all over me. Where the hell have you been?"

"Where the hell have I *been*?" Kit repeated vaguely, holding out her hand to help him up. "You look awful, Hector. What the hell are you doing sleeping on my doorstep?"

"Waiting for you, obviously. I didn't know where else to go."

"Why?"

"Because of this," Hector said, unwrapping what turned out to be a large gray raincoat to reveal a slim black case.

"A computer," Kit said wearily. It was way too early for this, whatever this was.

"Yeah. Sort of," Hector stated. "Can we go inside, please?"

Kit shrugged, unlocked and opened the door, then stood aside while Thistle hurtled her little black body out onto the landing. She came to a screaming halt when she realized Kit was standing there with a complete stranger, then proceeded to wrap herself around Hector's legs.

"You're a hussy," Kit said, picking her up and carrying her inside. She left Hector to close the door and went straight into the kitchen to turn on the kettle. "Do you want coffee?"

"Yeah, thanks." Hector slumped onto one of the bar stools, swung his bundle on the bench and laid his head down on it.

"You look like something The Cat dragged it," Kit said flatly, "and she's been known to bring home some pretty disgusting items."

Hector raised his head and stared at her. His eyes were red and bleary, he was in desperate need of a shave and his hair was completely deranged. "I have been on your landing since eight-thirty last night," he said slowly and carefully, as if that explained everything.

"How did you *get* on my landing, Hector?" Kit asked, imitating his tone. She poured some cat biscuits into Thistle's bowl.

"Credit card on the front door lock, O'Malley," he replied, and laid his head down again.

"So are you going to tell me why?" Kit got the milk out of the fridge.

"Are you going to get less grumpy than this?"

"I doubt it, at least not until I've had my coffee."

"Then I'll wait till you're sitting down," Hector said.

A few minutes later Kit took a seat and bent her head over her cup, hoping the caffeine fumes would help keep her awake. "OK, mate, what gives?"

"First of all," Hector said, turning to face her as he tied his hair back with the rubber band he'd had around his wrist, "you can't arrest me any more, can you?"

"No, of course not. Why would I want to anyway?" Kit asked, then added in a tone that suggested she didn't really want to know, "Hector, what have you done?"

Hector stared at the ceiling for a few seconds then unwrapped the computer again and dropped his coat on the floor. "I stole this," he said simply, then screwed up his face as if he thought Kit was going to hit him.

"Oh, Hector," Kit sighed. "I thought you didn't do that any more."

"Well, it was just lying around," Hector shrugged. "In that big crate."

"What big crate?" Kit asked, looking puzzled until it dawned on her what he was saying. She closed her eyes for a moment and shook her head. "You idiot," she said and then burst into laughter.

"What are you laughing at? It's not funny," Hector said desperately.

"Yes, it is," Kit managed to say. "I can't believe you have a guilty conscience about nicking a questionable piece of merchandise from a gang of ruthless murderers who have absolutely no idea who you are. I seriously doubt they're going to report it stolen. Why didn't you just take it down to the local pub and sell it, or add it to your own collection?"

"Because it doesn't work. I doubt any of them *work*," Hector stated. He pulled out his knife, flicked it open and lay it on the bench while he turned the laptop around and opened it. "And this is *not* funny, O'Malley," he added as he used the knife to undo the screws at each corner.

"Oh, my god," Kit said slowly as Hector levered the top off.

The key to the whole mystery, perhaps even the real reason for Celia's death, lay there as white as the driven snow, packed in two large plastic bags and taking up the space where the hard drive should have been.

Kit glanced at Hector, who looked genuinely scared, before pulling out one of the packets. "What do you suppose it is?" she asked.

"Scotch mist!" Hector snapped. "What the fuck do you think it is?"

"I meant is it cocaine or heroin?"

"It's death, O'Malley, that's what it is. I hate this stuff!" Hector snatched the packet from Kit's hand, threw it back with the other one and proceeded to screw the top back on.

"We have to take this to the cops right now," Kit said.

"No way. They'll probably arrest me for possession."

"Don't be silly," Kit said.

322

"O'Malley, I want you to tell me *who* those guys at that warehouse were, because I'm going to find them and make them eat this shit."

"If you want to kill them, Hector, I'm afraid you'll have to get in line," Kit stated.

"I am serious, O'Malley. They make me sick, those rich suits who wouldn't touch this stuff themselves except to exchange it for filthy money. I don't even care whether they're the ones who are responsible, I just want them to know that what goes around comes around."

"What are you talking about?"

"Those bastards, or some others just like them, killed my mother. I want them to die, and die in agony."

"Your mother? Oh, Hector, I had no idea," Kit reached out and clasped his hand. "What happened? Last I heard she'd gone into a detox program."

"Yeah," Hector said softly, his chin quivering as he tried not to cry. "She was clean for nearly two years. Then she met a guy. *Another guy.* He was a dealer and into it himself, and within three weeks she was hitting up again. Six months after that she was dead."

"Oh, god, I am *so* sorry."

Hector squeezed her hand and took a huge breath. "It was two years ago," he said. "Sorry, I thought I was OK about this now." He let go of Kit's hand and wiped his eyes.

"There's no need to apologize, mate," Kit said softly. "Besides, thanks to you I finally know what this whole sordid mess is all about. And what's more, with this," she tapped the laptop, "I can get Marek to do something about it."

Kit picked up her mug and stared at the contents while she tried to work out what to do next. Unlike Hector she wasn't worried about being charged with possession herself, but she was a little doubtful about the legality of her position of having approximately half a kilo of an illegal drug of dependence *in* her possession. Especially because *how* it came to be there would be another thing Marek would want explained. But it *was* hard evidence and now she had it she wondered how long it would take Marek to get his arse into gear. He'd have to bring in the drug squad and get search warrants because there was no question that it all came down to a police raid on Dalkeith's warehouse tonight. It was the only way to catch them all in the act.

Get your own arse into gear, O'Malley, she commanded. "Do you want a shower or something?" she asked Hector.

"Um," Hector sounded surprised. "I was going to go home."

"No way, Hector. I don't want you to go anywhere."

"What are you going to do?" Hector looked pained, as if he'd already been caught, tried, convicted and was on his way to J Division at Pentridge.

"Don't look so worried. I'm going to make a few phone calls, cover a few bases to cover our arses and then *we*," Kit emphasized, "are going to hand this stuff over to Marek. So get cleaned up. I could probably find you a shirt if you want one."

"Can I have a cigarette first?"

"Sure. Outside on the patio. Then have a shower. Second door on the right down the hall. You'll find a clean towel in the cupboard." Kit picked up her coffee, dragged herself over to her desk and slumped into her chair. What she really wanted was about three days' sleep but the likelihood of getting even a few hours had just become as remote as Christmas.

She flipped through her teledex, pulled the phone towards her and punched the number for Jenkins, Cazenove, Scott and Harris. She had to talk to Alex. She didn't *want* to talk to Alex but she had to. The plan she'd just formulated in her mind required Alex's assistance.

Who are you kidding, O'Malley? Of course you want to talk to her. That's *why* I don't want to, she thought miserably. She wondered why she felt so miserable. She wondered if Alex would take her call. She wondered when she'd suddenly developed this monstrous insecurity complex.

The ever-efficient Margaret Richards answered the phone and told her *Miss* Cazenove was meeting with a client and could not be disturbed. Kit breathed a sigh of relief while thinking "I knew it!" and then asked to speak to Douglas instead. He agreed to her plan so she rang off and pressed the autodial button for Marek's office.

"You wanted evidence, I got evidence," she stated when he answered.

"I hope it's not full of holes like the last lot," he laughed.

"Ha, ha, bloody ha! In about two hours you'll be laughing on the other side of your face, Jonno."

"OK, what have you got?"

"This is what I need you to do . . ." Kit began.

"Whoa, Trigger," Marek interrupted. "Tell me what you've got first."

"Marek trust me, OK? I want you to meet me at Douglas Scott's office at eleven o'clock. And you'd better bring Ray Lynch with you."

"Boscoe? What do you want him for?" Marek interjected again.

"He *is* still head of the Drug Squad, isn't he?"

"Yes," Marek said cautiously.

"Good. I also suggest you line up a magistrate to get a warrant organized to enter and search Ian Dalkeith's warehouse tonight."

"Oh, not that again. What have you got?"

"I'll see you at eleven. Oh, by the way, if I get pulled over for speeding on the way into town and then get arrested for possession of something that is definitely *not* baby powder I want you to know, in advance, that the stuff is not mine. It belongs to Geoffrey Robinson, Ian Dalkeith, Davis Whitten, Gerald Grainger, Malcolm Smith and a redhead named Maggie." Kit hung up.

She was still rummaging around in the mess on her desk when Hector shuffled back inside. "I doubt you'll ever find what you're looking for," he said.

"Finnigan's phone number," Kit said absently.

"That creep!" Hector exclaimed. "He nearly pulled my ear off when he dragged me out of that crate the other night. What do you want *him* for?"

"Because I suspect he's known about the drugs all along. If he really is who he told Alex he was then I think that's why he's here and I'd hate for him to miss out on the fireworks tonight. Besides, he'd probably throttle me. Ah, here it is."

It was a mobile phone number and the person who answered sounded as if he was sitting in a forty-four-gallon drum.

"Yo, Finnigan," Kit said.

"What?"

"What yourself," she countered. "Are you really a cop?"

"Oh, it's you, Girl Scout. What are you going to stuff up this time?"

"Nothing. That's why I'm calling you first. And don't be such a patronizing shit."

"What do you want, O'Malley?" he asked.

"Nice of you to tell me this was all about drugs," Kit said.

"You weren't conscious enough for me to tell you anything," he reminded her. "And I *did* tell you it was separate business."

"Yeah, well, it's not separate any more. It's time to get those bastards. So if you really are on the level and you want a say in what happens next you'd better meet me at Alex's office at eleven o'clock."

An audible sigh echoed around whatever it was that he was sitting in. "Give me the address," he said.

"I think we're going to need another large pot of coffee, please."

"Yes, Mr. Scott," Margaret Richards said as she closed the door.

Kit shook Douglas's hand, introduced him to Hector and then surveyed his office. She ignored Marek, who was glaring at her from one of the armchairs by the coffee table, and smiled at Ray Lynch, who threw her a friendly nod from his place in front of the window.

It had been a good two years since she'd last seen him but despite the graying hair and the few extra pounds he was carrying "Boscoe" Lynch was still a fine and imposing specimen of over-exercised manhood. Boscoe—short for proboscis and so-named partly for the size of his hooter but mostly for his ability to smell trouble from two blocks away—was as determined and as mean as a pit bull's owner when it came to the crooks in this town, but there was nothing he wouldn't do for a friend or any good cop. Kit had been in awe of him, and not just his reputation, when they'd first met six years ago but that feeling had soon given way to respect and admiration. He was, quite simply, one of the most honest guys she had ever met.

"Can we get on with whatever this is?" Marek asked, walking over to Kit.

"We're waiting for one more person," Kit said. "I think." The words were barely uttered when there was a short knock on the door.

Kit had no hope of maintaining whatever composure she thought she possessed when the person who opened the door was not

Margaret Richards or even Finnigan as she had expected, but Alex. She was followed closely by Finnigan, a strange reedy man in a dark blue suit and Margaret carrying another coffee pot, but it was nonetheless the unexpected appearance of Alex that caused Kit to stumble over her own feet in her attempt to make way for the procession of people through the door.

"Hello, Hector," Alex said with a smile. She turned to Kit, her gaze lingering for the briefest moment. "O'Malley," she nodded.

"Alex," Kit acknowledged with superhuman restraint. She stifled the grin that wanted to take over her face, and covered the flush of arousal that became a blush of embarrassment by running her hand through her hair several times and directing her attention at Finnigan's ghastly black and brown body shirt and unmatching tan trousers. She hoped, irrelevantly, that he'd been ransacking a local op shop for an undercover disguise because if not the man either had the most appalling dress sense this side of an ABBA revival concert or he was a genuine refugee from the seventies.

"What's this all about?" Alex was asking the question of Hector.

Hector rolled his eyes and shook his head. "Trouble," he answered.

Kit began the formal introductions, seeing she was the only one in the room who knew who nearly everyone was, but stopped short when she got to Finnigan. "Who are you really?" she asked.

He laughed and pulled out his wallet. "Liam Sullivan. US Drug Enforcement Administration, California," he replied, flashing his ID. "And this," he said, indicating the guy he'd walked in with, "is one of your own Feds, Detective Alan Sargent."

"Detective Sargent?" Kit repeated, trying in vain to hide her amusement.

"National Crime Authority actually," the man in question stated pointedly. "And there's nothing you can say that hasn't been said a thousand times before."

"I'll bet," Kit said, as everyone followed Douglas's lead and found places to sit around the table where Margaret was serving coffee.

Kit couldn't help but notice that Alex chose the chair furthest away from the one that she'd taken. And she knew it had nothing to do with the fact that Alex had something of great import to discuss with Douglas, who sat next to her, because they could talk any old time.

327

Nope, Alex had chosen the chair quite deliberately, just as she was now quite deliberately avoiding Kit's gaze by pretending to discuss something of great import with Douglas. I don't think I want to be here any more, Kit moaned silently, sagging into her chair. She was wondering who had let the air out of her tires when her personal space was suddenly invaded by Marek, seated to her right, who leant across her to peer intently at Hector.

"I know you, don't I?" Marek said accusingly.

"Ah, yes sir, Detective Marek, sir," Hector mumbled, as if he was guilty of every crime that had been committed in Melbourne in the past week, and then some.

"For goodness' sake, Hector, relax," Kit said. "You can start by opening up your little package."

Chapter 28

"I don't think this is such a good idea," Alan Sargent said an hour later.

"Why not?" Marek asked.

"It will compromise our whole operation."

"I don't see why," Boscoe said.

Kit let them argue for a while longer, narrowing her wide-eyed amazement at how it had come to pass that grown men had held so much power in the world for so long, down through a not altogether irrelevant wonder at how committees—being that they were usually made up of a number of people with their own agendas—ever got anything done, to the specific and probably unanswerable question of how Alan Sargent had ever been promoted past Sergeant Sargent. And a desk Sergeant Sargent at that!

Kit glanced at the other spectators of this tedious drama. Liam looked as though he was trying to figure out how to knock all three of them out with just one hit, Alex was still looking at everyone else in the room but her, Douglas resembled a bemused old grandfather who had never quite worked out what to do with the bickering offspring of the children he'd never wanted in the first place, and Hector was pretending he was an uncomfortable antique chair.

"Liam and my team have been working this case for months now. If, as Ms. O'Malley says, tonight's pick-up is the last of this shipment then we want to know where it's going," Sargent stated.

"Why?" Kit asked. "It's not even the same customer as last time, and I gather you didn't have that pick-up covered."

Detective Sargent actually flinched as if she'd hit a sore point. Liam, Kit noticed, was a picture of scowling pleasure, as if he'd made the point sore in the first place and was enjoying the fact that someone else was prodding it.

"If you'd involved us in this from the beginning we could have had all the bases covered," Boscoe stated.

"That was not my decision," Sargent argued.

Kit growled silently. She really wished she could make this guy stand in the corner until he learnt to fight his way out of a paper bag. He'd spent most of the meeting being obnoxiously unhelpful until Liam had pointed out they were all on the same side. Now he was just being annoyingly defensive.

"If I could have . . ." Sargent continued.

"Yeah, yeah," Kit interrupted, "and if Jacko's aim had been better none of us would be sitting here right now."

"Jacko? Who's Jacko?" Sargent asked, consulting his notebook.

"Sally Jackson. Inter-school hockey championship. She was a forward, I was captain. If she'd got that last goal, we would have taken the flag and I might have been inspired to try out for the Olympic team. At the very least I might have become a sports teacher instead of a cop."

"What's that got to do with this?" Sargent asked, his beady eyes rolling around their sockets in consternation, as if he thought he might find what he'd missed if only he could look in ten places at once.

"Absolutely nothing," Kit stated, managing to keep a straight face even though she was aware that Douglas had buried his snort of laughter in a very large handkerchief and Liam was hiding out behind a manila folder. "But," she continued, "what needs to be done here next is more important than what wasn't done before. So if you guys could save your demarcation dispute for another time it would be really helpful."

"O'Malley's right," Liam said. "It's time to pull the plug on these weasels."

Sargent rolled his head, either to remove a kink in his neck or to check that no one was spying on him from behind, and crossed his arms over his chest. "I don't know."

"I don't see what the problem is, *Alan*," Kit said, deliberately using his first name because calling him anything else, like Detective or Sargent or you-complete-moron, would have made her laugh hysterically. "I mean, it seems you have a unique opportunity here," she continued. "Correct me if I'm wrong, but doesn't a drug bust of this magnitude usually start with using the little fish in the pond as bait so you can hook the big fish? You know, follow the dealers to get to the suppliers."

"Yes, of course," Sargent sneered, acknowledging the obvious. "What's your point?" he asked, having apparently missed it on the way past.

"You've already got the sharks in this particular little pond; what do you want the minnows for?" Alex asked him before glancing at Kit. It was the first time she'd spoken during the meeting. It was also the first time she'd looked directly at Kit.

No, that's not true, Kit thought. It was simply the first time their gaze had actually met because, for some strange reason, each time it looked as if Alex *might* look in her direction Kit had turned her own attention elsewhere. Strange reason indeed, O'Malley, Kit thought desperately. Just as she'd known it would, that one look of Alex's had caused two diametrically opposed reactions: a deliciously uncontrollable thrill that resulted in the need for a cold shower and a fresh pair of knickers; *and* the revelation that when Alex ended it all, before it even got going, Kit would have no option but to join the Foreign Legion.

Her own expression, she knew, had said something truly embarrassing, like "I love you madly, let's get the hell out of here." On a scale of one to ten, however, those stunning gray eyes had registered a Cazenove unreadability factor of about 9.5 and Kit was convinced their expression, or lack thereof, did not bode at all well. She told herself to stop worrying, but herself was too busy thinking: "Worry. About Everything!"

"And all those sharks will be feeding in the one spot tonight," Boscoe was saying.

"OK, so we get warrants for this warehouse, for all their private residences and other places of business. That's going to take *some* organizing," Marek said.

"We should put the dogs on each of them. Immediately," Boscoe stressed. "*If* we can locate the ones you don't already have under surveillance."

"Geoffrey should be easy enough to find," Kit stated, returning to planet earth. "He *should* be attending his late wife's funeral from three p.m. today. And who knows, maybe some of his cronies will be there to lend support to the griefstricken widower."

"I did already have plans to keep watch over him during his hour of need," Marek stated flatly.

"It seems a waste of time and manpower to keep tabs on five or six people for the whole day when we know where they're going to be tonight," Sargent said petulantly, as if he actually realized that control of this operation, or perhaps his life in general, was slowly being removed from his reach.

"We *don't* know for sure that they're all going to front up tonight," Kit stated. "And *I* wouldn't want to be responsible for any of them doing a runner and setting up house in Majorca before we know they've even left the country."

"For that reason," Boscoe said, "we need to take the warehouse first, or coordinate all the raids for the same time. We can't afford to scare them off."

"We also need to let them load at least one box onto that boat before we move in or we've got nothing on Malcolm Smith," Liam stressed.

It suddenly occurred to Kit that they might be fitting an elaborate security system to the proverbial stable door when half the herd was already long gone. "Um," she said hesitantly, "were you guys watching the warehouse last night?"

"Not me," Liam stated. "I was watching Whitten and Dalkeith playing Black Jack at the Casino."

"Ah, I'm not sure," said Sargent, looking oddly anxious, as if a spiteful prankster had just made off with all his clothes and left him sitting there wearing nothing but a hint of complete incompetence.

"Why?" asked Liam.

"I've just had this horrible thought that Marek and I may have inadvertently scared them off already," Kit confessed.

"What do you mean, already?" Sargent demanded.

"Well, the last time I saw the dishonorable Geoffrey Robinson he was shitting bricks because his mates had screwed up their plan of making Byron Daniels's death look like a suicide," Kit explained. "Geoffrey now thinks, and quite rightly, that he may be a suspect in his wife's death. The fact that I also mentioned Grainger's name yesterday should give Geoffrey further cause for concern, and make them *all* wonder how much the police know about their many and varied dirty dealings."

"Oh, great! What a stuff-up," Sargent complained. "What did you do that for?"

"What did I *do* it for?" Kit asked, looking askance at Sargent. "Not being privy to the finely tuned strategies of your covert operation we were unaware, while doing *our* jobs, that we were treading on your toes."

"Your job, *Ms.* O'Malley," Sargent sneered nastily, "has quite possibly cost us months of work. They probably moved the damn drugs last night."

"I doubt it," Liam interjected.

"Personally I don't give a rat's arse what I've cost you. You at least knew *what* you'd been watching, and if you'd been doing that last night you'd know whether they'd been moved or not," Kit snarled impatiently. "That bunch of arrogant lowlifes you guys have been tap dancing around for the last couple of months are directly, by their own hands, responsible for the deaths of two innocent people. All I care about is nailing Geoffrey and Maggie what's-her-face and that disgusting Gerald Grainger for the murders of Celia and Byron. The drugs are all yours."

Marek put his hand on Kit's arm. "The drugs will help us nail them, Kit. They'll be falling over themselves to dob each other in if we catch them red-handed with a million or four worth of heroin."

"I know that," Kit said, trying to calm down. "But what about Andy?"

"Who the hell is Andy?" Sargent demanded.

"Our whingeing friend Mr. Bartoli," Liam replied calmly before turning to Kit. "We have Andy under wraps. I'd like to say he's helping us with our inquiries but I'd be surprised if he could help himself across the road. And I did go back on Wednesday night to make sure his buddy turned up to cover for him as he promised."

"What about the fact that we have a nice little share of their stock in trade sitting right here on my coffee table?" Douglas asked.

"I repacked the crate so the empty box was at the bottom," Hector muttered.

"Do you really think they may have moved the rest of the stuff already?" Marek asked.

Kit shrugged. "Finnigan, I mean Liam, is probably right. They can't be too worried if Dalkeith and Davis Whitten were out playing cards last night. And we still don't know for sure whether Celia's murder is incidental to all of this or just coincidental. Geoffrey might be shitting himself but the others mightn't give a damn."

"All things considered, however, we can't actually assume that the heroin is still there," Boscoe commented.

"Why don't you go in and look?" Hector suggested, quite bravely considering representatives of just about every level of law enforcement in the country suddenly turned their undivided attention in his direction again. "Well," he said, shrinking back in his chair, "if they've moved it already you're all going to look like right gits, aren't you?"

"I'll go in," Kit volunteered immediately.

"You can't go in, you're a civilian," Sargent stated.

"But *I* know exactly where the crate is, or was." Kit glanced at Liam who didn't point out that he did too which should mean that any further involvement on her part was unnecessary. "So *if* it's still there," she pressed on, "the raid can go ahead, and if not then I'll have saved you all a great deal of embarrassment. I don't need a warrant to go in and check. You lot do."

"What if you get caught in there?" Marek asked.

"Then the crooks can have me charged with trespass and you can arrest me."

"They're much more likely to beat the crap out of you to find out what you know then dump you in the river," Marek said.

"Don't make it sound as though it's something you'd like to see, Jonno," Kit stated.

"We could put a wire on her, just in case," Liam suggested.

"No way," Sargent declared.

"*Yes* way," Kit insisted. "Look, it's logical that I go in. Being a civilian means I can't compromise your case against these bastards because I have no jurisdiction. I would simply be a trespasser. And if they do catch me, then with any luck they'll do the decent bad guy thing and tell me exactly who did what to whom and why before they take me out the back and shoot me."

"O'Malley!" It was Alex's voice. "This is serious."

"I *am* serious."

It was one o'clock by the time Marek, Boscoe and Sargent had arrived at what they called a preliminary strategy and set off to put various wheels in motion. Well, Marek and Boscoe had left to organize warrants, surveillance equipment, strike teams and probably lunch, but Kit hoped that Detective Sargent was out trying to raise a posse to search for his personality.

"I reckon you must have done something quite dastardly in your last life," Kit said to Liam as they approached the foyer where Hector was sitting waiting for Alex to emerge from her office. She had offered to drop him in St. Kilda before going home to change for Celia's funeral.

"Dastardly?" Liam's hairy hound-dog face looked as if it was trying to work out whether that was an insult or not.

"How *did* you get lumbered with that guy?" Kit asked.

"Ah!" Liam laughed. "I arrived here—well, in Sydney actually—twelve weeks ago with a couple of leads on Whitten, a few suppositions, a great deal of intuition and absolutely no evidence whatsoever that anything was going down here. Consequently when I approached your federal boys they kindly assigned me their prize paranoid redneck as a special liaison officer. You know, he actually believes Australia is at risk of invasion by the Asians."

"Which Asians?" Kit asked.

"All of them, I think," Liam replied. "He maintains that citizens should be armed against the enemy, to protect their women and country from imminent rape and pillage."

"I see," Kit said flatly. "I gather that means only the men get the guns."

"Of course." Liam smiled, raking his huge moustache with his fingertips.

"It's probably just as well," Kit stated. "If I had a gun, Alan Sargent would be the first of the enemy I'd shoot."

"You . . . ah . . . noticed that he didn't exactly approve of you then?" Liam commented.

Kit laughed. "He's one of those poor bastards who feels personally threatened whenever he meets a woman who has no apparent need for a male in any area of her life. I'm sure it makes him feel quite impotent to know that I think I'm quite capable of protecting my country and my *own* women, thank you very much."

"Speaking of women," Liam grinned as he patted down all the likely places on his clothing where he may have put the thing he was looking for, "I got the impression you don't know the identity of your buddy Robinson's girlfriend."

"I know her voice and her first name but I've never seen her up close. I'm actually beginning to think she might be part vampire because her image hasn't come out clearly on a single photo I've taken," Kit admitted. Liam pulled a battered leather-bound notebook from his back pocket. "Oh, Liam, mate. You know who she is, don't you?"

"According to her driver's license and credit cards she is Margaret Easton."

"Her credit cards?"

Liam shrugged. "I lifted her purse in a cocktail bar one night, the second time I saw her with Robinson when he was drinking with Dalkeith and Whitten. I was curious although at the time we didn't even think Robinson was a player, let alone her. I thought she was a hooker but we ran a check and she has no form."

"That just means she hasn't been arrested or convicted," Kit reminded him.

"True. But I think it's a game they play," Liam said.

"A game?"

"Yeah. I watched him pick her up in the street one night about three weeks ago. She'd turned down three johns in ten minutes. They weren't low rent customers either; one was driving a Rolls. But she brushes 'em off, then gets in with Robinson and off they go to that little love nest of theirs."

"Are you saying she pretends to be a prostitute so he can pretend to pick her up?"

"Hey, each to their own," Liam said. "They probably call it foreplay. But I'm pretty sure it's their own private little game because I know she's got a key to that place. I've seen her come and go on her own while I've been watching Whitten and Dalkeith."

"Maybe she services them as well," Kit suggested. "After all, Geoffrey's also been in that place with a blond."

Liam looked at Kit as if she was completely daft. "It's the same woman, Girl Scout."

"The same?" Kit repeated. She couldn't have raised her eyebrows any higher if her life depended on it.

"Yep. She does a great line in wigs."

"Um, why were you watching her if you didn't think she was involved?" Kit asked, trying to cover how monumentally stupid she felt.

"I wasn't, exactly. I'd been making Whitten's business my own all day and finally tailed him to a photo studio in St. Kilda where he met Dalkeith and this Margaret broad. At eleven p.m. she and Whitten left together but he dropped her off a couple of streets away. Our favorite anal-retentive Fed had just arrived to take over the surveillance of Whitten, so when I noticed what she *appeared* to be doing I couldn't resist checking it out. She was a brunette that day, by the way."

"What was her surname again?" Kit asked, ignoring the dig.

"Easton," Liam replied.

"Maggie Easton," Kit said, trying to work out what tune the tinkling bells in the back of her mind were playing.

"You look as if you know the name," Liam said.

"No. Yes. No. I'm not sure," Kit replied vaguely. "It might be an alias anyway."

"That's a possibility," Liam said. "It *was* Sargent who ran the check and he may not have dug very deep. He couldn't see the point of checking out Robinson's bimbo when we were interested in Whitten and Dalkeith, and I must admit I didn't press the issue. It was about seven weeks ago and, as I said, we didn't think Robinson was involved then."

"Yeah, well, they're both most definitely involved," Kit stated.

"She might be involved by default just because she's Robinson's squeeze," Liam said.

"Robinson's *squeeze*?" Kit repeated, wondering which decade the man had beamed in from. "She is definitely his squeeze, Liam, but I am also positive that she killed Celia. Perhaps we could ask Sergeant Ramjet to do another background check."

"I can do it for you," Hector volunteered.

"You? How?" Liam asked.

"I could do it with just her name. But if you've got her license or credit card numbers written down in that little book of yours I could get you her life story in a few hours."

"How?" Liam repeated

"He'll probably surf the net or something," Kit explained.

"Ah, yeah," Hector said, bestowing on her a look he probably reserved only for the seriously technologically challenged, or maybe for the social workers of his acquaintance who claimed they really wanted to help people. "Or something," he agreed.

"Well," Kit blustered, waving her hands around.

"O'Malley." It was Alex, and the voice was cool, calm, collected, business-like . . .

Kit wanted to scream.

"May I have a word with you, please?" she enquired from the doorway of her office.

"Sure," Kit replied jauntily, wishing Alex at least had the decency to postpone her rejection until the sky fell in or hell froze over, whichever came first. "I'll catch you later," she said to Liam before turning back to find Alex's doorway empty.

You could just leave, she thought, as her feet took the rest of her down the hall. It's too late now. Take heed, O'Malley, if something

338

seems too good to be true it usually is. She wondered how much red tape was involved in joining the Legion, and whether they even accepted heartbroken women. She wondered if equal opportunity had made any inroads at all into that bastion of testosterone and, if not, whether it was a cause worth tackling. She wondered if it was raining in Maroochydore, and whether she cared or not.

The breath she took to help her cross the threshold towards sure and certain heartache was snatched away by the sight of Alex, who had just removed her black tailored jacket and was standing there looking at her, not to mention looking completely ravishing in a black skirt and pearl-colored silk shirt, one hand on her left hip, the other pushing her hair back behind her ear. *And* she was smiling, goddamit.

Maybe they'll let me start my own regiment, Kit thought desperately. "Nice office," she said, though she could have been standing in a concrete cell for all the notice she'd taken of the decor.

"That was unbearable," Alex exclaimed. She took two steps forward and reached behind Kit to push the door shut before pushing her up against it. Alex's mouth was on hers before Kit even had a chance to kiss goodbye the idea of traipsing through the Sahara wearing a funny hat. She kissed Alex instead. She locked her arms around the small of Alex's back and pulled her closer, while Alex kissed her mouth, her cheeks, her ears, her throat and managed to get her jeans undone and her shirt untucked so she could run her hands up Kit's back.

Kit's groan of desire when she felt Alex's thigh push between her legs, hard up against her crutch, was met with a gasp from Alex as their mouths and tongues came together again.

Katherine Frances O'Malley felt as if she'd just won Tattslotto, as if all her Christmases had come at once, or she'd just been made co-pilot of the first all-women space shuttle crew to Mars. And then she felt Alex's fingers inside her pants, inside her, sliding back and forth in the wetness, bringing her with a suddenness to an intensity that nearly made her pass out, until it flared out through her body, leaving her shaking and breathless. She was barely able to stand but her soul was singing show tunes and it wasn't going to stop until the sky fell in or hell froze over, whichever came first.

The look in those gray eyes now was wild and dark and full of undisguised lust.

"And I thought you were going to tell me last night was a mistake," Kit confessed.

Alex looked momentarily taken aback, then she smiled and brushed her fingers across Kit's mouth. "It would have been way too risky for me to look at you in Douglas's office," she said softly. "I may not have been able to stop myself from doing this," she moved her fingers inside Kit again, "in front of all those nice men."

"It wasn't only that," Kit gasped. "I just don't believe I could be so lucky."

"Trust me," Alex smiled.

Kit laughed. "I have to tell you, Ms. Cazenove, that's hardly a reassuring statement coming from a lawyer."

"It's not the lawyer in me who wants you, O'Malley."

Chapter 29

"Oh man, what a circus!" Quinn declared, propping herself against the wall beside Kit who was trying to be inconspicuous amongst the potted vegetation in the corner of the crowded lounge room. "There must be a hundred people here."

"Well, about sixty maybe. But there were certainly close to two hundred at the church. You seem surprised," Kit said.

"No, I just find it amazing how many people come out of the woodwork for a funeral. There are people here I haven't seen since I was seven, and some aunt or something who must be about thirteen-and-a-half times removed asked me how I liked England. I don't ever remember meeting her in my life yet she knows I've been working in London."

"I suspect your mother was a lot like mine," Kit stated. "In which case half of Melbourne probably knows your business."

"Where *is* Lillian?" Quinn asked, standing on tiptoes to scan the room.

"Last time I saw her she was armed with a bottle of champagne and on a mission to round up the attending members of the Class of '54."

"Oh good, Mum would have liked that." Quinn smiled, then stared down as she shuffled her feet. "Did I do OK at the church?"

Kit put her arm around Quinn's shoulders. "It was a lovely eulogy, Quinn, and a fine service. You also look very elegant, which I'm sure Celia would have appreciated."

341

"I scrub up OK, don't I?" Quinn grinned and gave a catwalk twirl to show off the cut of her dark green jacket and tight knee-length skirt. Then she leant over and whispered, "I'm not wearing any underwear though."

"What, none at all? Why not?"

"Well, surprising as it may sound, knowing that I was undie-less has enabled me to cope with my discomfort with these well-meaning but uncomfortable people who have no idea what to say when they approach me with their condolences. It's sort of a case of 'if only they knew maybe they wouldn't be so earnest.' Do you think that's awful?"

"No," Kit replied. "I think it's a little weird but I don't think it's awful."

"Well, that's not *why* I'm only half dressed, it's just a beneficial side effect. You see, I was trying to work out what to wear so I wouldn't be feel miserable and be squirming in my seat. I'd just rejected the idea of my Star Trek T-shirt and old jeans, knowing Mum *wouldn't* appreciate that, when I remembered her telling me about all these dreams she had after my father died. It started with the crematorium one where she ripped off all her clothes *except* her underwear and threw them on top of Dad's coffin. Then, nightly for nearly six months, she would dream that although she was exquisitely dressed to open a function or meet the Queen or eat in a restaurant she was always frantic with a fear that she was losing her mind because she couldn't remember where she'd left her undies. She wasn't worried that she didn't have them on, just that she didn't know where they were."

"That's why you left your knickers at home?" Kit laughed. "I doubt that dreams are hereditary, Quinn."

"I wasn't worried about that. Although, who knows, by actually doing this while I was awake I may have inadvertently put a stop to a worrisome little genetic imprint that's been bothering the women in our family for generations."

"That's always a possibility," Kit laughed. "Anyway I'm sure Celia would have found it quite a hoot."

"*That's* why I did it. If she's hanging around here watching any of this I hope she's having a really good laugh," Quinn explained. "Speaking of elegance," she added, reaching out to straighten the collar of Kit's white shirt, "you look absolutely gorgeous yourself, which is probably why that stunning-looking woman at the bar is trying to attract your attention."

"What woman?" asked Kit in surprise, searching the crowd. "Oh, her," she added as she spied Alex trying to indicate surreptitiously that Kit should be standing next to her instead of hiding out in the greenery. Kit didn't even try to disguise her pleasure. There was little point seeing Ms. Orlando was singing *Some Enchanted Evening* in her ear.

"You must have left quite early this morning," she commented.

"What?" Kit's attention snapped back to Quinn who just narrowed her eyes in response. "I . . . um . . . yes it was early," Kit acknowledged, running her hand through her hair.

"It's about bloody time," Quinn pronounced. "I thought I was going to be old and decrepit by the time you two worked out you were made for each other."

"Made for each other? I don't know about that," Kit said, gazing longingly at Alex who smiled engagingly back at her. Oh wow! *Across a crowded room*, Kit sang to herself. "And what do you mean it's about time?" she demanded. "You were the one playing along with that ridiculous wedding and divine Enzo nonsense. You deserve to be old and decrepit."

"What could I do?" Quinn shrugged.

"Well, I'll tell you what you can do now, and that's come and pour me a very large bourbon," Kit stated, taking Quinn by the hand.

"I would have thought that you'd want to be alone," Quinn teased but allowed Kit to navigate a path through a nattering clutch of pearl-draped Toorak matrons who were well on their way to semi-inebriation.

"Oh, sure. We'd have a better chance of being alone in a crowd of eighty thousand at a Collingwood–Carlton footy match. At least there the attention of the people in the immediate vicinity would be on an idiotic piece of pumped-up pigskin instead of on who's standing around them." Kit pulled Quinn in close. "Have you noticed how many of these people are giving each other the once-over to work out how they fit in, or whether they should? It's creepy."

"Try taking your undies off, Kit," Quinn whispered. "Then you can just smile knowingly at them when they look you up and down. I guarantee it'll throw them completely off balance."

"I don't doubt that for a minute," Kit said.

"You don't doubt what?" Alex asked, placing her hand oh-so-innocently on the small of Kit's back to help her find a nice comfortable niche at the bar. She left her hand there.

"Quinn thinks my state of mind would be improved if I was to wander through this gathering of snooty socialites and poncy social climbers without any knickers on," Kit explained, wishing the invisible little lust fairy would stop pouring warm champagne all over her body. It was very distracting.

"I understand," Alex said politely, looking beguilingly bemused. "I don't think I'll buy into this one."

"That's a very wise decision," Kit said.

Alex looked about her to make sure no one was listening. "Just before Marek left, about ten minutes ago, he asked me to tell you that everything is on line and to meet him at his office at six-thirty. He also said that he'd overheard some woman asking someone else who you were."

"Who *I* were, I mean, am?" Kit queried. "Who was asking?"

"That's what I asked him and he said he didn't know, *and* that the person who was being asked didn't know who you were anyway. They appear to have left because he couldn't point them out."

"It always astounds me how many people actually believe Marek when he tells them he's a detective," Kit said, shaking her head.

Quinn managed to organize their drinks before they were forced to move away by a large woman wearing an extremely threatening lemon twin-set who needed all their spaces to make her presence felt at the bar.

"Who's responsible for all this?" Alex asked as they checked out the long table set up in front of the open fireplace laden with a smorgasbord of taste treats.

"Rent-A-Wake, I think," Quinn quipped, then remembered that half the room was probably listening to her every word. "Uncle Douglas organized it," she amended seriously. "I assume it's Mum's usual catering company."

344

The intrusive sound of a mobile phone beside them was responded to with a remarkable display of dexterity by a young man whose life was probably a complete failure in every other respect. The quick-draw movement of the right hand on the phone was surpassed only by the coinciding fluid motion of the left as it selected a delicate canapé and stuffed it in his mouth. This last action spoilt the whole effect, however, as there are only a few things more embarrassing than answering a call by saying: "Hu-wo."

Quinn was saying: "Excuse me. I said excuse me."

"I'm talking here. Do you mind?" the guy replied.

"Yes, I do. Who are you?" Quinn asked.

"Hang on," he said to the phone. "Justin Beadman. Who are you?" he said to Quinn.

"Carmel Beadman's boy?" Quinn asked in surprise.

"Yeah," he replied impatiently. "Who are you?"

"The lady of the house. Where's your mother?"

"Um, over there," a mortified Justin Beadman stammered, waving his pointing finger around until he settled on someone who might claim him as her own—on a good day.

"Excuse me a second," Quinn said to Kit and Alex before taking a few steps into the throng. "Oh and Justin," she added, as he was raising the phone to his ear again, "if you really can't bear to be parted from that offensive piece of technology then, given the reason for this gathering, you could at least have the decency to turn it off. You can fondle it in your pocket if you get desperate or perhaps arrange to take your calls in the toilet, where the rest of the wankers are gathered."

Kit stared after Quinn who walked about ten feet before stopping as if she couldn't work out how she'd got where she was, shook her head as if to clear it, then set a course for Carmel Beadman.

"Ooh, that was spooky," Kit remarked, realizing that Alex was also standing motionless in astonishment.

"That wasn't spooky. That was Celia," Alex said.

Kit turned her back to the room in case she couldn't fend off the laughter attack that was threatening to undo her sense of propriety. She raised her glass to her lips, thinking vaguely that it was a dumb thing to do because she was quite likely to choke on her drink, when an all-too-familiar voice rose momentarily above the thrum of general conversation in the crowd behind her. She froze, resisting the urge to spin around and scan the room.

"O'Malley?" Alex whispered. "O'Malley," she repeated insistently, stepping into Kit's somewhat stunned line of vision which was directed at the blank wall behind the table. "For goodness' sake, Kit. Are you having a religious experience or something?"

Kit nodded and swallowed the bourbon that hadn't completely missed her mouth.

"Well, snap out of it, you're beginning to look mildly demented," Alex commanded, brushing her thumb across Kit's chin to clean up the bourbon that *had* missed her mouth.

"Alex, who is standing about ten feet behind me and just a little to my left?" Kit queried, clasping Alex's hand to stop her fussing and giving her a steady "please pay attention to me" look. "Alex? It'll be a group with at least one woman and two men."

"Well, Quinn's talking to Justin's mother and three men," Alex said glancing over Kit's right shoulder.

"No, no, my love. Try my other left," Kit suggested.

Alex smiled a warm, open, slightly taken-aback smile. "Why don't you look yourself?" she asked.

"Because I've heard a voice—no, I've heard *her*—voice and I need to pinpoint where it is. I don't want to lose my bearings by facing a room full of possibilities."

"You mean . . . ? Oh hell, what a nerve! You'd think she'd worry about being noticed," Alex said, apparently scanning the crowded room for a red-haired murderess in stilettos.

"Perhaps she's someone whose *absence* from these proceedings would be noticed. And there's no point looking for the obvious, Alex. I think she'll be in disguise; or rather, if you remember, the rent-by-the-hour persona *is* her disguise. So who can you see about ten feet in that direction?" Kit asked, pointing at her own left shoulder.

"There's an OHP contingent in a little conversational clique," Alex said, leaning to one side to get a clearer view. "There's Miles Denning, Adele Armstrong, that tedious Sandy Everett, Greg Fulton, Christine . . . um, the managing editor . . . Johnson, and Ma . . . Ma . . ." Alex glanced back at Kit with her mouth open.

346

"Ma Ma who?" Kit asked, turning around to see for herself. "Marjorie Finlay? Well, I'll be damned!"

"You don't think . . . ?" Alex was at a complete loss for words.

"That Marjorie Finlay is Margaret Easton?" Kit whispered. "Oh Alex, she is perfect! And I, *well*," Kit said in disgust, "I should have my license revoked. She's been right under my nose from the beginning."

"She *mightn't* be her," Alex said. "There are quite a few women in close proximity."

"Sure, and I'm Zsa Zsa Gabor. Come on, you have to introduce me to her so I can get her glass for fingerprinting."

"What? Who am I supposed to say you are?"

"Don't worry about it. You can strike up a conversation with one of them on our way past and then we can wing it."

"Wing it?" Alex exclaimed helplessly. "Kit, have I told you yet how exasperatingly adorable you are?"

"I am?" Kit grinned, momentarily confounded with unexpectedness.

"Yes, totally exasperating. Are you coming?" Alex brushed past her into the crowd.

"That's a very leading question," Kit stated, realizing the answer was diverting a little too much of her attention away from the more relevant question of how she was going to inveigle herself into the publishing scrum Alex had just interrupted by shaking hands with Miles Denning.

There was nothing more wallflower-inducing than standing on the outskirts of a group of people who were just that because they shared a common profession or workplace, and this bunch from OHP could have been a group of nurses, car mechanics or lapsed Catholics for all Kit had in common with their reasons for standing around in a little social huddle. Alex, however, was in the process of doing the polite, and in this case vital, thing of pointlessly introducing a single companion—"this is my friend Katherine"—to a whole group of people who have no interest in said companion because they're never likely to set eyes on them again. Each of them in turn gave Kit a courteous nod and, those so-inclined, a brisk handshake, then proceeded to ignore her, which was fine because she was still trying to work out how to get Marjorie Finlay's fingerprint.

The fact that the woman's glass was still half full ruled out the obvious tack of offering to get her another champagne. Kit was tossing up which conversational approach would make Marjorie drink faster: to say, "Alex tells me you're in marketing, that must be interesting," or to be up front and ask her, "Just how many wives *have* you knocked off?" when the voice of Tiger Robinson's inamorata solved her dilemma by speaking to her.

"I'm sure we've met somewhere before. Is that possible?" the voice said.

Kit stared stupidly at Marjorie Finlay, who appeared to be practiced in the fine art of ventriloquism, then came over all queer and nauseous as she turned disbelievingly to face Celia Robinson's killer. Margaret Easton, a.k.a. Oh-Maggie-yes-Maggie, Miss Enigma and the Dragon Lady, was standing there bold as brass in her Adele Armstrong guise, waiting for Kit to pull herself together and say something vaguely intelligent.

"Um," she said instead, then, remembering Quinn's advice about throwing people off balance, feigned the same sort of penetrating openly sexual look that Adele had cast over her three weeks before.

At least that was her intention. Kit realized that to make the moment work she probably should have at least imagined she'd taken her own knickers off. She hated to think what expression she really had on her face because, as she glanced provocatively from head to foot and back to that striking angular face, she was actually picturing Geoffrey's secretary in a miniskirt, in a blond wig, in a red wig, in high heels, bonking her boss on a warehouse dock in Footscray, and belting Celia over the back of the head with a champagne bottle then leaving her to drown in the pond just outside the very room in which they were now all standing.

"The James Berkeley-Shaw launch at the Hilton a few weeks ago," Kit said, lowering her voice half an octave. "We didn't actually meet though," she added, hoping Adele would infer from her tone that Kit had spent the intervening time wishing they had been introduced or knowing that fate would in fact present another opportunity.

And, by golly, here it was.

"Katherine Lang," Kit said, holding her gaze steady and trying valiantly not to lose her lunch all over the feet of the murderess whose hand she was shaking.

"Ah, yes," Adele said, as if she too remembered their not quite meeting. "It's a pleasure, Katherine," she added, the throaty voice softening deliberately as she said her name. She let go of Kit's hand and glanced at Alex before turning back. "What's your connection with the family?" In other words, who the hell are you really and why are you here? Kit had no way of knowing whether Adele's performance was as much an act as her own, especially seeing there was the definite possibility that the woman had gotten a good look at her the day she'd visited the Skintone Agency.

"My parents were great friends of Celia and her first husband, and Alexis and I used to babysit Elizabeth together when we were teenagers, before my family moved to Sydney," Kit said, giving Alex an almost dismissive look to let Adele know that was the extent of their relationship. It didn't escape her attention, however, that Alex had not only managed to engage Marjorie Finlay in conversation but was trying not to look at Kit as if she'd taken complete leave of her senses.

"So, are you living in Melbourne now or are you just down for the funeral?" Adele asked.

"I've been back about a month. I'm working at Aurora Press as assistant editor to Del Fielding. Perhaps you know her?" Kit replied, weaving some reality into her fiction.

"No, I don't believe I do," Adele replied. "But seeing you don't have to leave town perhaps we could have dinner. Tomorrow night?" Adele cut right to the chase, giving Kit a look which virtually removed all her clothes as it said "or better still let's go somewhere else *now*."

Oh, whoa! Reverse engines, Mr. La Forge! Kit thought, unable to determine whether Adele was trying to catch her off-guard because she knew or suspected Kit was lying, or whether the woman was simply a sexual predator of the first order with few morals, all of them loose, and absolutely no conscience whatsoever.

Kit glanced at Alex who, she noticed, had now managed to get hold of Marjorie Finlay's glass and was wearing a "mission accomplished, what the hell are *you* doing?" look.

"Dinner? That would be *most* enjoyable," Kit agreed, thinking it had to be the former. Adele must suspect something because Kit had never had this kind of response to any attempt at flirting in her life. In fact, she'd never thought she was that good at it. Alex, on the other hand, obviously disagreed because she was glowering at her as if she now had proof positive that there was, in fact, a good reason for the rumors about Kit's reputation—the one that preceded her, that is.

Jeez, O'Malley, Kit thought. Just get the woman's glass and get the hell out of here.

"That's a nasty bruise you have," Adele commented. "Can I ask what happened?"

Think fast, she thought. "Oh," she said, raising her hand to her chin then brushing her fringe aside to reveal the steri-strips on her eyebrow. "I had a violent encounter with a filing cabinet. It appeared to have been holding a grudge against me for all the times I'd slammed it shut. It waited patiently until we were moving it on Tuesday then flung its top drawer right into my face," Kit explained, allowing her actions to speak louder than her words as she flung her hand out in demonstration. It collided quite nicely with Adele's glass, emptying the contents all over Sandy Everett's right trouser leg.

"Oh, my goodness, I am *so* sorry," Kit exclaimed, looking from Adele to Sandy and back to Adele.

"Don't worry about it, Katherine," Adele said, trying not to smile. "It couldn't have happened to a nicer guy, believe me," she added softly, before turning on the unsuspecting Mr. Everett to shove a serviette in his hand. "Stop fussing, Sandy. It's just a little iced water. There was no Scotch left in the glass."

Exit stage left, O'Malley, Kit said to herself. "Let me get you another," she offered.

"No, I'm fine really," Adele said, waving the empty glass just out of Kit's reach.

"Please, Adele, I insist." Kit injected her tone with a seductive suggestion of . . . of . . . god-knows-what actually, Kit thought to herself. Whatever it was though, it was working.

"Thank you." Adele accepted graciously and surrendered her glass. "Scotch and ice."

Yes! Kit cheered. "I'll be right back," she said, before turning to Alex as if it was an afterthought. "Alexis, do you want another drink? Oh, I see you already have two glasses. Are you taking orders?"

"My god, O'Malley, have you no shame?" Alex asked when they were halfway across the room.

"What does that mean?" Kit asked, making a beeline for her mother who appeared to be directing air traffic at one end of the bar.

"That *woman*," Alex whispered as she clasped Kit's elbow, "practically had you undressed and on the floor."

"Tell me about it!" Kit exclaimed, raising her eyebrows suggestively.

"Can't you say no? Is that it?"

"Just call me Zsa Zsa," Kit stated.

"And what does *that* mean? Oh."

"Oh, exactly. It was very clever of you to get Marjorie's glass but, as it turns out, *this* is the one we needed." She placed the glass on the bar in front of Lillian who had finally managed to attract the barman's attention and was ordering another bottle of champagne.

"Hello, Katherine darling," she said.

"Could you not call me darling," Kit requested softly.

"Why ever not?" Lillian asked, peering at Kit to make sure she had in fact addressed her remark to the right darling.

"I'm sort of undercover and I need you to disown me for a while."

"Yes, of course, whatever you say, darling. Dear. Katherine." Lillian shook her head. "Are you still Katherine?"

"Yes, Mum," Kit said.

"Don't call me Mum if you don't want me to call you darling, dear."

"OK, Lillian," Kit said, glancing back to find that Adele was facing the other way, which was lucky because it looked as though getting out of here wasn't going to be as easy as she'd thought. "I need to put something in your bag so you can take it secretly out of the room for me," she added, reaching over the bar for a paper serviette.

"You mean I'm undercover too, dear?" Lillian said in delight as she grabbed hold of the strap on her shoulder to heft a frightening and incongruous leather thing, almost the size of a sea trunk, around into view. She opened the flap.

"You-know-who is *not* watching," Alex said helpfully.

Kit picked up Adele's glass, wrapped it carefully in the serviette and added it to the extraordinary collection of things her mother couldn't bear to leave home without. She closed the bag quickly, deciding now was not the time to ask Lillian why she had brought a can of blue spray paint and a pair of secateurs to a wake.

"Where are you taking that bottle?" Kit asked her instead.

"There's a few of us giving Chel a good send-off in the library," Lillian replied. "Are you going to tell me what's happening or is this on a need-to-know basis?"

Kit stifled a grin. "Need-to-know, for the time being. I'll meet you in the library in a few moments to retrieve that glass. Please don't touch it."

"She's looking this way, Kit," Alex said, before casually turning to the barman to order the necessary drinks.

"Mum, sorry, Lillian, can you point in the general direction of the library and pretend you're telling me something serious."

"James James, Morrison Morrison, Weatherby George Dupree," Lillian whispered somberly, as she waved her hand towards the doorway and fixed her daughter with a very serious look indeed.

"That'll do," Kit interrupted. "OK, now you don't need to *volunteer* this information but should anyone ask you who I am or where I went, just tell them I'm Kathy *Lang*, my mother's just had a turn and I've probably taken her home. And don't elaborate."

"Right," Lillian said emphatically, straightening her shoulders. "Now what? I go to the library and wait for you?"

"Yes, please," Kit said, wondering whether she had just blown the whole deal as she watched Lillian zigzag across the room like a diminutive Margaret Rutherford at her Miss Marple best.

"Oh, dear," Alex observed, turning back to the bar. "Now what?"

"I have to get out of here and get that glass to Marek. I'll throw Adele some kind of apologetic, back-in-a-minute type look on my way out the door, and then you could deliver the drinks a few seconds later with the story about my mother taking ill. It might be a good idea to continue your chat with poor old innocent Marjorie Finlay, at least long enough to allay any suspicions Adele may have. Then I suggest you find Quinn and fill her in about who I'm supposed to be, just in case. I wouldn't tell her about Adele though."

"OK. What if your latest conquest asks me for your phone number?" Alex teased.

At least Kit hoped she was teasing. "Take hers and tell her I'll be in touch. With a warrant and several large policepersons."

Alex grinned and picked up her tray of drinks. "Will I see you later?"

"Oh, I hope so," Kit said, squeezing Alex's shoulder gently as she leant over to give her a chaste farewell kiss on the cheek. "Wait up for me," she added softly, before turning to leave.

"O'Malley."

"Yes, Alex?"

"Please be careful tonight."

"You bet," Kit grinned.

"I'm serious."

Chapter 30

"We're going to fit you with an IAD."

"The *whole* department?" Kit asked, leaning away from Harry Costanzo and the sinister surgical implement he was waving around. She'd always thought Harry looked a little like Gregory Peck, but right now he looked like Gregory Peck auditioning for his role in *The Boys From Brazil*.

"I don't think he's talking about Internal Affairs, Kitty," Marek snorted.

"Actually I am, in a manner of speaking," Harry corrected him. "This," he added, holding up a very small something in a plastic bag, "is an intra auricular device. A hearing aid, of sorts, because it will be aiding O'Malley to hear us from as far away as half a kilometer."

"You're not really going to stick that in my ear are you, Dr. Mengele?"

"That *is* the general idea. And the beauty of this little thing is that even someone standing right next to you will not be able to see it, or hear what you hear."

"I don't know about this," Kit protested.

"I promise it won't hurt," Harry insisted. "It will, however, make you effectively deaf in whichever ear we put it in which of course may have an effect on your sense of balance."

"I don't have a sense of balance," Kit stated.

"Good, you won't notice it then. I *would* avoid climbing on anything, however," Harry said. "Now sit still."

"What I want to know is," Kit said, screwing her eyes shut and trying to distract her own attention away from the sensation of a cold and foreign something sliding into her right ear, "is . . . is why this van stinks of boys' socks. Don't you guys ever open it up and let some fresh air in?"

She was still cringing and jigging her knee up and down when Harry informed her that the procedure was complete.

"Is this when you tell me it requires major surgery to get it out again?" she asked.

Harry smiled menacingly and rolled his chair across to the console behind him. "It's time for a sound check. Here, Jenkins, take this outside and keep your voice low," he ordered, handing Nick a personal communicator. "Jonno, stand next to her and make sure you can't hear anything."

"Hailing frequencies open," Kit said, tapping her ear.

"You have no idea how long I've been wanting to get into your head."

"Very funny," Kit commented, surprised by the clarity of Nick's voice.

"If you're talking to Nick he can't hear you yet," Harry stated, his words echoing most peculiarly inside her head.

"Oh, Harry, please," she complained. "I can hear you *without* the mike."

"Sorry, honeylamb," he said, flicking a switch on the console. "Jonno?"

"I couldn't hear you or Nick but there's definitely something there, though I suppose it might be a flea nattering in her hair."

Kit whacked Marek on the leg and turned back to Harry. "How many voices am I going to have in my head?"

"Only one at a time. And no one at all unless it's necessary."

"Good. I don't need to feel schizophrenic as well as unbalanced. What about the transmitter?"

Harry dragged a box across the bench and onto his knees, before swivelling his chair round to face Kit again. "The choice is yours."

"Well, this is a far cry from having half a recording studio taped to your body," she said, marvelling at the selection of innocuous items which included a pen, a belt and buckle, a small torch, a cigarette case and a lipstick.

"State of the art, honeylamb, state of the art," Harry said joyously, as if they were his very own inventions. Considering how hard it would have been to get the money for them out of the annual budget his delight was understandable.

"I'll use this," Kit said. "I don't want something they'll automatically take from me if I get caught." She replaced her belt with Harry's hi-tech lifeline to the outside world, or rather the world inside the van. "Does it have an on/off switch?"

Harry leant forward and turned the buckle over to indicate how to turn it on while he tried to ignore Marek's outstretched open hand waving under his nose.

"Twenty bucks, Costanzo. No checks and no IOUs."

"What are you betting on this time, Marek?" Kit asked.

"Detective Costanzo was convinced you'd choose the lipstick," Marek explained.

"He obviously doesn't know you like we do." Nick's voice echoed in her head again, making her jump in surprise.

"Welcome to the party, Nick." Kit picked up the lipstick and shook her head. "This was designed by a *yobbo*, Harry. A clever yobbo undoubtedly but a yobbo all the same. Even if I did wear this stuff, *Flaming Sheila* would not be my color. And could you please turn Nick down a bit, he's going to make me deaf if he keeps cackling in my ear like that."

The back door swung open to reveal Nick looking apologetic, a hand over the mike on his headset. He stepped aside to usher Liam and Sargent into the van ahead of him.

"The boat's waiting," Liam said, straddling the one remaining stool. "Are we going to do this or not? It's nearly seven-thirty."

"We're almost ready," Marek stated.

"Oh, I nearly forgot," Liam said as he pulled out his mobile phone. "A call for you, Girl Scout. It's our surfing friend."

"Surfing? Oh," Kit said, taking the phone. "Hello, Hector. Hello. I think you lost him, Liam."

"Try your left ear, Kit. I'm in this one," Nick whispered helpfully.

Kit rolled her eyes at him and put the phone to her other ear. "Hector. What have you got for me?"

"It's about time! And it's nice to talk to you too, O'Malley," Hector grumbled.

"Sorry, but we're on a tight schedule here, mate. I hope you're going to tell me that Maggie Easton also goes by the name of Adele Armstrong."

"I sure am," Hector confirmed cheerily and, quite oddly Kit thought, without even a trace of disappointment that she already knew.

"So which name is the alias?" Kit asked.

"Neither. O'Malley, you're going to love this."

"Hector, I'm only going to love it if you can manage to tell me sometime this side of my sixtieth birthday."

"That's gratitude for you. Do you have to take all the fun-macadamia? Dunnowha . . ." Hector's incomprehensible words degenerated into a splutter of static.

"Shit!" Kit shook the phone uselessly. "Harry, I hope *we're* not going to have communication problems like this."

"Not with this technology, honeylamb."

"Which just leaves good old human error, or oversight." Liam pointed at Harry's console. "Doesn't that little green light indicate an incoming call?"

Harry grunted, flicked a switch then handed a spare headset to Marek.

"O'Malley," Hector's voice sang out from the phone in her lap.

"Hector, where the hell are you? And what were you saying about fun and macadamias?"

"I said 'fun out of it,' O'Malley. And I'm in . . . um . . . I'm in a friend's car. I was saying that I don't know why that feral Fed couldn't find this out."

"Find out *what*, Hector?" Kit said through clenched teeth, trying not to lose her patience, or at least sound like she wasn't.

"Armstrong is her married name. The name Margaret Adelaide Easton got when she married Bruce David Armstrong, a small-time drug dealer and pimp from Sydney."

"Great Caesar's bloody ghost!" Kit exclaimed. "She's Edwina's daughter. You're right, Hector, I *do* love it."

"That's not the best bit, O'Malley."

"It's not? What on earth could top that?"

"Maggie stroke Adele divorced her husband in 1989, a year after he got out of Long Bay where he'd done three for manslaughter. She came to Melbourne. He disappeared, went underground for two years. That is until he resurfaced, publicly at least, in Melbourne in 1991. He's the one with the alias, O'Malley."

"Hector, please don't play games."

"Three words, O'Malley," Hector teased. "Ian Munro Dalkeith."

"What? Well . . . I'll be a," she couldn't think of anything. "Well, fuck-a-duck!"

"That's charming, O'Malley."

"Hector, you're a genius."

"I hope you remember that when you're considering what sort of bonus I get for all this work."

"You bet. Tell me though, how did you know about Edwina? I mean why weren't you surprised when *I* made the connection?"

"Oops, converging trams, O'Malley. Gotta go."

Trams? Kit stared suspiciously at the disconnected phone until she realized Marek was grinning at her as if he'd just eaten the cat that had swallowed the canary. "What?" she asked him.

"We have a match."

"The fingerprints? I knew it!" Kit declared, clenching her fists in victory.

"You looked mighty pleased with Surfer Boy's news too," Liam commented.

"Oh, mate, my day just keeps getting better," Kit said with a grin. "Twist number twenty-two in this sordid little soap opera is a doozey. *Margaret* Adele Armstrong, née Easton, is the daughter of Edwina

Barnes, Melbourne's most famous madam. This explains why Edwina's name is on all their books even though she's been stuffed away in an exclusive sanatorium for several years. The same luxury nuthouse, I might add, where one Shirley Smith, sister of Captain Malcolm, has spent the last nine years, probably doped to the eyeballs to prevent her from doing the community a great service by bumping off her ex-husband Geoffrey Robinson."

Liam swivelled on his stool to let Detective Sargent know that the scowl on his face was meant for him and him alone.

"That's not all, guys. Twist number twenty-three, parts A and B are the icing on the cake. Adele's ex-husband *used to be* a piece of lowlife scum from Sydney called Bruce Armstrong. We, however, know him as a hotshot property developer and glamour-boy-from-Nowhere, and believe me there really is such a place. He's our very own drug smuggler, nasty piece of work, and all-round *respectable* businessman Ian Dalkeith."

"Shit," said Marek.

"That is an understatement if ever there was one," Kit pronounced. "How come you couldn't find this out, Alan? Or did you?"

"Me? I don't even know who you're talking about. Who is this Adele anyway?"

"Geoffrey Robinson's secretary. Celia Robinson's murderer," Kit stated.

He still looked blank.

"Robinson's bimbo," Liam said. "The one you said checked out as just some slut on the make."

Sargent's expression was as plain as recycled toilet paper as he rolled his paranoid little head around on the chip on his shoulder. It was hard to tell whether he was trying to work out how to get out of this one, or whether he really had no idea why everyone was staring at him.

"You got someone else to do the background check for you, didn't you?" Liam asked.

"Yeah. So?"

"We're not treading on someone else's turf here, are we?" Marek asked. "I hope we're not going to find out that our sharks are just little fish in an even bigger pond being watched by some of your colleagues from head office."

That would certainly explain why someone bearing Sargent's particular brand of toady ineptitude would have been assigned as Liam's liaison officer, Kit thought. No doubt he could be relied upon to liaise his little balls off, exchanging reliable data for misinformation without ever knowing the difference.

"No way," Sargent was saying. "I have complete authority in this. It's my case."

"So who goofed on the Easton broad?" Liam asked.

Sargent shrugged. "An old friend from St. Kilda CIB ran her name for me."

"We're dealing with local, interstate and international drug dealers here," Marek stated. "You have federal resources at your disposal yet you get some mate from the local cop shop to check her out?"

The disbelieving "oh sure" tone which had invaded Marek's comment suggested he too was thinking what had just occurred to Kit, that Sargent had been mighty quick to suggest the drugs had already been moved.

"You know, I've heard this nasty and probably unfounded rumor," Kit said lightly, as if she was changing the subject, "that if you don't want the crooks to nick off with the goods an hour before a raid goes down, then you don't give the Feds the time of day let alone anything more specific."

"What the hell are you inferring?" Sargent asked defensively, looking a lot like someone who'd just stepped in something sticky and on close examination of his shoes discovered it was his own brains.

"You *really* wouldn't want to know all that I'm inferring, but you obviously got the gist of my implication," Kit stated, at the same time realizing it was a pretty dumb theory because if Sargent *was* bending the rules in the wrong direction then Dalkeith and his cronies would have pulled up stumps weeks ago.

Liam obviously wasn't quite so ready to dismiss the possibility. "Just what are we going to find in that warehouse tonight, Alan?"

"How the fuck should I know?" Sargent protested. "You're the one who's been inside. You and your sidekick Tonto the dyke here."

The sound of a pin dropping was disturbed only by Nick's barely audible "uh oh" in her right ear. Kit seriously contemplated shooting the stupid prick right where he stood, using Marek's gun which he'd subtly offered by sweeping his jacket back off his hip, but she decided now was not the time. She wasn't worried about the four witnesses—in fact she had the feeling they'd probably help get rid of the body—she just didn't want to owe that many favors.

"So," she said, inhaling deeply as she sent out a mental sheepdog to muster up her self-control before turning away from Sargent towards Marek and Harry, "do we have the entire Victoria Police Force ready to secure this beachhead or is it going to be a nice intimate little commando raid?"

Harry Costanzo couldn't answer because he was busy trying to get his Zippo to light the cigar he'd stuffed in his mouth. Harry hated not knowing stuff and Kit knew he was wondering whether Sargent's insult had simply been the best thing he could think of at the time or whether it explained how Marek knew he'd win the *Flaming Sheila* bet. Kit smiled and gave him a slight nod because she knew that despite his age, which was pushing him towards retirement, and his sturdy working class background, Harry didn't have an ist or phobic bone in his body, and if he found one he'd probably have it voluntarily replaced with something more ideologically sound. Sargent, on the other hand, she decided, would benefit greatly from a compulsory and complete skeletonectomy.

"Are you listening?" Marek asked.

"What?" Kit responded.

Marek rolled his eyes. "We're keeping it small and personal. Counting you, for some strange reason, there's twelve of us. Boscoe is already on the ground with Dipper, Robbo and Smasher."

"Sounds like the cast of a Warner Brothers cartoon," Kit interrupted.

"Do you want to know this or not?"

"Yes, Jonno," she said sweetly.

"Harry, Sargent and I will also be on site, working from the van. You, Nick and Liam will go in the boat with Tony McCoy and Jenny MacKenzie. They'll take you up river and drop you and Nick at the back door."

"Oh great," Kit said. "I haven't seen Macka and Macka for ages."

❖❖❖❖❖

361

In reality Kit didn't know the detectives Macka from Adam or Eve but they welcomed her onto their plain-clothes police boat just the same. The Mackas, like their boat, were also disguised for an undercover mission, in garb appropriate for a leisurely cruise or a spot of after-dark bream fishing on the Maribyrnong on this perfect Melbourne summer night.

With daylight saving still in effect and still fading curtains in the homes of people all over the country who had no conception of what actually happened when they turned their clocks forward one hour, the sky low to the west was a pale blue-black reminder that Old Sol was probably only just now setting seven hundred kilometers away in Adelaide. Overhead was a Star Trek Universe of infinite suns and possible worlds although Kit had to admit that from where she stood, rocking around in the back of a boat on the narrow river which sepa-rated the city from the western suburbs, the celestial bodies in this neck of the galaxy were having a hard time competing with the millions of incandescent filaments throwing their artificial light willy-nilly out into the heavens.

Splendidly insignificant, Kit thought, admiring the sight that was Melbourne at night. Her gaze was drawn away from the illuminated heights of the city's skyline to the twisting span of the West Gate Bridge which arced over the Yarra and seemed to hover way way above the upper decks of a super tanker which was being tugged up the river by a boat one-hundredth its size.

Speaking of insignificant, she thought, as her attention was brought back to the here and now by the sound of Detective Alan Sargent doing the standard public service abdication-of-responsibility-but-only-in-the-case-of-something-going-wrong routine. He was stating for the record, for the thirteenth time, his objection to *Miz* O'Malley's involvement, and was therefore categorically dissociating himself from the fallout from any stuff-ups that may occur as a result of no one taking his objection seriously.

"Fine," Liam said. "In that case, when everything goes according to plan we'll make sure that O'Malley gets all the credit for busting an international drug ring."

Sargent looked fleetingly horrified and quickly rearranged his body into a semblance of macho posturing—chest out, shoulders back, one foot up on the edge of the boat, the other still on the jetty. "I was merely making it clear," he said, shoving his hand in his pocket to make sure he was still wearing his penis, "that I refuse to be held accountable for the thousand and one things that could go wrong because of the involvement of a female civilian in a police operation."

What did he expect to happen? Kit wondered. A niggly little worry worm uncurled itself in the back of her head. Did he know something they didn't? Was his paranoia contagious?

"O'Malley is a highly trained and experienced ex-member of the Victoria Police Force," Marek was saying. "She is not a hairdresser from Chapel Street or my elderly aunt from Wandiligong East. Nothing is going to go wrong."

Oh, yeah? Kit thought, making a list of the things that could. She could get caught, for instance. She could get killed. That wouldn't worry Sargent one little bit, but how would she explain it to Lillian?

"*Ex*-member," Sargent sneered. "I think . . ."

Kit grabbed him by his supercilious shirt front and held him precariously off balance between the boat and the jetty. "We don't actually give a shit what you think, Alan," she snarled, invading his personal space by pushing her face close to his. "And by the way, don't *ever* call me Tonto again. OK?" She let him go and watched with dismay as he recovered his balance and didn't fall in the river.

"I've got to hand it you, Girl Scout," Liam said as Jenny Macka piloted the boat northwards. "You showed admirable restraint. Wasted, but nonetheless admirable."

"Well, you must be a paragon of all things virtuous to have put up . . ." Kit began, then remembered she was wired for sound. She touched Jenny on the arm and pointed to the pontoon dock at the rear of the Freyling Imports Storage Company's main warehouse and drug distribution center, about a hundred yards ahead. The back door to the loading bay was closed and there didn't appear to be a soul in sight.

"This would be a good place to drop us, Jenny," Kit suggested, indicating a section of embankment where the boat could get close enough to allow them to jump off.

"Batgirl to the Batvan. Come in, Alfred," Kit called, bending unnecessarily to speak into her Batbelt buckle.

"Stop mucking around, O'Malley," came Marek's voice, as clear as a Telstra-connected call from his elderly aunt in Wandiligong East.

"I am not mucking, Marek. Nicholas and I are about to leave the relative safety of the Batboat and we would like the latest situation report, please."

Marek put her on hold while he called for the troops to report in so Kit ran an equipment check to make sure she had everything she needed. It didn't take long. She was only carrying a torch and a pick-lock, and they were still where she'd put them in the pockets of her army pants.

Despite being a highly trained and experienced ex-member of the Victoria Police Force it was the ex bit that Marek emphasized when he refused to lend her a .38 Police Special for the night. He'd given her Nick instead, which was actually a lot more reassuring because he was packing a .357 Magnum and a *very* attractive Armalite complete with nightscope. Not only was the lightweight automatic rifle the police sniper's weapon of choice, but this one was in the hands of an expert marksman.

Marek came back on line to report that: Dipper, hidden somewhere in the underbrush, had the police boat in view and there was no other activity on the river side of the warehouse; Robbo was on the roof (Kit wondered how the hell he managed that); and Boscoe and Smasher on the north side had counted one vehicle in the car park and one man from the opposing team on guard inside. "And so far there's no traffic or other movement in the street out here," Marek concluded.

"Great," Kit said. She grinned at her bodyguard. "Lock and load, Nick old buddy, it's time to go."

"This is a quick trip, Kitty, OK?" Marek reminded her. "Just get in, check that the stuff's still there, and then get the hell out again."

"No worries," Kit replied as she grabbed hold of the canopy, hauled herself up onto the side of the boat and leapt towards dry land. She landed neatly on two feet, turned quickly to witness the Maribyrnong River apparently leaving town in a surging hurry, then fell backwards on her arse. "Ow! Don't *climb* on anything?" she exclaimed under her breath, shaking her head to clear it. "Harry, you should have told me not to jump off anything either."

"I assumed if you didn't do one you wouldn't need to do the other," came Harry's voice.

Nick helped her to feet and dusted her off. Liam, who'd been having a good chuckle, slapped his hand over his mouth when Kit glared at him.

"Go catch some fish, you guys," Kit said, dismissing them with a wave. "And don't get too engrossed in what those boys in their pajamas are doing with that silly little ball," she added when she noticed that Tony McCoy had set up a portable TV, tuned into the cricket, in the back of the boat.

Kit supposed she should have been grateful it wasn't winter because if the stakeout team was watching a night footy match then all hell could break loose around them and they probably wouldn't notice. She'd always thought that the most extraordinary thing about cricket was that, despite the fact that it was a game where nothing at all could happen for hours and days on end, people actually watched it for hours and days on end. Thank god Liam was with them. He'd probably find the blank walls of a darkened warehouse a lot more exciting to watch than a boring bloody test match from Brisbane or Barbados or wherever.

"Don't do anything stupid in there, Girl Scout," Liam said as the boat pulled away and headed to the other side of the river.

Kit led Nick down the bike path, up over the rocks and under the ramp from the loading bay. No one, it seemed, had checked the perimeter as the section of fence she'd cut through was just the way she'd left it on Wednesday night.

God, that was only two nights ago, Kit realized with amazement. It seemed as remote as that first civilized breakfast meeting with Celia which, even right now as she scrambled around in the dirt under the dock and waited for Nick to follow, seemed the least likely thing to have gotten her into a fine mess like this, let alone to have contributed to Celia's untimely demise.

Just you wait, Adele Armstrong, she thought as she picked the lock on the side door of the warehouse. Nick, the Armalite slung over his back and the .357 in his hand, was a lot less distracting than her last accomplice on this breaking and entering lark.

Alex. Wow! she thought mushily, then felt a twinge of guilt at being pleased that something good had come out of this fine mess.

Before Kit opened the door, Nick checked in with Marek that all was still as it had been the last time they'd communicated, then they slipped into the quiet darkness of Freyling's probably never-used lunch room. Kit headed up the first hallway and glanced around the corner. The one man on guard inside had his feet up on the desk in the office upstairs and was reading a newspaper. Once again the only light in the place came from the office and the fluorescent strip over the staircase.

She gave Nick the signal to follow her dash for the stacks of crates on the right, and when they were safely out of sight again she indicated the direction they were going to head in. As agreed he kept her in sight but stayed one row behind her as she weaved her way down and across the dusty aisles to the place where, she hoped, the offending crate would still be sitting.

Kit stopped dead, as did Nick, when she heard an "um" in her ear. "Two cars just pulled in—a Mercedes and a BMW. Hang on," said Marek. A couple of seconds later he continued, "It's Dalkeith, Whitten and Grainger. If they're here the stuff must be too so get out now."

Kit shook her head at Nick, who waved his hands in objection but followed her anyway. Kit had to make sure. For all she knew, Geoffrey's cronies might just be here to do a bit of bastard rat catching.

She reached the last row of crates near the center of the warehouse and took a quick look back towards the office just as the exterior door at that end slammed shut behind Whitten and Grainger. Dalkeith was already halfway up the stairs.

Kit motioned to Nick to join her and then stay put, under cover, while she ventured out into the empty half of the warehouse. Even in the dark she managed to find the crate. Well, she found a crate. She could only assume it was the right one. She positioned herself so that the crate was between her and the office, lifted the lid enough to squeeze her hand in, then switched on her torch just long enough to verify the presence of several boxes marked Toshiba before easing the lid down again.

In the following nanosecond Kit registered three things happening—all of which she wished she hadn't still been around for. The spot she stood in was suddenly awash with light, Nick muttered "oh shit" in her ear, and someone was striding towards her.

She blinked. Davis Whitten was nearly on her and she had absolutely nowhere to go.

Chapter 31

"Who the hell are you?"

"I beg your pardon?" Kit asked, hoping she sounded surprised, confused or stupid rather than scared witless.

"Who *are* you? And what the fuck are you doing here?" Whitten shouted.

"Oh," she replied, looking about vaguely as if she hoped a suitable answer might materialize out of thin air. She couldn't see Nick anywhere, which was about the only thing she had in her favor at the moment. "I can explain," she stated.

"Damn right you will." Whitten grabbed her by the elbow and started dragging her towards a sure and certain death.

Not without a fight, Kit thought, trying to shrug off his hand. "I'm coming already," she snapped impatiently, trying to sound a lot more confident than she felt.

Whitten let go of her arm and pushed her towards the stairs. "Get up there."

Kit looked up to find two other members of Drugs and Murder Incorporated staring down at her from the top landing. Dalkeith looked ropable, while Grainger was obviously trying to place where he'd seen her before.

Don't climb on anything, she thought miserably. She gripped the railing. It was bad enough that this was the kind of staircase her vertigo hated most, but the miniature internal affairs department in her ear decided to make its presence felt by making it appear that the stairs were moving in three different directions at once. On top of that she had a boorish and obscenely wealthy American threatening to shove her onto her face.

She was helped up the last three steps by Grainger, who dragged her off her feet and propelled her into the office. Thank god, Kit thought, as she collided with the desk.

"Who is she?" Dalkeith asked Whitten as Grainger manhandled her again, this time into a plastic chair which nearly tipped over backwards with the suddenness of her arrival in it.

"I've got no idea," Whitten stated.

"Do I know you?" Grainger asked, peering at Kit from a pair of mean little eyes which were much too close together on either side of his oft-broken nose. His breath ponged as though he'd had three loaves of garlic bread and a slab of beer for dinner.

"No," Kit replied, which was almost the truth. She wasn't going to remind him that he'd been this close to her just a little over twenty-four hours ago.

"She might be a cop," Whitten suggested.

"I am not," Kit declared.

"Shit," Dalkeith observed. "Make sure she's not wired."

"I'm not a cop," Kit insisted as Grainger began rubbing his hands all over her body. She kicked him in the shins. "Get your filthy hands off me, you pervert," she shouted.

Their collective attention was shanghaied by the ringing of the red phone on the desk. Dalkeith snatched at the receiver and while he conversed with Malcolm Smith, who was apparently informing them of his imminent arrival, Kit tried to pretend that Whitten and Grainger weren't staring at her as if she had two heads.

With her back to the window overlooking the staircase, she had nothing to look at but a faded curling-at-the-edges girlie calendar, circa June 1972, which featured a naked blond with extremely large breasts straddling a Kawasaki motorcycle. Somebody had made a note to do something for or about "Mum" on the seventeenth. Dalkeith hung up the phone and asked Bill the guard to find something to secure the intruder to the chair.

He sat on the edge of the desk a few feet from Kit and fiddled

369

absently with the ring in his ear while Bill, obviously pleased to be of service, found some rope on the shelf behind him, pulled Kit's arms back and tied her hands firmly together and to the legs of the chair.

"Now, go open the back door. The boat will be here in a minute. And keep your eye out in case our friend here is not alone."

"Yes, Mr. Dalkeith," said Bill the guard, looking as though he'd much rather stick around to watch whatever it was they were going to do to Kit.

"Who are you?" Dalkeith asked.

"O'Malley. Katherine O'Malley," Kit replied. License to kill, especially scumbags like you, sadly revoked, she thought.

"Is that supposed to mean something to us?" Dalkeith asked.

"I don't think so," Kit said. She tried a smile to see what would happen.

"What are you doing snooping around here?" Dalkeith asked.

"Oh," Kit said, as if she finally understood what he really wanted to know. "I organized a date with Adele for tomorrow night and I just wanted to confirm it with her."

"You've got to be kidding," Grainger said.

"No," Kit answered, as sweet and innocently as possible.

Dalkeith's open hand whacked her in the face before she realized he'd even raised it to slap her. Not that she could have done anything about it.

"Ow! What did you do that for?" she complained indignantly.

Dalkeith slapped her again. "Who are you?" he demanded.

She could taste the blood in her mouth. "I told you. O'Malley. Katherine O'Malley."

"You have more incoming." It was Marek's voice. "Oh, Christ Almighty! They've . . ."

The rest of Marek's blasphemous pronouncement was drowned out by the screeching metal of the riverside roller door being raised by Bill the guard. This was followed by a commotion at the side door near the bottom of the stairs which indicated that the rest of the bad guys had arrived.

Oh shit, now you're really in trouble, O'Malley, Kit thought.

"Ian," Geoffrey bellowed.

370

Dalkeith slipped off the desk and went to the door. "What the hell? Where did you find them?"

"I'll have you know that this is kidnapping," came the last voice in the whole world Kit had expected to hear. It was the only voice in the whole world she wanted to hear but not now and not here, and certainly not being dragged along with its objecting owner up the stairs. If Kit hadn't already been rendered immobile by a well-knotted rope, the chill of dread that trickled down her spine would have paralyzed her with disbelief, or fear.

When Alexis Cazenove, who should have been at home waiting for Kit to return from a hard night's work catching crooks, caught sight of Kit tied to the chair she tried to break free of the grip Christo had on her arm. She didn't get very far. The threat of the dishy blond boy's gun waving in her face made her pull her head back and behave more sensibly. For his part Christo looked like a nineties yuppie version of Wilmer, the snivelling gun-toting hood in *The Maltese Falcon*.

This turn of events was completely ludicrous. If it wasn't so deadly serious Kit would have rolled round the floor in hysterics. As soon as someone untied her from the chair. Actually, the rising hysteria was such a peculiar combination of silent but deranged laughter and numbing fear that it was cramping her chest and making it difficult to breathe.

"What are you doing here?" she managed to ask politely, as if Alex was an unwelcome third party at a romantic dinner for two.

Alex only had time to shrug before Christo dragged her out of the way to make room for everybody else who had come to join the party. The next guest, who was hurled unceremoniously through the door, was Hector, followed by Geoffrey who had obviously done the hurling.

Kit groaned. "What is going on here?"

"That's my question," Dalkeith stated, slapping her again to make sure she understood. "What . . ." which was as far as he got before Christo interrupted with his two bobs' worth.

"Hey, you're that reporter."

"No, I'm not," Kit stated.

"She's not a reporter," Geoffrey said. "She's a policewoman."

"I am not," Kit protested, just as Adele made her grand entrance, red wig and all.

371

"What's she doing here?" Adele asked, pointing at Kit.

"That's what I was going to ask you about them," Dalkeith said, jerking his thumb at Alex and Hector.

"They were tailing us," Adele explained. "We managed to fool them into stopping and then we helped them out of their car."

"We caught *her* snooping around down there," Dalkeith stated. "She claims she had an appointment with you."

"Well, sort of," Kit volunteered. "I had to leave Celia's wake in such a hurry I thought it would be polite to drop by and confirm our date for tomorrow night, Adele. Or should I call you Maggie in this company?"

"What the fuck is going on here?" Whitten exploded.

"Calm down, Davis," Dalkeith ordered.

"Calm down? You want me to calm down?" He took two steps towards Kit and slapped her across the face. "Who are you?"

The left side of Kit's mouth felt as if it was being attacked by a swarm of bees. Bleeding bees. She ran her tongue across her lips and tried to glare defiantly at Whitten, although she couldn't see a damn thing through her watery left eye.

"She claims she's not that reporter that came to the agency that day . . . um . . . you know, the one I tried to run down," Christo informed Adele.

"That's not what I said, Christo. I'm just not a reporter," Kit managed to say. "Or a cop," she added, glancing at Geoffrey.

"And I'll wager you don't work for Aurora Press either," Adele remarked.

"No, actually I was working for Celia Robinson until you killed her."

Adele actually laughed. Geoffrey looked as though he was caught in a tiger trap, and Whitten began ranting about how he'd known that little episode was going to screw things up and good.

"Oh, shut up, Davis!" Adele commanded. "So what are you, some kind of private detective or something?"

"Or something," Kit acknowledged.

Adele was obviously intrigued by the notion. "And Celia hired you to do what?"

"Follow him," Kit replied, nodding at Geoffrey. "To find out about you."

Adele laughed again but Geoffrey was not amused. "That bitch," he snorted.

"Kitty," Marek's whisper echoed around what she realized was her aching head. The sound surprised her, she'd forgotten she had friends out there. "Don't tell them everything. Get something from them."

"That's all there is to this?" Dalkeith asked. "Geoff's wife asked you to find out who he was screwing?"

"Basically," Kit admitted.

"Enough of this shit," Grainger shouted. "Let's just get rid of them."

"Oh, that's a good idea," Kit said sarcastically.

"Jeez, Kitty, don't annoy them into confessing."

"Honestly!" Kit continued, ignoring Marek's advice "I don't know how you lot have stayed in business. You keep making the same mistakes."

"What do you mean?" Whitten asked petulantly.

"Who cares what she means? Somebody shoot her for Christ's sake," Grainger begged.

Christo raised his gun but Adele slapped his hand down. "Don't be an idiot."

Kit took that as a sign to continue. "It just seems," she said, "that you keep knocking people off before you've found out if they know anything."

"Like who?" Geoffrey asked.

"Like your *wife,* Mr. Robinson," Kit spat. "I mean, god only knows why you actually killed her, but you should have asked her who she'd been talking to recently."

"I did not kill Celia," Geoffrey stressed.

"Oh, sure. You're just an accomplice before, during and after the fact. And the *fact* is that your floozy here, as Celia called her, did kill her."

"How could you possibly know that?" Geoffrey asked.

"Hey! I just know. Believe me."

"But you can't prove anything," Adele smiled.

"Oh, I don't know," Kit said suggestively. "I have a lovely Scotch glass in my car that I lifted right out of your sticky fingers. And the cops told me they have a very clear print on the murder weapon."

"Nice try, *Katherine*," Adele sneered, "but I wiped the bottle."

Yes! Kit cheered silently, although the echo that bounced off her ear drum sounded just like Marek. "Now get the other one to confess, Kitty."

"Why did you kill her, Adele?" Kit asked softly.

"Believe it or not, it was an accident," Adele stated. "I didn't mean to kill her. Well, that's not entirely true." She ran her hand up Geoffrey's arm. "I just didn't mean to kill her *then*. I called in, on the pretext of having to deliver something to Geoff, to see if I could somehow find out if she had any idea what her husband or her butler were up to. I managed to orchestrate a woman-to-woman-type chat about the general problems we all have with men when I realized she was conducting her own little show."

"Why are you telling her this?" Geoffrey asked. "Why are you telling her anything?"

"Where's she going to go, Geoff? Who is she going to talk to?" Adele queried.

"I don't understand," Kit stated. "Or, having ascertained that Byron had no intention of blackmailing Geoffrey, did you think he was blackmailing Celia because of Geoffrey?"

Adele nodded and shrugged.

Kit shook her head. "So what was Celia doing?" she asked. "Don't tell me she was pumping you for info about Geoffrey."

"The woman was so civil," Adele said, almost admiringly, "that it took me some time to work out that she knew about me. When I realized there was probably no blackmail going on at all, just the likelihood that Celia's loyal little butler, in doing *her* bidding, would probably open a window on affairs that were *none* of her business I simply put a stop to her. Actually I just got very annoyed and hit her with the closest thing to hand."

"She didn't know about you, Adele," Kit said flatly. "At least, not you specifically. And as for poor innocent Byron . . ."

"What?" Geoffrey snapped.

"Innocent Byron?" Dalkeith repeated flatly. "You mean the guy wasn't following Geoff?"

Kit shook her head. Why was this so hard for everyone to understand? "Of course not. *I* was. I'm the detective, remember."

"So what was Daniels doing?" Geoffrey asked, still not convinced that he'd made a huge mistake.

"*Nothing,* Geoffrey," Kit emphasized, "except helping your wife compile lists of your known appointments, hangouts and acquaintances so that I would know where to find you at any given time."

"What a complete cock-up!" Whitten erupted.

"That's it in a nutshell," Kit laughed. "Geoffrey's wife just wanted to know where he was putting it when it was up." Kit pulled her head away from Grainger's threatening fist.

"Don't hit her again, Gerry," Adele snapped, drawing on the cigarette Geoffrey had just lit for her. "She can't finish this *very* interesting story if you beat her senseless."

"The boat's coming," said Marek.

"Good point, Adele," Kit said. "There you all were, running around like a flock of headless bloody chooks, thinking that Byron was accidentally going to blow all your sordid little deals with a blackmail plan that was, in actual fact, completely non-existent. So what do you do then? You get spunky trunks here," Kit said, nodding in Christo's direction, "to lure Byron to his death in a tacky little hotel room in what, or so I gathered from Geoffrey's agitated babbling yesterday, was supposed to look like a suicide."

Dalkeith threw Geoffrey a positively murderous glance.

Kit tried to give the love of her life a reassuring one, and actually received a wan smile in return even though Alex was rigid with fear, which was understandable seeing she was still being held by the juvenile delinquent with the gun.

"The boat's here," yelled Bill the guard from down below.

"But it seems things got a bit out of control, didn't they, *Mr.* Edwards?" Kit said, ignoring the interruption as she tried to bait Christo. It didn't take much. He even let go of Alex.

"Hey, I didn't do nuthin. He did it," Christo stated, waving the gun in Grainger's direction.

"Ah, yes," Kit said, "Mr. Gerald Grainger alias George Ryan. That was quite a mess you made."

"Shut the fuck up you smart-mouthed bitch!" Grainger shouted, smacking Kit in the face again. "Or yours will be the next throat I cut."

Kit screwed her eyes shut and waited for the stinging in her mouth and cheek to subside. The whole left side of her face felt as if it was stuffed with a throbbing butternut pumpkin. She hated to think what she looked like.

"See, see, I'm a gun man. I don't do knives," Christo was saying.

"Give it a rest, Christo," Dalkeith ordered. "Go and help Bill load the boat. And give me that gun, you little twerp."

Oh great, Kit thought, with a mixture of relief and trepidation. Now that Dalkeith had the gun Alex was no longer the primary target. She was.

"I've had enough of this shit," Grainger complained. "Let's just get rid of them."

"You see, there you go again," Kit mumbled. "You keep making mistakes. One after the other and they just keep getting bigger. You killed Byron because you thought he might have found out something. You killed Celia, I assume, without actually asking her if Byron told her anything he might have found out. And now you're going to do us."

"If only to shut you up," Grainger remarked.

"You have absolutely no idea what I know. Or who I've told."

"Perhaps we don't really care," Dalkeith said, rubbing the barrel of Christo's gun across the palm of his hand.

"Well, that would be stupid," Kit said. "Unless you're planning to leave the country tonight."

"That's a good idea," Whitten stated, pushing past Grainger. "This is a fucking mess. You lot oughta learn not to shit where you eat. You can clean up your own yard. I am outta here."

"Kitty, Kitty. Place him in the room," Marek said urgently.

"Mr. Davis Whitten," Kit said, shaking her head slowly.

"What?" he asked turning back.

"I hope you've got a passport in a different name."

"Now why would I need that?"

"It's just that a hacker friend told me the Feds were keeping an eye on an American businessman who happens to have the same name as you."

Whitten paled, and for a man his size that was no mean feat. The color just drained right out of his face and disappeared down his neck. Kit couldn't resist looking at his feet to see if he was standing in a puddle.

"How can she know all this?" Grainger asked, looking, for some strange reason, at Dalkeith and Adele. "She's got to be a copper. We should all get out of here. You are a copper, aren't you?" he asked finally turning to Kit.

"Oh yeah, sure," Kit remarked snidely. "And the whole place is surrounded, which explains why I'm still tied to this bloody chair. And I suppose my comrades out there just let you drag my friends in here for fun."

"Speaking of your friends," asked Dalkeith, who was so cool it was unnerving—it was almost as if he was amused by the whole situation—"What have they got to do with all of this?"

"Nothing," Kit shrugged. "They were *supposed* to be home taping tonight's episode of *Murder She Wrote* for me." She glared at Hector who, strangely enough, appeared to be the most guilty-looking person in the room.

Adele actually laughed again. Kit couldn't believe the woman. But, just like Dalkeith, she appeared to be completely unrattled by the unexpected turn the evening had taken. They made a fine pair, which made Kit wonder what on earth Adele saw in Geoffrey.

"Why are you telling us all this?" Miss Enigma asked.

"You said it, Adele. Where am I going to go? I might be trying my damnedest to reason with you, but I'm not stupid enough to think you're really going to let any of us walk out of here," Kit said. She tried to ignore the gurgle that came from Hector's general direction.

"Boxes on board, Kitty. Just annoy them for a couple more minutes. We're moving in." About bloody time! Kit thought. "So," she continued, "I just wanted to make sure, before you kill me, that you know what a bunch of complete fuckwits you all are. You've left a trail a mile wide."

"That's your opinion," Dalkeith stated.

"Hey," Kit asserted, "you're such an incestuous little bunch it wasn't hard to put this together. Tell me *Margaret*, does your mother enjoy a glass of special Endicott punch every arvo with Geoffrey's ex? And speaking of ex-relatives, Geoffrey, why don't you invite your brother-in-law, Captain Mal, up to join the party?"

Geoffrey collapsed with a groan into the only other chair in the office. Adele simply raised an eyebrow then kindly helped her Tiger close his mouth by lifting his chin with her finger.

"You're obviously quite good at your job, Katherine," Adele commented.

"I make a living." Kit smiled at her and then addressed Geoffrey, who was staring at her as if she'd stripped him naked and was laughing at his dangly bits. "I must say that the most interesting family connection in all of this was discovering that your floozy *Mrs. Adele Armstrong* divorced *her* husband Bruce shortly before he reinvented himself as Ian *Munro* . . ."

Dalkeith's hand, the one not holding the gun, knocked the wind right out of her. Kit gasped for breath. When she managed to sit up straight again Geoffrey's dumbstruck attention was still swivelling between Adele and Dalkeith. Obviously the stupid bastard had no idea.

Adele simply raised an eyebrow, shrugged, took a long drag on her cigarette then squashed the butt quite brutally under the toe of her red stiletto. Along with Tiger Robinson's ego, no doubt. Before Geoffrey had a chance to collect himself enough to say anything, Christo appeared in the doorway. "Um, Boss?"

"Is that boat loaded yet?" Dalkeith snapped.

"One of the boxes is empty."

"What?"

It was actually a chorus of whats, exclaimed by everyone in the room who cared that some of their merchandise had gone walkabout. Kit glanced at Hector to make sure he wasn't going to fess up out of fear. She needn't have worried. The lad was doing a great impersonation of the Shrinking Invisible Man. Alex had moved into the corner next to him and was gripping his hand as her gaze darted in the direction of anyone in the room who made any kind of movement, sudden or otherwise.

"I'll check it out," Grainger said sharply, barging his way out of the office.

"There's another thing, *Bruce*," Kit said, boldly going where probably only stupid people had gone before. "Did any of you give a thought to AWOL Andy? Perhaps you'd better check the other laptops to make sure your drugs are still there."

"Oh man!" Whitten exclaimed. "She knows everything. Kill the bitch, Ian, and let's get the hell outta here."

"No!" Geoffrey shouted. "That will only make things worse. We've got to stop this now. God, this is awful."

Kit stared at Geoffrey in surprise. The man was genuinely spooked. Obviously things had gone way too far for his liking. But then he wasn't a career crook like the rest of his little gang. Like Dalkeith, for instance, who was just sitting on the edge of the desk smiling at him. It was not a reassuring smile. It was contemptuous and mean. The guy looked like a taipan about to strike. The respectable glamour-boy persona of Ian Munro Dalkeith had been stripped back to reveal the small-time drug-dealing pimp who'd already done time for killing someone. This was a very ugly man.

Stay away from Dalkeith, he's a nasty piece of work. Kit remembered Liam saying that and *had* wondered what it meant exactly. She wasn't wondering any more and she was suddenly more scared than she had ever been in her life.

"Nobody's asking you to do anything dirty, Geoff," Dalkeith said calmly. "We've taken care of all *your* problems so far, haven't we? Even the imaginary ones. We can't let these people walk out of here and that's all there is to it."

"You're all fucked, and from several directions, whether we live or die," Kit insisted.

"Hey, maybe you're right," Dalkeith hissed in her face, "but you and your smart mouth won't be around to know one way or the other." He held Christo's gun by the barrel and pushed the butt between her legs. Kit's automatic reaction was to clamp her legs together so he couldn't move the gun any higher. Knowing it couldn't do any damage held like that did not detract from the fact that it was not a pleasant sensation.

Dalkeith ran his tongue across his bottom lip and then, as if he'd made a decision, he abruptly sat back, tossed the gun from his left hand to his right and waved it at Alex and Hector.

"Davis. Take those two down to the boat. You and Mal can drop them off out in the bay somewhere. And tell Gerry to check the stuff is still in the other boxes."

"Oh, shit," Hector moaned as Whitten grabbed him and Alex and pushed them across the office and out the door.

"O'Malley!" Alex cried out.

"It's OK, Alex," Kit called after her, wondering desperately what the hell was taking Marek so long.

"What about *her*?" Adele asked.

"It will be my pleasure to knock this bitch off myself." Dalkeith turned his snake-eyed attention back to Kit, caressing her right cheek with the side of the gun barrel. "Then I think I might torch this building. I've grown rather tired of it."

Oh shit, Kit whimpered silently. Nasty? He really loves this stuff. Visions of a baby Ian pulling the wings off flies which had strayed into his bassinet dissolved when the adult piece of work stood up and straddled her left leg, bending at the knees so that his crutch rubbed against her thigh.

Kit tried to kick out at him but he just laughed, stepped back and aimed the gun directly at her. Then he unzipped his fly. Oh god, oh god, Kit thought. Where's the fucking cavalry?

"I don't need to see this," Geoffrey said in disgust, knocking over his chair as he stood up.

"Oh, come on, Geoff." Dalkeith glanced at him as he reached inside his pants and started rubbing himself. "Don't you want a bit?"

"You're a sick bastard, Ian," Geoffrey stated. "Are you coming, *Maggie*?"

"Just get it over with, Ian," Adele snapped at him, moving to follow Geoffrey.

Kit pressed her body back in the chair as Dalkeith closed in on her, his hand still in his pants, the gun aimed at her forehead. She was vaguely aware that Geoffrey and Adele were arguing their way down the stairs but her attention was focused on the gun, waiting for the end. It was like watching a slow motion replay, over and over, from every possible angle. It had already been an eternity, certainly long enough for her life to be flashing before her eyes, so why wasn't she seeing anything but one-eyed death staring her in the face?

A disembodied voice, like a phantom in a waking dream warning her of danger—as if she hadn't realized that already, for Christ's sake!—was telling her to drop to *her* right when he gave the word.

Oh, Nick. Thank you! The word. What word? She jammed her right foot up against the front leg of the chair.

"Too bad," Dalkeith was saying, then something distracted him. A shout maybe, from downstairs.

"Now!"

Now? That was a good word. Kit lunged to her right, bringing the chair with her. As she went down she thought she saw Dalkeith flying backwards across the room. She crashed to the floor, screwing her eyes shut against the spear of excruciating pain that shot from one shoulder to the other.

Then all hell broke loose. All around her. There was noise coming from everywhere, not the least from inside her own head where she could still hear Nick shouting, "Now! Now! Move in now, goddammit!"

Kit opened her eyes. She stopped struggling uselessly against the ropes and stared at Dalkeith. The Armalite, she remembered, was a high-velocity high-impact automatic rifle. Nick used to say if you were to shoot some guy in the leg from as far away as 150 yards he'd probably die of shock. Ian Munro Dalkeith hadn't had time to be shocked. He had a small neat wound bang smack in the center of his chest, and would have been dead before his body slammed into the wall. And, judging by the mess splattered and smeared on that wall, a hollow-point bullet had taken the back right out of him.

Kit lay there for another eternity, her cheek squashed against the floorboards, staring at Dalkeith and listening to yelling voices and shots ringing out all over the place. She felt hands on her body and kicked out at them.

"Kit, Kit, it's me, Nick. Are you OK?"

"I don't know, Nicholas. How do I look?" she asked, squinting at him.

"Like shit warmed up, girlfriend," he said and grinned as he undid the ropes. She let him hold her for a moment, just to feel as though there was something normal in the world, then she struggled to her feet.

"It sounds like the Gunfight at the OK Corral down there," she muttered as she lurched towards the door.

"Yeah, round up time," Nick said.

Kit started very gingerly down the stairs, then froze halfway down when she heard a shout from the dock. "Let me go!"

It was Alex's voice. Kit slipped, slid and finally stumbled down the rest of the stairs then hit the floor running. She reached the loading bay in about fifteen strides, shrugged off the someone who tried to grab her on her way through the door and ignored Marek's shout from outside to get back. She skidded out onto the dock, straight into the middle of a standoff between three armed coppers and Davis Whitten who had his arm around Alex's waist and a gun to her head.

Kit stopped dead in her tracks and automatically held her hands out in front of her to show she had no weapon. She didn't need Whitten to shoot her for no reason at all, except maybe gross stupidity.

"Drop the gun, mate," Marek was saying, as calmly as possibly. He was standing at the top of the ramp about ten feet away, his gun trained on Whitten. And Alex.

Smasher, in a crouch in the doorway to her left, and Dipper just behind her and to the right, also had Whitten in their sights. Kit was standing in the best position to be shot by everyone.

"Don't do anything stupid, Whitten." It was Liam. He emerged slowly and unarmed from the warehouse and moved to stand next to Kit. "Let go of the woman and put the gun down."

"Screw you!" Whitten shouted, tightening his hold on Alex. "Get out of my way. You're going to let me get on that boat, and you're going to let the boat leave or I *will* kill her."

Kit glanced down the ramp. The *Shirley Too* wasn't going anywhere in a hurry. By the looks of it Jenny had rammed Captain Mal's boat with her own. She and Tony also had Mr. Smith, Christo and Bill the guard nicely covered with their shotguns.

Kit looked back at Alex whose face was frozen in fear.

"Get out of my way," Whitten shouted at Marek.

A small sound above Kit's head made her glance up. It was a split-second look but Whitten had followed suit, also catching sight of Robbo on the roof.

What happened next also took a split second. And about three hours.

Whitten moved suddenly, using Alex to cover himself from the overhead threat. In the same moment a shout snapped Kit's attention in the direction of Detective Alan Sargent who had materialized as if from thin air behind her. Even as she turned away from him, however, she was aware that Whitten had stumbled backwards. Then she heard the report of the gun. Whose gun? Kit spun back in time to see Whitten hit the ground, *his* gun falling from his hand.

Alex just stood there, stock still. Then she looked down at her right arm, an almost puzzled look on her face as she watched her white shirt sleeve turn red. Kit launched herself forward just as Alex's head lolled back and her knees began to buckle. Kit managed to break her fall but they collapsed in a heap on the ground.

"Oh shit, no. No!" Kit struggled out from under the dead weight of Alex's body, clutching at her and holding her tightly. "No, no!" she screamed.

"O'Malley. O'Malley!" Marek was shaking her. Kit didn't even know she was crying until she realized she could barely see him through her tears.

"She's not dead, you idiot."

"She's not?" Kit said stupidly.

"She fainted. The bullet went straight through her arm. It hit Whitten in the chest. He's the one in trouble."

"Good," Kit spat. She held Alex gently, stroking her face. She's just fainted, Kit thought. It's OK. She's just fainted.

"What the hell happened?" she asked Marek. And then she remembered Sargent. His gun raised.

He was still standing exactly where he'd been when he fired on Whitten, and hit Alex as well.

"Look after her, Jonno," Kit said, getting to her feet.

"Where are you going?" Marek objected.

Kit looked around the dock. She knew it was here somewhere. Ah there! Dipper had pushed it out of Whitten's reach and was now paying undue attention to the man who looked as though he'd bleed to death long before any serious help arrived. Kit bent down. Whitten's gun felt much too comfortable in her hand to be picking it up in anger.

To hell with it! she thought and rounded on Sargent, her right hand cradled in her left and the gun aimed at his head. "Is this the kind of stuff-up you had in mind, *Alan*?" she asked, bending her right elbow and drawing the gun back towards herself as she advanced on him. "Is it?" she demanded and grabbed his shirt front, the gun, unwavering in her hand, still aimed at his forehead.

Sargent, who had shat himself three times over already, was incapable of speech.

"Oh Christ, Kit, don't!" said Nick's voice in her ear.

Kit cocked her head slightly to one side and stared at Sargent as if she was trying to work out what species he was. "Just whose side are you on, you stupid bastard?"

"O'Malley." Liam was just behind her. "Give me the gun. Come on, Girl Scout, he's not worth it."

Sargent managed to get his shit back together enough to start blustering. "Get this stupid fucking bitch away from me."

"Shut up, you moron, or I'll shoot you myself," Liam snapped. "O'Malley, please," he added softly. "Give me the gun."

Kit relaxed her stance and snapped the gun back away from Sargent's face, holding it level with her shoulder in a gesture of surrender. She let Liam take the weapon and then she clenched her fist, aimed for a point *way* behind Sargent's head, about three miles north of Sydney, and punched him in the mouth. He was down and out for the count before he knew what hit him.

"And *don't* call me a bitch either," she snarled.

Liam peered over her shoulder. "I don't think he heard you, Girl Scout. Where'd you get a right cross like that?"

"I doubt I could do that again if I tried," Kit laughed.

"O'Malley?" The voice was weak, but it was Alex's.

Kit fell to her knees beside her.

"Am I going to die, Kit?"

"I don't think so, sweetheart," Kit said, helping her to sit up.

"What's all this red stuff then?" Alex asked uncomprehendingly. Marek had tied something around her arm but it too was now soaked with blood.

"It's a flesh wound, Alex. They're very melodramatic things."

"I'll say," she mumbled. "Do you think I'll be able to get the stain out of my shirt?"

Kit was about to point out that there wasn't a sleeve left to get a stain out of but it was too late. Alex passed out again.

"You OK, O'Malley?" Boscoe squatted down beside her.

"Yeah, thanks, mate," Kit nodded. "We do need an ambulance though."

"There's one on the way."

"So where are the rest of the crooks?" Kit asked.

"We've got Robinson and that screaming hellcat in a divvy van out the front."

"Hector!" Kit suddenly remembered. "Where's Hector?"

"Right here, O'Malley." Hector shuffled forward, wearing a look of extreme contrition and a lovely black eye.

"Who hit you?" Kit queried.

"That prick Grainger," Hector stated.

"Good, he saved me the job of punching your lights out. What the hell are you doing here? I assume Alex was the *friend* whose car you were in?"

"Hey, it wasn't my idea. Really. I turned up at your friend's wake to give you the information just as Alex was leaving. She was going to follow that Adele woman. So I kinda went along for the ride. I sorta figured you'd probably rather she didn't go on her own anyway."

"Oh sure, Hector. I'm really pleased you *both* got kidnapped and nearly killed."

"Can I do anything to help?" Hector asked, nodding at Alex. Even though he was trying to change the subject he was obviously genuinely concerned.

"Yeah," Kit said. "You can start by giving me the shirt off your back. This thing is soaked."

Hector ripped off his T-shirt and began tying it carefully around Alex's arm.

"Where *is* Grainger?" Kit asked, suddenly realising he seemed to be the only one unaccounted for.

"He's dead," Boscoe stated. "In the corridor in there. Found him face down in a bag of smack."

Kit's attention snapped towards Hector who was concentrating all his on the first aid task he'd been assigned. She tried to keep her expression passive as she turned back to the head of the drugs squad.

"Silly bastard," Boscoe said knowingly, casting a casual glance at Hector before smiling at Kit. "Looks like he tried to conceal the evidence by eating it."

Kit laughed. She couldn't help herself.

"Whoa!" Alex exclaimed, coming to suddenly and sitting bolt upright. "Is there something funny going on around here?" she asked, enunciating her words very carefully.

"Yes, Alex, there's a lot of funny going on."

"O'Malley?"

"Yes, Alex?"

"I'm serious."

"About what?"

"What about what? Oh. Didn't I ask you yet?"

"I don't know, Alex." Kit brushed Alex's hair back from her forehead and tried to keep a straight face. Alex looked back at Kit and smiled, that trademark Cazenove smile that said a million things and nothing at all. And then she laughed. "You should see your face," she said. "You look awful, Kit."

"Thank you, Alex. You don't look half bad yourself."

Alex frowned. "You're not going to be here today and gone tomorrow, are you, O'Malley?"

"No, Alex," Kit smiled.

"What does that mean exactly?" Alex asked.

"It means I'm not going anywhere without you. Ever." Kit said.

"Oh," Alex said, her eyelids failing her again. "Good," she mumbled and fainted again.

"Yeah, it's great," Kit whispered in her ear.

Then she shouted: "An ambulance would be a nice idea, about now."